The

Joining

Jacqueline Clark

For Carolyn and Leslie: The head and the heart in equal measure.
And for David. Thanks for your infinite patience and support.

Prologue

It was difficult to stand upright. Her young body jerked from side to side as the ground beneath her shook. She felt nauseous from the low frequency rumble that vibrated along her bones and into her skull.

The quake had lasted for an hour, but was the least of her worries. For five days and nights torrential rain had fallen, turning the ground into a carpet of thick, cloying, mud. Her psi-awareness tingled as blinding forked lightning split the sky in two. There was a loud crack, a shower of sparks and the tree in front of her burst into flames. The fire cast an eerie orange glow across the clearing.

'*Why is this happening?*'

Her people were lucky. They lived on the highland plateau and were safe from the rising flood water. Looking down from their vantage point, the tribe could no longer distinguish the path of the river from the surrounding countryside. It burst its banks on the first day of the deluge, turning the grassy plain into an ocean that spread as far as the eye could see.

That's when they spotted them. A small group of lowlanders were climbing up the cliff face towards their sanctuary. Fear ran through her mind, instantly comforted by the collective consciousness of her kin.

'*It will be all right, we will protect you.*'

How can you protect me? she thought. Everyone knows the lowlanders are bloodthirsty savages whose way of life is to kill or be killed. They're long-lived and slow witted, but they're also far stronger than us.

'*I may be a child, but I know death when it's staring me in the face.*'

When the lowlanders crested the top of the ridge, they howled in anticipation; the bloodlust in their minds fuelled by the raging storm.

From where she stood at the back of her family group, the girl could hear voices shouting to one another in an unfathomable language. Her people had no language, they communicated mind to mind. She strained to make out the meaning of the words, fascinated by this new experience.

'I wonder what it's like to speak.'

After a few seconds, she gave up her futile attempt at translation. The words uttered by the lowlanders didn't matter, the hatred in their thoughts was easy to read; they blamed the highlanders for the natural disaster that swallowed their home.

'It's not our fault.' she screamed, but the lowlanders' minds were closed to all form of telepathic transmission.

Discarding the heavy animal skins that hung around their bodies, the short, muscular lowlanders formed a line. Grinning at one another they raised their weapons and surged forward; the roar of battle exploding from their throats as they approached.

In response, her brothers, her uncles and even her father sprang into action, holding their staffs aloft in an attempt to deflect the oncoming horde.

Wood was no match for metal.

Within seconds the battle lines had crumbled embroiling everyone in the fight for survival. There was chaos all around.

Still the blanket of relentless rain pelted down.

Backing away from the carnage, the girl tried to find an exit route from the scene. It was then she noticed the conflict was also behind her.

Trapped.

'What shall I do?'

Pushed to the ground, she looked up and saw her eldest brother succumb to a fatal blow. In a flash his consciousness was lost from the group mind.

Her uncle, his leg severed above the knee, fell into the dirt; the muddy rain water splashing over her as he collapsed. He looked up at his attacker begging for mercy, but the psychic plea was ineffective. The barbarian cried

4

out with pleasure as he plunged his heavy sword into the man's chest.

Shocked by the deplorable scene, she swung around to see her father sent flying. He landed heavily in the mud, shaking his head and wiping the teeming rain from his eyes.

'Look out, Father!'

Before he could stand, one of the creatures jumped astride him, pinning him to the ground. The lowlander turned and grinned, then sunk his pointed teeth into her father's neck, severing the artery and releasing a fountain of bright purple blood.

Brain death followed an instant later.

Standing once again, the barbarian shook the blood from his sodden clothing and looked about. He spotted the girl close by and strode towards her.

She backed away.

Coming to a halt, the girl noticed for the first time that the quake had ceased.

At least I can stand upright now.

Rigid with fear, she stood in the centre of the clearing watching the slaughter around her. There was nowhere to run, nothing to do but wait for the inevitable. One by one her kin were slain until only her six sisters remained. Noticing their younger sibling alone and vulnerable, they rushed to her side.

Unknown to the lowlanders, the seven remaining females had one last form of defence. They huddled together, back to back in a circle, drawing on each other for support.

'Not yet,' warned the eldest. *'Not yet.'*

When the brutish male lowlanders attacked, they ran headlong into an invisible wall of energy, their cries of victory cut off before they left their mouths. Some were bruised by the impact. Most were thrown awkwardly to the ground.

She smiled to herself, savouring this small triumph.

Not believing what had happened, the men let out a series of angry shouts, stood and sprang forward once again. Once again they were repelled by the womens' shield.

Each time one of the lowlanders pushed at the energy barrier, the sisters pushed back with the power of their minds.

Stalemate.

Eventually the men gave up their pointless attacks. Encircling their prey like a pack of hungry hounds, they watched and waited. Time was on the lowlander's side, they were long-lived and slow, and waiting came naturally to them.

The rain died away, the lilac sky cleared and daylight turned to dusk. The young women could sense night closing in fast.

'We must stay awake.'

Leaning on her sisters for support, the girl could feel her eyelids become heavy with fatigue. How long has it been since I rested comfortably in my own bed? Three, maybe four days? The lure of sleep tugged at her soul, her resistance diminishing in the fading light.

She wasn't sure how long she slept. It was probably just a few seconds, but it was too long. With less power to sustain it, the protective shield dissolved to nothingness.

Suddenly the night was ripped apart by hysterical screams.

Then she noticed him staring at her, the same man who killed her father. He licked his lips and wiped a hand across his brow.

'No, please... no.'

She tried to run, but rough hands reached out and grabbed her slender shoulders. Her fragile frame crumbled under the man's weight, the stench of him filling her nostrils as she was pulled to the ground.

Wriggling beneath his bulk made him push down harder, until it was difficult to breathe. She tried to relax, but he was close... so close. She could feel his greasy hair on her face, the stubble of his beard scratching at her neck, his open mouth seeking hers.

When his weight shifted, she knew what was coming. Her mind rushed from her body, leaving the agony of torn flesh behind and seeking shelter amongst the stars.

The clearing was in total darkness when she returned to her body. Keeping her eyes shut tight, she listened to the sounds of the night. He was still there beside her, in a deep slumber brought on by the rigours of the climb, the fight and the violation. Others were close by too. She was flooded with relief when she felt the consciousness of her sisters; all asleep, but thankfully all still alive.

Now she must take a chance. She reached out her psi-awareness. The man held his sword in one hand, its blade resting on his chest. If he were disturbed there was no doubt he would strike out and kill her in an instant. Drawing in a slow breath, she surrounded her body in a psionic field and lifted from the ground until she hovered just above the squelching mud.

He groaned. She tensed. Then sighed when his breathing became regular again.

Slowly, she moved away from her tormenter, floating on a cushion of air toward safety.

At last, she reached the tree canopy. She flipped herself upright, grounded and ran at full tilt away from the clearing. She didn't stop to look back. Fear drove her legs forward into the dense forest.

As she ran, she could feel his seed within her, the moment of conception shocking her bewildered senses.

'It's not meant to happen like this.'

The muscles in her legs ached, her chest heaved. She could run no further. Sinking onto the soft ground, tears poured down stinging her cheeks. For a long time she lay there on the forest floor, sobbing into her hands.

The sun rose on a new day.

With a series of slow breaths, the girl steadied her troubled mind and looked up at the tree overhead. Dappled light bled down through the canopy warming her bones.

I recognise this. The leaves are familiar. Then she realised where she was. She had come to rest beneath the fabled Markless tree. Since the first stirring of her consciousness, she'd been warned of this plant's deadly qualities. One bite of the fruit was enough to kill a grown man.

Her mind searched through the foliage until she found the largest fruit. She pulled it free with telekinesis and floated it down into her hands.

'I know what I have to do.'

Gnawing at the thick skin, she peeled it back with her teeth to reveal the blue flesh beneath. Then she bit down harder, gobbling up the deadly feast. The taste was delicious. She wanted it to last forever. Licking juice from her sticky hands and fingers she devoured every last drop.

At first nothing happened. She sat with her back to the tree trunk and was beginning to suspect that the tales of poison were exaggerated to scare children, when the effects finally hit her. Swirling vortices of energy played around her mind. Her vision was ablaze: Colour, taste, smell, all sensation mingled into one.

'This isn't death, it's the most incredible life.'

She watched from a detached distance as the scene sped up. Her belly became swollen, the child inside her growing at an exceptional speed.

Soon, she was gripped by the first agonising contraction of childbirth. She curled into a ball and screamed.

******

Pain yanked her from the trance, her mother's mind receding into the distance as the telepathic bond was broken. Angeriana'asusilicana opened her eyes to the welcome vista of her family home. Thankful to find herself sitting crossed-legged amongst the colourful cushions, not doubled over on the forest floor.

'Well, child. What does it mean?'

'I... umm...'

Nyaseema stared down at her daughter. It was difficult to keep frustration from her thoughts. *'It's two months since we enrolled you at the Academy. The 'Tale of the two and the one' is the most basic of all the sacred texts. You must have some idea of its meaning?'*

Angeriana gazed down at her toes, trying to put the gruesome images aside. Why are the chronicles always so horrid? And why does my tutor insist that if I live them vicariously I'll understand them more?

'I'm waiting,' pathed Nyaseema impatiently. *'Your first examination is in three days time. If you don't pass this test, you won't move to the next level.'*

I have to please Mother, she thought. She won't stop asking until I say something.

'It's a warning...a warning of climate change.'

Startled by the answer, Nyaseema pulled up her shield. Her daughter's interpretation showed insight well beyond her age; a definite indication of her growing abilities. Not yet, she thought, unfulfilled longing playing with the edge of her mind. The time is not yet upon us.

Cutting herself off from her daughter's consciousness, she responded in words.

'No, no, no. Where did you get that idea? The sacred texts are not literal. You should know this by now. Have you been neglecting your studies?'

'But Father's thoughts...'

'Your father is an Elder of the Circle. It is not your place to interpret his thoughts. I will hear no more of this.'

'I'm sorry, Mother. I'll try harder.'

Unaware that her shield was slipping, Nyaseema let out a deep sigh and stared at her daughter. *'Why you? Why did I give birth to you?'*

Angeriana stifled a gasp of surprise, looked down and played with her hair.

There was a long pause.

'Well?' demanded Nyaseema at last. *'I can't sit here all day.'*

'It's about destiny. In the story the girl returns to the clearing with her daughter and the others welcome her home. She tells them about the magic tree and they all eat

9

the fruit. Her baby was the first of a new type of Manyarnern. It matured quickly, but was also long-lived. It had miraculous mental powers, way beyond anything the highlanders had before. This girl used her powers to heal the wounded land. The tribe was grateful and made her their Premier.'

'Go on...'

'If events had not unfolded as they did, she may not have come to the specialisation intended for her. This girl, the Premier, was born to fulfil a specific role for her people.'

Nyaseema's face lit up. 'Yes, my child, as we are all born to our specialisations.'

'But what if the Lenses are wrong? What if they make a mistake at someone's birth?'

'Never in all of history has a Lens made a mistake. There's no need to fear, your name was chosen wisely. You will make a fine healer.'

'But what if I don't want to...' She regretted it as soon as she thought it.

Nyaseema leaned down, her scarlet eyes blazing. 'Like the rest of us, you will do as you are told.'

She stood up, brushing her daughter aside with a thought. 'Now it's time for your meditations.'

Angeriana walked reluctantly towards the garden.

Everything I do, everything I say. It's never good enough, she thought.

Emerging into the afternoon sunshine, she glanced back over her shoulder. Her mother was leaning on the arched portal watching her intently; no doubt checking that she obeyed instructions. When Angeriana knelt down and started the cleansing ritual, her mother moved away, returning to her own duties.

For the briefest of moments she felt resentment in her mother's mind.

******

The world vibrates as the threads of our existence are pulled. As a child, I heaved on the cord which tied me to my life: only to feel the pull when I was old enough to know better!

The Chronicles of Angeriana'asusilicana

Chapter 1

I traced my finger around the edge of the terminal screen and sighed. How can a job on the forefront of scientific enquiry be so boring? This is the largest space station in the galaxy and nothing ever happens. It's almost as dull here as it was at the Manyarnern Academy and there are just as many pointless regulations.

Still, I've made it this far. Working as a catalogue tech may not be perfect, but it is something to call my own. That is what matters.

Jumping down from the stool, I walked across to the food dispenser and requested a beaker of Tralmark. As soon as the fabrication cycle was complete, I snatched up the drink and took a large swig. The colour was the same, the taste was the same, but my mind knew immediately that the psychotropic qualities which made this beverage special were missing.

Throwing the beaker into waste reclamation, I stomped back to my desk; my mind returning to memories of my childhood.

Mother and Father exploded the day they learned I'd quit the Academy. I knew I had let them down, knew they wanted, expected, more from me. I'll never forget the look of disgust on their faces.

'We can't leave you alone for a few hours without some major disaster happening,' pathed father, anger at my sudden announcement in the forefront of his mind. *'You are two years from graduation, leaving is not an option.'*

Unable to meet his fierce stare, I crossed my arms and looked at the floor. *'You can't make me go back. I never fitted in there. I'm no good as a healer.'*

Mother marched forward. For a moment I thought she was going to hit me.

'You cannot reject your specialisation. It is written in your genetic code.' She threw her arms into the air. *'We are Elders of the Circle. How dare you bring such shame on the family.'*

'You're not thinking of the family. You only think of yourselves. If it's all right for you to go off-world, then why not me? You want me to be a healer. I choose a different path.'

I have argued all my life with tutors and friends about Manyarnern philosophy. It was just such an argument that initiated my rapid departure from the Academy that afternoon. I understood what the Lenses told me about my personal myth, but for some reason couldn't bring myself to believe it. I might only be five years of age, but four years deliberating on the finer points of psionic manipulation had dampened any enthusiasm I once held for my specialisation. I wanted to be out there, anywhere, doing something different not wasting hours in pointless meditation. Mother and Father just didn't understand.

'We understand the meaning of duty and obligation. That particular lesson seems to have passed you by,' pathed Father.

My head jerked up. I fixed him with my hardest stare. *'Is that why you are leaving for the Gretin Station? Is it really your duty to serve on the O.P.U. Assembly instead of the Circle?'*

I felt uncertainty in their thoughts. I knew I had found the flaw in their argument that would serve my purpose. *'Take me with you, please?'* I poured my heart into the telepathic signal. *'Find me a position on the station. I can be dutiful. I'll work hard. I promise. Just give me a chance.'*

Whether they believed me or not, they found me this job as a catalogue tech working on the Species Recognition Programme.

I am trying to keep my promise. For more than a year, I've really tried.

A buzzer sounded and the entry portal appeared. Pulled from my reverie, I noticed the usual induction tech, Leela, approaching with a trolley.

'I've got a new specimen for you,' she called cheerily.

I stood up. 'At last. I thought they'd forgotten about me. Species?'

'Human male. The medics have just fitted his transceiver. He's still unconscious.' Parking the trolley in the centre of the lab beneath the inspection lights, she smiled and handed me a data tag. I swung around and placed it in the reader. The terminal sprang to life as it downloaded the alien's file.

Nodding in my direction, Leela trotted from the room. 'Enjoy.'

The portal disappeared behind her.

I looked down at the young man in front of me. His scrawny body barely filled the sleep-suit, and an unruly mop of light-brown hair covered his face. Not a promising specimen.

I turned back to the terminal and noted the results of his genetic screening. Several base pairs were similar to those found in the DNA of my own race. I had noticed this before. Various species in the galaxy have these tags. I added the findings to previous reports, however nothing happened. I presumed it was not relevant to the O.P.U.'s main objective. If the powers that be were interested they would do something about it.

Dismissing it as a random aberration, I got on with the next test.

He began to stir just as I finished a neural probe. His large brown eyes looked up at me. 'Shit!' he exclaimed, jumping to the floor and spinning around. 'What the fuck's going on?'

His thoughts bounced around in a crazy jumble of

13

fear and intrigue and it took a great deal of psionic control to keep him rooted to the spot. Entering the last few details of his test results into my terminal, I walked around to face him.

'Hi. I'm Angeriana'asusilicana. Rather a mouthful, I know. So you can call me Angie.' He did not respond. 'Your name's Iain... Iain McClellan.' I read his open, child-like mind easily. In the first few moments of consciousness he revealed the syntactic nature of his language as well as much of his personality. On the surface he was a practical individual, more of a doer than a thinker with conventional morality and a need to conform. His passivity bored me. Is this all that humanity has to offer? I probed deeper.

Below the surface, were characteristics he rarely showed anyone. He was clever, an idealist who lived in the shadow of those around him. He wanted to break free, to make his mark on the world. Self-reliant and determined he knew that one day he would do it. I smiled inwardly. Just like me.

Iain looked me up and down. 'Who are you?'

I felt both sarcasm and disbelief in the question and knew that it would take a while to explain. He was totally unaware of his new telepathic abilities.

I wonder why the scout ship chose him, I thought.

Glancing down at the terminal I checked the file. He had received no induction. That was odd. Maybe they fast tracked him through to the infirmary for some other reason. There would be time to look into this later.

I led him back to the bed. 'Iain, do you know where you are and how you got here?'

My question was met with silence, but his thoughts answered for him. He had the notion that this was an elaborate joke. That I was trying to dupe him into thinking he had been abducted by aliens. He was used to being the butt of his friend's jokes, it seemed the most likely explanation. At the same time, he did not quite believe it. Reading his inner confusion, I grasped that there was a particular friend, Sebastian, whom he believed, would be capable of pulling off such a prank. He had decided to play along for the moment.

'You're eyes are really cool. Where did you get red contact lenses?' He looked around. 'It must have cost a bundle to set all this up. Are we on a film set?'

'No, we are on the O.P.U. space station in the...'

I watched as he inspected the room again. Medical equipment way above his understanding filled the small cubical. There were diagnostic scanners and surgical induction units, imagers and bio-filters all pulsing and flashing their data. I read his mind. He had decided this was beyond anything his friends were capable of. It all looked too real.

'No. I won't believe it,' he said, under his breath.

Iain's body began to shake. His breathing quickened and muscles tensed as his metabolism went into overdrive. Thoughts tumbling out of control, he clung resolutely to the hope that this was some sort of dream or hoax, not abduction.

Despite his efforts, the realisation that he had, in fact, been taken by hostile aliens was rapidly causing a dangerous state of mind. Snippets of television footage and horror stories filled his thoughts. I caught a brief flash of a grey-green monster with complex exoskeleton and retractable mandible bursting from a man's chest - It was not unlike the Potriad race of the Cihan nebula. Next came giant machines rampaging across the surface of his planet, burning everything in their path. Unknown voices screaming in his mind solidified into one man's frantic monochrome pleading; 'there're not human, can't you see...they're here already!' In different circumstances, I would find his paranoia amusing. I did not have time for that now.

Iain's condition was reminiscent of an incident a few months earlier. On that occasion, the specimen in question had become violent, rapidly sinking into insanity. I requested immediate termination. Putting this hapless creature out of its misery was kinder than seeing it suffer, yet my medical training disposed me towards healing, rather than killing.

Gruesome images continued to parade through Iain's thoughts. His heart rate had tripled in response to the rush of adrenaline. I knew he couldn't withstand such high levels of stress much longer. Linking directly with his unconscious, I spread feelings of reassurance. Hoping that I could turn his fear into acceptance.

This better work, I thought.

'What're you doing to me?'

'Psionic suggestion. I think you would call it telepathy.'

'But I'm not...'

'Some of your people have limited psionic abilities, but in your case we fitted a transceiver.'

I held his terror at bay allowing the parasympathetic system to calm his physiology. It almost worked. As deranged panic subsided, anger rose up to replace it. I had not expected this from such a submissive specimen.

'A what?'

'A psionic transceiver is a device to allow telepathic communication between our races. It's fitted into the frontal cortex of the brain and connected to the hippocampus and speech centres.' I indicated the appropriate parts of his head with my finger. 'It's only because you have one that we're able to talk. Without it I'd find it much harder to speak and understand your language.'

Iain held his hands to his head. His previous assumption, that this was just a practical joke, was no longer a viable explanation.

'What've you done to me?' His hands formed into fists. 'You have no right. Get the fuck out of my mind, and get this lump of junk out of me too.'

Going into him once more, it surprised me to meet such indignation in one so young. We had given him a gift other species would be grateful for, but he thought I had abused and violated him in some way. With physiology still in a heightened state of fight or flight, I sensed a stronger mind here than other humans I'd catalogued.

I sighed. First encounters are meant to be straight forward. Why was this specimen proving so difficult to handle?

16

Despite the potential for something new and interesting, I still had concerns that he'd fail to make the long-term adjustment required to cope with his new life.

Regulations recommended termination following a poor first encounter. These specimens usually proved unsuitable for further study. Given the circumstances, such drastic action seemed rather extreme. I thought through my options. I could easily sedate him, delete the memories of our conversation - along with the vid-cam recordings of the past few minutes - and start afresh once he regained consciousness. Termination was still an option if that did not work out. I sighed. For some unfathomable reason, killing him felt wrong.

This human deserved the chance to prove himself.

What had come over me? I had never given credence to the Manyarnern obsession with fate, now I was considering following my instincts? I had never followed rules blindly, either. Did it matter why I had made the decision to spare him? As long as I made the decision soon.

Let's see whether my psionic suggestion actually works, I thought.

'This 'lump of junk', as you call it, is a very delicate instrument and I would have thought that you would be grateful for the abilities it affords you. Vocalisation is so primitive, so ineffectual. The psionic transceiver allows for much more mutual understanding. Its use will be greatly beneficial to us...'

His hands dropped to his sides, but his eyes still glared.

'That's crap. You have the advantage here. You took me and messed me about. Now you expect me to be grateful for it. Well lady, if you are a lady, you've got another thing coming. I'll never cooperate.'

'And what do you think non cooperation will achieve?' I pathed.

Iain's jaw dropped open and he turned away from me in an attempt at defiance.

'Turning your back won't stop me. Telepathy has no boundaries, no limitations. Once you adjust to it, you'll see

how much you missed before: how limited your knowledge of others was. After you've learnt how to shield personal thoughts, you'll feel much less vulnerable. We don't want to pry into your private life, Iain. All we want is to improve our knowledge of human society.'

His sarcasm was scathing. *'Is that all.'*

Iain's reaction to our first telepathic exchange fascinated me. I'd known telepathy all my life and took it for granted that conversation could continue when the parties involved were distant from one another. It was also second nature for me to pay attention to the nuances of a telepathic signal. The subtle emotional content that passes between linked minds is as revealing as the words themselves.

I had the clear advantage here I could interpret his thoughts without revealing my own.

'There are no hidden agendas, Iain.'

'Get the fuck out of my head. You may use this receiver thing to interpret my speech, but I don't see why you have to put words directly into my brain. I know when I'm beaten. I'll help just as long as you give me some privacy.' He sat down on the bed and played with the fabric of his suit. 'What would you like to ask first?'

The situation was quite comical. Did he really think that I had some kind of military objective? That a race so advanced would need to obtain strategic information from such an insignificant person? Still, it did seem unfair of me to delve too far into his private thoughts. I decided to avoid unnecessary intrusion unless he displayed signs of psychosis.

'I'm glad that you've decided to cooperate.' He hadn't, but at least he was calmer. 'I know how upsetting this whole experience must be. What if I was to promise not to use telepathy again, to stick to speech and only use the transceiver for interpretation? Would that be more acceptable to you?'

He nodded half-heatedly and I continued. 'Good. Let me tell you more about our Species Recognition Programme and see whether you're willing to aid us in our research. If at any time you want to stop, just say so.' I forced myself to smile and he visibly relaxed beside me.

At least the immediate danger had passed.

Overriding his body's physiological arousal, I placed the suggestion of fatigue directly into his mind. He yawned

'Look, Iain. I know you're annoyed that we fitted the transceiver, but I assure you it won't do any permanent damage. If, after we've discussed it further, you still want me to remove it I can perform the surgery immediately. Then we can resort to a less efficient, but more acceptable, means of communication. Why don't you sleep on it and we can chat tomorrow?'

By now he could hardly keep his eyes open. 'Okay then, as long as you promise to remove the bloody thing if I tell you.'

I helped him into a prone position and he fell instantly asleep. I'd bought myself some time.

I checked the terminal. The recording of our meeting was still sitting in the buffer. I hit delete. No need to give the Board any ammunition. A short telekinetic burst reset the counter on the vid-cam. Easy, the past few minutes never happened.

I looked down at Iain curled in a foetal position on the trolley. 'I'm risking my career for you, you better be worth it.'

Setting the transceiver to wake him in twelve Earth hours, I teleported him to his allotted room in the visitors centre.

There was no going back now. If this went wrong and he didn't adjust quickly, my days working on the programme would be numbered. Satisfied at last, I returned to the lab to write up my report.

******

I stared at the empty screen, mulling over events. I had broken quite a few regulations that day. It called for a little spin on the truth.

What if it doesn't work out tomorrow? What will I do then? I thought.

In spite of my distaste for regulations, I could still kill him and move on to the next creature in this cycle's inventory. And if he did calm down, I could begin my research in earnest.

'Computer record mode.' The machine beeped. 'Catalogue number 717250H. Physical profile...

******

'The human brain has two types of cells,' I began. 'You refer to them as glia and neurons. It's the complex nature of neurons, their capacity to exchange signals over vast distances, which gives us our consciousness.'

Iain nodded half-heartedly. Scanning him, I could tell that he was pretending to be disinterested. In reality he was as curious about me as I was about him.

At least this was a start.

It was his second day in the visitors centre and I'd managed to coax him into eating some food and sitting calmly while I continued his physical examination. At first he stubbornly refused to converse with me, but I knew he would not hold out for much longer.

'In human societies the mind is a private sphere to which no one else has access. In telepathic races things are subtly different. Although your neurons can send messages they require a physical connection, an axon, through which the electrical signal passes. In telepaths the signal uses psionic not electrical energy and this can move between the neurons of different brains. Of course we don't want this happening all the time, so we naturally shield our private thoughts, choosing with whom to communicate.'

His pupils widened, betraying his interest in this new information.

'The mind has a series of layers and we can decide how deeply we want another telepath to penetrate.'

'Like an onion.' He chuckled.

'What?' I scanned his lexicon. 'An onion is a vegetable.'

He sat up, more attentive now. 'I said *'like an*

onion'... Shrek, don't you get it?'

I was shocked when his mind filled with the image of a bright green creature. It had ears on stalks and a wide grin.'

'I didn't know such beings existed on your world.'

Iain let out a deep sigh. 'They don't it's Shrek.' He paused and gave me an irritated look. 'You people don't get out much, do you?'

Ignoring this strange line of questioning, I continued with my lesson. 'In order to shield you need structure to the neuronal connections.'

I looked down. On the floor below the table lay the magazine I'd brought him that morning. Using telekinesis I floated it up into my hand. The cover artwork read OK! in big letters.

'Did you enjoy reading this?' I asked. Iain shrugged. 'I imported it to make you feel more at home. I hope it was satisfactory.'

I tore the front page from the magazine. Holding it up between thumb and index finger, I jiggled it in the air. 'This paper is light, flimsy, weak.' Laying the paper down on the table in front of me, I rolled it into a tube and stood it on its end. 'Now it has structure it is much stronger.' Looking around once again, I noticed the plate of half-eaten food. It lifted and floated across until it balanced on top of the paper column.

'This is what you must learn, Iain, to bring structure to your neuronal connections. Then you will be able to control the layers of your mind.'

An unusual image suddenly impacted on me. He was thinking of something.

A brick wall.

He was thinking of a brick wall and shielding quite successfully from me.

'Very good.'

I was stunned that he had mastered the technique so quickly. This was going to give a whole new dimension to my work with him. Regulations stated that access must be available to the thoughts of specimens at all times. It was another type of control the Species Recognition

Programme imposed on its subjects.

Too late, what's done is done. I felt strangely proud of his achievements.

'Excellent, Iain. Now you'll be able to keep some mental privacy. What gave you the idea of such a structure?'

Iain's face showed total concentration. *'A brick wall. I must think of a brick wall...'*

*'I said **some** privacy.'* Brick by brick the wall crumbled away. *'I've been doing this a lot longer than you have.'*

We both laughed.

We were making progress.

******

Four days after Iain awoke in my lab, I took an even greater risk with my career.

This place needs shaking up a bit, I thought.

Leaving Iain's room in the visitors centre, we rounded the corner and came face to face with the Board supervisor. His race, although basically humanoid in shape, was visually very different to me. Beneath his uniform, the thick skin on his trunk and arms was dark grey and scaly. His muscular legs and feet turned outwards, the soft underside dotted with yellow and green spots. More amphibian than human, I believe his race has a semi-aquatic lifestyle. It must have felt very uncomfortable to live in the dry atmosphere of the station.

I glanced towards Iain. Thankfully, his mind conveyed fascination at this encounter, rather than the terror I'd expected.

'Where do you think you're going?' pathed the supervisor.

'I've decided that a change of scene would be beneficial to my research.'

'You've decided.' The supervisor's fibrous collar stood up in a ritualised threat display. *'Since when has a catalogue tech had the authority to make decisions?'*

'Since the Board neglected their duty.' I regretted it

as soon as I sent out the thought. What was I doing talking back to my boss? My position in the O.P.U depended on his opinion of me. If I wasn't careful he could downgrade me and I'd spend the rest of my career filing reports.

'How dare you!' He stepped forward. *'The Board has worked tirelessly to protect these foreigners. They are wild, dangerous animals that would ransack the station given half the chance. The regulations are there to prevent that happening. If everyone was as irresponsible as you, we'd have been overrun years ago.'*

During the brief exchange, I sensed Iain beginning to break into our link. It pleased me to be proven right for once, this clearly indicated his growing psionic abilities. The supervisor retaliated swiftly. Iain winced and I felt his pain.

'See. Even now the primitive is getting above his station. Regulations state that before you can make a request for movement all visitors are held in isolation for two full rotations. I've worked on this programme for decades and never before have the rules been so blatantly ignored.'

'Never before has a specimen shown such quick adaptation. Maybe it's time the regulations were changed? Has it ever been considered that it's our treatment of these creatures that caused their psychiatric problems?'

'Hah. Now you want to do my job for me.'

I just couldn't stop myself. I knew that I'd dug a big hole by answering back. The short time I'd spent with Iain had convinced me humans had more potential than we realise. My career suddenly seemed much less important than his welfare.

'I'm sorry, but I think you're wrong; at least about Iain. Next time there's an open session of the Assembly, I'm going to ask my father to put this debate on the agenda.'

I tried to reach into the supervisor's mind, curious to learn whether my arguments were having any affect. It astonished me to discover he'd thrown up an impenetrable shield. There wasn't time to speculate over what he was hiding his next statement took me by complete surprise.

'Angeriana, I hold you personally responsible for this human's actions. You have my permission to conduct him to a few limited locations within the humanoid sphere, but you must restrict his access to technologies of any kind. If you overstep these conditions you'll find yourself on the first Eilad heading back to Manyarner. One bit of trouble and your career in the O.P.U. is over. Do you understand?'

Shielding heavily to mask my true feelings, my demeanour returned to one of contrite composure. Acknowledging the supervisor's instructions, I headed quickly up the corridor. Iain trotted along behind me.

As we moved off, I felt him glancing back over his shoulder. This was the very first time he'd seen another species or witnessed a teleport in progress. It amazed me that he took it in his stride.

There was much more to this young man than met the eye. Now I had to convince everyone else of that fact.

******

Several exhausting hours later we found ourselves in the arboretum. This simulated garden was planted with specimens from across all worlds of the O.P.U. It symbolised the union between planets and gave those working here a welcome break from the austere surroundings of metal bulkheads and dermoplastic partition walls.

Sitting down on the soft carpet of synthetic soil, I indicated for Iain to join me.

'You've told me this place is a giant space station orbiting the outer reaches of a solar system close to my own.' I nodded. 'Who pays for it all?'

I pulled my waist-length hair away from my face, tucking it behind my ears. 'You mean money?'

'Yeah, cash, readies, wonga... This lot must've cost a bomb.'

I smiled at his use of slang. The English language alone could keep my research going for months.

'If I'm interpreting the term correctly, we don't have

money in the sense you mean. We do have credits, at least each planet does. These are acquired through a barter system.' I felt the confusion in his thoughts. 'For example. My planet, Manyarner, has a lot of mineral wealth - gold to be precise. It's just there lying on the surface. We don't have any use for it; at least we didn't until the O.P.U. was formed. Gold is a major component in space ship construction and quite rare in the galaxy. We exchange it for other commodities, like teleporters and food dispensers. The value of these items isn't always equal so as a planet we're in credit.'

'I get that, but whose credits were used to build this place?' He waved around us at the unfamiliar foliage.

'No planet alone could construct a space station this large. It took the combined knowledge of more than a hundred worlds. Over four thousand individuals live and work here in the humanoid sphere. Many more diverse species are housed in spheres just like this one, each connected by a cord of artificial gravity. The station orbits the Gretin star.'

He raised an eyebrow. 'So you say. I have to take your word for it. Nowhere we've been today have we seen a porthole or window. And come to think of it, apart from that grey guy we haven't seen any people either. What are you hiding from me?'

'Nothing. As I was trying to explain earlier, the Order of Planetary Unification is a conglomeration of worlds...'

'Like the United Nations?' he interrupted.

It took me a moment to acquire knowledge of this organisation, subtly, from his long-term memory. 'No, not really, there's no political affiliation. It's more like a university with lots of separate departments each engaged in research.'

'Researching what?'

'You, or people like you. When the developed planets in this sector of the galaxy discovered one another, they agreed to combine their efforts to map the rest of the known universe; to learn from each other and to share knowledge. A major part of the O.P.U.'s role is the

Species Recognition Programme. Scout ships embark on long missions to reach newly discovered worlds...'

'To seek out new life and new civilisations...' Laughing aloud, he rolled back on the ground beside me. 'To boldly go where no one has gone before.'

Giving him a bewildered look, I continued my explanation. 'The O.P.U.'s main directive is for the assessment of potential development on such worlds. Earth is just one planet marked out for special consideration. Many humans before you have been brought here. Unfortunately, early specimens died from a sort of culture shock. Unable to comprehend what was happening, they rapidly degenerated into mental illness. We learned very little from these people.

'The O.P.U. isn't a cruel organisation and disliked what they'd done. The program was stalled for some time while the ethical and moral implications were debated. In time the Board put a strong enough case to the Assembly to be granted an extension to their research. This permission held two conditions: First, that a way be found to minimise suffering, and second, that a more convenient system of information exchange be employed. After some initial experiments, they decided to fit future specimens with a psionic transceiver.' I shrugged. 'And here you are.'

Monitoring Iain's reactions closely during my account, his emotions rose and fell with each new revelation. He was angry and my mind perceived a strong visual impression of rats running around a maze. I'd been prepared for this, but he had other feelings as well. Hopelessness and despair mixed with anticipation and excitement. His psyche was complex and quite astonishing.

Leaning forward I took off my boots. 'I don't know how you people manage to wear clothes all the time. It's so uncomfortable.' I rubbed my toes to improve the circulation. 'I have to wear this uniform in the infirmary and multi-cultural areas, but usually get to spend my day alone in the lab. There I can take it off and really relax.'

I caught a mischievous thought from his mind and hurried on with my commentary. 'Of course out of courtesy to your culture, I'll continue to wear clothes when in your company.'

His reply was tinged with disappointment. 'Of course.'

'It's quite lucky that I'm wearing them today as this place is about to go into its dark cycle. Look up there.' I pointed up at the domed ceiling above us. The artificial sunshine was still intense, but a crack had now appeared on its surface.

'Every rotation, that's about a week to you, the whole station turns on its axis and this sphere points back into space. The shield is then opened and we have a sort of artificial night. It's quite spectacular to watch. That's why I brought us here.'

The sky above suddenly split open, plunging us into an uncompromising blackness. I watched his face as he looked up in amazement, relieved to feel a sense of wonder rather than panic. Stars became visible in the newly formed night sky, until the whole area was bathed in the blue brilliance of many millions of suns.

He lay back on the ground. 'Shit. Now I'm impressed,' was all he said for a very long time.

Without taking his eyes off the panorama overhead, Iain began to question me further. 'So why haven't we seen anyone else on our travels?'

'The simple explanation is that we're on foot. It's very rare for people to walk between locations, not when teleportation is so much easier. I must confess, though. I think they've cleared the corridors deliberately, to avoid you seeing too much.'

'And instructed you to only show me the crapiest places,' he added. 'With all this wealth of knowledge around us, all I get to see are a few plants and a very impressive view of the night sky. Where's the machinery that runs all this? How is the enormous amount of energy needed to power this place, generated? They're the things I wanna see.'

'I doubt you'd be able to comprehend it even if I showed you.'

He stood up. 'There you go again, treating me like

27

I'm some sort of retard. I'm taking science A levels. My teacher told me I've a natural aptitude with electronics. Maybe I'll surprise you by my amazing grasp of your technology. After all, the laws of physics are the same everywhere in the universe. Einstein proved that, right?'

I shook my head. 'This Einstein, to whom you refer. Is he the one mentioned in your history books who said that faster than light travel is impossible?'

'One and the same. The greatest man in science.' His eyes widened. 'You're not going to tell me that he was wrong?'

'No, not exactly wrong. He did remarkably well for someone with such a limited perspective. He figured out only a small part of the enigma. There's so much that he didn't know about the fabric of the quantum universe. I could try to explain our science to you, Iain, but it would probably take half your lifetime to understand the very basics. I thought you were in a hurry to get back home?'

Who was I kidding, the Board had never released a subject, and I doubted that one promising specimen would change their minds.

'I am but...Hey, how d'you know?'

'You must believe me when I say that I'm not deliberately reading your thoughts.' I gave him a sideways look. 'You've been thinking of Mum and Dad for days. Wondering what they're doing, wishing you could see them. It just pops into my head.'

'If you know that, then you also know...'

'How thrilling all this is? Yes, I understand. If we teach you about our technology you can go home and become famous.'

'But you won't, will you. It's against the rules.'

'Okay then.' I stood beside him in the darkness and pointed up at the starscape.

Let's see how he copes with this, I thought.

'Did you wonder how the shield was removed so rapidly? As I said when we came in, this arboretum is an artificial biosphere many hundreds of metres wide. It sits on top of a sphere the size of a small moon.'

'At this distance from the Gretin star there are huge

dangers from meteors, cosmic rays, and other kinds of radiation. The shield protects the sphere and all of us within it. This is not a crude metallic device like someone on Earth would produce. As we rotated into the darkness phase it appeared that the shield opened. This was an illusion. The shield is made of pure energy. Energy generated not by any apparatus, but by the minds of the people living on the station. Yes, there are some tools we posses that may be considered, in your limited definition, as machinery.' I pulled a teleport control from my pocket and held it up for him to view. 'But the vast majority of our 'technology' involves mental manipulations far more complex than your mind can even comprehend.'

'So why, if you people have super powers, do you need to kidnap the likes of me? Can't you just beam down and find things out for yourselves?'

I reached into his mind, there were still vestiges of his earlier anxiety, but he managed to exploit the tension and change it to anger. It didn't matter that he focussed this towards me; my concern was that anger unchecked could quickly turn to violence. 'You're annoyed again. I think we'd better return to your room and resume this discussion tomorrow.'

'Don't like it when I get angry aye? It sticks in your throat that even with all your fantastic talents to manipulate matter, you still can't understand the workings of human society. I get it now. Maybe you're not so *all powerful* as you like to make out.' He strode off into the darkness.

My psi-awareness could feel him running about, tripping over the plants that grew either side of the pathway in his haste to get away. After a while he stopped.

He was completely lost.

Probing his mind was fascinating. He felt enraged by my comments and stood forcing himself to take deep breaths, quelling the anger. I'd not expected so much from a primitive mind and couldn't wait to report my findings to the Board. Using the teleport, I materialised at his side.

'Can't you find your way back?' He almost jumped

out of his skin.

I let out a short telekinetic burst and a navigation drone rose from beneath the undergrowth. As it came up it brushed against the triangular leaves of a nearby bush; a pungent smell like rotting flesh filled the air. The drone stopped when it reached head height and hovered before us, shedding a pale blue light across the dense foliage.

'Is that better?' Iain nodded, taking my arm. 'I concede round one to you. Now, please show me the way out of here it's giving me the creeps?'

'Look, Iain. I know this is difficult to accept, but I do care for your welfare. In my medical judgement you've had enough stress for one day and need to rest. Let me teleport us back to your room and you can sleep for a while.'

My suggestion brought him relief.

I held up the teleport control, allowing him to watch me set the programme.

'Here we go.'

In the next instant we were back in the visitors centre.

******

I materialised in Iain's room two hours later; expecting to find him still asleep on the couch where I'd left him.

He wasn't there.

After checking the waste disposal facilities and the bedroom, panic began to set in. I looked up into the vid-cam and pathed to the duty technician.

'Where is he? Did they move him to another room?'

'Did you expect us to monitor the movements of catalogue number 717250H? The Board supervisor told us you were taking personal responsibility for this case and assigned us to monitor another specimen.'

'Yes, I did, actually. If he's not here then he must have found some way out of the room. How is that possible?'

I sensed the technician scanning through her

30

security logs. *'Records show unauthorised access to the door activation codes fifty minutes ago. This is most irregular.'*

'Idiot!'

I rushed outside, searching the nearby corridors. If the situation wasn't so dire, I'd marvel at Iain's ingenuity, but there wasn't time for such speculation.

I couldn't find him.

I paused to catch my breath. This was all I needed. The supervisor had taken me at my word and removed all surveillance. But it didn't add up. Throughout the day the absence of people on the walkways indicated that our every move was being watched. Everything said by Iain would have been recorded and analysed as part of the programme. Could the supervisor have another reason for allowing me such freedom? What could he possibly have to gain if Iain escaped?

Termination seemed the most likely outcome of that day's events.

By now I'd approached a terminal outlet. Set at a walkway intersection. I leaned close to the microphone.

'Recognition.'

The computer's stiff, mechanical voice responded immediately. 'Designation - Manyarnern female, Angeriana'asusilicana. Catalogue technician first class. Current assignment Species Recognition Programme. Awaiting request.'

'Level one internal security search, identify and locate catalogue number 717250H. Show visual display at this terminal.'

Tapping my fingers on the dermoplastic screen, I muttered to myself. 'Why do I always do these things? I can't just settle for following the rules, can't adhere to regulations. I have to drop myself in it by taking risks.'

The display focused to show the off-world traders market.

'How could he have got there?' The viewer zoomed in to one of the tents. Iain was climbing into a metal container stacked at the back of the small space.

'Gotcha. Computer, teleport me to location

displayed and close search parameters.'

******

Chapter 2

Materialising at the end of the market, I jogged up the busy street; between ornate tents displaying their wares in mini grav-nets. Nearing the centre of the market, the crowd became denser forcing my pace to slow.

'Come on... come on...'

I considered lifting above the crowd.

No, it would draw too much attention.

I pushed forward at ground level, searching for one tent in particular. Spotting the garish black and yellow stripes, I glanced around and slipped inside.

'And what do you think you're doing?' Raising the lid of a container, I revealed Iain crouching down amongst a glistening shipment of pond crystals. *'Trying to get me fired?'*

He looked at me angrily and climbed out. A few crystals had stuck to his suit. Snatching them up, he hurled them to the ground at my feet.

'You've been bating me all day. If this gets you fired for your own incompetence, then I'm glad. I know I'm fucked. There's no way out of this mess for me. But if I can take you with me, that suits me just fine.'

He projected his most deranged thoughts into my mind: Images of violence and death, feelings of intense hatred and malevolence. It's a tactic most animals use when cornered, suddenly turning on their captor.

How easily he'd penetrated my shield.

I was impressed.

I'll need to keep my guard up in future, I thought.

'Typical.' I took a deep breath and walked a few paces away from him before turning around again. 'You get me to agree to restrict my conversation to speech then you go and change your mind. What exactly do you want me to do?'

'You know damn well what I want.'

He lunged forward, his body weight knocking me to

the ground as he passed. In the next instant he'd ducked through the opening of the tent and disappeared from view. My heart sank and I lay back, panting heavily. Violence, whether mental or physical, **would** be picked up by the Board.

I didn't relish the idea of carrying out orders for his termination.

I rose and brushed debris from my robe, anything to postpone the inevitable.

A few seconds later, Iain ran back, hotly pursued by two security officers and the trader into whose tent we had trespassed. The closest guard raised his weapon.

'You are both under arrest,' he barked on a public channel.

I glared at the man. The report couldn't have been passed that quickly.

'On what charge?'

Realising that I no longer wore my uniform, I added. 'I am Angeriana of Manyarner, Catalogue technician, and this is a... a friend of mine. On whose authority do you place us under arrest?'

Now the small, hairy, creature spoke; his crooked nose twitching in time with his antennae. He wore a patchwork cloak, fastened under his neck with a huge yellow and black bow. Beneath this, shiny buckled boots protruded. I wanted to giggle, but suppressed the temptation.

'On my authority as owner of this stand and purveyor of those pond crystals which your 'friend' has just rendered worthless.'

This was unexpected. I decided to see where it took us.

'I'm very sorry about your crystals. I will of course reimburse you for any loss.'

The trader stepped forward and fixed me with a steely glare. 'Even if you are an O.P.U. operative, I doubt if there's enough credit in your account to cover the cost of them there crystals. They're valuable items that he's just trampled all over.' He snorted in Iain's direction. 'I tell you what, sell me this pet and I may consider dropping the charges.'

'As I said earlier, he's my friend, he's not a pet, and he's definitely not for sale.'

I grabbed Iain's hand, marching him rapidly towards the doorway, passing too close for comfort in front of the trader.

Putting out his stumpy arm he blocked my way.

'I don't know what you're playing at,' he pathed menacingly on a private frequency. *'I know what he did to you earlier and it didn't seem much like friendship to me. Either you give him to me or pay me my dues. Either way I'm not letting you two out of my sight until this is settled. D'you understand?'*

'Oh I understand very well. You're smuggling Garillian pond crystals into the Gretin system. They are, as you so rightly point out, rare and valuable artefacts. From my recollection they're also banned on most O.P.U. worlds. A psionic inhibitor, if I'm not mistaken? How is it going to look when I tell security the exact nature of the items you stock? Maybe I should recommend a further search. See what other contraband you have here in your tent.'

'Blah,' he said aloud, retracting his arm. 'Ok I'll let you go if you make some kind of payment; a reasonable payment to reimburse me for my trouble.'

'See, officers. There's nothing here but a misunderstanding. Please put your weapons away, they're making me very nervous. I assure you that I'll pay this respectable merchant whatever fair price he requests. Does anyone have a keypad?'

Losing no time, the trader snatched a credit transfer pad out from under his cloak. His fingers moved deftly over the panel as he typed in the transaction details.

'Now, lady. If you give me your name and designation once again I'll complete our business and let you and your friend, be on your way.' The trader smirked.

There are few times in my life that I've used my official connections, but this seemed a most appropriate moment. I bent down and took the pad from him, speaking into the mouthpiece in Manyarnern. 'Computer, recognise

Angeriana'asusilicana, daughter of Ambassador Voltin.' I turned towards the two officers. 'Who you know is senior representative on the O.P.U. Assembly. Call up credit rating and transfer requested units to this account.'

'Acknowledged, transfer complete,' replied the metallic voice.

I handed the keypad back to the trader.

'Will there be anything else?'

The security officers lowered their weapons and looked rather embarrassed. The senior of the two stepped forward to address me. 'Madame,' he bowed deferentially. 'I'm very sorry for this regrettable situation. If only you had identified yourself earlier we would not have treated you so…'

'There's no need for apologies. I promise to keep this little misunderstanding to myself. Now if you would excuse me, I've had enough excitement for one day and would like to return to my quarters.'

'Certainly, Madame. My team would be happy to escort you anywhere you wish to go.'

Patting him lightly on the shoulder, I smiled. 'Thank you for the offer, but I'm certain that you have other duties to attend to.'

Seeing my opportunity for a quick exit, I grabbed Iain's hand; pulling him out of the tent and into the commotion of the market street beyond.

Calling after us telepathically, I addressed the trader. *'Should have asked for double that price, you're losing your touch.'*

'And where would your eminence like her shipment of pond crystals delivered?' he replied, good-humouredly. *'I know when I've been had and it couldn't have been done by a lovelier creature than yourself. You'd fetch a high price at market.'*

'Flattery will get you nowhere, but thanks for trying. Keep the crystals in storage for me, at a reasonable cost billed yearly to my personal account. One day I'll come back and claim them. If you're still around?'

'Oh. I'll be here. Westler Topynkin, at your service, Madame.'

I looked at Iain, struggling against me as we pushed our way back through the crowd.

I'm sorry, but you leave me no choice, I thought. *'Calm down.'*

The psionic suggestion brought him under control. His eyes glazed over and his pace slowed. Now he'd settled down, I dragged him along behind me as I headed towards the nearest teleport stand.

******

I sighed, dropping down into one of the chairs in Iain's room. 'I don't ever want to go through that again.'

Iain looked at me, baffled by events. 'What exactly did just happen? I was completely lost after you started speaking in, what I guessed to be, your native language? All I remember was that dwarf wanted me in exchange for those funny looking bits of rock. He was under the impression that I was your pet. How on Earth did you manage to talk him out of it?'

'You really don't want to know. You came close tonight to getting your wish to leave the station. Only it wasn't Earth he intended to take you to. It was a slave market in the Gretin asteroid belt.' I paused. 'Perhaps it would have been better...'

It felt as though Iain's intense gaze could see right through me. I shuddered and pulled my shield up tight.

'Your planet may be R.A.W. - that means a restricted access world - but it doesn't stop the more unscrupulous races of the galaxy visiting Earth to collect specimens of their own. There are worlds where the taste for human flesh is becoming quite a delicacy.'

'You're kidding me, right? Advanced alien species are supposed to be peace-loving protectors of primitive races. Not barbaric cannibals looking for their next meal.'

I glanced across at the terminal, expecting to see the screen light up with an incoming message. Is it worth explaining, I wondered. It was only a matter of time before the order arrived. And then I'd have to...

'Angie, are you okay?'

Surely the orders would arrive at any moment, I thought.

Any moment now...

******

'I'm sorry I got mad,' said Iain.

'No need. Most of our guests react with hostility at some point during their stay.'

I looked at my chronometer, the order still hadn't arrived. Had they noticed his outburst? Perhaps they weren't monitoring us at all? I felt tired. Iain wasn't the only one stressed by the day's events.

He beckoned me towards the sofa and we both sat down. 'Have you examined many people before me? You said some didn't make it. How many others are here on the station working for you?'

I felt ashamed. The tale of his predecessors' demise wasn't a pretty one. Surprised by my own reaction, I wondered whether I should tell him the truth.

How would he take the news of so many deaths at our hands?

Iain, sensing my hesitation, shifted his weight and turned to face me. 'Is it that bad?'

'No. It's not that exactly. We've studied the Earth for decades. In the beginning we used cruder methods. We have, in fact, brought hundreds of your kind here before... '

His expression was incredulous. 'You're not telling me that I'm the only one?'

I nodded. 'Yes. I'm afraid so. No one else has survived this long. You're the first human taken outside his room who remained sane enough for further research.'

'Well, Angie, if I'm the only one then doesn't that make me a sort of Ambassador for my planet?'

'I wouldn't hold your breath, but I'll put in a good word for you with the Board.'

There was still hope.

I rubbed the back of my neck. 'I've never done so much walking before. Tomorrow we'll have to use the teleporter. By the way, how exactly did you get out of the room?'

He smiled. 'It didn't take me long to figure out that this gismo in my head does far more than just telepathy. Once I'd scanned the door mechanism, it was easy to link my mind with the control circuit and...' The wall in front of us shimmered as the hidden portal unlocked and swung open.

'Very ingenious of you.' I shot him a look of disbelief. It baffled me how such a primitive mind could master our technologies so quickly.

I had underestimated his resourcefulness.

Sending out a telekinetic signal, the door vanished once again. 'If it's that easy, we'll have to review our security protocols.'

He shrugged. 'Will you get in trouble?'

'When you went missing I carried out a level one security search. When the Board read the print outs I'll be called in to explain myself.'

I tried to conceal my fear. It was a miracle they haven't noticed his outburst back at the market.

Do miracles actually happen? I thought.

A few days ago, I would have willingly killed this young man. I must have been out of my mind.

I pushed the notion away. This conversation needed a more constructive direction.

'Are you going to tell me why you tried to run away? How far did you expect to get; a single human alone on a massive space station three hundred light years from your world?'

'Imagine you're me. One day I'm walking home from football, the next I'm whisked away and told that I've had some gismo put in my brain. That I'm a guinea pig in an alien's experiment and that most of my fellow humans turned into raving lunatics. Do you expect me to just sit here and take it?'

I pondered how to reassure him.

'I understand why you did it, Iain. If I were in your place I'd probably have done the same. I sense that even now that you don't fully trust us.'

'D'you blame me?'

I shook my head. 'Let me level with you. We need you... I need you. More than you realise. The programme has ground to a halt. Species worthy of our attention are too few and too widely scattered across the universe to make it a worthwhile use of time and resources.'

He threw his hands into the air. 'Why me, Angie. For fuck sake! Why me?'

'You were in the wrong place at the wrong time.'

'Or the right place... it depends on your perspective, doesn't it?'

Ignoring his sarcasm, I continued. 'It was chance, that's all. I must admit that since you arrived things have changed a bit.'

'Changed?'

'Ever since you opened your eyes on the medi-bed in my lab, I've sensed something else. You're special, Iain. You have qualities I've never seen in another human.' Taking his hands in mine, I looked deep into his eyes. 'I know it's difficult for you, but I ask for a leap of faith. Let me, willingly, into your mind and I'll explain. It's impossible to deceive when linked.'

He thought about my proposition for the briefest of moments before replying.

'Okay. What do I do?'

'Just go with the flow,' I replied, dropping my shield.

Summoning images from the initial days of the Species Recognition Programme, I allowed them to fill me up. I breathed life into the sights, sounds and smells of the early research then passed them across the psychic bridge into his mind. To begin there was a view of the very first specimen disembarking from one of the scout ships; technicians vying for the chance to study this visitor from a distant world. Then a scene from inside the Assembly chamber itself with ornate emblems of the many O.P.U. planets unfurled to rapturous applause. Finally I showed two non-humanoid creatures undergoing dexterity tests in a lab similar to my own; the technician struggling to communicate through a rough kind of sign language.

Iain experienced everything as if it were happening

right in front of him. I think he was impressed.

I hesitated, the images lost substance. Something was happening, something astonishing. My eyes widened. Iain had taken control of the link.

Dismissing these well-chosen scenes, he pushed through my consciousness, heading single-mindedly for one thing; my long-term memory store. Why I let this happen I don't really know. It angered me at first. He'd used my trust to gain an advantage, but could I blame him? Breaking the link would be easy, but curiosity got the better of me.

Once it began, I felt compelled to continue.

He searched through my memories looking for a way home. An escape route - something - *anything* that could get him off the station. What he found in the depths of my psyche neither of us expected.

The truth.

Pulling image after sickening image from my mind, he recoiled in horror.

The first human I'd experimented on lay face down before on the medi-bed; his head pulling against the restraining field in an attempt to look around at me. The laser-scalpel in my hand cut along the length of the man's spine. He screamed in agony, his body convulsing. Troubled by his reaction, I increased the pain barrier I'd established in his mind and he settled once again. A neurostimulator floated up from the trolley and into my hand. I leant down to attach it to the man's vertebrae. He let out a further piercing cry and died. With a sigh, I threw the stimulator down beside the other equipment and tapped my fingers on the terminal screen. Humans were obviously more sensitive than we thought. Stepping away from the bio-bed, there was a shimmering light as the teleporter disintegrated the corpse.

Another memory appeared to replace the first. A human female sat in the corner of her room. Curled into a tight ball, she rocked back and forth humming softly to herself. As I approached, I reached down telekinetically and pulled her hands free; they were covered in her own blood. Dragging the woman up into a standing position, I

41

noticed that she had scratches running the length her arms. Her long, red, fingernails had torn open the skin in some kind of self mutilation. She looked at me, eyes vacant, soul empty. There was nothing left here to study. I dropped her onto the ground and walked away. When I reached the far wall a force field appeared, dividing the room in two. There was a hissing sound as the air was sucked away. The asphyxiated women lay dead on the floor.

The violence of the next image took us both by surprise. A middle-aged man sprung from the medi-bed while my back was turned.

'Stop it. Stop right there.' I shouted. 'I've had quite enough of you...'

His attack froze in mid-air behind me. I turned slowly, angered by his actions.

The man's eyes betrayed him and I noticed a poorly concealed switch-blade jutting out of his sleeve. My mind took hold of the knife pulling it down and into his open hand. With telekinesis I curled his fingers around the knife until his index finger pushed on the button. The thin, metal blade sprung out. I could feel the hatred, the murderous intent, in the man's thoughts as his eyes fixed on the shiny cutting edge.

'Is this what you want?'

Controlling his arm, I moved it forward and around his body until he was holding the knife against his own throat. Now his eyes showed utter panic; darting down at his chin and then up towards me.

For a fraction of a second the image was replaced by a grinning barbarian sinking his pointed teeth into my father's neck. As quickly as the memory surfaced it flashed out of existence again, replaced by the scene of the human with the knife.

The man's arm suddenly yanked on the blade, cutting through the carotid artery with one stroke. A fountain of dark red blood poured out; showering me in warm stickiness.

'Damn.'

I shook the blood from my uniform and tapped the

terminal. The decontamination field fizzed around me. In the next instant my uniform and the room were completely clean. The man's body was gone.

******

'Holy shit!' Iain's consciousness retreated from the link.

I've lived inside someone else's mind on many occasions, sharing visions, memories and scenes from the sacred texts. This was different. Iain had just shown me my past through his eyes.

It was disgusting.

He hated me, and at that moment, I hated myself. How can I justify all this suffering in the name of science? I felt sick to the stomach and for a while thought I would vomit.

Having recoiled mentally, Iain now pushed himself away physically; toppling backwards over the arm of the sofa and landing heavily on the floor.

'I gotta get away from you.'

I crawled towards him along the cushioned seat. 'No, please. That's not me. Not anymore. I've changed. You've changed me.'

His jaw tightened, shoulders hunched with violent intent.

'I'm sorry. I never meant to hurt them. It was just my job.'

A wave of remorse overtook me. I pulled my legs up, cuddling them to my chest, rocking gently. A deluge of tears ran uncontrolled down my face. *'Go, get out of here. I won't stop you.'*

He didn't leave.

He simply stared, silently, at my outpouring of regret.

I couldn't read him. I didn't even try.

Minutes, maybe hours, later I used a meditation to regain some control.

'Forgive me.'

He still sat on the floor at one end of the sofa. I

reached down, offering him my hand, grateful when he accepted it; re-establishing the psychic bridge.

'I am Angeriana'asusilicana, daughter of Ambassador Voltin, Elder of the Manyarnern Circle.' I sent him an image of my home planet. Turquoise lakes and high, snow capped, mountain ranges set against a lilac sky: This tranquil vista a brutal contrast to my inner landscape.

I rallied.

'I swear I'll make every effort to ensure you're the last human brought into the Species Recognition Programme and I will never again, willingly, cause harm to those taken against their will and brought here.'

The tension subsided as he felt my pledge.

I was taken aback by the nature of my promise to him. In just one day, I'd completely changed the direction of my career. He'd changed too. Banishing thoughts of escape, he replaced them with a determination to exploit the O.P.U. in whatever way he could.

We couldn't stop the Species Recognition Programme, but we'd have a damn good try. Our thoughts mingled and we become resolute of purpose, almost single minded, in our desire for change.

Replacing my shield, I broke our telepathic link, let go of his hand and stood up.

'You rest. I have a difficult report to write before I go off duty.'

'Why bother? You said that the Board will call you in to explain how I escaped. If things are that bad, maybe we should make the most of it while we can.'

He was right, I'd probably lost my job already. I didn't care about me. If I could post a favourable report there was still hope for his future in the programme.

I shrugged. 'I suppose I can use the terminal in here, as long as you're quiet.'

'Cool. I'll get us something to eat. Let's see what this contraption can knock up?'

He walked over to the food dispenser and brought up the menu directory. I had intended to work on the report, but for some reason just couldn't keep my eyes off his every movement.

Then it hit me.

The intimacy of our link had stirred up new emotions. My people call this 'triptoy.' A moment in your life fated to happen: that you cannot deny and must act upon.

Watching Iain selecting items for us to eat, my mind wandered back to the day I learned about triptoy. It was a week after I'd advanced into the third level of the Academy. Grateful to be dragged from the tedium of mental agility classes, I flew with my tutor to our family temple in Vanya province. Almost as soon as we grounded, she started her lesson for the day.

'See this?' She waved towards the foot of one of the stone columns. A few centimetres above the floor was the carving of a tall figure. More tree than person, it's legs were embedded in the ground and it's arms reached up to form the branches. Amongst those branches was a symbol that I already knew; the symbol for Manyarner.

Her mind broadcast the most peculiar sense of awe at the sight of this image. I couldn't have been more disinterested, but nodded to keep her happy.

'This is you,' she said, pointing her finger more insistently toward the carving. I obligingly leaned closer. *'This glyph sequence appeared at the last full moon, but until yesterday the Lenses were not sure to whom it pertained.'*

I shrugged. *'Big deal.'*

For a moment she glared at me, her anger restrained beneath the propriety that comes with the specialisation of tutor. *'Yes, Angeriana, it is a big deal. Laid out before you is your personal myth. All the events of your life, all the dreams, thoughts and fears are written in this story. Aren't you even a little intrigued to know what's to come?'*

Shaking my head non-committally, I sat down on the stone floor; my back against the nearest column. *'Yeah, a little, but I already know what I'm going to do with my life. I'll spend the next two years at the Academy and then I'll be a healer. That's what the Lenses tell me and I*

45

doubt my chronicle appearing on our family temple will encourage them to reveal any more.'

'You may be right.' She walked forward and ran her fingers over the sequence of glyphs: touching the tree-person first and then tracing the outline of further carvings in the sequence. There were triangles and dots. Shallow zigzags mounted above spirals and curved serpents devouring tiny people. A few meters higher was a break in the pattern; an area devoid of shape or meaning.

'What's that?' I asked, nodding towards the smooth stone.

'Triptoy.' Her voice echoed around the temple, the word itself refusing to diminish until I had acknowledged the power in its utterance.

'Trip what?'

Avoiding my gaze, she took a few steps across the shrine and looked out at the countryside beyond. 'The Lens who read your specialisation was correct. You are to become a healer - if you keep your thoughts focussed on your studies.' A slight tingle of irony rippled through her mind, but was quickly pushed aside. 'There are a few individuals in our society, and you are one of them Angeriana, for whom the story is not fixed. These individuals have moments of triptoy in their personal myth that manifest themselves as breaks in the carvings. Triptoy is a moment in time where many different paths lie ahead and a choice must be made over which one to follow. These moments are fated and cannot be avoided, but the outcome - the choice - cannot be seen either: not until the temple rewrites itself.'

I left her to ramble on. My attention had been drawn by a Lava Beetle as it climbed skyward up the stones. The carvings must have been like mountainous obstacles in its path, yet it shuffled its many feet across the uneven surface with a fierce determination to get to the summit. As I watched, a mischievous thought sprang to mind and I reached out my psi awareness to feel the smoothness of the beetles back. A gentle poke of telekinesis, and I dislodged it from the stone. In a flash the beetle's back opened and gossamer wings unfolded from their hidden cavity. Glinting in the sunshine, it turned indignantly and flew away.

'Angie... Angie...' The demanding voice dragged me back to the present. 'I was asking if this is okay?'

I looked up at Iain and smiled. 'Sure, anything will do. I'm not fussy.'

So, it seemed that the threads of both mine and Iain's destinies had unknotted and brought us into that moment; full of potential, ripe with possibilities for the future. My mind raced through the likely outcomes of today's events. In the end I decided there was nothing I could do, so why worry about it. Damn Manyarnern philosophy. However hard I tried, I just couldn't get away from it.

Deep in thought, I accidentally pathed on an open channel.

'Triptoy.'

'What did you say?'

'Sorry. I didn't mean for you to pick up that thought.'

'I'm not so naive that I don't realise this form of communication is more natural for you.' Stunned by Iain's telepathic skill, I had no idea of how to respond.

******

Iain put down his spoon. 'That wasn't half bad. A bit bland, but okay. What did you call it?'

'Tesnet soup.' I wiped a finger around the rim of my bowl and licked it. 'This duplicated food doesn't taste anything like it does when it's cooked fresh. My planet's not known for its cuisine, so I rarely select Manyarnern dishes from the dispenser. I actually think this was an improvement on what I'd get back home.' I chuckled.

'And you're sure my digestion can handle it?'

I nodded. 'It's just a mix of roots, seeds and herbs, nothing poisonous.'

Pushing his bowl away, Iain leaned back in his chair. 'What's your planet like? You showed me a picture of it earlier and it looked pretty unspoilt. What's it like living there?'

'Tranquil, spiritual, idyllic.' I sighed heavily. 'The sky is always a perfectly cloudless shade of lilac. Grassy plains stretch across huge swathes of each continent, interspersed with pockets of forest. In some areas the open-cast mining has left exposed rock, but even this has a natural beauty of its own; flecks of gold sparkle in the endless sunshine.'

'What about cities? Where do people live? What do they do?'

'There's no big, noisy urban sprawl like you have on Earth, no heavy industry or other kind of manufacturing. We don't need to work to survive, but we do follow our specialisations. Some people are creative artists who inspire our minds through colourful exhibits or music, others are artisans who weave delicate fabrics and fashion them into simple gowns or soft furnishings for our homes. Everything else we acquire from off world. We also have environmentalists who manage the weather and some who induce plants to grow; so they can be harvested from the countryside. And there are healers like me, who are needed on the odd occasions when someone has an accident or to help with childbirth. Sickness and disease have been completely eliminated.'

He wiped his hand through his thick hair. 'So who cleans the toilets?'

'There was a time, before the O.P.U. was founded when we had labourers; people who performed maintenance and other menial tasks. These days we use imported technology to do those roles.'

He didn't look impressed. 'It sounds almost too good to be true. You gave all that up to come here?'

I shifted uneasily in my seat. Could he read through my shield? Did he know that I had gladly left this behind in exchange for the excitement of working for the O.P.U.?'

'There is no hardship, Iain, no poverty or hunger. No pollution, homelessness or intolerance. Extended families live peacefully together on large estates, sharing every aspect of themselves; both day and night.'

He shot me a cheeky grin. 'Every aspect?'

I sat up. 'Sorry, Iain, I'd love to spend time telling

you about my home world, but I still have that report to write.' I sensed his disappointment. 'Ask me another day, and I'll tell you some more.'

He stood up and collected the soiled bowls and utensils. 'Okay, I know when I've been told to shut up.' He walked away from the table, smiling to himself.

******

The Board in charge of Species Recognition sits in open session twice every cycle. More like a tribunal than a review, cross examination was enough to test anyone's nerve. The members - there are twenty in total - represent founding planets of the O.P.U., each chosen for their consummate telepathic skill. Caught in the intensity of their combined stare, it felt almost as bad as the examinations given at the Manyarnern Academy... almost.

Although the Board reports back to the Assembly, they're fairly autonomous in decisions made regarding individual specimens. My previous unsuccessful cases resulted in short, superficial, interrogation.

Ian's case was different.

I'd come through the first panel by the skin of my teeth; thankful that they didn't bring up his aggressive outburst at the off-world market. This time I was 'sticking my neck out' - such a curious human expression - even further.

'As you know from my reports, catalogue number 717250H has demonstrated remarkable adjustment to his new environment. He's cooperated fully at every formal interview panel and willingly undergone numerous medical and psychological tests.' Attempting to read their reaction, it didn't surprise me when my mental probing revealed nothing. It's decades since a technician reported such a successful first encounter. They're probably taking their time to consider his case.

Unsettled, I rushed ahead with my request. *'Iain, I mean catalogue number 717250H is a quick learner. I've run out of things to do with him.'* Their continued silence made my anxiety rise further. *'What I mean is... I can't find* anything new to talk about if we just walk in the market or arboretum every day. I need to put obstacles in his path and watch how he reacts to them.'

'Will he behave himself this time?' they pathed in unison.

Damn it, they did know about Iain's earlier outburst. I hoped I'd got away with it.

The Board supervisor coughed. 'Your mother is not without influence here.'

My heart thumped. Resentment and gratitude mixed uncomfortably in my mind.

I couldn't meet her gaze.

'What exactly are you proposing?' asked the supervisor.

'In my opinion, we've forgotten the purpose of our own research. The programme was designed to look for developmental potential on R.A.W. planetary systems. I believe that due to previous negative incidents, we've become too restrictive on the few who do show potential. Iain's not a threat, he's proved that. So far he's exhibited amazing psionic ability. Allow me free access to all areas of the station and let me show him our technology. Then I'll be able to study him in more detail. I will, of course, accompany him everywhere.'

There was silence while they deliberated. I noticed the Board supervisor repeatedly glancing towards me, and I was certain he told them about our encounter in the corridor. It didn't bother me too much. I'd decided to resign as soon as Iain's assessment was complete. I was more concerned about their intentions toward him and his planet in the long-term.

'Very well, Angeriana, show catalogue number 717250H around the rest of the station. Challenge him and see how he reacts. We are not unmoved by the tragedies that have gone before. To lose another specimen, especially one with such a remarkable mind, would damage us all. We do not intend to neglect our duty to him and his kind.'

The phrasing of their response was clear evidence that the supervisor had indeed told them of my earlier comments. It surprised me that they decided so quickly, especially when I'd been openly critical of the regulations.

At that moment I felt rather disappointed. I'd geared myself up for another argument, relishing the opportunity to raise my misgivings over our treatment of the primitives. Now they'd robbed me of that platform. Still, they had agreed to extend my research with Iain and that was a definite victory.

'Thank you. I'm certain that this will prove a great opportunity for us to further our knowledge of Earth and its dominant life form.'

******

For six months we worked together, usually conversing sub-vocally. On more than one occasion, I caught Iain thinking about the dreadful images he'd extracted from my mind.

I felt ashamed.

When this happened, I allowed him to pick up my pledge regarding the programme. It helped to quiet his concerns. Our friendship deepened and I learned a great deal about human society. That didn't mean I fully understood his culture, his reactions could still take me by surprise.

'You look unhappy,' I said, as I entered his room one morning.

Iain sat on the end of the bed, scuffing his bare feet on the floor. The previous day, I'd bought him some new clothes from the market. It cost a considerable number of credits - almost half my weekly allowance - to procure jeans, T shirt and training shoes from one of the merchants. How this individual came by human garb was something I didn't enquire too closely about. As I approached the sleeping area, I noticed the little pile of garments untouched beside Iain on the bed.

A wave of regret flowed through my mind. I'd hoped to please him with my purchases; making him feel more at home. Instead of pleasure, they seemed to be causing him pain.

He looked up as I crossed the room. 'What day is it?'

'D'you want the date in the Manyarnern calendar or the O.P.U.'s chronology?'

'I said day, not date. What day of the week is it?'

Something definitely bothered him. Sadness underpinned his words.

'Designating individual days with a specific name is something unique to your planet. Here on the Gretin Station we do not have days as such, only dates.'

He shrugged. 'Thought so.'

I sat down beside him and approached the problem from another angle. 'What day do you think it is?' He shrugged again. 'Oh, come on, Iain, you've got to help me out here. Something's upsetting you and I can't make it better if you won't tell me what it is.'

'Saturday. I think its Saturday.'

'Is there something significant about this day? You mentioned once that your people celebrate the date of your birth. Is it your birthday?'

He transmitted a subtle ripple of laughter.

I was relieved.

'No. It's not my birthday. If it was I'd expect a cake'. In response to my puzzled expression he sent me an image of a sweet confectionary, decorated with a sugary paste and little sticks of wax, each topped with a tiny flame.

'So what is the significance of Saturday?'

'Football. I bet I've missed the Premier League and the F.A. Cup.'

How strange, I thought. These leagues and cups held great significance for him.

'Iain, can you please drop your shield? I...' My mind filled with one of the most unusual images I've ever seen: Two groups of eleven players taking part in some kind of sacrament. All male, his memory did contain rare views of women players. They kicked a spherical ball around on a rectangle of turf. The ball was made from the skin of a domesticated animal. Intrigued, I watched this ritualised hunt through his eyes. During the game, the players spent

much of their time on the, pitch, forcefully projecting the ball towards a wooden enclosure covered with a net. In front of the net stood a man called the 'goal keeper'.

'Aha. This is a kind of sport, an entertainment?'

'It's much more than that.' Now I sensed his excitement, the exhilaration while watching a game, the jubilation when his 'team' won.

'This game is usually played on a Saturday?' He nodded and gave me a weak smile.

Even though I didn't see any real purpose to these events, I could sense that he held the succession of competitive fixtures in the highest regard.

Jumping up, I walked over to the hidden vid-cam *'Are you there?'* I pathed to the duty technician.

'You have a request?'

'Please arrange for a screen to be brought in here and patch me through to the communications hub. I need to access some transmissions.' I looked back over my shoulder. Iain's face lit up. If only everything was that simple, I thought.

******

Chapter 3

Iain completed his research schedule and I kept my promise; resigning from the Species Recognition Programme. Downgrading to the post of medical tech meant I wasn't involved with any more specimens brought to the station. I did retain membership of the O.P.U. which gave me continued influence over their policy and practices via a free vote in public referendums.

Resigning was a risky decision. Neither of us knew if, once the schedule was complete, the Board would allow us further contact. They debated Iain's future for months; planning and refining ground-breaking policy. There was nothing we could do, so we took advantage of the delay; spending as much time together as possible.

My new position meant long hours waiting in the infirmary for a patient to present themselves for healing. It was mind-numbing. To relieve my boredom, Iain and I spent the time chatting about his world and mine. He was fun to be around.

On days when I was busy, he filled his time studying information about the O.P.U.

A week after the panel granted my request, Iain dismantled the food dispenser in my quarters. The refurbishment team took ten hours to repair it. The Board soon gave him more complex tasks to turn his attention to.

Sitting in the infirmary one day, discussing Manyarnern history, Iain caught a thought from my mind. 'Your parents don't approve of our relationship, do they?' he said.

I'd taught him well how to shield his personal thoughts. Caught up in the conversation, I forgot to shield my own.

'No, they abhor the idea of me mating with anyone from such a backward race.'

'Mate! Who said anything about mating?' He scanned up and down the curves of my naked body beneath the flimsy gown I was wearing. 'I mean they don't like it that we spend so much time together and are such close friends.'

He wasn't thinking of friendship.

'But you said relationship. I thought you meant...' My face and arms flushed deep purple. Turning towards the terminal, I tried to disguise my embarrassment.

A few minutes later, my thoughts were back under control and I looked up. 'Mother and Father have considered the possibility of us becoming closer. The Manyarnern race has some peculiar rules regarding choice of Joining partner.'

They had, in fact, had countless family gatherings on this topic; all of which ended in an argument. It was made quite plain to me that the genetic material of our species could not be diluted with human DNA.

'They're worried because our paths have become entangled,' I added.

He gave a deep sigh and this time it was his thoughts that betrayed him.

'You still want to leave?' It shocked me that I hadn't picked this up before. 'Why didn't you say?'

'It doesn't matter, they'll never let me, will they?'

Why is life so difficult, I thought.

'It's never happened before, but that doesn't mean it can't happen. Perhaps if we...'

Who was I kidding? He knew as well as me that the O.P.U. wouldn't allow a primitive to return to their home world. News of our intentions escaping onto R.A.W. planetary systems would be disastrous for the programme.

'Is that what you really want, Iain, to go home? It's just that we've become so close...' I reached out and touched his cheek, opening my mind fully. The intensity of the moment nearly knocked him off his seat.

'Shit. I never...'

I completed his sentence '... realised how you feel? I'm ashamed of you. What do you think has been happening between us these past few weeks? Were you so innocent that you failed to notice the rapport growing daily?'

'Rapport?'

'Love. The word translates into love in any language.'

'But I can't be in love with you. You're... I'm... I mean you brought me here to... I never meant for this to happen.'

He knew his comments upset me. 'Are you saying that you can't love someone so different?'

'You're twisting my words. That's not what I meant.' His residual shield made me wonder if that was exactly what he meant.

'I'm sorry, Angie. I didn't mean it to come out that way. Let me open up to you again. Please?'

Tenderly at first, then with more determination, I sensed his consciousness reaching into mine. His intelligence and strength of will I'd felt before, but now they were tinged with something else. Youth, inexperience... fear? In all our months together I'd forgotten one basic fact. He was just a boy.

There had to be a way to set his mind at rest.

How old d'you think I am?' He shook his head and shrugged. *'This might come as a bit of a shock, but I'm actually only seven years old.'*

'But you look...'

'My people grow at an accelerated rate. For the first year, it's about three times the speed of a human child. When we get a little older it slows down. Seven Manyarnern years makes me the equivalent of seventeen human years. Isn't there a human expression...' I paused to retrieve the information from his unconscious mind. *'...never judge a book by its cover.'*

Iain smiled. This was a saying his mother used. Thoughts of her brought him comfort.

'Our true ages don't matter. It's how old we feel that counts. Neither of us can predict the future, so why waste energy worrying about it. Let's make the most of what we have. Here and now.'

'This is weird...'

He looked at me. I felt his passion. His head moved forward and then stopped just in front of my face.

56

'May I?'

I didn't know what to expect, so I nodded...this was interesting.

Iain pressed his lips to mine for the first time.

It was most pleasurable.

Kissing is peculiar to human courtship. Originating from a mixture of grooming behaviour and the mother's need to pre-masticate food for her young, it evolved through learning processes into a ritualised activity. It floods the pleasure centre of the human brain with Dopamine and is as addictive as a drug.

Manyarnerns don't have the same biological mechanisms. Our sexual practices are centred in the mind, not the body. Closing my eyes, I went with the new sensations, their intensity surprised me.

After a short while he broke off and hugged me to him. Now he could express himself.   'I've never even had a girlfriend. All this feels far too quick. It's been great fun living here, and I do like you, but I could never be completely happy. I need to go home, Angie, to see my parents and friends again.'

'There might be a way. We can ask for the Joining ceremony.' I knew this would cause trouble with my family. 'It's a marriage ritual. Once it's been performed, they can't keep us apart. Then we'll return to Earth together.'

Iain's thoughts flew in all sorts of directions. He undoubtedly found me attractive and there was more than a hint of sexual curiosity, but he couldn't consider Joining.

I went into him to try and gauge his feelings more accurately. Pair bonds were definitely the norm on his world, although there did seem to be some differences in how a mate was chosen.

Regardless of whether Joining was an acceptable custom, he wasn't sure about the idea of committing to me. I was shocked to learn that his expectations were for something called 'dating' and that this ritualised courtship could take months, even years, to perform. How different it all seemed to my own world where, once rapport was established, the pair would Join almost immediately. I put my curiosity aside for the moment, aware that he was trying to formulate a reply to my suggestion.

What he said next, was not what I expected.

'Look at yourself, Angie. It's impossible.'

What did the way I look have to do with this?

I recalled his responses to questions put to him by the Board. How he'd described outward appearance as holding far more sway on his world than an individual's mental profile.

A solution sprang to mind. Delving deep into my cellular tissue, I completed the transformation in one subtle fluid motion.

'Didn't know I could shape change, did you?'

Iain stood dumbfounded. My eyes were now dark brown, my hair shoulder instead of waist length, and my skin a human shade rather than its usual gently translucent purple.

'Fucking hell! How did you do that?'

'It's something I was taught at the Academy. If I can manipulate the living tissue of others in order to heal them, what's stopping me from manipulating my own? I've rearranged the material in the cells of my skin, hair and eyes. I'm still the same on the inside. It takes surprisingly little effort. I can stay like this for the rest of my life.'

'I'd never want you to do anything just to please me. You're Manyarnern and I'm human and that's something we can't change.'

'I don't care. I intend to keep this shape. We have rapport, Iain. Whether you understand it or not, rapport is a strong emotional bond that once formed can't be easily undone.'

He didn't bother to shield as he mulled over my words. The past few months had forced him to accept new information and concepts he'd never dreamed of before. He wasn't on Earth, so why did he need to live by that planet's, or his parents', standards. Perhaps this Joining was the best thing that could happen to him?

I was relieved when he finally acknowledged his own rapport towards me.

'They'll never let us leave…'

******

When we approached my parent's office in the administrative area, they already sensed my changes. They cut Iain off as he tried to follow me into the room, blocking his access to our telepathic argument.

Try as I might, their control was absolute.

'You want to do what?' boomed father, from behind his terminal.

'Iain and I have rapport and seek the Joining. It's well within the law; you can't stop us.'

He looked across at Mother who had, until now, sat impassively on the couch at the far end of the office. 'Did you hear that Nyaseema. Our daughter has gone mad. She's talking about Joining with a non-telepathic race; a barbarian from a R.A.W. world.'

Mother stood up. Lifting her feet an infinitesimal amount from the metallic floor, she floated across the room. Her silken gown undulating gently as she moved. Ignoring Father's remark, she addressed me in a calmer tone.

'Angeriana, you know full well that this request cannot be granted. The citizens of our planet may be spread across half the galaxy, but physical distance is not the issue here. We share a unique genetic inheritance. Our very essence has been fashioned into the specialised roles we take today. Human DNA is primitive, uncontrolled, and subject to too many genetic variations. A Joining between two such different races is impossible. Such a union would be fruitless. You could never produce viable offspring.'

I couldn't contain my anger any longer. 'Rubbish. That's just a load of religious clap trap. No one knows how our two races' DNA will interact because no one's ever tried. And if it is the case, then why make a fuss about me Joining with him? What's really bothering you is that I want to go to Earth. It's my choice, you can't stop me.' I turned towards the door.

'Oh yes we can.'

Father's telekinetic grip spun me around to face

him again. *'If you would stop being selfish for once in your life, you'd realise how much Manyarner needs you. Over the past thousand years the population has been dwindling faster than we can replace it. Those few still following the ancient teachings are so rare that the planet is under serious threat. How can we maintain the full range of specialisations with such a small gene pool? You don't know how privileged you are to be allowed off world to work here. If it wasn't for our respective posts on the Assembly we'd all be home and you would be a mother by now.'*

The anger pulsed within me.

'But I'm not home, and I'm not a mother. I can't Join with a brother I don't have.' I stared at Nyaseema. *'Her career was always more important than family.'*

'Angeriana.' Father's mind raged with inconsolable fury. *'I don't care who you are, insolence like that will not be tolerated. You're not too old to be fitted with an inhibitor, marched straight back to our family temple, and Joined with one of your cousins.'*

'You can't tell me what to do with my life. The constitution says I have the right to leave Manyarner and go to live on Earth. And that's exactly what I intend to do.'

I tried to turn around again. Now Mother's mind held me immobile. Her thoughts remarkably calm. *'This is typical of you, Angeriana. Never in your life have you settled to one thing and actually seen it through. First you dropped out of the Academy. What was so wrong with being a healer? Then you begged us to come here and work for the O.P.U. Do you know how many strings we had to pull to get you onto the Species Recognition Programme?'*

I started to reply, but her telepathy cut me off.

'That wasn't good enough for you, you had to resign on some feeble ethical grounds. Now you want to jump into bed - and I do not use that human phrase lightly - with this primitive. Your track record speaks for itself. If you go to Earth you'll be stuck on that world for ever. When, not if, you change your mind there'll be no means of escape. The Joining is not something you can run away

from. If he were a Manyarnern we could know his mind and be sure that his intentions towards you were true. We're worried that's all; worried what you're letting yourself in for.' She scanned my physical changes. *'Just because you look human, doesn't make you one.'*

I knew that the balance of life on Manyarner was precious. That somehow we'd brought our own planet to the brink of destruction. I was young and impulsive. All I could see before me was a dull life on a parochial world. It was true that I'd never settled to one career, but this was different.

Everything told me that my future path involved Iain and his planet. They just couldn't see it.

Mother sighed and walked over to the terminal. Touching the monitor lightly she flicked through the glyphs until she displayed Iain's file. Without looking up she pressed execute.

'I'm sorry, but this has to stop. I'm issuing the order. I should have done it months ago. In a few days time you'll forget all about him, then we'll return to Manyarner together.'

'No!'

I rushed forward and leaned on the desk. *'Please. Mother, Father, don't kill him. I need him. I beg you don't do this.'*

Father tried to comfort me, but I brushed him aside. *'Child, you are young and shall find rapport again. This creature can never respond in the way one of our own race could. Let him go, come back with us. It's been a long time since we felt the group consciousness. Once we return home all this nonsense will be forgotten.'*

'But I don't want to forget him. I want to spend the rest of my life with him.'

This time it was mother who attempted to placate my growing hysteria. *'It's done. You'll just have to get used to the idea.'*

I leant across and flicked through the menu, desperate to find confirmation of the termination order. Eventually the file was displayed, it's delicate glyphs overshadowed by the Assembly's official emblem.

'Damn you. I'll never go back. You can't make me Join with anyone else.'

Pushing myself away from the desk with a burst of telekinesis, I flew backwards out through the doorway. I came to rest beside Iain in the corridor. Without saying a word I sunk down into his gentle arms.

'I won't let them do this,' I sent.

But I knew in my heart there was nothing else I could do. The orders had been issued and it was only a matter of time before the guards came to take him away.

******

At the end of my shift, I teleported to the refectory to eat in the company of strangers; hoping that the cacophony of emotion found there would distract me from my sullen mood. After toying with my food for a few minutes, I pushed the bowl away and sighed. Despite being surrounded by numerous exotic creatures that shared the Gretin station, I couldn't have felt more alone.

Iain's face haunted my thoughts.

Forcing myself to continue the journey back to my quarters, I decided that some exercise might do me good and strode off towards walkway three.

The humanoid sphere, like most of the spheres that make up the Gretin Station, is created from a series of interconnected modules arranged in a spiral pattern. Each module is designated for a specific function be it medical, technical, administrative, or accommodation. In the very heart of the sphere is the chamber of the Assembly.

People working and living within the station usually move around by teleport. There are also moving walkways that run between certain sectors. The refectory was deliberately linked to the accommodation module by the station's designers. Humanoids have legs, I guess they thought we'd want to use them. Walkway three runs around the inside of the outer shell. It has observation platforms at regular intervals where weary travellers can rest and enjoy the view. Despite this attraction, it was rare for anyone to use it. I didn't mind, solitude was a welcome relief from the emotional turmoil of the past twenty-four hours.

When I stepped onto the walkway, it accelerated my pace to five times usual walking speed. The hubbub of the refectory receded into the background and the walls took on a familiar bland uniformity. It was a considerable distance from this sector to the accommodation level, even at an accelerated speed. On foot it would take the best part of a rotation.

I didn't care. No one would miss me.

Setting a fast pace for the first few hours, I shut down my conscious mind focussing on the rhythm of my stride.

Something pricked the edge of my psi-awareness, causing the hairs on the back of my neck to stand up.

A siren started to wail.

The force of the explosion was tremendous. It ripped through the fabric of the station in an instant making the bulkhead shudder. The walls contorted, pulling panels from their mountings and the percussion wave knocked me to the ground. I instinctively curled into a ball to protect myself from falling debris and lay there shaking.

Power conduits throughout this sector overloaded causing a series of deafening secondary explosions.

The Assembly went into emergency link; their collective mentality controlling the worst of these blasts and lending support of the station's superstructure. The intensity of this energy field saturated the air making my skin tingle.

Gradually the noise abated.

Rising, I sensed survivors trapped in the storage bay I'd passed moments before. Without a second thought, I flew back along the walkway.

Pushing through the shattered remains of the entrance, I found myself transfixed by the devastation before me. Under normal conditions this compartment would be stacked with storage canisters; each suspended in a grav-net. An automated cradle in the ceiling selected items for teleportation to the requested sector of the sphere. With no power these cases had collapsed on top of one another to form a mangled mess on the floor.

Beyond this, a huge rupture in the outer wall gaped ominously, revealing the deadly void of space.

A shout from somewhere close by dragged me back from my abstraction. Locating the source, I rushed over to help a group of technicians pulling themselves from beneath the wreckage.

In the back of my mind I could feel the grip of the Assembly weakening. Knowing that when failure came, death would follow for everyone trapped here.

A senior systems engineer, who introduced himself as Loftori of Paldrin, was the closest to me. Once I'd healed his head wound, he started to use a grav unit as a stretcher. Muttering to himself, what I guessed to be Paldrinian profanities, he wrestled the bulk of his Lorian team leader onto the rig. He took great care not to put stress on the temporary repair I'd made to the team leader's side.

Meanwhile I busied myself with regeneration of a severed limb of the next patient. Despite my preoccupation, I had time to appreciate the care this gentle giant took over his colleagues as he moved them off towards safety.

I worked on alone.

With a thunderous screeching sound, a bulkhead against which I'd leant some of the wounded collapsed. Leaping clear, and momentarily stunned, I awoke to find myself pinned beneath a piece of panelling. The engineer returned and together we tried, me with telekinesis and him with brute strength, to dislodge the heavy weight.

'Where's your teleport unit?'

I indicated the pile of scrap metal beside me. 'Under that lot, somewhere.'

'I'll go for help.'

'No time, get the others back to safety.'

He pulled an unconscious colleague, blown clear as the bulkhead collapsed onto the grav unit, alongside the others already lying there. His mind was full of remorse, but he understood the logic of the situation.

'You sacrifice will be remembered by myself and

my people. Before I rest I will repay this debt of life. It is a sacred bond between us.'

Without glancing back in my direction, he pushed the injured towards the walkway, leaving me alone with my thoughts.

'Weird,' I said aloud. 'I wonder what Paldrin is like?'

Glancing down, I noticed for the first time the barbed edge of a cradle arm embedded in my side. The wound oozed dark purple blood, which trickled slowly across my new skin.

Defeated resignation overtook my heart.

At least I'm spared a life of drudgery, I thought.

Dismissing any temptation to repair myself, I looked around. Through the gaping hole in the outer wall, the blackness of space was revealed. Millions of distant suns winked at me from their varied locations in the cosmos, each one a constant reminder of my isolation.

Disassociating my mind from my body, I floated upwards until I could see the vastness of space before me.

I studied the star formations for a short while, attempting to locate the sun that shone down upon Iain's home world. It was no use. Overtaken by fatigue my mind slipped back into my body as I lost consciousness.

******

I came round to find myself on a stretcher just outside the infirmary. Injured people lined the corridors as far as the eye could see.

'Welcome back,' said Iain, kissing me on the cheek. 'You had us all worried.'

Something was wrong. I tried to think. Then I realised, my psi-awareness was gone.

'Don't strain. You've only just come out of your cocoon. The medics said that it'll take a while for your powers to come back.' He smiled. 'I guess you'll have to communicate like a human for a while.'

'You're alive, what happened?'

He cleared his throat. 'There was an explosion, a

bloody huge explosion. It took out a large section of the station's humanoid sphere. The shock wave was so big, it registered on sensory equipment half way across the sector. The rumour is that it's deliberate. I didn't know you people had terrorists?'

'We don't, not that I've heard of. Who could've done such a thing?'

'How should I know? Does the O.P.U. have any enemies?'

I shrugged. 'How did you get away?'

'With the station half wrecked, the Assembly linked and drew psionic energy from every available O.P.U. member. Everyone answered the call for assistance, including the security forces. With them preoccupied, I slipped away unnoticed.'

I couldn't believe it. He'd been dragged from my quarters by half a dozen security officers the previous day. Images of his distraught face as he was wrestled up the corridor burned into my mind. I shivered.

Why didn't they kill him immediately? I thought.

'I don't know. I guess bureaucracy works slowly everywhere in the galaxy. It's the catalogue technicians who usually terminate specimens. You're my designated technician.'

This was terrible. I was as open as a child. I couldn't shield, I couldn't feel his emotions. I found myself wondering how people managed without psi-awareness.

Iain paused, pushing a clump of matted hair back from his face. 'D'you want me to explain what happened next, or not?' I nodded, shocked that he could read me so easily. I guess the tables were turned.

'Realising your predicament, I stole a teleport control and entered the damaged sector. Once there, I pushed my way through the debris until I found you.'

'How on earth did you get me out?'

'I don't really know.' He shrugged. 'I can't remember it very clearly. I guess I got a huge dose of radiation. I do know that I carried you back along the walkway until I met a rescue party.' He looked towards the ceiling. I could see the concentration on his face as he tried to recall the details. Glancing back down, he shook his head. 'Does it matter? You're safe now.'

Talking intently, neither of us noticed my parents approach up the corridor. Catching sight of them, Iain backed away. 'Crap.'

With no psi-awareness, I found the emotional backdrop a complete blank. The emptiness angered me. I needed to know what they were thinking.

They walked over to my stretcher and smiled. Mother lifted my hand and rubbed it gently. Father looked across at Iain. 'If you took our daughter to your home planet what exactly would she do once there?'

Iain's mouth dropped open. 'But... but your orders.'

'We have rescinded the termination order. It is no longer an issue.'

Iain swallowed. His eyes darted back and forth between them and me. 'Well, Sir,' he replied. 'She hasn't completed her studies of Earth culture and I believe the O.P.U. would gain valuable insights into my world if an operative was allowed to study it firsthand.'

They looked at one another, exchanging a private thought.

I strained to read them. It made my head hurt.

'Will you swear never to tell the Earth authorities about the O.P.U.?' Iain nodded, his sincerity apparent. 'How could you guarantee her safety in such a barbaric society?'

'Can you guarantee it? Under the circumstances the Earth seems less dangerous than being here on the Gretin station. My feelings for Angie are strong. I've already shown that.'

'Yes. You have demonstrated remarkable resourcefulness and impressed us with your loyalty,' began Mother. 'But will you remain faithful once back amongst your own kind? You could make quite a name for yourself, if you gave away her true identity. She would be particularly vulnerable left alone on such a hostile world and rescue from a R.A.W. planet would be impossible.'

'Angie means the world to me. I promise you, I'll guard her with my life.'

'You've already shown us your willingness to put her safety above your own,' replied Father.

Iain smiled down at me. 'The only thing I could do for my future Joining partner.'

******

And so we found ourselves standing naked beside the temple of the fourth continent, two kilometres from my family estate, overlooking the lake that borders Vanya province. At that time of year, the lake was a particularly appealing turquoise. I longed to dive into its cool depths. To be swallowed up in the uniquely sensual qualities created by the molecular structure of the water flowing across my skin.

'Why are we undressed?' asked Iain.

'Most ceremonies are performed this way. It's just something you get used to. Living in a society where your inner consciousness is on daily display the most naked you can feel is when a stray, derogatory, thought slips through your shielding. The Manyarnern weather control system creates a warm and stable climate so clothes are hardly necessary.'

I stretched and looked up into the sky. That day felt hotter than usual. The sun beat down fiercely, causing beads of perspiration to form in my hairline. I fought back an irresistible desire to run headlong towards the water's edge. I knew it was impossible for the weather to be hotter than during my childhood. Maybe it's anticipation of the Joining that's making me sweat, I thought.

'If my parents could see me now they'd die of embarrassment.' Iain blushed, keeping his eyes fixed on the distant mountain range. *'No, I take that back. They would've had heart attacks long before this.'*

He hadn't asked about the Manyarnern marriage ritual until a few minutes before it began. I quickly explained that during the ceremony we'd have our brain patterns scrambled - there's no better English term for it - then reformulated in synchrony. Thankfully he accepted this without further comment.

Wriggling my toes into the grass, I allowed the living patterns of energy to tingle against my senses. Beyond this, the group consciousness infused my soul with acceptance. It felt so good. Raising my gaze towards him, I smiled.

'I think they're about to begin.'

He nodded, and we walked, hand in hand, into the shrine.

There are no walls to Manyarnern temples, just a central platform surrounded by seven curved pillars. Iain pointed towards the complex designs as we passed.

'Some stones depict individual's myths,' I pathed, *'others contain images from the sacred texts.'*

Passing beneath them, Iain gazed up at the columns. *'It looks like they're about to fall on us.'*

'Don't worry, all the temples are like that. They've been leaning inwards at that unusual angle for centuries and none has ever collapsed.'

The temples' construction is one of those things scholars have argued about for centuries. Those kinds of debates didn't interest me, but I admit there was something special about this place, more than the unique nature of the structure, something mysterious and strangely overpowering.

'What now?' he sent.

I signalled towards the ceremonial procession, led by my father and two Lenses, which had approached unnoticed from the south. The small group climbed the few steps to join us on the platform.

We knelt, lowering our heads to receive my father's touch.

******

Iain sat down on the grass at the foot of the temple steps, watching as the last of the Lenses dematerialised.

'So now that's over with, do we just hop on the next space ship heading for Earth?'

I sat down beside him. 'It's not that simple. Earth is R.A.W. When we get back to the station, I'll book an Eilad and see whether my request is granted.' I wriggled closer. 'As my Joining partner, you're now considered Manyarnern and subject to its laws. Clause Thirty-One gives us the right to choose our specialisation and where we want to live. So we both choose Earth and hope for the best.'

He cocked his head on one side. 'You're sure about this?'

I tried to sound convincing. 'Yeah, it'll be fine.'

Iain lent closer to my face. 'At weddings there's usually a moment when the vicar says *you may kiss the bride.'* He swept me into his arms, the kiss lasting for minutes before he caught his breath.

'Wow! What was that?'

I giggled. 'That's the Joining. Our brain patterns are the same now. It goes way beyond telepathy. Everything that one partner feels is shared by the other. At first it's going to be a little overwhelming, but in time you'll get used to it.'

He pushed away from me. I could sense apprehension in his mind.

'What's wrong?'

'You mean I can't keep anything private? You'll know everything? What if I want to buy you a present, or throw a surprise party?'

I pecked him on the cheek. 'Layers, remember? You can still shield particular thoughts. The joining is something more fundamental than telepathy it's a much deeper psychic bond. Everything between us will seem more intense, more vivid. Let me demonstrate.'

Throwing my arms about his neck, I pulled him down onto the grass.

'I believe that human marriage isn't permanent until it's been consummated.'

He tried to sit up, but I held him tight. *'What, here, now? Someone might see us.'*

Opening up my psi-awareness, I scanned the surrounding countryside.

'Do you feel anyone?'

He shook his head. *'No but...this is all so different.'*

I giggled again. *'Trust me.'*

******

Chapter 4

Our return to Earth was filled with anticipation. The final days of the voyage waiting for the Eilad to drop out of hyperspace made us increasingly restless. When the window shield retracted, I pressed my nose up to the vidscreen and sighed.

What a beautiful planet. From space Earth is a bright blue-green world, with swirling vapour clouds floating above a patchwork of diverse continents and sparkling ice caps at the poles.

Iain stood beside me and I felt his heart rate jump. Relief washed through his mind. We'd spent five weeks alone on the little ship talking about his planet. In all that time, he carefully concealed how he felt. Now it became clear. He thought he'd never see his home again.

To avoid detection, the Eilad made a rapid and acute descent; touching down at dusk in a remote part of Dartmoor in the county of Devon, England.

We stepped from the access ramp. I looked around me. My excitement became disappointment.

I'd expected to see luscious green valleys and flaming sunsets. Instead my eyes met a bleak and unkempt landscape. Apart from thick, matted, grass and little clusters of grey rocks, the vista seemed inhospitable.

It was a stark contrast to Manyarner.

No elegant buildings interrupted the grey horizon, no exotic fragrances filled the air and no concert of telepathic transmissions sang in my soul. Instead it was cold, very cold.

Watching the Eilad disappear into the sky, I shivered. Nothing could escape the angry, penetrating, wind.

'Come on then. No time to waste.' He pulled the bundle of fake bank notes from his pocket and waved them in my face. 'Let's hope these work.'

'They will.'

Putting away the money, Iain picked up the packages at his feet.

At his insistence, I'd bought a coat from the market before embarking on our journey. I considered it a waste of credits at the time. Pulling up the collar, I snuggled down into the fleecy lining, thankful for his forward planning. He took my hand and we strode out across the landscape, my mood lifting with each step.

This is the first day of my new life. I'm going to enjoy it, I thought.

We arrived by train in Iain's home town early the next day. His apprehension grew as we marched along streets frequented during his childhood and up the gravel drive of a large red brick house. I didn't understand his anxieties until I saw the look on his mother's face as she opened the front door.

'Hello, Mum, I'm back.'

She slammed the door.

Give her time.' I pressed the bell again.

Opening the door once more, her shocked expression turned to delight. Without speaking, she ushered us into the lounge.

Julia McClellan stared at her missing son for a long time.

'Aren't you pleased to see me?' he said. She dashed forward hugging him to her breast. 'Oh Mum, stop that.'

Then she found her voice. Questions tumbled out in quick succession, each expertly fielded with our planned cover story. Yes, he'd been in London. Yes, he'd run away to avoid the pressure of his exams. No he hadn't told anyone, not even Sebastian, where he was. Yes, he was back for good.

Then came the tricky one... Yes, he did stay with someone and here she was.

That last answer didn't go down as well as we'd hoped. But there was time yet.

Tony McClellan arrived half an hour later, his stressful thoughts reaching me well before he entered the building.

'What's the matter?' he called, as he removed his coat in the hallway. 'Your message sounded urgent.' Walking hurriedly into the lounge, he couldn't believe his eyes. 'Oh my god!'

Half a dozen cups of a beverage they called 'tea' later, everyone felt more at ease. I liked them, they were straight forward and very easy to read.

It transpired that they'd reported Iain missing a few hours after he failed to return from football practice and a large-scale man hunt had ensued. The police questioned strangers in the vicinity; they even made a TV appeal. Iain's disappearance baffled everyone. For the next few weeks, local people gathered in shops and public houses to speculate on his demise.

Meanwhile, Julia and Tony spent hours preparing flyers and posters bearing Iain's image. Eventually, in typical stoic fashion and with all leads exhausted, they gave up. Shelving the emotional side of the trauma and appearing to get on with their lives. Nothing could have been further from the truth.

'What's Seb doing now?' asked Iain, once the initial shock of his return had subsided. 'Maybe I should give him a call?'

Tony ran his fingers along the crease in his trousers. 'Sebastian finished at sixth form months ago.' He felt let down, but I couldn't understand why. 'He got a fancy job up in the city. I think he lives there now. When you first disappeared he called here all the time asking for news. But we don't hear from him these days.'

Iain's mind felt pain. The loss of this friendship was difficult for him.

'There's nothing stopping you from making contact now you're back.'

'I guess so.'

I didn't understand Iain's reluctance, but decided to put this aside for another day.

'I think it's a lot more important for you to call the police,' commented Julia, sipping at her tea.

Iain shrugged. 'I don't see why?'

'Don't see why,' shouted Tony. 'You go waltzing off,

god only knows where, causing a lot of suffering for your mother and even more trouble for the authorities in a wasted man hunt...'

'Okay, Dad. I get the point.'

'Good. I'll make the call.' Tony jumped up and headed from the room.

Julia shot us a concerned look. 'It's for the best.'

Two uniformed officers arrived shortly after lunch. They questioned Iain at length, listening to every detail of his story with fixed expressions and disbelief in their thoughts. He stuck to the assertion that he'd run away due to the pressure of his imminent exams.

During the interrogation I remained in the background, drawing as little attention to myself as possible. After two wasted hours, I hastened the end of the interview with a psionic suggestion. We'd done enough to satisfy them, what good would it do to prolong the discussion?

When evening fell, Iain took my hand leading me towards his bedroom. This behaviour was met by strong opposition. I think his parents were more shocked that he stood up to them, than by the fact that we were sleeping together.

A heated argument ensued regarding his intentions towards me. It was obvious from the tone of their thoughts, they considered him far too young and inexperienced for a full-time relationship. It wasn't their fault, they were the product of their environment; small minded people from a small minded town.

I don't know what I'd expected by coming to Earth with Iain, but this wasn't it. The more they argued, the more isolated I felt.

I soon realised Iain must have suffered the same feelings when he first came aboard the station.

'A stranger in a strange land,' he pathed.

'What?'

'It's the title of a book I read once. It's about a human raised by aliens, who comes back to Earth and doesn't fit in.'

'Written by a human?' Iain glanced towards his

parents before nodding. *'Interesting...'*

'It's probably still on my book shelf. Remind me to dig it out for you to read.'

We'd decided before arriving that we daren't tell his parents about our Joining or where I came from. Now I understood why.

'But we don't know her,' snapped Tony. He looked me in the eye. 'She could be anybody.'

'I know her. That's gonna have to be good enough.'

'You can't bring a complete stranger into our house and just expect us to accept it without question.'

I went into them. They weren't bad people and didn't mean me any harm. They saw the world as ordered, everyone fitting neatly into boxes. They expected their only son to finish his education, get a mundane job, meet a 'nice girl' and get married; eventually providing them with two or three grandchildren. It was Iain's dogged independence that scared them.

I'd always thought genetic specialisation was restrictive. This seemed far worse.

The argument dragged on well into the night. I considered influencing the outcome with a suggestion similar to the one I'd used on the policemen, but decided, for Iain's sake, it would be better to let him resolve this dispute in his own way. In the end, it was his adamant assertion that if I left he was leaving with me, never to return, that eventually brought about their resignation. With reluctance they agreed to let me live in the house and we headed upstairs together.

I begged him not to be angered by their reaction. It was, after all, not unlike my own parents' behaviour.

Dawn broke on the third day of my new life.

******

For three months we lived with Julia and Tony McClellan in the back room of their four-bedroom house in Godalming, Surrey. It wasn't a big house by Manyarnern standards and living so closely with non-telepaths gave me a constant headache. Every petty little thought; had the washing up been done, did the grass need cutting, what should we eat for Sunday lunch...all impinged on my mind.

I knew I would never take personal shielding for granted again.

At first, Iain and I crowded into his single bed in a room most unsuitable for habitation by two people. The room was hot and stuffy and covered in hideous wall art that he called graffiti.

A week later, after his father found me walking around naked in the lounge, they agreed to move us to the much larger guest room which had a little seating area and an en-suite bathroom. I knew I could never reveal to Iain what his father was thinking as he watched me. It was quite inappropriate by human standards, although less so by the customs of my own planet. Including this in my first O.P.U report, I dismissed it from my conscious mind.

One of the early problems, apart from wearing clothes that blistered my skin and shoes that strangled my toes, was what to tell people about my background. I currently held the position of O.P.U. field operative engaged in anthropological research. It sounded rather grand, but in reality the posting was more down to my parents' influence than my own ability. This might have been my job, but it wasn't something we could tell any of the humans about. So after some discussion we decided upon a suitable course of action.

******

The sash window rattled as Iain lifted it and squeezed inside. For a moment he tensed, listening to the noises of the night. Satisfied that no one was around, he dropped forward and onto the floor of the registry office.

'Is all this really necessary?' I asked as I lifted myself up and also climbed through.

'Yes. Now get a wriggle on before someone spots us.'

Standing beside him in the darkness, I reached out my awareness and scanned the room. There were two desks on our right, covered with box files and folders full of paperwork. On the far side of the room was a row of filing cabinets standing beside a hatch that connected this space with the waiting room beyond.

Iain tiptoed across and pulled at the handle of the nearest cabinet.

'Locked,' he pathed.

'It's what we expected.'

Nodding, he moved his awareness into the mechanism and turned the hidden tumblers. The click as it opened sounded deafening in the silence.

Moving forward, I started to rifle through the contents of the top drawer. *'Remind me again, what we're looking for.'*

I felt him sigh. *'You may have hacked into the tax office to create a national insurance number with that fancy computer of yours, but that alone is not enough to prove you're a real person.'*

'But why do we need to prove to your government that I'm real? I can use a psionic suggestion with anyone I meet.'

Iain moved past me and started searching through the next cabinet. *'Because...'* He pulled out four leather-bound pads of blank documents. *'Aha. Found you.'* Peeling off the uppermost sheets from each, he walked over to one of the desks. *'Because you won't be able to meet every official in person. The tax office is only one of a number of government departments we need access to if we're gonna provide you with a back story.'*

Despite the darkness, I could tell he saw the look of confusion on my face. *'You said you want to stay here forever?'*

'Of course I do. '

'Sooner or later, you're gonna need a proper job, or to claim benefit or even a pension when you get old. All those things call for supporting documents.' He pulled a fountain pen from his pocket and started to fill in the first of the blank birth certificates. *'D'you have the list?'*

I held out the data tablet I'd carried in my bag. His face shone with reflected glow as he peered at the screen.

The tablet contained the names of fake parents we'd identified for me. These were people who died years before and would be difficult to trace unless someone was very determined.

There was a loud bang behind us. We jerked upright, and swung around; ready to flee the scene of our crime. Realising that the noise was just the window shutting, Iain let out a deep sigh and glanced towards me.

His eyes widened.

'What's that?' He pointed towards the conical device I was now holding out in front of me.

'Just a stunner.' I shrugged and returned it to my bag.

'You brought a weapon with you?' Smirking, he turned back to the task in hand. *'I don't recall seeing a stunner on the list of approved items for a field operative.'*

'You didn't think I'd come to a hostile planet without some kind of protection.'

'You never cease to amaze me, Angie.'

******

Settling into life on Earth wasn't easy. Every time I thought I understood human nature, I'd experience something quite baffling which threw me into utter confusion. The use of half-truths, innuendo, and threats was common even in simple social exchanges.

The river Wey was close to Iain's parents' house. Meandering through the countryside it had broad grassy banks with overhanging trees that dipped their branches into the dark water. The river was unlike the clear waters of my home planet, yet still enlivened my senses at is rippled past. Iain and I walked there most days, watching the wildlife that frequented the banks while we discussed Earth customs and cultures.

During the first of these walks, I attempted to catalogue the species of plant and animals I encountered. I hoped that it would make a useful addition to my initial O.P.U. report. Within a few minutes, I was forced to give up. The bio-diversity was astounding and in total contrast to my world.

'That's an Oak,' said Iain, pointing at a large rounded tree ahead. 'And there's a Willow by the water. An Elm, a silver Birch and conker... I mean horse chestnut, over there on the edge of that field.' He looked about. 'Oh and over there I can see a Pine and that bush is Hawthorne.' He chuckled to himself. 'I never knew that Scout badge would come in handy.'

I shot him an irritated look. I could sense that he was enjoying this far too much.

'Do you want me to try and identify the birds and other wildlife too? Of course, these are just the ones here in England. It said in my biology text book that there are between thirty and fifty million species on Earth. No one has actually counted them all. D'you wanna give it a go?'

I shook my head and hurried along the path.

******

Further on, I noticed a man jogging with an animal on a leash.

'That animal is called a dog, isn't it?' I sent.

Iain looked across at the opposite bank of the river. *'Yeah, that's right. It's a breed called Golden Retriever.'*

'Why does it stay with him when it's so upset?'

'What?'

'The dog's unhappy to run along like that when it's hungry.'

'D'you read everything, including all the animals?'

'Yes, I read the feelings of all creatures in the immediate area, unless they're shielded of course, it just slips into my mind. If the thoughts I detect are boring, I filter them out. With animals they're so base, so instinctive that I can't help myself.'

'All those unwanted thoughts must get bloody confusing.'

'No, it seems quite natural to me. I sort them out unconsciously and either respond or ignore them.'

I looked along the path at a couple hand in hand. *'From the outside they look pretty happy, wouldn't you say?'*

He followed my gaze and stared at the couple. The man tenderly touched the woman's face then bent and pressed his lips firmly on hers. She reciprocated and soon they were in a deep embrace.

'Now go into them...' I grabbed Iain's hand, linking our minds, then stretched out towards the couple.

'Stop that!' He jerked his hand away and stared at me. 'That's invasion of privacy.'

'Oh come on. Don't be so righteous. You'd love to know what they're feeling. You can't deny it.'

'Yeah, you may be right.' He shrugged. 'I'm curious. But it doesn't mean we have the right to stick our noses into everyone else's business just because we can. On your world...'

He switched back to telepathy. *'...You may be very open and honest and feel there's nothing to hide, but here we think privacy is important. I wouldn't want every Tom, Dick or Harry to know my inner most secrets. You often shield from me so I'm sure you feel the same.'*

I could sense his irritation rising and didn't want it to end in an argument. Turning back to the man with the dog I resumed my original line of questioning. *'So, why does the dog stay? I'm sure you don't mind me reading the helpless creature?'*

'I suppose it's got something to do with domestication of certain species. We live in a sort of symbiotic relationship. In return for food it stays with us as a companion. I've never met a dog that really minded. Try reading it again now he's let it run free.'

I looked across the water. The man had unfastened the leash. While he gasped for breath, the dog bounded around enthusiastically. I went into it. Iain was right; the animal didn't choose to run away. Neither did it feel compelled to stay. Rather it thought of the human as a leader of a pack who commanded respect.

As I stood concentrating on the dog I didn't notice the man throw a stick into the air. The dog suddenly sprang off the bank, landing in the river with a huge splash.

Caught up in the thrill of the moment I too launched myself into the water.

I'm not sure who was more surprised Iain, me or the courting couple a few metres away. Rising to the surface I indicated that I was fine and began to scramble up the muddy bank.

Pulling myself upright, I stood there, cold, wet and dirty. Iain started to laugh.

'What's so funny?'

'That'll teach you not to read people, or unsuspecting animals. You said you can control the feelings. I think they just controlled you.'

'Yes, well... I did sort of get carried away.'

'I thought you were going to retrieve the stick yourself.'

'Very funny.'

I gave him a good-natured slap and we started off towards home; chuckling to ourselves as I squelched along.

When we approached the front door of the house, Iain turned and kissed me lightly on the cheek. He had a very mischievous expression on his face. I guessed what he wanted to know.

'He was thinking she wasn't as good in bed as his wife.'

I slipped inside and hurried upstairs to get myself dry.

******

Later that same week, Iain suggested we accompany his mother on a shopping trip. It seemed like a good idea at the time, but soon turned into a clash of both wills and cultures.

'What's this?' I picked up a round meat product from the chilled cabinet and turned it over in my hand.

'Huh?' Julia finished selecting something from the shelf opposite, then trotted across the supermarket aisle towards me. 'Haven't you heard of haggis?

I shook my head. 'I don't eat much meat.'

'It's a mixture of lamb, onion, oatmeal and suet cooked together in a sheep's stomach.'

I grimaced and placed it back onto the shelf. 'Yuk.'

Julia leaned across me, grabbed the haggis and placed it into her trolley. 'Haggis, neaps and tatties happens to be one of Iain's favourite foods.'

'Hello there.'

We swung around. Waddling towards us was a very overweight woman. She was dressed in leggings and T shirt; two sizes too small for her bulk. 'Is this her?'

Julia stepped to the side. 'Yes, this is Iain's... This is Angie.'

I held out my hand as the woman approached. 'Pleased to meet you.'

She ignored my gesture. How rude, I thought.

'Scrawny, isn't she. Where did he pick this one up?'

Julie turned toward me. 'Be a good girl and get some of the fizzy pop Iain likes so much. It's in the next aisle. You can also choose some breakfast cereal.' She shooed me away.

I couldn't believe it. She was actually dismissing me in order to gossip in private. Didn't she realise I knew what she was doing? I hesitated. If I left then I'd be condoning her bad manners, but I was curious to know how she interacted with another human.

Pulling myself up straight, I gave the newcomer a curt nod and walked away. Once out of sight I stopped and closed my eyes, scanning the supermarket aisle as they continued their conversation.

'Oh Betty, it's been a nightmare. After all we've done for him, he brings home this little tramp. He's always been such a good boy, you know he has. He was doing so well at school. Might have even got into Cambridge. He threw all that away and ran off with her.'

The other woman made soothing noises of agreement.

Hardly stopping for breath, Julia continued. 'And her manners... well, I don't know where she comes from, but her parents couldn't have brought her up very well. She's so surly, so rude. Hardly smiles or passes the time of day with Tony and myself.'

'Oh yes, it must be terrible for you... such a waste... I can hardly believe it of him. Where did he pick her up, London wasn't it? Do you think she's one of those...' Her voice dropped to a whisper. 'Ladies-of-the-night?'

'I can't work out what she is or what she's thinking. Her face is just blank, as if she's staring right through us. The saving grace is that she spends most of her time skulking in their room... I don't know what he sees in her.'

Julia's words infuriated me. Did she hate me that much? Had I offended her by my mere presence in the house? I rushed into her, expecting to find dark thoughts. What I actually found was rather intriguing. Her mind was quite calm. She'd accepted me; relieved that I'd taken care of Iain and returned him safely to her. So why did she complain about me to the other woman?

Preoccupied by my scanning of the encounter, I didn't notice Iain approach from the opposite end of the aisle. He grabbed my arm, making me jump.

'What's up?'

'Shhhh, I'm listening.'

'Listening to what?' He looked around.

'Your mum and some woman called Betty. They're round there talking about me. It's not very polite.' I paused. *'I don't think your mother likes me very much.'*

Iain's face cracked into a broad grin. *'Course she does. If it's the Betty I'm thinking of, that old battle axe is the biggest gossip in town. No one's safe from her tittle-tattle and bitchiness. Mum's probably just playing along to get rid of her.'* He grabbed my hand, pulling me towards his mother. *'Thing's aren't always what they seem, Angie. You have to give things time.'*

'It's all so confusing.'

Iain stopped and burst out laughing. *'Getting a taste of your own medicine at last... You'll get used to humans eventually. Let's get this over with.'* He led me back towards the two women.

Life here was definitely more challenging than I'd anticipated.

******

It was a Saturday afternoon on the fifth week after our return to Earth that we sat together on the little couch in our room.

'Sure you won't come with us?' asked Iain, wrapping a garish red and white scarf about his neck.

'I'm fine. You and Sebastian don't want me tagging along spoiling the day.'

He stood up, pulling on his jacket. 'You're probably right, but I'd like you two to meet soon.' He checked his pocket for the match tickets. 'Right then. You know where I am if you need me.'

I walked with him to the front door of the house and we kissed goodbye.

'Have fun.' I waved as he walked down the drive.

As soon as the door was closed I ran back to our room, pulling the A to Z and teleport control from their hiding place in the bedside cabinet.

Could I manage to programme this from a map reference alone? Turning to the correct page, I shrugged. What was the worst that could happen? I end up miles from where I intend and have to walk back.

When I arrived inside the football stadium, I could hardly believe my eyes. There were thousands of people crowded together in the oval structure. Some stood beside the pitch, chanting and singing to one another. Others were seated on tiered concrete benches engaged in ritualised socialising or munching on warm meat pies. Backing away from the crowd, I leaned against the concrete wall beside the turnstile, waiting for Iain and his friend to arrive.

As I scanned the mob, the seething mass of humanity began to overwhelm my senses. I'd never in my life been in the presence of so many minds. There were thousands, maybe even tens of thousands of people here.

Buttoning my mind up tight made it feel like I perceived the world through dense fog; but even dampened psi-awareness was better than the full force of so many unshielded souls.

Eventually I spotted Iain and Sebastian enter through the gates and head towards their seats. I moved into position three rows above them where I could get the best view of their behaviour. Watching the match was the last thing on my mind, but once it began the excitement around me became infectious. Iain and Sebastian cheered and shouted along with the crowd. They jumped up when one of the players scored a goal, throwing their arms into the air in celebration. I found myself copying their actions.

When the match was over, the crowd started to surge towards the exits. The crush was phenomenal. I remained on the bench watching Iain and Sebastian's slow progress through the crowd. Suddenly someone lost their footing and fell over; stumbling against another fan, knocking them off their feet.

'Watch it mate!'

The rabble pushed forward again, crushing those closest to the gates.

'Oi. Get the fuck out of my face.'

Another shove from behind and those in the lead went down, Iain amongst them. One second I could see his mass of light brown curls, the next he dropped out of sight. I stood up, craning my neck for a better view and reaching out my dulled psi-awareness the best I could.

The crowd's mood blackened, excitement giving way to violence. There was a fierceness here, festering just beneath the surface, that could spill over at any moment.

Thrusting a hand into my coat pocket, I felt for the stunner.

I doubted the weapon would be enough to subdue them all, but it might give me time to push my way towards Iain and teleport him to safety. I stared more intently. He was on the ground somewhere amongst that group, only where?

Then I noticed faint singing coming from the back of the crowd. The mob in front of me noticed it too. Heads started to turn, voices began to rise as they took up the song.

'Oh when the beans,

Come out the tin,
Oh when the beans come out the tin,
You put the bread in the toaster,
Oh when the beans come out the tin.'
I looked about me. More and more people were joining in the club chant. As they did so the violence in their minds dissolved into nothingness.

Iain's head bobbed back up again. He slapped Sebastian playfully on the back and both men started laughing and smiling as they also sang along.

I was amazed. Humans have the ability to switch mood so abruptly and it was definitely heightened by the presence of others.

Three hours later, I was lying on the bed at home, eagerly entering my observations into a data pad. Iain trotted into the room and unzipped his jacket. He was still humming the club chant to himself.

I feigned disinterest.

'So what did you think of the match?' he asked, grinning from ear to ear.

I looked up, my mouth dropping open in disbelief.

'Did you really think I couldn't spot my Joining partner's mind in the crowd?'

******

The next few months ticked by quite uneventfully.

One morning I wandered into the bathroom, glancing at myself in the mirror as I passed. I stopped dead.

Something was different. Scanning my internal structure for signs of disease, nothing appeared to be wrong. I was about to dismiss the notion when my attention focussed on my lower abdomen. One of Iain's colourful expletives came to mind.

'Fucking hell, I'm pregnant!'

I couldn't pin point the precise moment of conception - some Manyarnern women can - but I knew this was going to cause us problems. We'd always assumed my parents were right in their assertion that

87

human and Manyarnern DNA couldn't mix, so we didn't bother to 'take precautions' as humans called it.

They were **definitely** wrong.

I walked back into the bedroom. Iain lay diagonally across the bed, his left leg tangled around the dishevelled sheets. He lifted his head. I could tell his mind was still half asleep.

'What's up?'

Sitting on the end of the bed, I stroked his leg while gathering my thoughts. There was no easy way to say this.

'I'm pregnant'.

He felt no excitement, no concern. He just lay there wearily, snuggling into the soft pillows.

'Did you hear what I said? I'm pregnant.'

Now I had his attention. Sitting up, he grabbed my arm and pulled me closer. 'What did you say?'

Third time lucky, I thought.

'Pregnant, I'm pregnant.'

'Bloody hell.' He paused. 'That's wonderful.' His tone was surprisingly up-beat. 'Scary, but wonderful. You said it couldn't happen. Wow. Great.' Pulling me close, we kissed.

'Wait till I tell Mum and Dad, they'll be...'

In an instant the excitement had vanished. Looking deep into my eyes he asked the question I'd been dreading.

'Will it be human?'

'I doubt it.' I put a finger to his lips. 'Before you go telling anyone, there's a lot more you need to know.'

Switching to telepathy, I continued. *'This child will be a mixture of Manyarnern and Human DNA. It might have psionic abilities, it might not. It could look human, or it could look ...'* concentrating for a moment I simultaneously locked the door to the room and changed my shape *'...Manyarnern.'*

His gaze panned up and down my amethyst skin eventually fixing on my scarlet eyes. *'Oh shit, that's not good, is it?'*

I shook my head. *'The child's appearance is the*

least of our problems. Tell me, how long are human pregnancies?'

'Nine months, why?'

'The Manyarnern gestation period is just three months. Your parents will notice. What's more, when a Manyarnern child is born, its growth rate is accelerated, doubling the infant's body weight in the first few hours after birth. That won't be easy to hide. Your blood is red, mine is purple. What would a doctor make of that?'

I could feel his rising panic. 'So what're we going to do?'

'The only logical thing we can do. I must leave here as soon as possible.'

'Okay then, we'll find an excuse to tell Mum and Dad.'

'No, Iain. You've only just got home. I love you and want you to share this but... I understand that you want to see our baby born, but it's madness for you to return with me. Your life is too precious. I won't let you risk it.'

'What am I supposed to do, just sit here and wait? Bloody hell, Angie, you opened me up to the wonders of the galaxy, and now you're dismissing me. Alien or not, this is our baby. Yours and mine.'

I understood his anguish. But I also understood the situation. He'd got away from the O.P.U. once.

I doubted it could happen again.

His face burned into my mind. I felt his pain.

'I'm sorry...'

******

Chapter 5

Mother was smug when she met me in the arrivals lounge of the Gretin Station. She didn't need to say, 'I told you so', her thoughts said it for her.

'It was lucky that merchant vessel was close enough to pick up your signal,' she almost sneered with self-satisfaction. 'So, you're back. What do you expect to do now?'

'I'm not back, not really. I've just come to... to visit.'

I felt her scanning me. Blinded by her own arrogance, she knew that something was wrong, but couldn't figure out what it was.

I took a deep breath. 'I've returned for the sake of my child. Believe me, I wanted to remain on Earth, but safety during and immediately after the birth was far more important than my pride.'

Her psi-awareness focussed on the developing embryo in my womb; maternal instinct taking over.

'Is it conscious? Have you sensed it? Does it generate a psionic field?'

'Patience, Mother. All in good time.'

Rushing back across the concourse, she suddenly stopped and gasped. 'A Lens, we must summon a Lens to name him.'

Smiling to myself, I picked up my bag and followed her towards the infirmary.

It's funny how you can go from wayward child to responsible adult in one thought.

******

I wasn't prepared to admit it, but I was worried the child might suffer from unpredictable mutations. I'd never forgive myself if it was born with no psionic abilities. Such a life would be hollow and empty - a prison sentence for the soul.

The O.P.U. medics did their best to placate these fears. Even they didn't know what to expect. Shortly before the birth, I felt the child's consciousness stirring within me and all my concerns disappeared.

In due course our son was born.

Looking down at the child in my arms, I was overcome with longing. Iain should've been there.

If he were Manyarnern he could've shared the birth mentally. Distance was usually no barrier to Joined minds. I'd chosen to spend my life with a human and had to face the consequences of that choice. Iain's telepathy was due to the psionic transceiver and wasn't strong enough to reach this far across the galaxy. The difference between us never seemed so acute.

The Lens dispatched from Manyarner tried to read the child's specialisation and I felt sorry for her as she struggled day after day to find a clear path through his tangled genetics. Eventually she admitted defeat and asked me to choose a name.

For historical reasons, names are very important to my people. When a Lens identifies a baby's specialisation it usually forms the basis for the given name. Females have a long form, something like *educator and conveyer of words* - a tutor at the Academy. Boys, on the other hand, have simple one-word nomenclatures that hint of the specialisation, often in a cryptic way. For example, Thunder, for someone destined to control the weather.

I had a boy, how difficult could it be to find a one-word name?

On the third week after he was born, I sat at the terminal in my room, the child asleep beside me on the couch. I'd spent most of the day working through the O.P.U. data base of human names, looking for something suitable. One jumped out at me as familiar. It was Serbian in origin.

'Andranovich,' I said aloud. 'It sounds like the Manyarnern word for water. I rather like that'.

Andranovich opened his eyes and looked at me.

'Do you like it?' I pathed. The child gurgled contentedly.

'Hello, Andranovich.'

******

'He must remain here.' She straightened the straps of her gown; a deliberate gesture to distract me from my purpose. This was nothing new.

'No, Mother, Andranovich is my son and I'm taking him back to Earth.'

'He may look human, but in a few weeks his powers will emerge and then what will you do?'

'Fit him with an inhibitor if I have to.'

She snorted in disgust. *'A mind in chains. No grandson of mine is going to suffer that fate. You've attuned to his telepathic frequency. His psi field is off the scale.'*

'Yet, the Lens could not identify his speciality.'

I could feel her anger growing. She withdrew for a moment, no doubt using a Manyarnern meditation to calm her mind. When she continued she had regained her equilibrium.

'You know full well that Andranovich is a special case. The genetic engineering that fashioned our lives does not apply to him. We cannot know the extent of his genetic corruption until each trait exerts itself.

Corruption! Now I'd heard everything.

'Whatever you think, he's my son and he carries our family's genes. You might not like that he's half human, but you have to accept it's a miracle he was even conceived. Andranovich might be the only grandson you get.'

I glared at her. Grandmother or not, I wouldn't have him treated like he was some kind of freak.

She took a deep breath. *'This Tony and Julia that you live with, do they know who and what you are?'* I shook my head. *'I thought as much. How will you explain that you suddenly have a one year old son?'* I frowned, puzzled by her comment. *'You're forgetting. By the time you reach Earth he will be the equivalent of that age. And when he suddenly floats across the room, or anticipates their speech, what will you tell them then?'*

I hadn't really thought of the practical implications of taking him home. I decided to call Iain. It wouldn't take long to set up a hyper-spatial link to Earth. He'd be so disappointed if I returned empty handed.

'Iain will have to get used to it.'

I shot her an angry look. How dare she read through my shield.

'A few months on that backward world has dulled your senses, my girl. What will a lifetime there do for my grandson?'

Nodding slowly, the truth in her words was finally hitting home. Covering up Andranovich's alien ancestry would be difficult, not impossible, but cruel in so many ways. I was sure Iain would see the sense in this suggestion.

'Good, then we have an accord. We'll keep him here on the station, sending him to you when he's old enough to control his powers. I think a year will be long enough. During that time, your Father and I will provide some basic psionic training.'

She came forward, placing an arm awkwardly around my shoulder. *'I know how hard this is, no mother wants to let go of her child. Andranovich's needs must come before your own. We'll take care of him. I promise you. He'll want for nothing and will be loved unconditionally.'*

'A year?'

'Yes, it's for his own good.'

'I've not agreed yet. This is Iain's decision too.'

******

The day the Eilad delivered me to the rendezvous, it felt like truly coming home. Iain ran up the ramp, sweeping me into his arms and spinning me round in a manner not unlike the old black and white movies he liked to watch.

We avoided the difficult topic of Andranovich's absence, neither wanting to acknowledge our mutual loss.

When the Eilad moved out of view above the cloud cover, I watched it go with longing in my heart. The tiny ship somehow representing a lifeline to the child we had, yet didn't have.

'Come on, let's go home.' He drew me to him. We were close - joined minds could be nothing else - but we were standing still. My pregnancy should've given our relationship a new dimension. Returning to the Gretin station for the birth made it feel as if nothing had ever happened.

While I was away, Iain used the time to finish at sixth-form college and gain entry to university. He stunned his school teachers by completing three A Levels in a year; achieving an A grade on each. No one knew about the mind training technique I'd shown him, no one needed to.

This put him back on track with his contemporaries and gave us an excuse to leave Godalming. It was time to move on, to live an adult, independent, life.

'You're going to love the digs I've found. They're close to the Uni so we can spend time together between lectures. The lounge overlooks a park with lots of trees. The kitchen's a bit on the small side, but we don't have to cook much.'

I let him chatter away, thankful for something new to focus on.

******

In addition to his studies and moving to our new home, Iain had been seeing a lot of Sebastian while I was away. We'd agreed early on to keep my origins a secret from his family. They were too closed minded to handle the truth. Sebastian, Iain assured me, was different.

'Seb's not like them.' He drained the last dregs of milk from the carton in his hand. 'He's never been racist. He's been living in London.'

'What's London got to do with it?'

I scraped some more butter over my burnt toast then took a bite from the corner. It wasn't very appetising, but would do for now. By ten o'clock I'd be in the university canteen with a huge piece of cake and a large latte. I felt myself salivating at the thought and chewed more rapidly on the toast.

'London's much more...' I felt Iain searching for the right word. 'Mixed up. Racially, I mean. Living there, someone has to be really open and tolerant. '

'You're sure he can handle it?'

Iain nodded and looked up at the clock. 'Shit, I'm late.'

He pushed away from the table and scanned the room. Spotting his jacket on the floor beneath the sofa he bent down to retrieve it.

'Now we've agreed to tell him, we might as well get it over with.' He stood up, pulled the jacket on over his T shirt and headed from the room.

'I'll give him a call and invite him round for a drink tonight,' he shouted from the hallway.

I wasn't really sure that we had agreed, but decided not to make a fuss. I'd met Sebastian in passing a number of times, but we'd never been properly introduced. They'd been friends for ten years. Iain knew what was best. Besides, I could always erase his memory if things didn't work out.

Dashing across the lounge, I peered into the hall. 'What does he drink?'

Iain paused half way through the front door. His face had a crooked smile. 'Anything wet. Just go to Tesco and buy the cheapest beer they have.' He slammed the door behind him.

******

Sebastian was an athletic man, thick set with dark eyes and jet-black hair. I could have easily mistaken him for one of my own kind. All he needed was purple skin. His most noticeable, and definitely non Manyarnern-like quality, was a permanent grin.

Unaccustomed to many human expressions, I found it difficult to know when he was serious and when he simply found things funny. Once I knew him better, I realised that this man had a permanent smile because he did, in fact, take life as one big joke.

'So, you've started Uni. I can't believe it, you always hated school.' Sebastian took a large swig from the bottle in his hand.

Iain aped him in typical macho style, gulping down his own beer. 'Did not, that was you.'

Sebastian grinned. 'Oh yeah, so it was. You showed real promise going AWOL like that. Now you're back to Mr. boring; towing the parental line.' He looked across to where I sat at the back of the room. 'Married, too. Thought you'd be married to a computer long before you married a human. I bet that caused a riot with Mummy and Daddy.'

Iain coughed nervously. 'Yes, well, they don't actually know we're Joined.'

'Joined what?'

'Married, it means married. They don't actually know about it, so please keep your voice down. If the neighbours hear anything they might spill the beans. Mum and Dad didn't like the idea of us living together at first, but there're cool about it now. You know how they can be. We thought we'd keep the marriage bit a secret until I'm older.'

'You haven't told them?' His face cracked into a broad grin. 'Welcome to the club, it's about time you joined the rest of us lying, scheming bastards.'

Iain beckoned me towards them. 'Can you be quiet for a minute, there's something else we need to tell you. Being married is the least of it. It's something we've not told Mum and Dad, and can never tell them.' He put his right arm around my waist as I approached. 'But we've decided to tell you.'

'I don't believe it, you...'

Iain held up his hand. 'Stop right there, Seb. This is serious. Just listen to me for once.'

'Keep your hair on, mate.' Taken aback by Iain's tone, Sebastian's smile faded. 'Okay, tell me this dark secret of yours.'

'Angie isn't just my wife – Joining partner, we'd say.

She also happens to be an extraterrestrial. That's where I went for nine months. I was living on a space station out there.' He pointed up at the ceiling. 'This might sound crazy, but it's the truth. Angie is an alien from another world.'

Sebastian tried unsuccessfully to choke back a mouthful of beer. It spluttered out from beneath his teeth and dribbled down his chin onto the carpet below.

'Shit,' he mumbled. Wiping the sticky froth from his face and clothes, he continued. 'That's bullshit. You're joking me, right?' Looking at each of us in turn, he noticed our very serious expressions. 'No... come on... pull the other one... She looks pretty human to me.'

'He thinks you're making it up,' I sent.

'Let's surprise him. Can you...'

I needed no more encouragement and flowed back into my natural form.

The poor man fainted right there on the lounge rug, his smile replaced with an expression of complete shock.

******

While Iain attended lectures, I spent my time studying Earth history at the university library. I found it a little tedious, but couldn't avoid the duties imposed on a field operative. It wouldn't matter that I considered Earth my home, if the Board decided to cancel the research I'd be recalled immediately. To avoid this ever happening, I conscientiously compiled a monthly report and transmitted it back to the Gretin station for archiving.

One particular day, I sat on a bench propped up against a window, allowing the winter sunshine to warm my back. A data pad lay discarded beside me. I was happily day dreaming about a glass of Tralmark - a Manyarnern beverage used in rituals. It has an hallucinogenic quality that sharpens the psi-awareness - when the thoughts of another person drifted into my mind.

'Iain was that you?'

'What? No... I'm in the middle of some rather fine tuning of this oscilloscope for my next practical. I'd rather

be left alone for now.'

I received a quick view of the room he was working in. Other students busied themselves around him and a rather attractive girl leaned close to ask a question. His eyes wandered down to her cleavage and I sensed a slight tingle of excitement.

'Yes that is a rather fascinating piece of equipment.' He blushed both physically and mentally. Good humouredly I sent. *'I'll have a stiff talk with you later.'*

Cutting off from him, I scanned the area for another telepath.

'Who's there?' This was a public frequency used by most O.P.U. races. As far as I knew, no other operatives were currently on Earth. Although I couldn't rule out the possibility that someone was sent to spy on me.

'Who's there?

I received a garbled image of the refectory; flashes of people's faces and indistinguishable snippets of conversation. This was not a trained mind. Could it possibly be a human?

The O.P.U. had already documented a few cases of humans with limited telepathy, but this was something else. Despite the garbled content of the transmission, the signal itself was strong. If this was coming from a human then it had serious implications for the Earth's future. Once I reported back, the Board would be obliged to follow it up.

My heart rate quickened. What would that do to my research? Would they recall me, sending in a more experienced team? Or resume their abductions spurred on by these revelations?

I soothed my mounting fears. Establish the source of the telepathy first, and then speculate about the consequences. I hadn't come to Earth to make a name for myself. Being a field operative was just a convenient way to remain here with Iain. Maybe it was best to leave well alone. I didn't have to report everything.

Whatever happened, the decision was mine for once and intriguing enough to warrant further investigation. Shoving the data pad into the lining of my jacket, I headed into the busy street and across to the dining hall.

Pushing through the door, I looked around. There were hundreds of garbled thoughts surrounding me, but I was scanning for a particular consciousness. In a booth on the far side of the room sat an attractive redhead. She talked intently, between sips of steaming coffee, with another student. I marched over and sat down beside her.

'Do you mind?' She gestured to the seat. 'We're saving that for someone.'

This was going to be difficult. How do you broach such a delicate subject - excuse me I was just reading your thoughts - without being laughed at as a lunatic? I had to find a starting point.

Her mind was completely open, just as Iain's had been on our first meeting. In a flash, I picked up enough information to begin a conversation.

'Jennifer, don't you remember me from school? Fitzwilliam County Grammar.'

I gave the other person at the table the suggestion that she needed to do something urgently, she made her excuses and left.

I slid further along the seat.

Jennifer lifted her glasses and looked down her long, angular nose. 'I don't remember you. Were we in the same classes?'

'No, I was two years below you. But I remember that remarkable performance you gave in the school play as Lady Macbeth.'

Warm memories of those care free days flooded into her mind and her whole face lit up. 'Yes. I was rather good, wasn't I? So what brings you here?'

'I'm doing some research. Are you studying drama?'

'Don't be silly. Acting was only a hobby. I'm doing teacher training.' She looked at her watch. 'Sorry, I've got a tutorial in half an hour and I've got to get some books from the library.'

She stood, pulled on her coat and picked up her bag. 'It was good to meet you, even if I don't remember you.'

I couldn't let this go.

'Come to think of it, I need some books too. Mind if I tag along with you?' I could feel that she did indeed mind and invented the library as an excuse to get away from me.

Let me try a more direct approach, I thought.

'How long have you been hearing the voices?'

'Wh…What?'

'The voices in your head. Have you always heard them or have they started in the past few years?'

'I don't know who you are, or what you're talking about,' she lied. 'But I'd appreciate it if you left me alone.' She turned and strode out of the canteen.

I scanned the room. The back of the booth was quite well hidden from public view and everyone else was engrossed in their own conversations. Deciding to take a chance, I pulled the teleport control from my jeans pocket.

The next instant, I was standing among the trees on the far side of the campus. I watched Jennifer descend the stairs and approach me.

I stepped onto the path in front of her.

Stopping dead, she looked about. 'You again. Where the hell did you come from?'

'If you can spare a few minutes, I'll tell you.'

Lowering her gaze, she walked forward and pushed past me. 'Please leave me alone. I've got to get to the library.'

I grabbed her arm. 'No you don't. That's just an excuse. You don't have any lectures for the rest of the day. I'm not going anywhere until you tell me about the voices.'

Jennifer stared at my hand clamped tightly around her upper arm. 'Well as you seem to know so much, is there any need for me to explain?'

'None what so ever.'

Jennifer's eyes widened in astonishment. Delving into her memories, I extracted the information directly from her long-term store. 'So they began on your tenth birthday. Let me put your mind at rest. You're quite sane. Despite what you've read in psychiatric journals, the voices are the thoughts of other people not mental illness.'

Her mind raced through all kinds of possibilities. Could I have quizzed her friends to gain so much personal information? Was I a psychiatrist sent to hospitalise her? She finally concluded that I was a figment of her own imagination.

'I'm quite real. You can pinch me to make sure if you like.'

I released her arm and took a step backwards.

Suddenly she darted around me and broke into a run; her coat flapping behind her as she dashed across the grass.

I sighed and rubbed my forehead. Why were humans so complicated?

Jennifer approached the main road, dodged the traffic as she crossed, then disappeared around the corner. I followed at a discrete distance.

A few minutes later, I walked back into the domed concourse of the university library.

I'd left here fifteen minutes before and wondered if anyone noticed my sudden return.

I looked about. The atmosphere in the building felt thick; as if the air itself is weighed down by the accumulated knowledge housed there. Dust particles floated across the room, suspended in beams of sunlight that streamed down from high windows. My senses flitted around the space, in and out of writing booths, up and down aisles of regimented tomes. A group of students stood opposite, balancing books and folders in one arm, while their dextrous thumbs spelled out text messages on an array of state-of-the-art phones. They leaned close, hissing their conversation to one another. There was a beep from one of the phones and a ripple of laughter filled the silence.

A cough drew our attention.

Behind the desk sat a neatly dressed librarian. She pointed towards the 'Quiet please' sign. The students nodded, motioned towards the door, and pushed past me as they left; swallowed up by the roar of traffic outside.

Then I noticed Jennifer. She was half way up the

stairs to my right, leaning against the aluminium hand rail as she rummaged through her bag.

Unfortunately, the librarian's cough had also drawn her attention. She spotted me just inside the door, panic consuming her mind. Turning on her heel, she shot up the carpeted stairs to the floor above. I also broke into a run.

'Shhhhhh,' hissed the librarian. I waved my apologies and trotted up the stairs at a more leisurely pace.

Reaching the top of the steps, I scanned the area. Directly in front of me, the narrow aisle led the eye forward. Light oak veneers at the end of each shelf reflected the artificial strip lights above. The effect was similar to that created when one mirror reflects another; the diminishing images stretching away to infinity. At the top of each of these wooden panels were orange and black plaques displaying a series of numbers. The first one read: 000 - 099: computer science, journalism and rare books, the next; 100 - 199: Philosophy, Epistemology and Psychology.

Walking slowly forward I glanced to left and right down each row. They were stacked from floor to ceiling with volume after volume of multicoloured works. At the end of each aisle were round tables set against the exposed brickwork beyond. Surrounding these, red fabric chairs were occupied by students bent over writing pads or laptop computers.

The first three rows were empty. In the fourth was Jennifer.

She was standing with her back to me, somewhere between A History of Parapsychology and Dream Analyses. Whether deliberate or coincidental, it seemed as good a place as any to continue our conversation.

'Hello again, Jennifer.' I imbued the message with as much sympathy and understanding as I could. She jumped and swung around. I could feel her frenetic thoughts.

She's not real. This is a hallucination; a psychotic episode. It feels real, but it isn't. I deny you. Go away. Leave me alone to my misery...

'I know this is scary, that you think you're mentally ill. You're wrong. Please give me a chance to explain.'

This is my mind trying to trick me; distorting reality, changing my perceptions. Thought insertion, that's what it is. She closed her eyes tight, wrinkling her face into grotesque lines. *There's no one putting these words into your head. It's you doing it. You've finally lost the plot. You've got to get some help.*

This was taking too long. I had to find a way to get through to her.

While I deliberated, she broke into a run once again; heading rapidly towards the end of the aisle. No one was around so I took a chance. Lifting myself a few centimetres above the nylon carpet, I flew after her.

I'd almost caught up when two students walked around the corner and bumped onto Jennifer as she fled.

'Hey, slow down. Where's the fire?'

She ignored them and dashed out of sight.

Now they looked towards me.

'Damn,' I muttered under my breath.

I grounded with a thud and continued on foot.

'You didn't even see me.' The psionic suggestion instantly wiped their memory as I trotted past.

At the end of the row of shelving, the room opened out into a brightly lit foyer. I looked around. Students studied at desks lit by flexible lamps, the silence broken only by the scratch of turning pages.

Coming to a halt, I focussed my psi-awareness, searching for Jennifer's thoughts. Her consciousness wasn't hard to find amongst the minds of those present. She'd made it to the stairwell and was heading towards the ladies toilet. Calmer now, a sort of defeated acceptance had descended on her mind. She was about to do something very stupid.

******

'I wouldn't do that if I were you.' I pushed my way into the end cubicle. Jennifer was crouched on the floor beside the toilet, her finger poised on the send button of

103

her mobile phone. 'If you call an ambulance it'll make things much worse.'

'It can't get much worse than this. I'm holding a conversation with my delusional mind.'

I considered my options. A psionic suggestion would bring this debacle to a rapid conclusion. But would it help her in the long run? No, she had to accept this on her own terms.

Jennifer watched as I stepped over her, closed the lid and sat down on the loo.

'You're not making things easy for yourself, Jen.' She shrugged, but remained quiet. 'Let's say you do call an ambulance and explain to the paramedics that you're hallucinating and hearing voices. They'll section you and lock you up pending further tests. Your career's down the drain, your life here at Uni is thrown away. Do you want that?' She shrugged again. 'Now let's speculate. Maybe I'm real. Maybe the voices you're been hearing since you were ten are the result of telepathy. That's something you never even considered. All those times you picked up other people's thoughts you believed you were mad. If I'm right, all you have to do is let me explain and then you can get on with your life. Agree to listen and when I'm done, I'll go away and never make contact again; although I'm hoping that won't happen.

'Telepathy. Is that how you're putting the words into my head?'

'Yes.' I smiled. *'My lips aren't moving but you can still hear me.*

'That's easy for a hallucination to say.' Her finger hovered over the send button once again.

'Unlikely as it sounds, telepaths do exist. Something must have happened when you were ten, something clicked into place and allowed you to be able to pick up others' thoughts. What harm will it do to humour me for a few minutes? If I don't convince you then you still have the option of making that call.'

Her mind filled with sorrow, the sadness cutting deep. 'We were coming back from our birthday treat at the zoo when the accident happened. The other car didn't stop

104

at the lights. Greg, my twin brother, was tickling me at the time. I tried to stop him. To reach me he took off his seat belt. He died right there on the seat beside me. I still remember the sound of his neck snapping before his body went limp. It was my fault.' She looked up, sniffing back her tears. 'I've never told anyone about it before.'

'You were ready to tell someone.' I stroked her troubled mind with my own. *'It's amazing you managed to keep this bottled up for so long.'*

I was acting just like a Lens.

With a creak the outer door to the toilets opened. We tensed and leaned forward, glancing around the side of the cubicle. I felt Jennifer gasp.

'Do you know her?'

'It's Melissa Smith, she's on my course,' she whispered.

'So you acknowledge that she's real.' Jennifer nodded. *'Okay, here's a choice. Stand up now, confess to her that you've lost your mind and hope she sits in the ambulance with you when they come to take you away. Or take my hand, let me link our minds and I'll show you how telepathy works.'*

We listened as the other women entered the furthest stall. There was the rustle of clothing, the tinkling sound of urine hitting porcelain then the rumble of the spinning toilet roll. All the while, I was aware of the internal argument occupying Jennifer's mind.

'It's make your mind up time.'

Reluctantly she raised her arm towards me. I smiled and took her hand, rubbing my thumb gently across the knuckles. I dashed into her mind, forming a link between us. When it was established, I reached out towards Melissa.

She was thinking of... her unsightly thighs. How her knickers dug into the top of her legs leaving an ugly red mark. Should she buy some more in a larger size or go on a diet? Ice cream sundae... Now she was thinking of her evening meal. Steak, chips, peas followed by a huge sundae at the cafe in the centre of town. Would Tom, her favourite waiter, be there? He was so fit, nice bum...

maybe she should go on a diet, then he might actually notice her.

By now she had left the cubicle and was washing her hands at the basin. Jennifer stood up awkwardly and led us both out into the main area beside the wash stand. We were still holding hands, the link between us stable and comforting.

Melissa noticed movement and looked around. 'Jenny. Hi. What're you up to?' Her gaze fell onto our joined hands. *Oh my god. She's a dyke!*

Jennifer and I burst out laughing as the thought entered our minds. The tension of the past half hour vanished in the warm glow of instant friendship. Startled by our reaction, Melissa turned around and headed towards the door, grabbing a paper towel from the dispenser as she passed.

We were still laughing some minutes later as we emerged from the library into the afternoon sunshine.

Waiting at the kerbside for the traffic to pass, I took stock of the situation. Jennifer had come through the crisis remarkably well. Now it was time to take it to the next level.

'There's a bench over there.' I pointed further along the path. 'I know its a little cold. Can you sit with me for a while and I'll explain everything?' She nodded agreement and let me usher her towards the seat.

'Where did you come from? What do you want from me?' She asked once we were settled.

I smiled warmly, extending my hand in the traditional human custom.

'Hi, I'm Angie McClellan.' Then switching to telepathy I added. *'All I want is the chance to put your mind at rest. I'm quite real, made of flesh and blood. Where I come from is a little more difficult to explain. If you can spare an afternoon I'll tell you all about it.'*

'So I'm not mad?'

'You're as sane as me, which probably isn't saying very much.' We both laughed. *'We share a unique and remarkable ability. We can read other people's minds as well as communicating directly. I thought Iain and I were*

the only telepaths in the vicinity. We'll have to be more careful now we've found you.'

'Iain? There are more of you?'

'He's my husband. At the moment, he's working over in the engineering faculty. Would you like to say hello?'

'I don't know…all this is so strange… How do I…?'

I went into her, forming the bridge between us again.

'Stretch out your feelings towards him like this.'

Images of the lab swam in our minds, gradually coming into focus. I felt Iain gasp when he noticed the unfamiliar mind sharing the link. In a flash I transmitted the day's events and he relaxed again.

'Hello, Jennifer. It's good to meet another telepath. I was beginning to feel a bit of a freak.'

For a moment she experienced shock that another mind was inside her own - or perhaps it was the other way around? Taking a deep breath, she dismissed the fear plunging headlong into the experience.

Her fortitude was remarkable.

'What does he mean?'

'There's no need for me to answer your question. If you focus more intently on his mind you can glean the information directly.'

Reminiscent of a child taking her first few steps, Jennifer's early exchanges were clumsy and lacked confidence. Sighing with relief, she decided she wasn't mad after all.

'This is like waking from a nightmare.'

It didn't take long for her to master telepathy. We discovered the next day, over coffee at our flat, that she also had substantial telekinetic abilities. Enthused by her gifts, she quizzed us for hours about every possible use of psionics.

'No kid's ever going to pull a fast one with me again,' she remarked. 'My teaching practice supervisor won't know what's hit him on Monday.'

Iain looked concerned. 'Aren't you scared he might find out?'

'How can he? I lived with those voices for nine years and never figured it out. Besides, if you've got the skills, you might as well use them.'

******

We introduced her to Sebastian shortly after that. It was obvious from their first meeting that they too had a special connection. It surprised me that they got along so well, he was flippant, irresponsible and maddening at times, she was ordered, direct and kind.

'Opposites attract,' remarked Iain. 'Stranger things have happened.'

Over the next few months, our cosy foursome went everywhere together. Teleporting around the country visiting galleries, concerts and many, many, pubs.

They were good days.

Their romance blossomed and our love for them deepened. Iain wouldn't have called it love, humans don't like to express their emotions so openly, but that's exactly what it was.

During the Easter break in Iain's first year at university, we gathered one evening after a pleasant meal at a local restaurant. Returning sated to Jennifer's rented house, she and I continued a conversation we'd started earlier. Sebastian lay on the couch with Jen below him on the floor. We sat opposite them in two floppy armchairs; the stuffing worn thin by years of abuse.

While Jennifer was deep in discussion, Sebastian absent-mindedly played with her hair.

'I wish you'd stop doing that.'

'Stop what?'

Iain put down his wine glass and scratched the palm of his hand. 'You're sending a ticklish feeling as you do that with her hair.'

'I wasn't doing anything. You're the telepaths. It's not my fault if you pick up unwanted sensations when reading my mind.'

Seb resumed the gentle stroking motion.

'This isn't the first time we've shared more than

108

words.' Jennifer lifted her glasses and winked.

'Hey what's going on?' Iain looked across at Sebastian who sat up, more interested in this new line of conversation. 'Is there something that you're both not telling us?'

'D'you remember a few months ago when you skipped classes and came home for - how shall I phrase it? - sex,' began Jen.

Guessing what was coming next, Iain squirmed uneasily in his seat.

'I was over five miles away on teaching practice that day. The emotions were so intrusive, I had to excuse myself and sit in the ladies loo for nearly an hour.' She sent us an image of her, hot and sweaty, squatting in the little cubicle; trying unsuccessfully to block the feelings of arousal that flowed into her mind.

Sebastian took a while to catch on. 'You mean that every time they do it you...' He trailed off at the realisation, and then looked across at me. 'And you knew about this, Angie?'

'Yes, I had a fair idea. Sometimes we just get carried away in the heat of the moment.'

'But you told me that you could shield your thoughts even from each other.'

I shrugged. 'We can. Sometimes it takes an effort.'

'There must be some way to stop yourselves from doing it. I mean sending the thoughts not the other.'

For the first time since we'd met, I felt him blush. No stupid jokes? I thought. That made a change.

'If you were a telepath like the rest of us,' remarked Jen, 'you'd understand the closeness of sharing these things. I was startled the first time it happened. Now I quite enjoy it.'

Looking into her eyes, Sebastian appeared distressed. 'Jen, I'm surprised at you. I thought I was dating a nice girl. One I could take home to my mother.'

Shocked by his comment, Jennifer's thoughts quickened and a flush spread across her face. Then his features cracked into a broad grin and she realised he was just teasing.

109

Typical Seb, I knew he couldn't remain serious for long.

Jennifer reached up, slapping him playfully with a cushion. 'Damn you, you almost had me then.'

Feigning injury, he rolled off the sofa and lay on his back beside her. Gazing up at me he asked. 'D'you pick up pain as well as pleasure? Would you know if she was beating me?'

'Yes. Probably. But in your case I'd assume you deserved it and take no notice.'

He turned to Iain. 'It's not fair. The women are ganging up on me. Can't you do anything to control your wife?'

Iain picked up his glass and took a large mouthful of wine before replying. 'I daren't tell her what to do for fear she'll turn me into a frog.'

'Are you implying I'm a witch.' Grabbing a cushion, I used telekinesis to launch it towards him. It bounced off his forehead and onto the floor.

'A hundred years ago you would've been burnt at the stake long before this,' laughed Iain.

Our carefree banter continued for some minutes.

After a while, Jen and Sebastian stopped play-acting and started kissing. I watched them closely, reaching out my psi-awareness.

Sensing my intentions, Iain leaned on the arm of my chair. 'Oh no you don't,' he whispered into my ear. 'What they're thinking is private.'

I pulled away from him, pouting. 'But they look so happy, so...'

Jen and Sebastian stood up.

'Leaving so soon?' teased Iain. 'We were just settling in for the floor show.'

Sebastian grabbed Jen's hand, pulling her towards the stairs. As they headed up to bed, Jen peered back over her shoulder. *'We hardly need to be in the same room for you to get a ringside seat.'*

Once they were gone, Iain looked puzzled. 'What did she mean by that?'

'I think it was an invitation.'

'An invitation to what? Oh I see.' He grinned. 'You're not thinking of taking her up on the offer are you? What would Seb say?'

'What he doesn't know won't hurt him.'

'You dirty little voyeuristic nymphomaniac.'

I sighed contentedly as we also headed for bed. How wonderfully Manyarnern this felt. Although it was the first, it was definitely not the last time we all shared more than each other's thoughts.

******

I reached across the table, grabbing the last piece of bacon from Iain's plate and stuffing it greedily into my mouth. The crisp, salty taste felt comfortable on my tongue. Noticing the silence, I looked up.

Jen, Seb and Iain were staring at me with open-mouthed astonishment.

'Of all the sensual pleasures enjoyed on Manyarner, food has never been one of them.' I licked the greasy residue from my lips.

'She eats like a horse,' said Iain from beside me.

'If she doesn't watch out she'll end up looking like one.'

'Seb,' chastised Jennifer, 'don't be horrid. Angie's got a lovely figure. I wish I had...'

'It's just a trick of molecular biology. Remind me to teach you some day.'

Jen pushed herself away from the table. 'If you'll excuse me, I need the loo.'

'Put the kettle on, on your way past,' called Iain, as she disappeared through the doorway.

I pointed towards Sebastian's plate. 'Are you going to finish that?' He shook his head. The corner of toast lifted, wiped itself around the residual egginess, and then floated across the table into my mouth.

'Yum.'

Iain and Sebastian burst into fits of uncontrolled laughter.

'What's so funny?' I asked once they'd calmed

down.

'hmmm…aahh…'

'Iain, did you hear that?'

'hmmm mmmm… heeee...'

'There it was again. Is everything alright, Jen?'

She trotted back into the room. 'Fine, thanks, I was only gone a minute.'

'Seriously, there's something...'

I scanned the room. We were the only ones present.

Going deeper I sensed the fabric of the chairs, the wood grain in the table, the artificial fibres of the carpet.

Still there was nothing out of the ordinary.

What I'd experienced was telepathic; inarticulate and weak, yet real. I was certain of it.

Deeper, I must go deeper, I thought.

The air around me came to life, oxygen and nitrogen moving in a chaotic dance. Nothing was out of place.

I took myself further, into the atomic structure; protons, neutrons, electrons spinning... Now I felt the bonds of energy holding this subatomic world together. There it was... something... something...

'Mummy help me.'

I grabbed Jen and Iain's hands, drawing on their strength.

'Andranovich!' we exclaimed in unison.

'I'm going to kill that woman when I get hold of her. How could mother do this.'

Breaking the link, I dragged my mind back to the macro world.

'Seb. Teleport control. Under our bed. Get it NOW!'

He ran from the lounge and I heard him scrabbling about in our bedroom. When he returned with the control, I handed it to Iain. 'You know what to do, widest field possible, maximum dispersal.'

'It's too fucking dangerou...'

I cut him off. 'He's our son. DO IT!'

Colour bled from the world, sensation diminished.

The teleport pulled my body out of reality.

Wrenching, tearing; spreading my essence.
Nowhere, everywhere.
Void.

******

Chapter 6

The universe was mud, think congealed mud in my mind. Did I actually have a mind? I guess not. My physical body was torn into a billion, billion pieces, scattered somewhere in between the matter that constituted our lounge. Andranovich was there too, his essence pure energy without shape or form.

I knew I could find him. I'm not sure how or why I knew, I just did.

Instinct driving me on, I reached into the void.

A thought popped up, 'flesh of my flesh'. It was a phrase from the Joining ceremony, its significance startled me.

We were connected; two entities, yet both parts of the same whole.

I gathered him to me.

Now I had to find a way back. Concentrate. There was a mind close by. Concentrate. A mind so familiar... Concentrate. A mind joined with my own.

With a blinding flash and a deafening crack that split the air, we materialised on the floor at Iain's feet.

Curled in the foetal position, I cradled Andranovich in my arms.

When reality hit, he screamed, thrashing about wildly. Ignoring this, I held him, just held him close until his terror subsided.

******

I don't know how long we stayed there. The others wrapped us in blankets, forced warm liquids down our throats, embraced us until the world was right again.

'Angie... Angie... Are you okay?' I nodded. *'How did you...?'*

'I haven't got a clue. I just knew, instinctively, that I could do it.'

114

Remembering how close we'd come to losing our boy, my anger returned. *'What possessed Mother to send a child through a three hundred light year teleport?'*

'She said it was a duty, a lesson,' pathed Andranovich.

'A lesson in what? How to die.'

'Angie,' snapped Iain, on a private frequency. *'You're scaring him.'*

I smiled down at the child in my arms. *'It doesn't matter, you're home now. Andranovich, this is your father.'*

'Climcheck d'na rap'toor phushiim.'

'What?' said Sebastian.

'He's speaking Manyarnern.' I looked into his eyes. *'Andranovich, scan their speech centres. Feel the meaning.'*

'Hello, Father. May your senses be enlightened and your dreams be fulfilled.'

Staring at the son he'd longed to hold for over a year, I could tell that Iain didn't know how to respond. In his mind, he'd expected to see a baby. The child before him resembled a three year old. He had a soft round face and curly light brown hair. His eyes were a piercing blue.

He looked human, yet everything about him was alien.

I felt Iain struggling for words. What could he say to the son who'd grown up so far away?

He reached forward, took Andranovich's hand and smiled. Tears welled up, the emotion overwhelming him.

'Hello, son,' he said gently.

*****

'To me, to me.'

Seb kicked the football across the park. Iain caught it on his upper thigh, allowing it to bounce once before it floated down onto his upturned boot. Next he flipped his legs and the ball rose again, high over his head. His legs kicked backwards and he caught the ball behind him, then up and over his head again.

'Show off,' shouted Sebastian running forward.

I looked down at Andranovich beside me on the picnic rug. 'Don't you want to play?' He shook his head. 'Daddy would like it.'

'No thank you.'

I wasn't surprised by his dismissive tone. He'd been back with us for ten months and it was an uphill struggle to interest him in anything human. I looked up. Iain sensed it too. The football fell uncontrolled to the ground.

'Give him time. He'll get used to us eventually. Think what it was like for you when you first arrived on the Gretin station.'

'I'm trying to be patient, Angie. We're his family that should count for something.'

'You're not my real family.'

Football dismissed from his thoughts, Iain bounded towards us, followed by a confused Sebastian.

'What the f...?'

Andranovich looked up, his bearing portrayed a person well beyond his years. *'I understand your hostility, Father. You're human and I can forgive those frailties. Family is not a role you can just assume. You have to earn it. Nyaseema and Voltin taught me that.'*

His resentment towards us cut deep. We looked at one another, unable to respond.

I hadn't left him on the Gretin station by choice, it was Mother's idea and she'd used the opportunity to steal him from us.

'She taught me psionics and it brought us close.'

'You're reading through my shield again, that's not polite.'

'But sometimes necessary.'

I fought back my anger. This is her talking, not him.

Maybe he was right. On the station he shared thoughts and feelings all the time. It would feel like being amongst family. We must have been dull by comparison.

'So dull that he rejects us.' Iain's mind was flat, unemotional. *'There's no point in anger. We know where we stand. We can't compete.'*

Seb came closer. 'Is the game over?'

Standing, Andranovich took our friend by the hand.

'I think Mummy and Daddy need to be alone for a while. Buy me an ice cream?'

Iain nodded towards Sebastian.

'Okay, what flavour?'

'Pineapple.'

We stood together watching our son walk away.

******

A year later we were sitting under a tree outside the block where we now rented a flat. By now a truce had fallen between us and Andranovich. We knew he didn't want to be on Earth and he knew he couldn't leave. The only solution was to make the best of it.

Using telepathy as often as possible, we encouraged him to join in discussions with Seb and Jen. It wasn't the same as group consciousness, but it helped.

It was a lovely day in early summer. A vibrant green had returned to the trees and there was birdsong all around. The blue sky overhead hinted of warmer days to come. Iain had just one month until his final exams. I usually busied myself with O.P.U. reports while he was studying. Today was far too warm for work, so I lay on the ground playing telekinetic chess with Andranovich.

'You could've gone with them, you know,' Iain mumbled without looking up from his book.

'A trip to the sea side did sound tempting, but I couldn't face three hours stuck in a traffic jam in that wreck of a car your Dad drives.'

I felt a ripple of laughter drift from his mind. 'He considers it a classic, but I know what you mean. Mum says he intends it to outlast him.'

I smiled at Andranovich as his knight lifted into the air to check my king. 'Besides, I'm enjoying playing chess...' I stared down at the board. 'Even if I'm being beaten.'

A sort of contentment washed over me. Who needed excitement when there was so much joy in motherhood?

Iain's thoughts returned to his studies.

A few seconds later he doubled over in pain. 'Shit!'

Picking up our belongings, we rushed indoors and up the three flights of stairs. Slamming the front door of our flat, I dropped the blanket, chess board and pieces onto the hall floor. Iain put down his books and started a frantic search for his wallet and house keys. They weren't on the hall table, so we moved into the lounge searching amongst the piles of paperwork and discarded magazines that littered the floor. Andranovich watched us from a discrete distance.

'Aha,' exclaimed Iain, pulling the wallet from behind a cushion on the dishevelled sofa. I smirked at him then headed into the bedroom, he followed me. At my telekinetic command, a storage box slipped out from its hiding place beneath the wardrobe and the lock clicked open. I knelt down to inspect the contents.

'What d'you think?' I asked. Iain shrugged.

Reaching inside I retrieved the teleport control and a stunner.

'Let's hope we don't need it.'

I handed him the small weapon and he checked the charge. 'Better safe than sorry.'

Andranovich appeared in the doorway, holding out the bunch of missing keys.

'Good boy. Stand close while Daddy programmes the teleport.'

Materialising in the lounge of the Godalming house we scanned for Tony and Julia's thoughts.

'Nothing. They aren't here,' sent Iain. *'I know what I felt was intense pain and injury. They must've been in some sort of accident.'*

Andranovich looked confused. *'Human Gran and Grandpa aren't telepathic. How do you know?'*

'Human families can be as close as Manyarnerns. You haven't given their culture enough thought to realise that fact.' I felt smug and tried to hide it. *'I tuned Daddy's transceiver to them a long time ago. It made it easier for us to live here.'*

Ignoring us, Iain rushed into the front garden, scanning the local area for their presence. Catching up with him a moment later, Andranovich and I added our strength to his efforts.

'Three heads are better than one.'

While we stood motionless amongst the early summer roses, a police car pulled around the corner. It stopped in front of the house. Before the officer had climbed from his vehicle, we'd gleaned information about the motorway accident from his anxious mind.

Dashing back inside, Iain reset the coordinates on the teleporter.

******

We materialised, in a busy casualty department, thankful that the chaos covered our unorthodox arrival. Hiding the control in his pocket, Iain strode towards the admissions desk. We followed.

He tapped on the glass panel to catch the receptionist's attention. 'Where can I find Julia and Tony McClellan?'

'I'll just check for you.'

His impatience grew as she looked up his parents' details. 'Sorry, but there's been no one by either of those names admitted recently.'

'There must be. The police told us that following the accident they were brought here.' He scowled at the girl.

'I'll take another look.' She sighed and turned back to her computer screen.

It was Andranovich who noticed first. He pointed excitedly towards a burly paramedic disappearing into the trauma room. 'Over there, over there.'

We dashed across the waiting area, leaving the receptionist talking to herself.

'No one's allowed in here,' snapped the paramedic as we tried to push our way into the room.

'My parents are in there and they need me.'

'No. What they need is the doctor right now. He'll let you know when you can see them.' To make his comments final, he stepped across the entranceway and folded his arms.

'I don't have time for this.' Iain lifted the stunner up to the man's face.

'What are you going to do with that?' He gestured at the strange looking device. 'Don't make a fuss, your parents are in good hands.'

A stream of energy burst from the stunner, instantly freezing the man.

Entering the room I read the situation. Luckily Iain, blinded by his anguish, couldn't sense the severity of their condition.

The consultant looked up from his examination of Julia. 'Who let them in here?' When no one responded he turned toward us. 'I would expel you myself, but I'm a bit tied up right now. Who the hell are you anyway?'

'That's my mother and father.'

The doctor's expression tightened. 'I'm very sorry, but there's little I can do for them. Their injuries are just too...'

This was too much for Iain, he swept the stunner around the room, freezing all the staff.

I moved over to one of the trolleys and placed a hand on Tony's head. He'd been dead for several minutes. Iain grabbed at my arm, demanding that I try to help.

'I can't bring him back to life. It's too late for that.'

'You must. He can't die, he just can't.'

Turning to the other trolley, I rushed into Julia. She had many broken bones, and some extensive internal injuries. These I could satisfactorily heal. Most worrying was the damage to her head. The skull was completely crushed on one side and oozed with semi-congealed blood.

Iain noticed my hesitation. 'Get on with it.'

'I can heal these injuries. The head trauma is too severe. Even if she came round from the resulting coma, the brain damage would be... terrible. She'll be a vegetable for the rest of her life.'

'Just read her bloody cell structure and repair the damage, will you.'

'I can do certain things, yes, but I can't replace the material stored in the cells. I can't give her back her mind.'

This was not what he wanted to hear. 'Fuck you.'

Thumping the trolley, he grabbed Julia's hand. Reaching into her with his limited telekinetic powers he began to rejuvenate some of the tissue.

'Don't be so stupid, you can't do it by yourself. It won't do her any favours in the long run.'

Placing my hand gently on his, I went into him. He clung stubbornly to hope for her recovery. *'There's nothing more we can do. You must let her go.'*

Another mind approached. Comforting thoughts spread through our link, focusing on the root of Iain's pain. Looking down, I smiled. Andranovich now stood between us, his hand on top of ours.

This was what families did for one another.

Iain's grip weakened.

I glanced towards Andranovich. *'Thank you.'*

'They'll be waking in a few minutes.' I gestured at the transfixed medical staff.

Iain bent down to kiss his mother tenderly on the cheek.

Reluctantly stepping away from the trolley, he took the control from his pocket and pressed execute.

We disappeared.

******

During the next few weeks, Seb and Jen were great. Their mere presence in the Godalming house seemed to help Iain cope with his loss. At first, I tried to assist with the funeral arrangements, but my efforts were pretty ineffectual. I made a mental note to learn about human burial rituals.

My greatest contribution was keeping Andranovich amused while they made endless phone calls to registrars, undertakers and distant relatives. Most of which I'd never even heard of.

The morning after the funeral, I walked into the bathroom to find Jennifer brushing her teeth. She was dressed in the fluffy cream bathrobe Iain had bought me for Christmas.

121

'You don't mind do you?' she asked, white froth dribbling down her chin.

'I thought there was a familiar consciousness here last night.' I smiled. 'No, not at all. It's nice to have the company.' I glanced back into the hallway. 'Where's Seb?'

She rinsed the brush under the tap, popped it into the toothbrush holder and then wiped her face on a nearby towel.

'He's gone to the local shop to buy some fresh bread and milk.' She turned around and smirked. 'Have you seen the state of the fridge?'

I shrugged. 'When we lived here, Julia took care of that sort of thing. She was the old fashioned housewife, not me.'

'I know. I'm sorry.' She sighed. 'What'll you do now? Move back here or live in your flat? Iain's exams start soon.'

Walking further into the room, I perched on the side of the bath. 'Your guess is as good as mine, Jen. He refuses to talk to me about anything. Now, if you don't mind, I'm busting for a pee. I didn't want to wake him by using the en-suite in our room.'

'Oh, sorry.' She headed towards the door, then suddenly spun around. 'Would you like us to stay? Just till the dust settles.'

'That's the best suggestion I've heard all week.'

******

A few days after the reading of the will, we discovered we were quite wealthy. As well as the Surrey house, Iain inherited an old hunting lodge in Scotland. It once belonged to Tony's uncle and was situated in an isolated location in the Western Highlands, on the shores of Loch Ossian. I knew we were lucky, that I was lucky. The inheritance delayed our need to find proper employment.

The house in Godalming was valued at £690,000.

'Is that a lot?' I asked, once the estate agent had left. Iain didn't respond. The loss was still too close.

'What's wrong with Daddy?'

'He's quiet because he's sad. Selling the house reminds him of Gran and Grandpa. Humans believe they must grieve alone. Give him time, he'll come out of it.'

I was pleased to see Andranovich's compassion for his father.

'In time, all wounds heal.'

I paused and looked down at my son. Perhaps a change of scene would do us all good. *'Andranovich, would you like to go on an adventure?'*

******

Travelling overnight to Fort William, we booked into a hotel. It may have been summer, but Scotland was not as temperate as Southern England. Tomorrow's forecast was for warm sunshine, much better for walking in the highlands.

Early the next morning we caught the train to Corrour Station. Throughout the journey Andranovich's excitement was infectious. His thoughts buzzed around us as he posed question after question. Who was the great uncle who once owned the house? Had Daddy ever seen it before? Would we be staying forever?

With a resigned shrug towards one another, we admitted there were no answers. He'd have to 'wait and see'.

When the train pulled away we understood why the guidebook described this as the remotest station in Britain. There were no roads and apart from a small wooden bunkhouse and almost idyllic youth hostel, situated at the water's edge, the place was quite uninhabited. The only way to reach the lodge, which was located at the far end of the loch, was on foot. I found myself wondering how Edwardian country gentlemen and their ladies had managed this journey.

Following a track that steadily climbed in altitude, we came parallel with the loch. The view from here was breathtaking. Wild stags drank lazily from the shallows, their image reflected perfectly in the stillness of the water.

They smelt our approach and looked up, hearts beating, muscles ready for flight. A psionic suggestion dismissed their fear. This was a sight few humans ever saw. I was determined to enjoy it.

Regimented lines of pine trees covered the bank on our right and ahead, the distant U-shaped valley led up to wilder country; dark and foreboding.

It took almost three hours to reach the lodge. As we trudged wearily up the unkempt gravel drive, past the remnants of old flower beds, their rhododendrons still heavy with bright pink blooms, images of black and white photographs floated through Iain's mind. His father had spent his school holidays playing amongst the heather that covered the mountainside. These happy snaps depicted Tony posing in handmade costumes or swimming in the chilled waters of the loch.

They gave Iain comfort so I left him to his thoughts.

Clearing the last of the bushes, we came to a halt in front of the lodge. I looked up at the grey, stone building and was reminded of my family home on Manyarner. It was a large fronted granite house with three stories and a tiled slate roof. Two massive bay windows looked down across the now overgrown garden and out towards the distant mountains.

The house was extremely run down. Ivy covered most of the right side of the structure; its spindly tendrils pervading every crevice and window frame. Here and there, holes gaped in the roof and I wondered how the structure would hold up through the forthcoming winter.

According to the deeds for the property, the house came with over two hundred acres of land. Iain and I turned around to survey the view and could just discern the roof of a distant building protruding above the pine forest.

'How long has it been since anyone lived here?' I asked.

'Dad's uncle died six years ago. Mum and Dad came up to visit once, but decided it was too far away from town to be used, even as a holiday home.'

Unable to contain his excitement, Andranovich

darted out from between us and bounded up the few steps that led to the large oak door. Not waiting for us to meet him with the key, he used a burst of telekinesis to open the rusted lock and enter the cool interior of the hallway.

'Come on.'

'Well, what d'you think?'

I shrugged and we followed Andranovich into the house.

On the left side of the hall was an equally impressive inner door. Iain pushed it open and we found ourselves in the sitting room. Dust sheets covered the dilapidated furniture, and the atmosphere was thick and musty.

At the end of the room was a huge stone fireplace, above which a carved sculpture depicted a highland scene. I approached to examine the carving in more detail. It showed hunting dogs prancing amongst the heather in pursuit of some helpless prey. Despite its gruesome nature, the artistry was impressive. I brushed a hand over the surface, dislodging a layer of dirt, to reveal bright paintwork beneath.

'This place hasn't been cleaned in a very long time.'

Iain walked further into the room, lifting a sheet from an old chair as he passed. Clouds of dust billowed up like smoke, catching in our throats and making us both gag.

'You know, I think we could be happy here,' he said, once his cough had subsided. 'It's far enough from civilisation for us not to be noticed. We can use the money from the other house to do it up.'

This was the first time that he'd shown interest in anything since the funeral and it was good to see him smile.

'That's exactly what I was thinking. It'll take a lot of work, but the bones of the building have a good vibe.'

We met in the centre of the room and embraced; linking our minds and sending our psi-awareness foraging amongst the ruins of the house.

Momentarily, we caught a glimpse of ourselves standing in a temple beside the loch. The unexpected flash caught us both by surprise.

'Did you see... Was it the future?'

I nodded. *'One of many possible futures.'*

'Is fortune telling another of your people's abilities?'

I shook my head. *'Whatever it was, this is where we're meant to be.'*

I shielded, my mind in turmoil. This should only happen to a Lens during the blending. Why was it happening now?

I knew the vision meant something; something I'd been running from all of my life.

Was it possible that my speciality had been misinterpreted? Dismissing this dangerous thought, I shelved the inevitable internal dialogue; dragging myself back to the here and now.

I was not living on Manyarner so whether there had been a mistake wasn't important.

Andranovich burst into the room.

'Did you see it?' We nodded. *'Was I there? I couldn't see myself.'*

I walked over and crouched down, thankful for the distraction. *'It doesn't matter where you were. The fact that you shared the vision from another room solves a big mystery.'*

'It does?' He cocked his head, eyes full of excitement and wonder.

'Now we know your specialisation. You're a communicator, Andranovich. I didn't want to speculate before. Now I'm sure. A communicator can work anywhere in the galaxy. I'm so proud of you.'

I turned towards Iain. 'I agree. We will be happy here.'

******

We spent the next few months making arrangements with a local building firm. We also had to sell the house in Godalming to pay for the renovations. Every time a prospective buyer came to view the property I felt Iain's anguish.

126

In the end I turned to Sebastian for help. He was remarkably mature about it.

'Seb, this is getting really difficult. I'd like to ask you a favour?'

'Sure, what's up?'

'If I was to take Iain and Andranovich for a holiday, could you take over renovations of the lodge?'

He paced up and down our lounge. I could sense him thinking through the proposition.

'When you say take it over, what exactly do you mean?'

'We'll leave you with our power of attorney. You can spend the money in any way you see fit, just as long as you don't let Jen near a shoe shop.' We both laughed. 'And as long as there's a home for us to come back to.'

'How long will you be away?'

Now it was my turn to think. Travel time, five weeks, six months to let the dust settle and then five weeks back.

'About ten months. Maybe a year.'

'Wow, where exactly are you three going?'

'Where do you think?'

******

Chapter 7

Walking into the strange ship, we put down our bags and looked around. Its design was reminiscent of other O.P.U. vessels I'd travelled in; most likely manufactured in the same ship yard.

Iain gripped my hand tightly, a ripple of caution running across his mind. In contrast, Andranovich could hardly contain his excitement.

'It's okay. We'll be fine,' I pathed.

'Hmmm. Welcome.' An inner door swung open. *'Welcome to my vessel.'*

A tall, hairy creature rushed forwards.

'Bloody hell. It's Chewbacca!' sent Iain on a private channel.

'He's a Repellan, most likely from Repos Four, although it could be Repos Two. I get them mixed up.'

'Hmmm. My name is Captain Fern.' He flicked his head towards us, the long fur of his upper body rippling with the movement. *'I was astounded to receive a telepathic transmission from this world. Hmmm. You're a long way from O.P.U. controlled space. Setting down on a R.A.W. planet is very costly.'* He studied our clothing and baggage. *'Hmmm. Very costly indeed. How can I be of assistance?'*

'As I said in my message, we'd like to buy passage on your ship.'

Captain Fern rubbed his chin. *'Hmmm. That's what I thought. Are you O.P.U. citizens?'*

Iain stepped forwards. *'We are citizens of Earth. My Joining partner works for the O.P.U.'*

'Hmmm. And how do you intend to pay? I'm afraid I cannot accept O.P.U. credits.'

'That's blown it.'

'Sshh, Iain, I've got this covered.'

I switched back to the public frequency. *'Captain Fern, I'm certain that you are a respectable and law*

128

abiding tradesman. I would not wish to insult your integrity. I hoped you might consider a less orthodox form of payment?'

'Hmmm. I'm afraid I do not require the services of a concubine at present.'

I laughed aloud. 'No, no. That's not what I had in mind at all. I do have access to a shipment of pond crystals, Garillian pond crystals. Would they be of use to you?'

His ears twitched with excitement. 'Hmmm. Are you proposing a trade?' I nodded. 'How many pond crystals are we talking about?'

'Enough to buy passage for three to Manyarner.'

'Hmmm.' He waved us towards the inner door. 'Come inside where we can discuss this in comfort.'

******

Repellan vessels, like many others in the galaxy, use Hyperlight drive. This kind of propulsion system phases the ship out of normal space-time, clipping the edge of hyperspace. Neither here nor there, we moved at great speed within the energy field that holds matter together. Inside the ship there's no evidence of the tremendous velocity. In fact, it hardly feels like you're moving at all.

Once Iain got used to Captain Fern's appearance, he spent a great deal of time in the engine room or on the flight deck. He hadn't finished his degree, I know he regretted it. Learning all he could about this new technology made up for that. Captain Fern seemed pleased to have the company.

'Hmmm. I don't get many visitors.'

I spent my time discussing Manyarnern philosophy with Andranovich. Mother and Father had already taught him most of the stories held in the sacred texts. Encouraging him to interpret these for himself, I soon learned that his views were badly tainted by theirs.

Our conversations regularly ended in an argument.

'The chronicle of Grimloch is one of the longest.

Why do you like it?'

Andranovich pulled the hair from his eyes, a gesture very similar to his father's. 'I like the part when Grimloch blows the mind of the liberationist soldier, and the bit where he fights Trynax. They tear each other apart with telekinesis.'

'What are you teaching him?'

We looked up as Iain entered the room. 'It sounds too violent for a child of his age.'

'And this comes from someone who spent his childhood watching *Alien* and *The Thing*!'

He shrugged. 'So who was this Grimloch character?'

'The Lenses call him and his sister Fayuun the architects of Manyarner,' I began 'They were the ones who took control at the end of the psionic wars. They used the Archive of Knowledge to reshape the Manyarnern way of life. She was a geneticist and instigated the genetic engineering programme, or so they say.' He gave me a puzzled look. 'The chronicles aren't historical documents. They're stories, metaphors with a hidden message.'

'So, Andranovich, what's your opinion of the Grimloch chronicle?' he asked.

This was going to be interesting.

Andranovich drew himself up and took a deep breath. 'I think it warns us against change. The psionic wars were fought to bring about Clause Thirty-One of the constitution, giving everyone the right to live the life they chose. Yet, Fayuun engineered the race to follow their specialisations. They ended back where they started. What was the point? Our personal myth is set at the moment of our birth. We have no choice but to follow it to its inevitable conclusion.'

The words were straight out of mother's mouth. She may have called this education. I called it indoctrination.

Iain shook his head. 'It doesn't mean anything to me. You two can discuss this as much as you like. I'd rather get on with my life. Is it lunchtime yet, I'm starving?'

'You're right, enough for one day.' I stood and

looked down at Andranovich. 'Let's eat.'

******

Andranovich had matured significantly since he returned to us. He now looked the physical equivalent of a human child of ten; although mentally he had always seemed much older. Sending a message ahead, we arranged for him to spend a few months training at the Academy. I shuddered at the thought of endless days spent in meditation.

'That doesn't mean he won't thrive in such an environment,' commented Iain. 'He's a tough kid; he'll cope with the strict regime.'

After five weeks on board, we dropped out of hyperspace. Andranovich applauded as the observation window filled with the view of my home world. The second continent had just entered its daylight phase and the glow of the surrounding psionic field could be seen above the upper atmosphere.

'Wow,' exclaimed Iain. 'So that's why you glow purple.'

I'd returned to my natural state shortly after we left Earth. It was a long time since either of them had seen me like this. Iain couldn't resist stroking my arm at every opportunity, watching the colours change beneath his fingers.

Captain Fern grinned. *'Hmmm. Such a shame to live a lie; hiding what you are from the humans.'*

Touching down on the fourth continent space port we said our goodbyes and prepared to disembark.

The door slid open, bright sunlight hit my face, I gasped. There was something carnal here, something primitive and erotic that I'd taken for granted before. I knew this was only the edge of the group consciousness. It felt wonderful.

Looking down, my heart sank.

'What are they doing here?' I mumbled.

'Take a deep breath,' pathed Iain from beside me. *'There's probably a very good reason.'*

131

I stomped angrily down the ramp towards Mother and Father. *'I bet there is.'*

Emerging from the ship, Andranovich broke into a run. He flew past us and was swept up into my mother's outstretched arms.

'Nyaseema...' He raised his shield, cutting off his telepathic voice.

I was stunned. They hadn't seen each other for three years. What could they possibly have to talk about in private?

We'd only just arrived and she was already scheming.

Father read my anger. Stepping forward he held out a container of Tralmark.

'May your senses be enlightened and your dreams be fulfilled.'

I grabbed it from his hand and drank deeply of the sweet liquid. This was the one pleasure indulged by my people that I'd craved during my time on Earth. In a few seconds its psychotropic properties took effect. Anger gave way to pleasure as my senses extended to their fullest.

Letting go of his grandmother, Andranovich walked over and took the beaker from me. He grinned, taking three large swigs of the drink before offering it to Iain.

'Do I have to? It's a hallucinogen.'

I shrugged and walked towards the waiting hover vehicle. 'Please yourself.'

Lifting the beaker tentatively to his lips, he sipped at the Tralmark and then handed it back to Father. 'Thanks.'

At Father's command, the beaker and its contents disappeared.

Hover vehicles are unlike anything found on Earth at the time. Resembling an open topped buss, there are no wheels, and come to think of it, no engine either. The floating platform is controlled by the minds of the passengers. Taking a seat at the back of the vehicle, I was irritated when mother sat down beside me.

'We're so pleased you've enrolled Andranovich in

the Academy. We knew you wouldn't want to remain here, so we've returned to personally oversee his education.'

'He's not enrolled, not fully. We just arranged for a few months training to help him realise his potential as a communicator.'

She flew into a rage. 'A few months! What good will that do? It takes four years for even the most basic specialisations to develop. A year of that will be spent addressing the damage done to him on Earth. Andranovich will stay here and complete his education properly.'

'STOP!'

We stared at Iain who sat on the seat in front of us.

'Both of you stop it right now. I won't allow you to ruin our holiday with your bloody squabbling. We can discuss Andranovich's education later.' He stared at Mother. 'By we, I mean Angie and me. We're his parents. It's our decision to make, no one else's.'

Mother shook her head and turned to face her grandson. 'Would you like to stay here and go to the Academy? It's not like being in a human school. They'll train you to extend your abilities beyond anything you've ever imagined.'

'Yes, Nyaseema, I'd really like that.'

Looking up, she had a smug expression; she knew she'd won the battle. 'I think someone has just made the decision for you.'

Iain fumed.

The vehicle lifted into the air.

By now the Tralmark had taken effect, opening our minds to the energy patterns around us. Andranovich stared over the handrail at the splendour below. 'There are thousands of other beings here I can feel them. If I stay, I'll never be alone again.'

Iain shot him a disapproving look.

'Don't be angry, Dad. There's so much love. Can't you feel it?'

I knew he could, but he wasn't prepared to admit it.

Eventually Father broke the silence. 'Your mother and I have organised a family blending. We hope you, Iain *and Andranovich will attend?'*

I sighed. I hadn't taken part in a blending since I was three. The haunting memories of that day are still with me. A blending is one of the most sacred rites performed on my planet. I didn't believe much Manyarnern philosophy, but that didn't stop me enjoying the deeply spiritual and uplifting nature of the rituals.

Despite my attempts at concealment, they knew I couldn't resist taking part.

'Who's commanding?' I pathed.

Father grinned, pleased by my quick acceptance. *'Trillia'fortunecta.'*

'What, silly Trilly?'

'She's not so silly these days,' pathed mother. *'Last year she graduated as Lens. Earlier this year, she Joined with Faltron. The blending will be her first major test as a novice.'*

Trilly was my uncle's the first-born. Being of about the same age, we'd trained together until my posting to the Gretin station. She was my best, and only, childhood friend.

With the exception of Iain and Andranovich, she was the only one I was truly happy to share my mind with.

******

The vehicle set down on the small grassy clearing beside our family home. The house was built into the side of a hill; the curved frontage protruding from the stone as if it was a natural feature of the bedrock. Arched doorways faced outwards overlooking the lake of Qualmarth - which means tranquillity. On one side of the structure grew a large expanse of Fructa bushes, their wispy fronds rustling in the light afternoon breeze.

Familiar scents filled the air. Sweet and spicy they stirred memories of my childhood. I bent down to pick a small blue flower, surprised to see a cluster of this unusual plant growing so close to the house. Standing up, it made a gentle tinkling sound, like distant bells, as I tucked it into my hair.

134

'And she shall have music wherever she goes,' sent Iain, his humour returning now we'd grounded. *'It must have been a magic childhood to play amongst this beauty.'*

'I wouldn't go that far. Playing is something Manyarnern children don't do very often. I may have meditated in the garden, but my eyes were always turned inwards.'

'Your people don't do very much, do they?'

'Yes, they do.' I answered the question a little too quickly. Iain gave me a knowing look.

'We meditate, we take part in rituals. We relax, swim, and have fun.'

'Boring.' He smiled and looked up at the stone structure in front of us. *'What I mean is they don't really do much work. We just flew over eighty kilometres from the space port and this is one of only half a dozen buildings I saw. It's very impressive and blends into the countryside, but there's nothing else here.'*

I opened my mouth to respond, then shut it again.

This was an argument I could never win. Dismissing the topic, I walked into my childhood home.

The house itself had five levels; hewn from the rock by successive generations of our family. Our ancestors had lived on this estate since the Age of conflict; the bloodline stretching back to Grimloch himself.

The ground floor had an open courtyard that led into a large brightly-lit living space. The layout was circular with a sunken area in the centre; liberally covered with cushions in a multitude of colours. Around the edge, the walls shifted with moving patterns of light.

When their commitments to the O.P.U. allowed, my parents used the rooms on the second level. Mother had prepared quarters for us on the third floor and we carried our belongings over to the back of the circular space.

'Where are the stairs?' asked Andranovich, looking around him.

'There's no need for them here.'

I lifted myself, and the bundle I carried, up into the air.

His face shone with delight as he also used telekinesis to lift himself to the upper levels.

******

It was a glorious morning, the atmosphere at home was charged with excitement at the imminent family gathering. We ate breakfast quickly; Riolta cake and fruits picked from the garden, washed down with a large cup of what I can only describe as Tralmark milkshake. I'd missed this psi-enhancing drink during my time on Earth, but that was all. I knew that the food we ate today would most likely be the same tomorrow, the next day, and for the entire holiday. I found myself drooling at the thought of bacon, egg and beans.

Doesn't anyone ever get fed up with the monotony around here? I thought.

'What's up?' asked Iain, through a mouthful of cake.

I shook my head. To him this was all new and exciting. 'Nothing.'

He didn't look convinced, but let it pass.

I dismissed the thought too. What we ate didn't matter, today was going to be fun.

******

Stepping from the hover vehicle, I looked around me. A small crowd was already milling about in the warm sunshine. Apart from our immediate group, there were aunts, uncles and cousins, their Joining partners, children and grandchildren. About thirty people in all.

Andranovich had adjusted well to his nakedness. Iain had not. He fidgeted nervously on the edge of the crowd, trying to cover himself with his hands.

Pulling him into an embrace, I wiggled myself against his body in an overtly sexual manner. *'See? No one's looking. No one even cares. Relax and you'll enjoy it a lot more.'*

There was a shout from behind me. 'Greetings,

Angeriana, nice to feel you amongst us again.'

'Trilly. It's been so long.'

She ran over to me and we embraced.

Stepping back, Trilly shook Iain's hand. 'I'm pleased to meet you, Iain. This is my Joining partner Faltron.' A tall, wiry man walked over and nodded towards us. 'It's a shame I was busy at the time of your Joining.'

'What you really mean is that Mother and Father didn't invite anyone,' I sent on my old childhood channel.

She blushed. *'Nothing ever changes, does it?'*

Letting go of Trilly, Iain reached out and shook Faltron's hand. 'It's nice to meet a friendly face. Since we arrived everyone's been avoiding me. I thought they were just giving us space, now I realise they're not particularly interested.'

Faltron smiled warmly. *'It's their way.'*

He had a warmth to him that comes with age, and from the intonation in his thoughts, I guessed that he came from the third continent.

Iain took a step backwards and looked around at the countryside. 'We left straight after our Joining. It's only now I realise how amazing this place is.'

'In that case, after the blending, we'll have to show you more,' pathed Trilly.

In the years since I'd last seen her, Trillia'fortunecta had matured into quite a beauty. My recollections were of a plain, melancholic, child. Now her soft round features were set off by a brilliant sparkle in deep crimson eyes. She was taller than I remembered, with hair plaited into a long braid that reached almost to the ground. Amongst its silky blackness long threads of gold and silver had been entwined, making it glisten with reflective light. The overall effect was quite ethereal.

I could sense Iain was impressed by her magnificence and her nakedness.

'What exactly does a Lens do during a blending?' he asked. I felt him trying to keep his eyes on her face.

'The commander is the main link and flows the group mind through her own. It's my duty to see that everyone participates fully, but also that they keep a thread of their individuality. We'll share visions, relive memories and experience personal insights into our life.' She paused. 'I sense your apprehension.'

'I do want to join in, but it's just so…'

'… Unnatural?' She smiled.

'Yes, exactly. On Earth, the last thing I'd want is to share my mind with one of the family. Most of my relatives can't stand each other, so we never really bother to meet up, other than for weddings and funerals.'

Iain's last few words were tinged with a pang of grief.

'Here you let strangers share everything. It's all too... too personal for my liking. I've been Joined to Angie for years now. I thought I'd got used to telepathy. When we arrived yesterday I realised how big a gap there is between our cultures.'

'Stop worrying, Iain. Everything's going to be fine,' she pathed.

My mind caught the edge of her subtle psionic suggestion. Iain relaxed.

'Thanks, Trilly.'

She turned and grinned at me. 'Now if you'll excuse me. It's time to begin.'

People fanned out until we stood around the rim of the temple; Iain and Andranovich opposite me in the large throng. Trilly walked to the centre and stepped onto the raised platform.

She looked up as a stream of pinkish light, emanating from the stone arches, flowed down to surround her body. One by one we took each other's hands until the circle was complete, then walked forward a few paces and knelt down.

For a fleeting moment I was aware of the thoughts of all those present. I saw the circle of people from many different viewpoints that gradually melted into one view; looking outwards from the centre.

For a short while my mind filled with pictures of distant planets and civilisations, one of which was the streets of London teeming with people busily going about their business. Another seemed to be the peaceful hills of the Scottish highlands and a third, the high plateau of the first continent.

This cacophony of individual feelings swirled around my consciousness then solidified into images from my childhood.

I was surprised that the blending should have brought such seemingly banal memories into my cognisance. Trusting to the process I decided that reliving a memory from my youth would be intriguing.

******

'Look at me, Angie.'

Trilly skipped up and over the Fructa bushes, her feet touching their feathery softness as she passed.

'I can fly like a bird.'

Glancing down, I noticed that I was wearing a yellow wrist band. These bracelets indicated a pupil's status at the Academy. Yellow meant I was in the second level.

This was the day we skipped classes.

I let go of the present and became the child.

******

I wasn't confident with the art of lifting and ran along through the undergrowth trying to keep up with my friend.

'Wait for me, Trilly. Please let me catch up with you.'

She grounded in a clearing beside a rock outcrop. The sun had warmed the stone and ground and it seemed as good a place as any for us to relax. Small animals scurried away in fright as we approached.

I sat down and opened a large leaf I'd been carrying. Inside were a handful of Markless fruits.

'If you hadn't scooted off like that we could've picked more.'

'I'm sorry. Can I still share them with you?'

Laying on our backs, we watched the birds circle

above us as we ate the fruit. They were dark blue, roughly the size of a plum and covered in a thick scaly, skin. Beneath this tough exterior was soft, sweet, flesh. Eating like this made the juice trickle down our chins. We giggled.

After a while we became aware of the effects. Sharing ourselves, we drifted into a dream. For hours we lay side by side on the warm soil while our minds wandered through fantasies of other worlds; sharing a longing for excitement, an escape from the rigid discipline of our daily routine.

Eventually I sat up. *'What've they taught you recently?'*

'Nothing much.' She rose up onto her elbows. *'They say it'll take months before I can even begin to channel energy. It's really frustrating. I saw a novice the other day practising in the gardens behind the hall.'*

She sent me an image of a teenage girl, her hair fluttering in the wind. The waiflike figure lifted her hands and caught a shaft of sunlight.

'I bet I can do things like that. They said I mustn't. It's not fair.' She looked up at me, resentment in her eyes and thoughts. *'You already practice your art, but I spend most of my time in meditation.'*

'I only get to heal little surface wounds.' I picked up a stick that lay on the ground beside me and snapped it in two. I focussed my mind, reached into the plant's tissues and joined the damaged ends.

'See... You can do things. I'm not allowed any fun.'

She jumped up, raising a hand above her head.

'Watch me.'

Forked lightning cracked across the sky towards us. It passed over our heads and I felt the static charge tingle my skin. Sensing danger, I leapt out of the way as it struck the rock face above us.

Trilly had been too preoccupied with her summoning of the light to notice the lightning's trajectory. When it struck the cliff, splinters of stone spewed out and began to rain down on her. She looked up at them and started to scream.

'STOP!' I shouted.

To my surprise the rock fragments obeyed my command, freezing in mid air just above her head.

Suddenly aware of an eerie silence, I looked about.

Then I realised that they were not the only things that had stopped. There was no breeze on my face, no bird song and Trilly stood absolutely motionless.

I was very afraid.

I rushed to her side and saw that she was transfixed, open mouthed, in a silent scream; the rock fragments looming ominously overhead. Pulling at her arm with all my strength, I managed to move her a few paces to the left. As soon as I'd accomplished this, the whole world started up again.

'...Aaaah.'

The rocks crashed down where she'd just been standing.

'What happened?' Trilly looked at me like a frightened animal. *'I was sure that they'd fall on me.'*

And with those words the joyous afternoon was suddenly gone; its serenity replaced by my inner confusion.

'You were so scared I pulled you out of the way.' I said, shielding so she could not read my true feelings. 'Anyhow, now you know you can't control the power and why they told you not to use it. We better get back.' I turned and walked away.

We trudged our way back to the Academy in silence, Trilly in the lead with me dawdling along behind.

I felt how shaken she was by the incident. She had no idea what to make of events and kept glancing back over her shoulder towards me.

I spent the journey trying to decide whether to tell her what had happened, or to figure it out alone.

As we approached the outer buildings of the Academy we were swept up in the hubbub of daily life and, thankfully, the decision was taken out of my hands.

******

Stretching, I noticed the circle begin to wake. Iain

141

smiled and trotted over, eagerly sharing his experience. He'd also relived moments from his childhood. It gave him the opportunity to say goodbye to his parents.

The blending is good for helping people deal with grief. I was pleased he gained so much from the experience.

I searched through the crowd looking for Andranovich, eventually noticing him sitting on the steps with a group of children. He didn't tell me what he saw that day, but afterwards there was little debate about his decision to remain on Manyarner.

It was well into the afternoon. People brought food from their vehicles, laying them out on the lawn for everyone to share. We spent the next few hours picnicking and discussing our visions.

'Mum.' I looked across at Andranovich who still sat away from me with the other children. His human appearance had taken on a gentle psionic glow. *'D'you mind if I go for a swim?'*

'Of course not, sweetheart. It's your holiday too.'

The group of children jumped up. Holding his hands, they rose together into the air. I watched, curious to see his reaction. For a few seconds he was anxious, then realising the thrill of lifting his fear was replaced with joyful laughter.

'Have fun.'

He waved and flew off across the trees.

Iain handed me a glass of Tralmark. 'Is it safe?' I nodded. 'He seems at home here already, doesn't he?'

It was hard to accept, but we both knew we'd lost our little boy for good.

I'd been aware of Trilly watching me for the last half hour; she now approached and sat on the grass beside us.

'What did you see in the blending?'

'I hardly think that you need to ask. How long have you known?'

She gave me a sideways glance. *'Do you realise what you did?'*

Even without telepathy I knew there was far more

142

to this question than met the eye.

Iain moved closer and looked at our intense expressions.

Feeling his curiosity, I shared with him the events of many years ago.

'So what did she do?'

Trilly took a large gulp of air.

We waited.

'You stopped time.'

As soon as the words came into my mind I knew the truth in them. The whole sequence suddenly made perfect sense.

'I am now convinced, as are the Elders, that your specialisation...'

'Yes, I know,' I interrupted. *'My specialisation was misinterpreted. I should really be a Lens. But I'm not and it's a bit late to go changing now.'*

Trilly's face cracked into a broad grin. *'Nothing so mundane, dear friend. You are not a Lens. Your name may imply that you are a healer, but in reality you are so much more than that.'*

The party around us fell quiet as they perceived the importance of our exchange.

I tensed.

'You are the Premier.'

I couldn't believe it. I'd suspected for some time that I was probably a Lens. That I could handle, but Premier? No way!

Mother and father's thoughts filled my mind. *'Yes, our daughter, you are the Premier. We are humbled in your presence.'*

'The what?' pathed Iain, confusion and concern mixing in his telepathy.

Father's commanding mind silenced his enquiry.

'Daughter, you know how our planet has suffered, how it is still suffering. It is in need of someone with the power to repair its wounds and bring stability again. The Circle of Elders offers the Premiership of Manyarner to you. It is your rightful place and more than that, it is your duty.'

This was more than I could stomach. Why couldn't they just leave me to live my own life?

Iain grabbed my hands and swung me forcibly around to face him. *'What are they talking about?'*

'They think I'm some kind of super being prophesised in the sacred texts. The whole idea's ridiculous.'

A tight knot of fury began to swell within me. My body shook as the anger grew.

Iain placed a reassuring arm around my shoulders, the physical contact soothing my rage. The thing I've always loved is his ability to put me first; even when he was out of his depth.

'Losing it won't help the situation. Ignore them, take a deep breath and tell me what all this means,' he said.

'You know how our race was genetically engineered thousands of years ago.' He nodded as the significance of the information became apparent. I felt myself relax a little, the words focussing my intent.

'Well, there's this legend that says in a time of crisis an exceptional individual will be born to lead the planet and solve its problems. And they think that's me.' I glanced towards Trilly. *'Although I can't believe that this single incident is any real evidence. I've been genetically mapped dozens of times, and no one's noticed anything weird about me before.'*

'Who wrote this legend?' asked Iain.

He also looked towards Trilly. She shrugged.

'We don't know,' I began. *'There are many different stories carved on the temples' walls. Every few hundred years the glyphs undergo subtle changes and it's the Lenses who interpret them for the people.'*

With eyes still fixed on Trilly, his thoughts now rang of betrayal. *'So you only have **her** word for it?'*

'That's right.' The truth finally sunk in. *'It's the Lenses who originally predicted all of this. So it's them who must have decided I'm the Premier.'*

Trilly moved closer. *'You were named as the one who would heal wounds and bring cohesion two days after your birth. I'm sorry it took so long for us to reveal the* truth.'

My anger was rising again. *'You mean they knew.'* I glared at Mother and Father. *'I don't care about my name. You're all wrong and you just have to accept it!'*

To emphasise my point I stood and strode off into the undergrowth.

It was mother's thoughts that pursued me. *'Ever since you were young you've fought us at every turn. Becoming a healer was not good enough for you. You had to travel off-world and work for the O.P.U. Then you resigned from the Species Recognition Programme and joined with this... this human.'*

Frustration fuelled my flight from the oppressive scene. *'I joined with the man I loved. It was my choice to make. Clause Thirty-One gives each and every Manyarnern the right to choose what to do with their lives. The last time I looked, I was still Manyarnern so that applies to me as much as it does anyone else.'*

I lifted as high as I could into the air, then shot off across the countryside.

A crushing weight suddenly bore down on my mind, forcing me to ground again. It was the collective consciousness of the whole planet. When my feet sunk into the soft grass, I paused to take a huge breath. The insistent voices in my head were becoming painful.

With hands curled into fists, I held them against my temples.

'Go away.'

'Every Manyarnern that lives or has ever lived forms part of a greater whole,' pathed the people. *'We are all born of the same stuff, and we are all dependent upon one another for our existence. Now that we know you are our Premier any attempt to flee from this destiny is impossible.'*

I tried to shield from the combined thoughts of so many intellects. With every second that passed independent thought became more difficult.

How could this far-fetched idea have started?

'It was meant to be,' responded the mob.

What gave the Lenses the right to tell everyone?

'The planet needs you.'

What did I know about ruling an entire world, I'm not a politician?

'You are the Premier.'

If it were true, what would become of my life on Earth? What would become of Iain?

'What is one life?'

I knew with certainty that unless this clash of ideologies stopped soon I would go completely mad. Subjugation of my will seemed the only way to cease the attack.

Giving in was not an option.

In one last-ditch attempt to block them I screamed. *'LEAVE ME ALONE!'*

At last there was silence. A silence more acute than I'd ever felt.

This absolute solitude created both relief and terror in the same moment.

I lost consciousness, collapsing amongst the tall grasses of the central plain.

******

Familiar lips pressed against mine, their tenderness pulling me back from the abyss. Beneath me I could feel the soft, damp ground. I shivered and opened my eyes.

I looked up into Iain's familiar face. 'We must stop meeting like this,' he said. 'Are you cold?' I nodded. 'It dropped to almost freezing last night. Here...' He pulled a rucksack off his shoulder and dug around inside. Retrieving a colourful robe, he helped me sit up and put it on. 'Better?' I nodded again.

'What time is it?'

'Almost morning. At first I thought it best to give you some space. When you didn't come home, I started searching for you. I've been at it all night. I was beginning to worry.'

I gave him a weak smile. 'Sorry.'

'It's okay. I've found you now.' He sat beside me on

the ground, pulling me closer to his body heat. 'Have you calmed down? I've never seen you so mad. Remind me never to get on your wrong side.'

'What d'you mean? What happened?'

'Don't you know?' I shook my head. 'When you told them to get lost, I guess you really meant it. That scream of yours packed quite a punch. The whole planet's suffering from one hell of a headache.'

'I did that?'

'Sure did. I'm sorry such a lovely day was spoilt by Trilly's announcement.'

'I still don't accept what she says, you know.'

'You might have to. That display of power fuelled Nyaseema's insistence that you're the Premier. I had a real barney with her after you left. In the end it was Trilly who calmed everyone down. She said...' I started to interrupt, but he held up his hand.

'She said, whether or not you accept the position of Premier, they can't keep you here. The constitution is still on your side. I had a long chat with her about it. She believes your personal myth is still changing, that destiny will lead you along the right path. If you decide to come back to Earth then it's meant to be. Your mum and dad might be Elders of the Circle, but even they won't go against the Lenses.'

'Damn them. They've known about this since I was born. They made me suffer all those endless classes at the Academy. I never wanted to be a healer... I was never any good at it. Why didn't they tell me the truth?' He shrugged. 'Why me, Iain. For fuck sake, why me?'

'Maybe it's the luck of the draw. It's in your DNA.'

My body stiffened as the anger returned. I didn't follow the religion before. No one's going to force me to follow it now.

'Calm down. I don't buy this religious rubbish any more than you do. But everyone else around here does, so I'm playing along to keep them quiet. Okay?' I nodded and he continued.

'Trilly said that if you're determined to return to Earth, she'll back you up. I like her, she's really sweet.' He smiled and I relaxed a little. 'I also got your parents to agree that they won't discuss it unless you mention it first. We came here for a holiday and that's exactly what I intend to have.'

'But... how?'

'I used reverse psychology on them.' He beamed. 'I told them the more they hassle you, the more likely you are to leave and never come back. Manyarner's managed all this time without a leader, it can do it for a few more years. They can't afford to drive you away forever.'

I was astounded. When we Joined, Iain was young and naive. Now he'd grown into an assertive adult who not only understood my world's complex philosophy, but could also handle my very pushy family. I'd lived at the university amongst his contemporaries for three years and I'm certain none of them would've been capable of the maturity Iain now displayed.

I'd always known he was special.

'Thank you. How did I manage before I met you?'

He smiled. 'You didn't. If it wasn't for me, you'd still be doing that dull technicians job back on the Gretin station.'

'Would not.'

'Would too. You needed someone to give you a kick up the arse.'

I grinned at him. 'I guess so.'

He pulled me closer. 'Have I told you lately how much I love you?'

A wave of sadness washed through my mind, tears following behind. Why was I crying? Wrapped in his arms and his love I should have felt blissfully happy. Perhaps I was mourning my lost childhood, for the life I wanted, but never had.

In his usual matter-of-fact style, Iain waited for my tears to subside.

'Better now?' I nodded.

We sat together amongst the wispy leaves of the grass, watching the sun rise over the plain in a crescendo of pinks and mauves.

'What about Andranovich?' I said at last. 'Do we let

148

him stay?'

'Yeah, why not? He won't talk about his experience during the blending, but somehow it's changed him. We can't pass up the opportunity for his education at the Academy. He'll miss out on so much if we take him back with us. Later, when he's older, he may choose to return to Earth.'

'What if he decides to never come back?'

'Stop worrying over things that might not happen. There's nothing to stop us visiting him. With this accelerated growth you people have, he'll be an adult in no time and that would be hard to explain to the authorities back home.'

'Yes. I suppose you're right.' I sighed. 'I guess it's time...'

He jumped up and lifted me to my feet. 'You're sure?'

'I have to face them sooner or later. Let's get it over with.'

We lifted into the air and flew back towards home.

******

The months on Manyarner flew by. No one mentioned the belief about my calling and after a while I almost forgot about it myself. That was, until Faltron took us on a trip to the Third Continent to attend an arts festival. As I walked around, people gave me strange looks. Some of them even started to bow when I approached. Sensing my obvious irritation they turned away, embarrassed.

'You're a celebrity, get used to it,' teased Iain.

At first, he hadn't wanted to attend the arts festival. It took a while to persuade him to accompany me. *I don't wanna waste time looking at a bunch of bloody paintings. You go, take Andranovich. I'll sunbathe.'* I read him easily. His concept of Manyarnern art couldn't have been further from the truth.

'There was a time you couldn't bear to be separated from me.' I deliberately looked hurt. *'You can at*

149

least fake some interest in my culture. Faltron's gone to so much trouble to make you feel welcome.'

'Oh all right then.'

He stood up and wrapped a towel around his waist. Together we headed into the house.

Looking at me, he grinned. 'I've learnt one thing on this trip.'

'What?'

'It doesn't matter where in the galaxy you come from. All wives nag their husbands.'

******

'What's this one called?' Iain wandered over to stare at the living patterns of colour and light. The configuration shifted; twisting and turning about in the air - one second vibrant, sparkling and exquisite the next dark, ungainly and depressing.

'Paradox.' I watched as his expression changed. 'How does it make you feel?'

He wrinkled his face and ran a hand through his hair. 'I'm not sure. I can't put it into words. I feel uneasy, confused... a little scared. Like you do on a dark, spooky night when you think someone's following you.'

'Good, very good. That's a strong emotional response.' I glanced sideways at him. 'Glad you came now?' He nodded.

'Mum, Dad, over here.'

We span around to see Andranovich dancing up and down with excitement. He stood under a patch of light that changed from orange to brown as we watched.

'What's up?' asked Iain as we neared the exhibit.

'Come in and see. It's called Sensation. It's fantastic.'

Iain stepped into the pool of light. His eyes widened and mouth opened in astonishment.

'Bloody hell, I've never... chocolate. The most sweet, creamy... delicious... No wait... now strawberry.' The light changed to red.

I smiled. 'It's not even designed for human

150

physiology and you're both addicted already.'

'Premier.'

The telepathic voice swung me around. Anger at the interruption from a happy family moment rippled through me.

'My sincere apologies.' The young man started to back away. *'Our arts committee thought that you might join the panel as a judge. I can see that you're busy with other things. I'm sorry to have disturbed you.'*

'Go on, Angie,' pathed Iain on a private channel. *'He didn't mean any harm by it. Judging one competition doesn't mean you're agreeing to anything. People see you as someone special, that's all.'* He smiled down at Andranovich. *'And so do we. '*

I felt ashamed at my reaction. I suppressed my irritation and sent the young man my warm apologies. *'It's okay. It really is. Give me a while longer to enjoy the exhibition and I'll be happy to.'*

******

Iain rolled over on the sun lounger. My eyes were closed, yet I could sense the intensity of his stare and the unrest in his mind.

'What's up?' I asked.

'Is this all there is to do around here? I'm not complaining, but we're on holiday and it's different. Don't Manyarnern's ever get fed up with lounging around drinking Tralmark and sharing themselves? I don't know what that stuff's doing to my system, but my head hasn't felt clear in weeks.'

I ignored him.

A few minutes later, he sat up. 'You know what I fancy doing? Watching a good movie.'

Now I let me head loll sideways. Opening one eye I gave him an amused look. 'When was your taste in films ever good?'

'Seriously, Angie. You people share so much mind to mind contact that nothing's new anymore. There's no entertainment industry at all.'

151

If I don't respond, I'll never get any peace, I thought.

I sat up on my elbows. 'Do you think Manyarner needs one?'

'Yeah, actually I do. Someone could open a theatre, put on a play or two; show a film imported from the O.P.U. It might take your mind off things for a while?'

'What things? Manyarnern's have nothing to worry about, nothing to think about other than our specialisations.'

He dropped back down onto the sun bed and let out a sigh. 'That's my point exactly.'

******

One afternoon I lost myself in private reflection. Walking through the garden and along the shoreline of the lake, I let my feet choose their destination while my mind mulled things over.

People residing on Manyarner tended to be the most devout followers of the faith. Given the circumstances, the behaviour shown towards me at the arts festival was restrained. I could forgive them for that.

What was wrong with me? I sounded like I believed it too.

My eyes blurred, the countryside around me grew fainter. I found myself standing beside a temple on the shores of Loch Ossian. The bitter highland wind stung my face. Rain sodden hair stuck to my neck and shoulders. Shivering, I looked up at the curved stones; their oppressive mass like a heavy weight in my mind.

'What do you want from me?'

Then the vision was gone.

Call it fate. Call it destiny. It didn't matter. Something was pulling me back to Earth.

Taking a deep breath, I walked on.

Emerging from the cover of a thicket of trees half an hour later, I noticed Mother leaving the temple. She hesitated on the steps, and looked around. There was something furtive about her behaviour.

I wonder what she's up to, I thought.

'May your senses be enlightened and your dreams be fulfilled,' I pathed.

She jumped.

Spotting me, she walked across. 'May we talk?'

'Okay, walk with me. I'll listen, but I can't guarantee to agree with anything you say.'

'As you wish.'

She was definitely up to something.

'Trilly tells me you're leaving at the next full moon.' I nodded. 'Is there nothing we can do to persuade you to stay?'

'We've been through this before, Mother. Earth is my home now. I won't deny I feel obligated to Manyarner, but I also feel compelled to follow my own path.'

'Yes. I accept that.' She stopped walking and turned to face me. 'My child, you have a difficult course ahead. Be assured the Circle will support you in all that you do.'

Her shield was low. I couldn't detect an ulterior motive. Perhaps she was coming round to my way of thinking? No, that was never going to happen. More likely she'd given up on me.

'Angeriana, Daughter. We may not see each other for quite some time. Can we call a truce? Make the most of the next few days? For Andranovich's sake, if nothing else?'

She was right. It couldn't be doing him good seeing us bicker all the time.

'I guess I can do that.' I smiled. 'I haven't thanked you for agreeing to oversee his education.'

'We would do nothing less for any of our grandchildren.'

'Huh?'

'Don't you feel them?' She placed her hand on my abdomen and went inside to feel the growing embryos. 'Twin boys. There haven't been twins in the family in a long time.'

'Hey, how did that happen?'

'I think that question is best answered by your

Joining partner.'

I laughed. She laughed.

We were actually sharing a joke. Well, there had to be a first time for everything.

******

Chapter 8

It was high summer when the Eilad sank slowly to the bottom of the loch. We'd decided to slow sleep the tedious return journey. It made the travel time pass in the blink of an eye, and saved us from weeks of emotional turmoil dwelling on Andranovich's absence. Lifting the lid of the sleep chamber, I looked around me.

'Welcome home.'

'Jennifer. How on Earth did you get in here?'

Iain answered for her, from the other side of the cabin. 'I programmed the computer to wake me as we entered the solar system, then sent a message for them to meet us.'

He was unloading the things we'd brought back with us from their storage compartment. Sebastian was there too, busily placing each item onto the teleport pad.

'You seem to have things under control. If someone can give me a hand, I'll take a look around the house.'

Jennifer helped me extricate myself from the harness, which had tangled itself around my left arm during the flight. Once free, I climbed from the chamber.

She looked down at my swollen belly. 'We got the message to prepare for some new arrivals. How long?'

'A week, maybe two. They're getting impatient to join us.'

She took my hand, placing it against her own abdomen. 'We'll have a full nursery in just over six months.'

I went inside to feel the foetus sleeping peacefully in her womb. 'That's great. You'll have to make an honest woman of her now, Seb.'

'Already have.' He glowed with pride. 'You're looking at the new Mrs. Phillips.'

Jen held out her left hand, revealing the glistening wedding band. 'My parents flew over from Canada for the week. It was a lovely spring day.' We embraced one another, sharing images of their wedding day. 'The only sad thing was that you two weren't here. I got quite lonely without your thoughts buzzing around my head. Seb's been brilliant and we often link to converse sub-vocally, but it takes a lot of effort when there's only me.'

I walked across to the food dispenser, requesting a large beaker of Tralmark. Although this synthesised food substitute would taste the same, I felt strangely disappointed that it would lack the psionic enhancing qualities of the real thing.

I wonder whether anyone has researched just how addictive Tralmark is? I thought, returning to join the others on the far side of the cabin.

I held out the beaker towards Jennifer. *'May your senses be enlightened and your dreams be fulfilled.'*

She accepted the drink and smiled. One by one they solemnly joined in the Manyarnern greeting ceremony.

Once finished, I looped my arm around Jen's. 'Now then, let's go see our new home.'

Iain walked back towards the teleport pad. 'Sorry, you'll have to wait until we finish unloading.'

Looking up at the view-screen, I noticed for the first time that we were under water.

'Where are we?'

'The bottom of the loch. Seb and me decided it's the best place to hide the Eilad from prying eyes.'

'Surely the Eilad is going back?' I stared at him in disbelief.

'Not this time. Your Father gave it to us.'

I tensed as my anger grew. What gave them the right to organise this without my knowledge.

'If they want you back, they have to provide the transport.' Iain flashed me a crooked smile, the one that meant he was up to no good. 'Besides, it'll be great to have our own flying saucer. Think of the day trips we can take?'

'You conned them out of it!'

'Well... not exactly.'

Sebastian coughed. 'What's all this about you

becoming Premier?' He had his usual mischievous expression. I'd missed that face during our year-long separation.

'Damn you Iain, did you have to tell them everything.'

'Actually, I didn't tell them. Jen picked it up from my subconscious.'

'I've not become anything. They wanted me to take over running the planet. I turned them down. For some unknown reason I've decided to spend my life here in the Scottish Highlands with you lot.'

Sebastian's face cracked into a broad grin. 'If my liege will permit her humble servant to continue with his duties, she can enter her castle and inspect the throne room.'

He gave a huge bow. Jen followed his lead and curtsied.

I laughed at the absurdity of the situation. It was good to be home.

******

An hour later, we finished a tour of the house. The builders had made a good job with their renovations; the decoration was clean and simple. In many ways the lodge was unrecognisable compared to the wreck we'd left behind. There were eight bedrooms in all, each with its own en-suite and sofa. These additions seemed a little unnecessary, but I didn't bother to comment.

The bedroom at the back of the house looked more lived in than the others. Clothes draped across a large floppy armchair and a neat row of shoes under the window indicated that it was occupied by Jen and Seb.

Jen walked into the room and straightened the duvet. 'I hope you don't mind. We've been using this one for the past year.'

Iain smiled. 'Cause not. As long as you haven't left us with the box room.'

'Certainly not.' She dashed up the hallway and threw open another door. 'We had your things put in here.'

We raced after her and peered into the room. It had cream walls and cascading blood-red curtains at the window. The material tumbled from the ceiling, forming a complex swirl like rose petals on the floor. Beneath this was a deep crimson sofa that seemed to have one arm missing.

'It's called a Chezlong,' pathed Iain. *'That's French.'*

A neat pile of red and cream linen sat beside three suitcases in the middle of the king-sized bed. On the floor were a stack of cardboard boxes, a flat-screen TV and a pile of paintings I recognised from the walls of the Godalming house.

'We'll take it,' said Iain happily.

At the end of the first floor corridor was a brightly-coloured nursery. The room had three identical cots, each standing beside a different wall, accompanied by a matching chest of draws. The ceiling had been painted with a star field. Model space ships and planets dangled on wires above our heads. They swayed in the disturbed air when we entered the room.

'It seemed rather fitting,' commented Sebastian, when he saw my expression.

'It's perfect. Thank you both for taking such care over the place.'

'I think there's something we ought to tell you,' began Jennifer.

We walked down the stairs and into the large, comfortable lounge. 'We've decided to live here too, that is, if you don't mind.' She sat down beside me on the leather sofa.

I immediately realised the importance of the decision - and the reason for three cots. The vision that Iain and I shared had a sense of community. The threads of that future path were inexorably drawing together, yet the overall pattern was still unclear.

Wondering where this would lead us, I smiled across at Iain. *'Jennifer, you are as much a part of our family as those unborn children. It will be an honour to share our house and the rest of our lives with you.'*

'No need to be so formal,' interrupted Sebastian, 'a

simple yes will do.'

'Yes,' we said, emphatically.

******

Iain plumped the cushion behind him. Spotting the label which read *Harrods*, he raised an eyebrow. 'So, how much did this lot set us back?'

'Well, if you deduct my Porsche, the yacht, Jen's designer wardrobe and Cartier jewellery...'

'I don't give a shit, Seb. If you've bought those things then you deserve them. I just wanna know how long I can hold off from getting a job.'

'If I have my way, forever.'

'What.'

Sebastian crossed his legs. 'You know how my Dad works for a city bank.' We both nodded. 'He advised me to invest your money with his firm. It's making a modest income, enough to support us and...' He glanced towards Jennifer. 'D'you want to tell them?'

'I've got us a Nanny come housekeeper.'

'We don't want strangers sniffing around, especially after the twins are born,' I protested.

'Mrs. Henderson isn't a stranger. She was my nanny when I was a kid.'

Iain chuckled. 'I didn't know you moved in such exclusive circles.'

'When Dad came over to England, he and mum had to attend lots of official engagements. They employed this Scottish nanny to look after me. It wasn't 'til we came up here that I looked her up. I remember the state of that flat of yours. You two were never tidy.'

I shrugged. She was right.

'I don't want to get lumbered with doing everything around the house as well as looking after the baby. Mrs. Henderson is a very nice lady. She'll stay in the old gamekeeper's cottage on the other side of the hill. Seb's installed security cameras throughout the estate, so we'll know when she's coming our way. Why don't we give it a try and see how things work out? She'll be arriving from

159

Edinburgh a week on Monday.'

'It all sounds cosy, but we can't have that much in the bank. We only started with a few hundred grand.'

Jen broke into a broad grin. 'That's not strictly true. I never realised how useful telekinesis could be until Seb took me on honeymoon to Las Vegas.'

'Holy shit, you didn't?'

They started giggling like naughty school children. 'You should have been there, Angie. It was hilarious. My darling wife...' Seb kissed Jennifer on the cheek. '...Cleaned them out.'

'And there's some more,' added Jen.

'More! You've not had her mugging old ladies as well, have you?'

'I've got a part-time job at the local school in Roy Bridge. It's a bit of a trek across the hills. In the winter I'm hoping you'll let me use the teleport.'

'By winter, you'll have had the baby.'

'I know, Seb. That's why I've engaged Mrs. Henderson. I told you before we moved here. I'm not going to waste my teacher training.'

'God woman, I never took you for a feminist.'

'And I never took you for a Neanderthal.'

Sebastian scoffed and changed the subject. 'During the renovations, the builders discovered some interesting things about this house. There's a secret room hidden below the study. I've had power run down there. Iain can use it as a workshop.'

'Why do I need a workshop?'

'For your inventions... or rather the gadgets your about to invent. You see, we've not only invested our... your money, we've also set up a company. You're looking at the Managing Director of McClellan Industries.'

'Seb, what's come over you? You must be an imposter. You're certainly not the same man we left a year ago,' I teased.

He looked thoughtful. 'No, I'm not.'

'Before Seb gets all philosophical on us,' said Iain. 'I'm dying for a cup of proper coffee. It's been so many months my body has almost forgotten what a caffeine hit feels like.'

'I've got that covered.' Jen jumped up and motioned for me to follow. 'Let me show you the kitchen. All mod cons, no expense spared.'

We hurried from the room.

Returning a few minutes later, we trailed a tray containing coffee pot, chocolate cake and four mugs behind us. Settling down on the table, the pot began to pour out the steaming brown liquid by itself.

Sebastian interrupted his intense conversation with Iain. 'That'll have to stop when Mrs. Henderson arrives.'

'Only when she's around. Of course, I'll have to fit the twins with inhibitor bands when they're born, and most likely change their appearance too.'

'I never thought of that.' Jennifer seemed very worried. 'Andranovich looked so human that I forgot...'

'You should see him now,' muttered Iain under his breath.

'Oh dear she'll have a heart attack if she sees them with red eyes. I'll phone and tell her not to come.'

'You'll do no such thing, I manage to maintain a human appearance and with a little effort I can change the boys' shapes too. At least until they're old enough to do it themselves.'

******

Early Monday morning, Iain and Sebastian left for Edinburgh. We waved them goodbye as they dematerialised.

I'd become irritated by their incessant talk about future plans for the company. In contrast, they seemed enthused by every little detail. Working as a catalogue or medical tech had been a job, but neither post held my full attention. Humans get so much out of their work, both physically and emotionally. I doubt I'll ever fully understand why.

Still, it was good to see that time apart hadn't dulled their friendship.

It began shortly after lunch, a sharp stab of pain in

my lower abdomen. Jennifer was in the kitchen at the time. Sensing what was happening, she shot up stairs to find me lying on the bed in our room.

'Should I call a doctor?'

'No, a doctor would guess in an instant that I'm not human. Besides, it'll take hours for anyone to get here. You'll have to deliver them yourself.'

She went quite pale. 'But I can't... I don't know how.'

'I'll give you the knowledge you need. Come over here.'

Sitting on the floor beside the bed, I transferred the information directly into her long-term memory.

'So it's that quick. Okay, I know what to do. You just relax.'

Twenty minutes later Gabkhan was born, quickly followed by Kohlarn.

Iain and I had chosen these names whilst still on Manyarner. I was thankful that I wasn't having girls. Deciding on the long-form would've been much more difficult. Iain had found the name Gabkhan, which means mirror, in one of our old family records.

'If they're identical then they'll be a mirror of each other,' he joked.

I'm not sure whether he meant the name as a serious suggestion, but once it was put forward it just felt right.

Kohlarn means follower and also had an irony to it.

I recall the look of disgust Mother gave me when she found out. She saw my actions as yet another rejection of Manyarnern culture. Her telepathy was full of disapproval.

'I understand it's difficult for you to wait until a Lens can name them. I cannot believe that you won't even try to read their specialisations yourself.'

'I don't have the training.'

She glowered angrily. *'You're the Premier, you don't need it.'*

Wrapping the infants in towels, I lay them side by side on the bed and then went to the bathroom to clean myself up. Sensing the tingle of a teleport in progress, I wasn't surprised to find Iain and Seb in the bedroom when I returned.

'Thanks Jen. I wish I could've been here to help.' Iain turned towards me. 'Why didn't you call us?'

'It all happened so fast.' I could feel the disappointment in his mind. 'You didn't miss much. You'd probably have fainted anyway.'

'Oh no I wouldn't.'

Taking his hand, I led Iain over to the bed. The babies rose into the air. He reached out and cradled them to his chest, tears running unchecked down his face.

'Hello you two, Daddy's home.'

Sebastian pushed past Jen and looked at the twins. He also found it impossible to hold back his tears. 'They have the most amazing eyes, and their skin... their skin is glowing.'

'The glow is psionic energy. They'll be surrounded with it for the next few days while they grow. The immediate problem is how we explain this to Mrs. Henderson when she arrives.'

******

The monitor in the hall flicked on and a gentle buzzer sounded.

Iain lay Kohlarn down for a nap. *'Right on time.'*

It was 11.30 am ten days after the twins were born. Jen had managed to persuade our new employee to take a few extra days to settle into her cottage, but now the moment of truth was upon us all.

'At least the old battle-axe is punctual.'

'I heard that. She's not an old battle-axe, and if you come down to meet her you'll see what I mean,' pathed Jen.

I looked up from the chair where I was feeding Gabkhan. 'I think you hurt her feelings.'

We all met in the hallway a few minutes later.

'Why do I feel nervous?'

I opened the door wide.

163

Mrs. Henderson was a small woman no taller than five feet. I estimated her age at about sixty-two. Her hair was cut into a neat bob and she wore a nanny's uniform.

'See, I was right, she looks like something out of the dark ages.'

Jen shot Iain a disgusted look before stepping forward.

'Mrs Henderson, it's wonderful to have you here at last.' They embraced. 'Let me introduce Mr. and Mrs. McClellan. You've met Sebastian before.'

I shook her hand. She had a firm and authoritative grip. 'Mrs. Henderson. Welcome to our home.'

'They're fine Scottish names you have there, but please stop calling me Mrs. Henderson. My name is Clara and I know that you are Iain and Angie.' She took off her hat and cape, placing them down very deliberately on the hall table. 'Now, why don't I make us all a nice cup of tea in that fancy new kitchen of yours and we can get better acquainted before I meet the two bairns upstairs.'

She marched off in the direction of the kitchen as if she'd lived in the house all her life.

'Well, she seems to have the run of the place already.' Her familiarity shocked me.

'While you were away she came up for a look round. She claims to be psychic and says the house has a good feel. When I was a child her intuition always astounded me.'

'Are you sure that she's not telepathic and picking up everything you send?' warned Sebastian.

I stretched out my psi-awareness, scanning Clara's thoughts. She had the most wonderful sense of purpose and an extraordinary feeling of curiosity. *'No, she's not telepathic. I can feel her mind. It's normal for a human although she's highly intelligent. I wonder how a woman of her intellect came to be a nanny.'*

Clara returned carrying a tray with tea and biscuits.

'Come, come, have ye not yet settled yourselves down? This will not do at all. Nursing mothers need all the rest they can get.'

We let her lead us into the lounge.

******

'Woohoo,' shouted Sebastian as the Eilad shot into the sky. 'This is great.' He glanced down at Iain who sat in the pilot's seat. 'Can I have a go?'

Pressing a few buttons, the small craft levelled out. 'Sure.' Iain stood up and Seb took his place. 'Hold this lever down with your left hand and turn that dial with your right. You can see the flight vector displayed here. Keep the green blob - that's us - between those two red lines,' Iain instructed.

Seb obligingly did as he was told.

'It's like the flight simulator on the play station,' added Iain with a grin.

'Yeah.' Sebastian's mind was as excited as a child's.

I glanced down at Gabkhan and Kohlarn crawling on the floor at my feet. They seemed to be racing one another with their favourite toy trucks. For a moment, my mind returned to my own childhood. By this age I was already being groomed for the Academy. Play was never an option. I sighed, dismissing the thought.

'Hey look down there?' We turned toward Jennifer who stood beside the vid-screen. 'Isn't that Clara?'

'What d'you think she's doing this far from the Lodge?' remarked Iain.

Jen lowered herself into a nearby seat. She was heavily pregnant and since starting her maternity leave had been finding every day a little bit more awkward. 'It's her day off, she's free to do anything she likes.'

'Yeah, but she must be ten miles from home,' said Iain.

Jen rubbed her back. 'Just because she's old, doesn't mean she's not fit and healthy. You didn't think you'd like her. Hasn't she proved to all of us that she's full of surprises?'

Concern stabbed at my mind. 'You don't think she saw us do you?'

Iain reached forward and pushed one of the

buttons on the console. The terminal lit up. He read off the data. 'We're at 1000 feet. We'll be in the clouds soon. If she spots us, we'll look like a small aircraft.'

I moved closer to the vid-screen, increasing its magnification as I approached. Clara could be clearly seen plodding up the stony path. She wore a raincoat, heavy walking boots and a rucksack. 'We might look like a plane now, but five minutes ago you were showing off to Seb skimming the top if the pine trees.' I shot Iain an irritated look.

'Lighten up, will you,' said Iain. 'Even if she did see us, whose going to believe her?'

With a wave of his hand, he ushered Seb out of the pilot's seat. 'Let's get some juice into this baby. Next stop Mars.'

I walked back and sat beside Jennifer. 'You better be right.'

She looked across at me and shrugged.
'Boys and their toys.'

******

A hand shook me awake. 'Angie. Angie!'

Opening my eyes, I gazed up into Jennifer's anxious face.

'The baby's coming,' she hissed. 'My water's broke yesterday and I thought I'd make it through the night, but...'

Iain stirred beside me. 'Baby.' He sat up and looked toward the clock. It was 3 a.m. 'The baby. Here, now?'

Jen nodded. 'Yes Iain. But not immediately, so don't panic.'

Throwing back the quilt, I swung my legs onto the floor and pulled on my dressing gown. 'Does Seb know?'

She nodded again. 'He's gone downstairs to start the car. I told him it's a waste of time. The snow's three feet thick. I'm not risking my child in some fruitless attempt to make it across the hills to hospital.'

'You didn't mention this to him last night?' I pathed on a private frequency.

'You know he's always been dead set against a home birth. Now he has no choice.'

I returned to speech. 'You're right, of course. Iain, trot downstairs and tell Seb that I'll deliver the baby.' I turned back to Jennifer. 'You go and... lie down, or walk about; whatever feels natural. I'll shower and dress.' She started to leave. 'Contractions?' I called as she scuttled up the hall.

'Five minutes apart and increasing rapidly.'

'I better make that a quick shower.'

Two hours later we were all crowded into Jen and Seb's room. The twins initial excitement had diminished as sleep overtook them. They curled up together in the large armchair by the window. In contrast, Sebastian paced anxiously in front of Jennifer who squatted on the floor beside me.

'Everything's all right, Seb,' she growled. 'You're getting very annoying. Ahhhhh.'

I started counting in my head. 'That one was much longer.'

Jen nodded, screwing up her face. 'Much stronger. Much more painful.'

Seb dived to the floor and rubbed her back. 'Push down, sweetheart. That's what they told you at the anti-natal class.'

She looked into my eyes. *'Can you do anything about... Ahhhhh.'*

I'd not given much thought to the difference between human and Manyarnern pregnancy. Women from my home world don't have the same muscle groups as humans. We use telekinesis to augment delivery rather than waiting for the mother's body to force the baby out. Jen already knew this as she had delivered the twins a few months before. I wrapped my mind around the child, its head was fully engaged and I saw no point in further delay. When the next contraction began, I gave a gentle telekinetic pull.

With a startled cry, Edward Phillips joined our family.

Grabbing a towel from beside me, I roughly

cleaned him up, severed the umbilical cord, then handed him to Jen.

'May your senses be enlightened and your dreams be fulfilled.'

******

Life settled into a fairly ordered routine after that. Clara arrived at seven on the dot each morning and prepared breakfast while Iain and I fed, bathed and dressed the twins. Meanwhile Jen and Seb settled Edward down in the nursery before she headed in her new jeep along the jagged track to school.

After our meal, Sebastian and Iain left by Range Rover for their office in Edinburgh. In fact, they drove just out of sight down the drive and then used the teleport to take them the rest of the way. Here they established the head office of McClellan Industries. They also bought an old factory to manufacture the first of Iain's inventions.

I spent my days with the twins who grew rapidly into toddlers. It was odd comparing their development to Eddie's. At ten months old, he was still a babe in arms and took up a great deal of Clara's time.

I found myself wondering how human women cope with the burden for so long.

We told Clara the twins had Hutchinson-Gilford Progeria Syndrome, a rare hereditary disease that accelerates growth and ageing. She accepted this with great compassion and never questioned me further about it. Thankfully, she also failed to ask about their apparent quietness and how I knew exactly when they needed my attention.

'It may not last for long, but I will give these two bairns the best life they can have,' she muttered under her breath when I told her of their condition.

One day, we were playing together under the large pine trees that grow at the bottom of the lawn, when I forgot momentarily where I was. It was early autumn and the twins now resembled three-year-olds.

Gabkhan threw his ball onto the air and it lodged in

168

the branches of the largest tree. He started to cry at the loss of this toy and Kohlarn, sensing his brother's feelings, joined in the wailing.

'Don't be upset. I'll get it back for you.' Although the inhibitor bands prevented them from using telekinesis, their telepathy had grown stronger in recent months.

'Yes, Mummy, get the ball, get the ball.'

I looked up into the branches, feeling for the toy. Loosening the surrounding foliage, I freed it from its perch and it began to float down towards us. Just as it reached my eye level, I became aware of someone behind me.

I swung round. Clara stood there, her eyes transfixed on the ball, which now hung in mid air between us. She balanced Edward on her left hip.

'What are you doing out here?'

'I was watching from the lodge and thought that you'd like another pair of hands. I can see that you've managed quite well without me.' She stepped forward and plucked the ball from the air with her free hand, then handed it to Gabkhan. 'Enough football for one day. Time to go back indoors.'

He obligingly threw the ball towards the house and they both ran after it, their feet tossing about the thick carpet of pine needles as they scurried away.

Shifting Eddie's weight to her other hip, Clara turned to look at me. 'I think that it's time we had a wee talk, don't you?'

We walked back to the house in silence.

How was I going to explain this? Maybe I should erase her memory? It might be easier on her than the truth.

I watched as she placed Eddie back into his baby carrier. She's bright, she's tough. She can probably handle it.

Settling ourselves down on the sofa, where we could watch the twins playing with the colouring pencils Seb had brought them the previous day, I took a large breath.

Okay, decision made. Let's see how this goes, I thought.

169

'I suppose you want me to explain how I managed to free the ball?' She nodded, but remained silent. 'And how I got it to float back down from the tree?'

'And everything else. I've been working here long enough to realise that this isn't an ordinary household. Why your husbands' keep up the pretence that they drive to work each day baffles me when there's so much else around here that's highly suspicious.'

It was my turn to nod, she continued. 'Like what you all do in that hidden room under the study? And why, when you sit at dinner, there's rarely any conversation; of the variety I can hear.' She smiled and I felt the tension seep from my body. 'Shall I continue, or would you like to explain one thing at a time?'

I laughed to myself. How little we'd kept secret from her.

'Please, go on. I never realised you'd figured out so much.'

'Don't get me wrong, dear. I haven't worked out how you do everything, but it's clear that you possess powers beyond anyone I've ever met. Take the boys for instance.' She looked toward them sitting on the hearth rug. 'They've grown at a rate which frankly isn't quite human, is it? I checked up on Progeria and they don't seem to be suffering from any of the other symptoms. I presume that this quick maturation is a normal trait for someone of their ancestry.'

'Yes. You're quite right. Their rapid growth rates are completely normal.'

Clara turned back to face me. 'But they're not normal, they're not even human; and neither are you? The others, Jen, Iain and Sebastian are human, although they seem capable of some remarkable feats themselves. Would you like to tell me where you come from? I assume you're not of this world?'

'I'm from a planet called Manyarner.' I said flatly. 'You're right the others are human. My sons show too many signs of their true inheritance. Now you know the truth, what do you intend to do? If you go to the authorities our lives are over.'

My heart beat faster, my mouth went dry.

Why did I feel as if this woman held my future in the palm of her hand?

I could wipe her mind, make her disappear or even kill her, but I knew I wouldn't.

I raced through Clara's consciousness as she considered what to do next. At first she was in shock that her suspicions were true. This was quickly followed by a moment of apprehension while she thought about my possible hostile intent. Finally, she came to a conclusion that startled me as much as it did her.

Clara's face lit up. 'I would never dream of turning the little darlings over to the government. No, no. That wouldn't do at all. I just wish you'd trusted me earlier.'

I broke down and hugged her to me. 'Thank you, Clara. You're wonderful. We don't deserve your kindness.'

Eddie started to cry fretfully. Clara walked over and lifted him into her arms. Returning to sit beside me, she started to bounce him on her knee.

'There, there. Don't be upsetting yourself.' She looked up at me. 'I'm not really a Nanny, you know.' My mouth dropped open. 'Jennifer just assumed I was because she remembered me being around when she was a child. Her father worked for a company that undertook a great many government contracts. They had to take certain security measures. I was Jennifer's body guard. Don't get me wrong, I love being a nanny and housekeeper to you and your family. It's a huge relief to tell you the truth at last.'

I laughed aloud. 'You're much better at keeping secrets than we are.'

Her face became serious once again. 'All I ask is that you treat me with a little more common sense, and I'll be happy to remain in your employ for many years to come.'

I regained my composure and told her the story of how I met Iain. This took the better part of the afternoon. I even removed the twins' inhibitor bands so they could use their powers freely. They whooped with joy and lifted around the garden; the two of us running after them in an attempt to get them back down.

When Seb, Jen and Iain returned, later that evening, we met them in the hall, each of us surrounded by a gentle psionic glow.

Clara beamed with pride as the two little boys lifted to kiss them hello.

It was Iain who spoke first. 'What the f...hell is going on around here?'

'To summarise a very long story, Clara knows everything.'

Iain's eyes widened. *'Everything?'*

'Yes. Absolutely everything. Most of it she guessed for herself. I only had to fill in a few of the details.'

Seb let out a huge sigh. 'Welcome to the club, at least now I'll have an ally who understands what it's like to live amongst telepaths and not be one.'

Jen took Eddie from Clara's arms and we walked together into the lounge.

'And I understand why they call the valley the UFO capitol of Scotland,' remarked Clara, pulling two lollypops from her apron and handing one to each of the twins. 'There have been so many sightings of your...' She looked up. 'What did you call it?'

'Eilad,' mumbled Iain.

'There have been so many sightings of your flying saucer that UFO spotters from all over Britain have flocked to the area. The village may be on the other side of the Glen, but it's still too close for comfort. Bill in the pub at Spean Bridge has rented out all of his rooms, even this far out of season.' She paused and smiled. 'I think that you'd better be more discrete with your pleasure flights from now on.'

We looked questioningly at one another. It was true that our favourite pastime of late was to fly around the solar system, admiring the splendours of the planets and asteroids.

Sebastian sat down beside Clara on the sofa. 'How do you know about our flights?'

'My hobby is hill walking. I go out most evenings and climb as far as an old woman's legs will carry me up the mountain path. For the last few months I've repeatedly seen this metallic-blue object coming over the hill then turning to sink beneath the surface of the loch. None of you have mentioned it, so I dismissed it as an old woman's folly. When Angie revealed herself this afternoon everything suddenly made sense. I put two and two together; the craft that I saw must be yours.'

Going into her, I picked up her thoughts. Sharing these with Iain and Jennifer I posed the question she was longing to hear.

'Would you like us to take you for a ride?'

Clara's face lit up. 'My dear, I thought you'd never ask.'

******

Putting down his knife and fork, Iain leaned back in his chair. 'That's the best Sunday roast I've had in ages. Well done to the cook.'

'Here, here,' said Sebastian from the other side of the dining table.

'Ear ear oast,' added Eddie from his high chair. He picked up his spoon and jabbed it into his father's ear.

Everyone laughed.

Clara stood up and started to clear the plates. 'Well I hope you boys have room for some pudding. It's jam roly-poly with custard.'

'It sounds delicious, I'm sure my brothers will enjoy it greatly.'

We swung around to see Andranovich standing in the doorway.

'What the hell are you doing here?' blurted out a shocked Iain.

Andranovich stiffened. *'As I recall, in your last hyper-spatial communication Mother invited me to visit.'* He pulled a teleport control from the pocket of his gown and started to reprogram it. *'I left the Eilad in a high orbit. If I'm not welcome here then I'll head straight back to Manyarner.'*

I glared at them both for their stupidity.

173

'Andranovich you are our first born and always welcome here. You just caught your father off guard.' I switched to a private channel. 'You're the trained communicator. How did you expect him to react when you arrive unannounced? Now put that thing away.'

'Sorry, Mother,' he replied.

'And you, Iain, should apologise for being so curt.'

Iain nodded towards Andranovich. 'It's good to see you.'

Realising that there was more to my son's quick temper than a misunderstanding with his father, I studied him more intently. I was suddenly aware of a shielded Manyarnern mind close by. The others felt it too and we looked questioningly at Andranovich.

'This is Lara'fortunecta, my... girlfriend,' he pathed, walking further into the room.

The pretty young girl stepped out from behind him and bowed. She wore a green wrist band indicating that she had reached the fourth level at the Academy.

'Premier. The Circle sent us to discuss urgent matters with you. I will speak with you immediately.'

'That can wait,' I snapped; my mental voice more abrupt than I intended. I smiled at the young woman and took a calming breath. 'We haven't seen our son for two years. Let us celebrate his return before we waste time discussing Manyarner.'

She struggled to shield her anxiety. 'As you wish, Premier.'

Jen came running into the room. 'Did I hear...?' She noticed our new arrivals. 'My god, Andranovich. Welcome home.' She rushed forward and hugged him to her.

I stood up and coughed noisily. 'Clara, this is our first born, Andranovich, and his friend Lara.' For the past few minutes, my mind had been too preoccupied to notice her standing transfixed at the far end of the table. Now I read the amazement in her thoughts.

'He's, she's... pink. Are you?'

I flowed back into my natural form, changing the twins at the same time.

'Is it a bit of a shock?'

174

Taking this new disclosure in her stride, she shook her head. 'No, it's beautiful.'

I smiled. 'Okay, then. Let's celebrate.'

Everyone looked up as two bottles of champagne and seven glasses floated into the room.

'It might not be Tralmark, but it's the best we can do.'

With a pop and fizz the party started.

******

Later that evening, I noticed the front door ajar. I walked across the hall and looked outside. In the half-light I could just make out Andranovich standing by the loch. He was staring into the water and although I couldn't read him clearly, I knew he was deeply troubled.

Leaving the babble of happy voices behind me, I wandered down to join him at the water's edge.

'Is everything okay?' I said as I approached.

He jumped. 'Sorry, I didn't hear you.'

'You were miles away. Is something wrong? Are things going alright at the Academy?'

I felt him tighten his shield. 'No... I mean yes. Things are fine. It's just this place reminds me of... of the day we visited after Gran and Grandpa died.' He swung around to face me. *'Premier, Mother. We need to talk. Lara and I were sent here on a very specific mission.'*

His face betrayed the anxiety in his mind.

I stepped closer and put my arm around his shoulder. *'It's okay. I've got over my shock at being called by that title. Go ahead and deliver your message, I'm listening.'*

'The Circle formerly requests your return to Manyarner. There's something wrong with the planet and they believe only you can ascertain what it is and how to put it right.'

'Wrong?' He nodded. *'What sort of wrong?'*

Andranovich sighed heavily. *'Well, the trees do not bear as much fruit as they used to. The rivers overflow their banks from time to time. The flocks of Phenel Geese*

175

*that usually migrate from the second to third continent
have remained immobile this year.'*

I couldn't stop myself from laughing. *'They sent you
all this way to tell me about Geese?'*

*'It's not just that. People are uneasy. The group
consciousness has taken on a darker tone. The Circle
believes that if you were present on the home world it
would help to calm their growing fears and bring solace to
the group mind.'*

It was almost dark now and I could just make out
the seriousness of his expression.

I pushed my laughter aside. 'Things like that
happen on Earth all the time. Has the Circle not
considered that these changes are minor fluctuations in
the ecosystem? All planets evolve, it's part of the natural
cycle of life. Manyarner's been kept artificially stable for
too long.' I bent down and picked up a stone, turning it
over in my hand. 'You know I can't go back. My life is here
with your father and the twins. But I will meditate on the
situation and send my suggestions for the planet and its
people. Perhaps that will help.'

I knew I'd let him down, but couldn't think of
anything else to say.

An oppressive blanket of night rolled towards us
across the water.

'I'm going back inside. Are you coming?'

He didn't answer.

I hurled the stone into the air, waiting for a few
seconds until I heard the gentle plop as it hit the water.
Slowly I turned and walked towards the house.

******

It felt good to have Andranovich with us again. I
didn't ask how long he was staying and knew in my heart
that it wouldn't be forever.

A few weeks would be nice, I thought.

Everyone else was suffering the effects of too
much champagne and the house was quiet that morning.
Walking down the stairs I could hear raised voices coming

from the study.

Tension prickled at the edge of my psi-awareness. The voices were Iain and Andranovich and I knew something was terribly wrong.

'They're not going with you, they're too young. This is my final word on the matter,' shouted Iain.

'What are you so scared of, Father? Do you think that once they realise the wonderful and idyllic life they could have on Manyarner they'll want to live there rather than in this dump?'

I heard a thud. Scanning the study I relaxed when I realised Iain had kicked the side of his desk. The action had done nothing to quell his fury.

'You sound just like her. That's why I can't let you take them. Nyaseema is a manipulative cow and I'm not letting her get stuck into your brothers like she did with you.'

'Grandmother has been nothing but kind to me all these years. She has taught me so much about psionics, about philosophy...'

There it was again, something shadowy hidden deep in my son's psyche.

I could feel Iain trying to calm himself. 'I'm not saying that they can't come to visit when they're older.'

'By then it might be too late.' Andranovich sounded shrill with hidden tension. 'If you'd let her come back instead of keeping her here...'

'I'm not doing anything. Your mother is a free agent with a mind and a will of her own.'

'Free. None of us are free. Whether you like it or not, her place is on Manyarner. If it wasn't for you, she'd see that.'

I sensed someone behind me and looked around to see Lara a few steps away.

'Premier. Can I help?'

I sighed. *'Yes. Please. Go down and find some excuse to stop this ridiculous argument before one of them says something they'll regret. I can't be seen to take sides.'*

'Certainly, Premier.' She glided past me down to

177

the hall, and then ducked inside the study. A few seconds later she emerged hand in hand with Andranovich.

Spotting me, he looked up, holding my gaze for a few seconds. *'I'm sorry, Premier. It is time for us to leave. Please inform Gabkhan and Kohlarn that they are welcome to visit Manyarner any time they wish. All they have to do is contact me via the O.P.U.'*

I wanted to beg him to stay, but knew it was impossible. I'd always hoped that the gulf between him and his father would vanish with time. Now it seemed wider than ever.

I waved. 'Have a safe journey.'

The words sounded pathetic, but my mind was too disturbed to think of anything else.

Before I'd reached the bottom of the stairs they had teleported away.

******

Chapter 9

The plane shuddered as it lifted from the tarmac. I looked out of the window at the ground diminishing below. How different this was from the Eilad. Not only was the vista tiny by comparison to the vid-screen, the lumbering metallic bird strained to gain any altitude.

I wondered whether it was really safe.

No, stop, I thought. Today I'm travelling like a human. I must think, act and speak like a human. Iain said that air travel is one of the safest forms of human transport. He must be right.

I had six hours ahead of me on the plane and considered what I could do to pass the time.

Looking around, I noticed the other passengers were settling into their seats; pulling novels from handbags or opening news papers. Following their lead, I picked up the in-flight magazine and started flicking through the glossy pages.

An article on wine production in France - not interested. An article on some business man I've never heard of - even less interested. Photos of women wearing the most excruciatingly painful shoes. Yuk.

I put the magazine back where it came from.

'What now?' I mumbled. 'Work, maybe I should get on with some work.'

I opened up my bag and pulled out a data tablet. The screen lit up as it loaded my last entry.

I'd started this project the previous year; ten months after Sussia'ficalasa - Susie, was born. She was a little darling, with shocking crimson eyes and jet black hair. In some ways she looked even more Manyarnern than me. Quickly learning to maintain a human appearance, her big brown eyes and dark hair were just as dramatic. She had a feisty personality too. Always pushing the boundaries at home, and manipulating her father to get away with it. Whenever there was disorder, Susie was the ring leader. She caused trouble not only for her brothers and Eddie, but also for Jen's youngest, Charlotte. The two girls were born within a week of each other and soon became inseparable. We adored them.

Even though my three had grown rapidly they never baulked at the differences between themselves and the human children. We lived as one big happy extended family.

Wondering what life would have been like if Andranovich has stayed, I chastised myself for getting maudlin.

I enjoyed motherhood, but my kids hardly needed me by then. They turned to Clara for guidance and support. She was a remarkable woman, and helped when I delivered Charlotte. Forcing me to acknowledge midwifery as one of her many talents. My children's special abilities never fazed her and I'm certain that even the Academy couldn't have taught them the directed control she instilled.

McClellan industries had gone from strength to strength too. Iain wasn't really inventing anything new. He was just exploiting what he'd learned of O.P.U. technology. For the first year, whenever the company released a new device onto the market, I sensed the notion within him that he was somehow cheating. With each new success, these feelings diminished until he hardly thought about it at all.

Of course, it wouldn't take a genius to realise that some of these gadgets defied the current laws of physics. Processors that worked well beyond the specifications of their components, data chips the size of a pin head yet big enough to house an entire library's worth of information.

No one asked the pertinent questions, because no one could guess the technology's origins. The gadgets and gismos sold in their millions. We quietly accumulated rather a lot of personal wealth.

We were comfortable, we were happy and life was carefree, what else mattered?

With Iain and Seb engrossed in the company and Jen job-sharing the role of head teacher at the school, I had little to fill my days. I'd toyed with the idea of practicing as a healer, but Seb pointed out that a psychic who could actually cure her patients would soon make a name for herself.

One ordinary Saturday afternoon, Susie was causing her usual ruckus in the house when we unexpectedly caught a thought from Eddie's mind.

'Can't find me...'

'Jen. Did you hear that?'

Her excited response flowed through me. *'He's got the gift, hasn't he?'*

'Don't get ahead of yourself. We need to test him first.' I reached out and found Eddy hiding in my bedroom wardrobe.

'Edward Phillips,' I pathed on the public channel. *'Can you hear this?'* I sensed his astonishment. *'No, don't answer out loud, think it.'*

'Angie... Mummy... I can do it... I can do it too.' It was painful.

'Yes, you can,' replied Jennifer. *'Now please stop shouting.'*

So that was the beginning of my project. If Eddie had inherited psionics from his mother, it showed that she was not a freak of nature. There might be others somewhere on Earth with the same abilities.

I plunged myself into the research. Investigating every incident of reported paranormal activity from the past fifty years. What I found was very interesting. Earth's history and literature was overflowing with reports of people with unusual mental gifts. From comic book heroes to ancient Aztec gods, no continent on the planet seemed free of the bizarre and wonderful tales. I spent six months at the terminal in our study accessing everything I could find on the internet. It was Seb who suggested I take the next step.

I started close to home with *Bessie Dunlop, The Witch of Dalry*. She was a wise woman with power to heal who was burned at the stake in 1576. Then there are the *Finfolk of Eynhallow* - nomadic shape-shifting sorcerers of the Orkney Islands and *Thomas of Rhyme*. No doubt a real person, he prophesised the future. The power given to him by the queen of Elfinworld.

These were just the local stories, in Britain there were hundreds more. The strangest thing was that such tales died away in recent years, usually replaced with ghost stories or tales of alien abduction. Those ones made me laugh aloud when I read them.

After a year, I took my search into the wider mythologies of other countries.

So here I was on my very first flight in an aeroplane.

'Cool tech,' said a voice.

'What?'

I looked up. Across the aisle a smart-suited business man was leaning towards me. He had nice eyes and muscular build. Hmmm, quite attractive, I thought.

'Nice technology.' He pointed at the key pad in my hand. 'I've never seen one like that, is it the latest model?'

I pursed my lips. 'You could say that, yes.'

He sprang from his seat and came over to sit in the empty chair beside me.

'Hi I'm David Davidson.' He held out his hand and grimaced. 'I know what you're thinking. My parents weren't very imaginative.'

I was confused. Should I read him? I was trying to be human. I could manage one conversation with a stranger.

'Weren't they?' I replied.

He was still holding his hand out to me. 'You are...?'

'Oh, sorry... I'm Angie McClellan.' I shook his hand.

'So, Angie, what's a nice gal like you doing on a plane bound for Cairo, business or pleasure?'

Don't panic. You can handle this, I thought.

'A bit of both, actually. I'm doing some research.'

'Archaeologist?'

'Anthropologist. But this is a private project.'

'Well, don't work too hard. There's lots to do and see in Cairo. Where are you staying?'

'The Grand Hyatt, why?'

'Good choice. It's easy to find yourself in one of the lesser hotels. My company has an office out here, so I'm a frequent flyer. Perhaps we can get together for a drink? I know my way round the city, I can be your unofficial tour guide.'

I didn't need psi-awareness to guess what he was after. He intended to show me more than the city. He glanced down at my left hand.

I laughed. He wouldn't find any wedding ring there, but that didn't mean I was easy prey.

'What's so funny?'

'Nothing, I was just thinking...' I rushed into his mind. Just as I thought, wife and four kids back home. How pathetic. The sexual customs of Manyarner may be more open than Earth, but they were far less sleazy.

'Thinking what?'

'That your wife, Claire, is it? And the kids Ben, Anthony, Katie and Mimi. They wouldn't appreciate you picking up strange women on a plane.'

The colour drained from his face. He opened his mouth to comment, then shut it again.

That's better. Now trot back over to your own seat and go to sleep.'

In response to my strong psionic suggestion, he practically climbed from the seat beside me, back to his own.

Okay, that wasn't very human, I thought. But he had it coming. I turned my attention back to the keypad in my hand.

When the plane touched down six hours later, I called over the flight attendant.

'The man in the seat opposite me is still asleep. Maybe someone should wake him up?'

The cabin staff were still trying to rouse him as I left the plane.

******

The leather-jacketed man stalked through the police station shooting indiscriminately at anyone he

183

caught sight of. Short bursts of automatic weapons fire echoed down dark, shabby corridors and distant voices could be heard as the assembled officers fled for their lives.

Meanwhile, the slim, blond woman, her face wearing a mask of terror, crawled beneath the metal desk in the detective's office. As she cowered in this futile shelter, her breathing was fast and shallow. Would she survive this next encounter with the assassin dispatched to kill her?

Did I care?

'Coffee?' I pathed, standing and looking down at Iain sprawled on the sofa below me.

His eyes were transfixed on the large plasma screen, mouth drooling in anticipation of the carnage ahead. *'Huh?'*

'D'you fancy a coffee?' My thoughts were slightly more insistent this time.

'Not right now.' Iain pointed towards the screen. *'It's just getting to the good bit.'*

I shook my head and strolled towards the lounge door, turning the handle telekinetically as I approached. Pausing in the doorway, I looked back over my shoulder. Iain had experienced the wonders of the galaxy, walked on distant planets, even owned his own flying saucer. Yet he still found himself drawn into the narrative of any movie containing the slightest hint of science or fantasy.

'I'll be back,' I pathed.

Laughing softly to myself, I headed out into the hallway.

The comfortable familiarity of home negated the need to scan my surroundings so it was a creaky floor board that gave the twins away. In response to the loud crack, I spun around just as they reached the top of the stairs.

They froze, mid step.

'Where have you two been at this time of night?' They turned slowly and I took in their bedraggled appearance. 'And what've you been doing?'

It was Gabkhan who spoke first; a little too quickly

to deceive. 'We went out for a bit and got wet.'

I shot them my *'I don't believe a word of it'* look. 'Is throwing yourselves fully clothed into the loch at midnight some new-age craze I've not heard about?'

'Don't be silly,' began Kohlarn. 'We went to...' Gabkhan's eyes flared and I felt the tingle of a private telepathic exchange. 'We went out, that's all. No harm done,' he continued.

'I'll be the judge of that. Come down here.' They glanced at one another before descending the sweeping oak staircase to the flagstone hall below.

Wrapping my mind around them as they neared, I sensed the coldness of their sodden clothing, the slight shiver developing as their body temperatures fell and the... the teleport control hidden in the lining of Gabkhan's jacket. Pulling it free, I summoned it into my outstretched hand.

'How did you get hold of this? It was locked in the workshop away from prying eyes and troublesome teenagers.'

Gabkhan pulled himself up, pride displacing the fear of his imminent scolding. 'It was no big deal to bypass the bio-molecular circuitry on the safe. All I needed was to invert the polarity of the actuator node.'

I looked them up and down. 'How many times have we warned you about unsafe teleports? You're nearly seven and perfectly capable of following the rules.'

I felt the frustration in Kohlarn's mind at being chastised for something they didn't in fact do. 'We programmed it to take us to dry land; it was after we arrived we got wet.'

Now everything became crystal clear. 'You went to Disney again! Which one this time Florida or California?' Gabkhan opened his mouth, but I didn't give him time to respond. 'It doesn't matter. You're old enough to understand the dangers in teleporting overseas. What if you had an accident?'

'Please, Mum. Not another bloody lecture!' pleaded Gabkhan. 'We know the risks. Nothin's gonna happen.'

My anger flared. 'Yes, you are going to get a

lecture.' Gabkhan slouched and let out a huge sigh. 'You'll get far worse if the humans find out who and what you are. If you're unconscious you'll revert to your true form and I won't be able to help, not from 5000 miles away. Do you two want to be laid out on a butchers slab and dissected?'

'Give us a break, Mum. There's nothing to do stuck here in the middle of nowhere. You're as bored as we are, that's why you keep flying off on research trips.'

Kohlarn flashed his twin a wry smile. They knew this issue had been a topic for hot debate within the family for the past few months. 'What Gab means is... Like you, we need something to do. We're old enough to take care of ourselves and can handle it out there in the 'big wide world'. You were working on the Gretin station when you were our age and that place has lots more inherent dangers in it than a trip to a US theme park.'

'Indeed, but...' Sudden movement at the top of the stairs caught my eye. We all looked up as Eddie rounded the banister and paused on the top step. Dressed in baggy Spiderman pyjamas, his hair sticking up in all directions it was obvious that something was wrong. With low shielding he broadcast intense fear.

'What's up, sweetheart?' I called.

'I had a bad dream. Mummy and Daddy are asleep. Can I have a drink of water?'

Smiling, I beckoned him down the stairs and towards the kitchen. 'What about some hot milk? Then you can tell us all about the nightmare.' Sensing the twins' intention to escape my wrath, I looked over my shoulder. 'You too, boys. You could both do with warming up.'

Five minutes later we were seated around the kitchen table, each cradling a mug of steaming milk. The creamy scent of sweet nutmeg wafted past my nostrils, reminding me of Julia who had sworn by this recipe as an aid to restful sleep.

Sipping at his drink, Kohlarn nudged his young friend in the ribs. 'So what's up, Ed?'

'I dreamt we were being chased by the Darlinks. Me and Charlie. We ran round and round the house shouting for Daddy, but he didn't come.'

186

Kohlarn smiled and I could feel him spreading reassurance towards the child. This was a talent I'd rarely sensed from him before. 'Have you been watching TV with Dad again?' You're a right tool. You know the Daleks aren't real. And if they were, me and Gab wouldn't let anything hurt you or Charlie.' The twins nodded emphatically.

Screwing up his face, Eddie didn't look convinced. 'Yeah, but there are bad aliens, Daddy said so.' He looked across the table at me. 'Angie's an alien, isn't she?'

The inference in his tone took me by surprise.

'Ouch,' pathed Gabkhan on the family frequency.

After a few seconds, Kohlarn broke the intense silence that had filled the kitchen. 'Yeah, she is, but she's a good alien. She's like the Doctor... in fact she is a doctor. The worse she'll do is make you stay in bed when you're ill or tell you off when you're naughty. You've not been naughty have you?' Eddie shook his head. 'That's okay then.'

Gulping down the last dregs of his milk, Eddie carefully placed the mug on the table and peered at me. All previous fear had dissipated and he now broadcast an intense feeling of admiration. 'Are you really 'The Doctor'?'

'I'm a healer, yes,' I winked at Kohlarn. 'But I'm not a Time Lord. Those sorts of people don't exist. When I was young, about your age, I trained in the specialisation that would allow me to make sick people well again. I still use the skills taught to me at the Academy, but I don't work as a healer. Not anymore.'

'What do you do?' asked Eddie, blissfully unaware of the significance of the question.

'I um... I do research about Earth. I learn things about the history of your world and send the information back to a space station 300 light years away.' I looked up at the kitchen clock. 'Enough for tonight. Its twelve thirty; time you were tucked up in bed. If you want to know more, we can talk about this after school tomorrow.'

Eddie stood up and the twins followed suit.

'Not so fast, boys. You two have never been to school and don't know the meaning of getting up early in the morning. But it's not too late for you to learn. I think we'll stay here until we decide what to do with you.'

The look of terror in Gabkhan's eyes was hilarious and I could barely restrain myself from laughing aloud. 'You're not gonna to send us to the Academy? No, Mum, please. We won't nick the teleport again or go anywhere overseas. We promise.'

'Sure,' added Kohlarn, his voice cracking with the strain. 'We'll stay at home, be quiet as mice, just don't send us there, please.'

At last, I thought, they're considering the consequences of their actions.

'Okay, off to bed with all of you and we'll talk about this in the morning.'

Gabkhan started to reply but was nudged towards the door by his brother. *'Come on Gab, she won't budge tonight. We'll work on her tomorrow.'*

I smiled mischievously as I broke into their private link. *'Not if she finds you some proper work first.'*

With heads hung low, the twins pushed Eddie from the kitchen and all three headed silently towards their respective bedrooms. I followed them to the doorway and watched as they climbed back up the stairs.

'I think you enjoyed that a little too much.' Iain's telepathy made me jump. *'It's going to be an interesting morning.'*

Trotting back into the lounge, I settled beside him on the sofa. For the next hour he watched the film while I sat in silence thinking over the previous conversation.

As hard as I tried to dismiss it, Eddie's comments kept playing on my mind. I couldn't believe that Seb considered me bad or evil, but the fact that he'd discussed this with his children was perplexing. We'd lived happily in the lodge for years and I'd assumed Eddie and Charlie understood who and what I was. Maybe it was time for a frank discussion with all of them about the darker species in the galaxy.

But this wasn't the only thing bothering me. A bigger question had come to the surface. What had I done with my life? Iain and Seb ran the company. Jen had her teaching career. Anthropologist was a label I'd used when I first came to Earth, but these days I hardly bothered to report back to the O.P.U. My specialisation was something I'd left behind a long time ago too. So what had I achieved in the past few years? If I didn't define myself in terms of a job or vocation - and nothing I ever tried had felt right for me - then what, and more importantly *who,* was I really? Maybe Eddie was right and I was an evil alien? I knew he hadn't meant any harm, but somehow he'd made me question everything about myself.

When the film's end credits finally disappeared I turned towards Iain. *'Can I ask you something?'*

He glanced at me sideways. *'I know that look, what's up?'*

'If you had to describe me, what would you say?'

Iain put his arm around my shoulder. *'It's what Eddie said, isn't it?'* I nodded. *'He was right, there are malevolent aliens out there.'*

'I know that, but he implied that I was evil. Seriously, Iain, if you had to describe me what qualities would you say I have? I was once a healer, but we both know that role wasn't right for me. We also know some of the horrendous things I did in my life as a catalogue tech. Am I gentle or aggressive, patient or intolerant... Do I really have the potential for evil? I've been struggling to think of a way to describe myself and to be honest, I can't think of anything.'

I felt Iain's mind racing through all kinds of jumbled thoughts. Would he upset me if he told the truth? What exactly was the truth? He knew that I could be cruel and thoughtless sometimes, but wasn't everyone? Job roles were often used by people to define themselves, but were they really important? It's the qualities inside that count. So if he really tried to think of some adjectives to describe me, what ones fitted me best? This is all so difficult...

Reaching out, I removed a curl of hair that had fallen across his eyes. *'Don't worry about it,'* I pathed, *'It doesn't matter.'*

'If it matters to you, then it matters to me too.' His face suddenly lit up. *'Unique... that's the word that best*

describes you. Like I said, once, you're a stranger in a strange land: a distinctive individual who is one of a kind.'

I felt heartened by his attempts to soothe my uncertainty. *'Being unique, doesn't answer my question. Do I have the potential to be evil?'*

He sat up straight. 'Dwelling on this won't make it any clearer. No one is that black or white; we're all shades of grey. We don't know what we're capable of, not really. All we can do is our best and wait to see what fate has in store for us.' He sensed the tension in my mind. 'Okay, fate was probably a bad choice of words. You're far too sensitive about this Manyarnern personal myth crap and always have been.' I nodded. 'Look, Angie, if you want to understand yourself you can go and ask Trilly. I know you don't want to do that, so as long as you're here on Earth you'll just have to put up with not knowing. Accept it and get over it. You're unique and that's my last word on the subject.' He jumped up. 'Now, come on, it's time for bed.'

Iain had attempted to use psionic suggestions on me before and we both knew they didn't work. On this occasion, there seemed little point in fighting the power in his words. I hesitated momentarily and then shrugged.

'You're right, of course. Things will seem a lot clearer in the morning.'

I stood and let him lead me from the room.

******

It was a bitterly cold winter's day five years later that the pattern of my personal myth revealed itself a little further.

To an outsider we probably looked insane swimming outdoors when there was two feet of snow on the ground and icicles hanging from the eaves of the house. Such an onlooker would be more astonished by the fact that there were no foot prints leading to or from the loch.

Gabkhan, now a young adult, had developed the speciality, like his father, for mathematics and engineering. He quickly took over maintaining and enhancing the equipment we employed around the lodge. His first new project was to design a force field to divide the shoreline of the loch from the rest of the water and heat it to a comfortable swimming temperature. The force field had the second function of keeping wildlife away from the shore. We didn't want to destroy the natural habitat just to give us a pleasurable swim.

The family used this natural hot-tub all year round; even when the Scottish climate was severe.

I can't recall where the suggestion originated, but I was soon railroaded into agreeing that we hold a family blending ceremony.

Susie surfaced and wiped the hair from her eyes. Spotting me a few metres away she glided across the water towards me. 'Go on, Mum, I've never been to a blending before. Gabkhan and Kohlarn did on their holiday last year. Charlotte and Eddie have enough telepathy to join in too. It'll be so much fun. Pleeease?'

I looked over at Iain. 'What d'you think?'

'Don't we need a Lens? Someone to command the blending.'

'Of course not,' said Kohlarn. 'Mum's the Premier she can do anything.'

The others nodded in agreement.

'Where did you hear that? No one's mentioned my calling in years.'

They looked sheepish. I sensed a private telepathic exchange. It was Gabkhan who eventually answered my question.

'Everyone we met on holiday was thinking about it. We didn't understand, so we asked Andranovich.' I ignored the further telepathic chatter. 'He said that you'd rejected the idea of being anything special and that we mustn't let on that we know. Are you angry?'

What could I say? They'd innocently stumbled onto my secret and after all these years the notion of whether I was Premier hardly seemed important.

'Don't be silly.' They relaxed. 'I guess we can try to hold a sort of blending, and I'll do my best to channel, but it won't be quite the same as having a Lens.'

I was a little nervous, but couldn't show this to the family.

I pulled up my shield.

'I can't promise anything, but if you want me to I'll give it a go.'

******

Later that day we were seated in a circle on the floor of the lounge, linking our consciousness.

From within my trance, I was aware of Sebastian and Clara, sitting by the window, watching our silent communications.

'You know what, Clara? I sometimes wish I could be a part of all this. My children get more alien every day.' Sebastian looked out at the snow covered mountains. I felt the pain in his thoughts.

Daddy. You are and always will be a part of all of us. Charlotte's maturity and strength was astounding.

Sebastian swung around to stare at his daughter, his mind unsure whether the telepathic voice was really that of his youngest child.

I smiled to myself. Seb would understand, one day.

The blending lasted for almost three hours. Coming round, I stood up to stretch my legs.

The fire, which had been blazing in the hearth when we started, now smouldered gently. A short pyrokinetic burst brought it roaring back to life; spitting and hissing and bathing the room in a warm glow.

The content of everyone's visions suddenly sprang to mind. In shock I turned to face two of my children.

Gabkhan shuffled across the floor, taking his sister's hand.

'We've had rapport for weeks now. You were all too blind to see it.'

'Bloody hell!' Iain pushed his hair away from his face. 'You're brother and sister, that's...' He swallowed hard. 'That's incest. It's not only illegal, it's immoral.'

'It's not illegal on Manyarner.'

Of the twins, Kohlarn has always been the

introvert. He sat back whenever there were family squabbles, silently watching for which way the argument would go. Now his thoughts had a confident authority that caught us all by surprise.

Jennifer recovered first. 'Where did you get that idea, Kohlarn?'

'I spent a lot of time chatting with Andranovich. He instructed me in many of the finer points of Manyarnern law.'

I felt a pang of guilt. Perhaps I'd neglected their education by raising them amongst humans? There was so much we'd never discussed about the intricacies of a psionic lifestyle.

It was my duty, yet I'd left it to their elder brother.

My vision filled with the image of Andranovich holding court with his younger siblings as he expounded the ancestral knowledge.

It hadn't struck me before, but the disparity between them was never more apparent.

Andranovich began life with mostly human characteristics. Now he was unmistakably Manyarnern. He shone with the violet brilliance of one who manipulates psionic energy at an unconscious level. His eyes had also changed from blue to deep red, a consequence of his Joining with a Lens. Since that Joining, he'd become further entrenched in the religious and political doctrine of the society. A doctrine he fervently adhered to.

In contrast, the other children had mastered the ability to maintain a human appearance. They showed no outward signs of their alien biology and until now had shown very little interest in the customs of Manyarnern society.

My unshielded mind wandering, Iain's elbow nudged me in the side.

Gabkhan was speaking.

'Thank you, Mum, for reminding us of Andranovich's Joining partner. You approved of their union. It was within the family, wasn't it?' He looked around. 'They're cousins aren't they?'

'Second cousins,' corrected Clara from the far side

of the room. 'It's perfectly legal in Scotland to marry a second cousin.'

Iain shot Clara an angry look. 'Andranovich's situation is very different. He isn't on Earth, you two are.'

Gabkhan's eyes were fixed on his father, yet his mind sought me out. *'And what about Nyaseema and Volitn? Juliana and Frintin before them. '* He pathed on a private frequency. *'Joining between siblings is a tradition in our family. But you've never told Father, have you?'*

'I... You can see why. He's just not ready yet.'

'Will he ever be?'

Dismissing me with a thought, Gabkhan switched back to speech. 'Well, second cousins is still family. If it's okay for them to Join, why not us?'

We all began to comment at once.

Iain held up his hand for quiet. 'Stop right there.' The room fell silent. 'Whose turn is it in the kitchen tonight?'

Charlotte and Susie stood up and headed from the room. *'Promise you won't talk about it while we're gone,'* they sent as the door closed behind them.

******

We resumed the heated debate after dinner.

Sebastian insisted we hold off until Edward and Charlotte were in bed. He pointed out that by human standards they were still too young to be involved in such adult conversation.

I smiled at his naivety, he didn't realise they were most likely listening in to everyone else's telepathic transmissions, and a lot more...

We watched Jennifer lead them from the room.

As the door swung closed, I could feel the disquiet in Iain's thoughts.

He leaned across the table to address Susie. 'It should be your bed time too. Remember, in reality you're only seven years old. That's the same age as Charlotte.'

'That's human years.'

His expression softened and he reached across the

table towards her. 'In my mind you're still a child and should be doing childish things, not talking about getting married.'

Now Gabkhan took up the campaign. 'She's the same age as Mother was when you met her. In developmental terms, Susie's the equivalent of 16 years old.'

'Yes, I agree she looks older, but she's only had seven years life experience. It's not enough to know what she wants.'

Susie started to rise. 'Thanks for talking about me as if I'm not here.'

I grabbed her hand, pulling her back down into the chair.

'Fight one battle at a time,' I sent.

Susie took on her most angelic expression, one she'd used on countless occasions to manipulate her father. 'Oh, Daddy, I know you can't help it, but you're still thinking in human terms. I may have lived for only seven years, but I've shared seven people's experiences during that time.'

He frowned. 'Living vicariously through someone else's senses doesn't count.'

Now it was my turn.

I switched to telepathy for greatest effect, pouring all of my emotion into the comment.

'Doesn't it?'

Iain's confused expression said it all.

'Our bodies grow quickly, how do you think our minds mature? Other people's experiences form a major part of Manyarnern education.'

******

The discussion went on well into the night.

Iain was intransigent, but Clara eventually agreed that most of the objections raised against such liaisons were due to possible genetic mishaps producing malformed offspring.

'These issues were screened out by my people five

195

thousand years ago. That's why we have our specialisations.'

Clara looked at me from the other side of the dining table. 'I'm very sorry, dear, but you will have to excuse an old lady for her ignorance. Could you please explain this to me?'

I wasn't convinced by her apparent lack of knowledge, but knew she rarely asked a question unless there was purpose to it.

'After the psionic wars, it was decided that the best way for my people to cope with their powers was for each individual to specialise in the way they applied them. They had specialisations before the war, but these were arbitrarily assigned jobs. Now the idea was taken to a whole new level. Everyone was screened genetically and their personal characteristics mapped. It was so effective that it became possible to identify personality traits and particular qualities during the first few months of life.'

Sebastian looked shocked. 'Are you telling me that a group of scientists sat down and genetically engineered the whole race? Deciding what people should become without them having any say in the matter?'

'Yes. That's exactly right.' I reached into the fruit bowl, grabbed a grape and popped it into my mouth. 'The project was instigated by a scientist, but soon after, reading and interpreting someone's specialisation became part of the role performed by a Lens. And it still is today.'

It was Clara who brought the subject back on track. 'Thank you, Angie, but what has this got to do with being able to marry, I beg your pardon, Join, with a close relative?'

'It's an interesting by product of the genetic engineering. Once the authorities had mapped everyone's DNA sequences, they could plan ahead and predict, almost control, what qualities would be bred into the race in the future. They built a sort of self-correctional mechanism into our DNA. If a potential deviation is detected it never comes to fruition.'

Clara nodded. 'I suppose it does make sense. If you have the technology to prevent genetic disease, whatever the social implications were to the culture, I…'

Iain suddenly butted in. 'There's one thing you're forgetting.'

Angered by his abruptness, we stared at him.

'Sorry, Clara. Did you have something to add?' he said, guiltily.

'No, dear. You go ahead.'

'I'm not Manyarnern. My DNA's never been messed with and it certainly doesn't carry a self-correctional system built into it. So my children, including Gabkhan and Susie, may carry all kinds of genetic mutations. We can't be absolutely sure that this Joining wouldn't lead to problems in the future. Am I right or am I right? Angie, what do you say?'

'Yes you are righ….'

'See, told you so. This whole idea is bloody ridiculous.'

Crossing his arms, he leaned back from the table.

'If you would please let me finish. You're right in saying they may carry genetic mutations. But the technology still exists to add the screening sequences into their cells. This problem can be easily overcome.'

Iain stared at me menacingly. It was an expression I hadn't seen since our early days on the Gretin station. 'You may think your Premier, but that doesn't give you the right to lord it over the rest of us.'

He launched his chair back from the table and stood up.

Jennifer, who'd sat passively on the sidelines for the last half hour now spoke up, her comments stopping Iain in his tacks.

'Even if you can prevent mutations, that's not the issue here. Incest is illegal. We can't ignore the laws of our own society just because they're inconvenient to us?'

'Jen has a point,' added Sebastian. 'Whatever we decide it will have to be within the mandate of British law.'

The argument went back and forth for another hour. Iain prowling around the room while the rest of us sat at the table.

In the end it boiled down to two issues.

Should Gabkhan and Susie live by human codes of practice, as we were residing on Earth? Or Manyarnern law, as this was their lineage?

Could they Join and remain amongst us, which they clearly wanted to do? Or should they live on Manyarner for the rest of their lives?

'Daddy, you already break many human taboos. Sebastian and Jen frequently share your bed when either you or Mum is away from home.' Susie looked around at her brothers and smiled. *'We feel it happening, it's just a consequence of the intimacy we have with each other.'*

His shock at the revelation that our private life was on display to all the children was more than he could bear.

'Shit!'

Shielding heavily, he stomped from the room.

I waited for the door to close. 'Don't worry about that, I'll talk to him about it in the morning. I must say, young lady, if you push your father too far he'll retreat into his human value system and you may never talk him around. Remember, you need him to carry out the Joining.'

She nodded. 'Sorry, Mum. It's just that sometimes, he seems so old fashioned.'

Clara now stood to take her leave of us. 'Child, you are not the first teenager to think that her parents are old fashioned. As for this business of marrying your brother. That particular custom may be acceptable on your world, but in my opinion, as long as you live in Scotland you should abide by its conventions. I have to agree with your father. Whether you dress up the facts with details about your fancy genetic engineering program, the law is still the law. Now if you will excuse me it's time I was in my bed.'

A few minutes later I arrived in my own room. Iain was snoring loudly as I climbed beneath the covers and snuggled up to his warm back.

With all this debate about Manyarnern customs and genetics I'd almost forgotten the joys of our first family blending and the apparent ease with which I'd channelled so many minds though my own.

I knew in my heart of hearts that by commanding a

blending, I'd taken a step towards acceptance of my calling as the Premier.

One day soon I would have to face up to my responsibilities. When that happened my life would never be the same again.

I shuddered.

A human would say it felt as if someone walked over my grave.

******

A few weeks later, I wandered into the conservatory, which had been built at the back of the house to give us additional living space.

My eyes were fixed on a remote display pad that floated before me. It showed the details of my recent research trip to Japan.

Looking up, I saw Susie and Gabkhan in the centre of the floor.

From the dishevelled nature of their clothing, and the silky sheen of sweat covering their faces, it was obvious what they'd been doing just before I entered.

'Carry on, I'm no prude.'

Trying to appear disinterested, I settled down in one of the comfortable wicker chairs.

'Although I'd make sure your father doesn't find out what you're up to.'

They looked at one another, and then stood up.

'Sorry, Mum. We'll be more careful next time.'

I smiled. *'Susie, I do remember what it felt like to be young and in love, you know.'*

Gabkhan cleared his throat. 'Dad is funny.'

'How d'you mean?'

'Well it's… you know... when Seb and Jen and you… I mean...'

He flushed with embarrassment.

I smiled to myself. He wasn't as grown up as he thought he was.

'Are you talking about when we have sex?' They both nodded. 'I see. Do you often pick up our thoughts?'

Nodding again, it was Susie who replied. 'Yes. It makes the whole house feel really close. But it's just that… Well, we think Dad's a hypocrite. Sharing each other as you do is very Manyarnern, isn't it? Andranovich told us a lot about what people do on Manyarner; the customs and acceptable practices. Humans definitely don't do that sort of thing, do they? Well, not as far as we know. But when it comes to us doing it, then the rules change and we have to live by British laws. It's just not fair.'

'What can I say?' I shrugged. 'You're right, some of the things we do, the intimate things, are very similar to how we'd behave on Manyarner. Even though humans don't usually do such things, there are no laws against it. The rapport between you and your brother is very different. It's unquestionably illegal and breaks a fundamental biological taboo which is deeply embedded in all cultures of this world. Normal, human siblings would never dream of falling for each other because they're programmed not to. You two don't have those inhibitions. Personally, I have no problems with the idea of you seeking the Joining. But your father comes from a totally different culture. He can't rid himself of his biology so easily.'

I returned my attention to the display pad. There has to be a way out of this mess, I thought.

******

Iain stood by the window, his body stiff with anger, arms folded across his chest.

'What about your next trip?' he demanded. 'The flight's booked, the hotel's sorted.'

I pulled a small case from under the bed and opened the lid. Clothes emerged from cupboards and floated towards me. Grabbing them from the air, I started stuffing then into the case.

I glanced up. 'This is much more important. The future of our children is at stake.'

'You said you were happy here and would never go back.'

'I never said *never*. This is different. I'm not returning because I'm the Premier. I'm going back for their sakes. Can't you see how unhappy you're making them? They want to please you, to live by British law, but they can't ignore their rapport.'

'Damn it, Angie. I don't know why I'm being portrayed as the villain in all this. Like it or not, you agreed to abide by human rules when you came to live here.'

I stopped what I was doing and gave him a quizzical look.

'Did I?'

Silence hung in the air between us.

I resumed my packing.

After a few seconds, Iain continued to rant. 'The kids have to accept that life on Earth can never be the same as it is on Manyarner.'

'They do accept it. That's why they've agreed to this trip.'

'Once they get there they can... you know... do it openly.' He grimaced. 'It makes my skin crawl. If they stay here they'll get used to the idea that they cannot be together!'

'Just listen to yourself. You accused me of lording it over people, now who's the dictator?'

Iain started pacing up and down the bedroom. I'd never felt such confusion in his thoughts. He was caught between worlds, wanting to please everyone and hating himself for it.

I found myself wondering whether we'd rushed into Joining.

Shocked by the notion, I couldn't derail the train of thought once it had begun. Perhaps the gulf between our two cultures was just too big to overcome. There was so much we'd never discussed - that I didn't explain before we Joined.

I took a deep breath and looked up. 'If I'd had a brother I would've been expected to Join with him. It's one of our family traditions.'

He stopped dead, taking a few seconds to assimilate what I'd said. 'You...expected?'

'I didn't mention it before because I saw no point. I don't have a brother and was lucky enough to work on the Gretin station where I met you. Gabkhan and Susie don't have that luxury.

'Look at this sensibly, Iain. If they don't Join with each other, then who do you expect them to Join with? D'you remember the date Kohlarn had with that girl from the village? He showed her a little telekinesis and she ran away screaming. There's no one on this planet, their own age, who they can reveal their true identity to. It's inevitable that they'd be drawn to each other. I'm ashamed I didn't think of it before. If they spend some time on Manyarner they might just meet someone else. I've never known rapport to be broken so easily, but I owe it to them to try.'

I could feel him mulling things over. This was better than the blind rage in his mind a few moments earlier.

'So why the hurry? And why are you taking Seb and Jen with you? What am I expected to do here all alone?'

'You're not expected to do anything. I thought you'd come with us. The company can run itself for a few months.'

He turned towards the dressing table. Picking up one of the many cans, aerosols and bottles that littered its surface, I watched as he ran a finger along the edge of the label.

'I'm not coming. If I go with you it's like I sanction their behaviour. I can see the logic of the trip. But...' Putting down the can, he turned and leaned across the bed, closing the lid of my case. 'I have a question for you? What if they don't meet anyone else? You know how erotic Manyarner can be. What if the sensuality of the planet takes them further? Do you expect to come back and for me to perform the Joining?'

I walked around to face him, placing a hand on each of his shoulders. 'I've lost one child already. I can't face losing Susie and Gabkhan too. I hoped you could understand this. If they don't find anyone else and still want to Join, I'll ask a Lens to perform the ceremony. What we do after that... where we live... well, I'll cross that bridge when I come to it.'

I didn't mean my words to sound so final, but it was too late.

'Then fuck off! Fuck off back to Manyarner and leave me in peace.'

He marched from the room, slamming the door noisily behind him.

'If you change your mind you know where we are. Transmit a message via the O.P.U. and I'll send the Eilad back for you.'

I don't know whether he heard me. He'd shut his mind away behind an impenetrable wall.

My decision to leave was breaking his heart. I knew it, but I couldn't stop the events that I'd now set in motion.

Once he realised how lonely the house was without us, he'd come round.

He had to.

******

Chapter 10

Sebastian leaned on the desk. 'How can our journey be cancelled? The Premier's Eilad has had its flight plan scheduled for weeks.'

The technician shifted uneasily in his seat before replying.

'I'm sorry but my orders are quite precise. There's too much hyperspace interference since the Jamplaythese star system went nova.'

He touched the teleport control on the desk before him and vanished.

Seb turned to face us.

'So the rumors were right.' He sighed. 'What do we do now? This was only meant to be a short stay.'

'We can give it a few more days and try again. They can't keep us here forever.'

There was more to this than met the eye. I pulled my shield up tight.

'Until then, we might as well make the best of it and extend the holiday,' I suggested.

'Hooray,' shouted Eddy. 'No more school. No more cold rainy mornings. No more wearing shoes.'

He grabbed Charlotte's hands, spinning her around in a circle.

Jen adjusted her sun glasses before looking down at them. 'Okay, a few more days holiday, but any longer than that and I'll start teaching you myself.' They stopped playing and pouted. 'It's either lessons from me or enroll in the Academy.'

The apparent jollity of the situation did nothing to quell my fears. The Circle of Elders had tried to get me here for years, I thought. Surely they wouldn't be stupid enough to try and keep me here indefinitely? Not using hyper-spatial interference as the excuse. What about everyone else scheduled to leave the planet?

Jennifer looked at my worried face. 'How d'you

204

think Iain's been coping, rattling around in that big house all on his own? He hasn't even got Clara to cook him a decent meal.'

Sebastian laughed. 'Pizza Hut's profits will double.'

'Yes but even Iain will get fed up with pepperoni eventually.' I sighed. 'We'll send him a message. He can make our excuses to the relevant authorities and call Clara back from Edinburgh. At least he won't be alone.'

I tried to sound upbeat. I should have heard from him by now. He was a pig headed idiot sometimes. I knew he was mad at me for suggesting I'd choose the kids over him. It was a cruel thing to say, I didn't really mean it.

I had to bring Susie and Gabkhan here. It was necessary, it was logical.

It hadn't worked.

Iain was right. Manyarner had the opposite effect on their relationship. Instead of introducing them to new prospective partners, they'd been thrown together both mentally and physically.

If he'd been there, I would've said I was sorry.

I fought back my anguish. We didn't even say goodbye before I left.

Jen sent me sympathetic thoughts.

'It'll be all right. He loves you, he'll forgive you.'

'Thanks.'

She pulled her bag up onto her shoulder. 'I hope Gabkhan and Susie aren't too disappointed by our return. I got the impression this morning that they were itching to have the house to themselves.'

'They'll be alright. Privacy isn't the easiest thing to find on this planet. It's something they'll have to get used to if they want to live here for a while.'

'What about Kohlarn?' Jen flashed me her most motherly smile. 'We've hardly seen him these past few days. Since he made friends with that group on the second continent, he's seemed much more...'

'Himself?' I interrupted.

She nodded. 'Yes, that's it exactly. He was always so quiet.'

'Kohlarn has found his specialisation. Only here will

he perfect his talents as a creative artist. I think my children have grown up.'

We walked on in silence.

'Let's go down to the lake for a picnic,' I suggested.

Sebastian patted Charlotte affectionately on the head. 'The lake it is then.'

We walked back towards the waiting hover vehicle.

******

I sat in the stern of the little boat, my right arm dangling over the side. The cool water swirled around my hand, causing ripples of incandescence to spread out across the perfectly still carpet of turquoise.

Seb sat in the bow opposite me trailing his own hand into the lake. His eyes transfixed by the patterns of light as they formed around his finger tips. The vibrant colours multiplied tenfold as he watched, shaped themselves into meaningful patterns, then dissolved into nothingness.

Stretched out at his feet was Jennifer. With eyes closed and head in hands, her naked body had a luminescence only the Manyarnern sun could give.

I don't know how long we'd drifted. The passage of time didn't matter anymore. All I knew was peace and a profound feeling of contentment.

Manyarner can do that to a person.

This lake is called Qualmarth which means tranquillity.'

A gentle breeze blew across my face.

The boat rocked from side to side.

I sat up.

Jen shook her head, pulling herself into a sitting position.

'That's the first wind I've felt all day.'

'Have you been eating too many Partchi fruits again?'

I looked about, everything seemed normal.

Except... Clouds were forming in the upper atmosphere.

206

Following the direction of my gaze, Seb saw them too. 'Where did they come from? It was perfectly clear a few minutes ago?'

The boat rocked; more forcefully this time.

Picking up the paddle, Sebastian turned us back towards shore. 'I think it's time to head home.'

We started to bounce around more violently, tossed by the waves as the swell increased.

A deafening clap of thunder rolled around us, followed by brilliant forked lightning.

'What the hell.'

It was almost dark now. Huge black clouds sped across the sky above.

Another clap of thunder and the heavens opened. Torrential rain pelted down. 'Faster, Seb. Paddle faster,' shouted Jennifer.

Our progress towards shore was painfully slow.

'I thought the weather was controlled?' said Seb.

'It is. Something must be wrong.'

Seb drove the paddle deep into the water. 'That's the understatement of the century.'

Within minutes the surge had increased considerably. The small craft reared and bucked as it was lifted up at the bow then smashed down onto the unforgiving waves. Each time we hit, water crashed over us, draining the residual heat from our bodies.

More lightning flashed down from the sky, burning our eyes with its brilliance. The raw energy gnawed at the edge of my psi-awareness making it difficult to concentrate.

This wasn't just wrong, it was very wrong.

For the next few minutes we were preoccupied with keeping ourselves afloat. We'd taken in a lot of water. Jen and I tried to bail out using telekinesis. We'd lift the water between us, edging it over the side. Just when we thought we'd achieved our goal, another wave crashed over us immediately refilling the boat. Meanwhile Seb struggled to steer us towards shore.

A mixture of static charge and gale-force winds whipped my hair into a frenzy, slashing it across my face and eyes. I just managed to pull it clear when Jen screamed.

'Oh my God!'

I swung around. A wall of water ten metres high was racing across the lake towards us.

I stretched out my mind, trying to create a protective energy shield.

Too late.

Overtaken by the force of the tsunami we were thrown from the boat.

******

A heavy weight was pushing down on me.

I must breathe.

There was something within me, inside my chest, straining to get out.

The need to breathe clawed its way up my throat, persistent in its demands.

My lungs were empty, they needed to be filled.

Breathe.

Giving in to the overwhelming desire I opened my mouth and inhaled.

My eyes bulged in their sockets.

Water! I'd breathed water.

Weighted down by the intake of water, my body lost buoyancy, plummeting to the depths of the lake.

******

I watched Angeriana sinking away from me.

Physical form didn't matter, here there was no pain, no bodily needs, just pure thought.

There I go...

No! That's me... I'm drowning. I'm dying...

I was suddenly aware of Jen and Seb dying close by.

Emotion overwhelmed me.

They're my friends, I love them. I can't let them go.

I focussed what was left of my mind, grabbing hold of their unconscious bodies and pulling them towards me.

Up. I must swim up. But which way is up?

Everything went white. Dazzling energy pulsing, surging.

The static charge shot upwards, seeking out the supercharged air above. As the lightning bolt ascended so did I, dragging my friends with me.

We burst upon the surface just as the water flash boiled.

I didn't hang around; streaking away from the turbulent scene I flew towards shore.

******

'Breath damn you woman, breathe.'

'Jen, inhale.'

She gasped life back into her body, then instinctively rolled over and emptied the contents of her lungs onto the ground.

There wasn't time to assess her condition. I turned towards Seb lying beside her on the wet sand. Taking a huge breath, I leaned down, clamped my mouth over his and exhaled. His lungs filled with my warm breath.

'Your turn, Seb, do it for me... please.'

His mouth responded, the kiss taking me by surprise.

He opened his eyes as I pulled away.

'I dreamt I was kissing an angel. I woke to find it was you.'

Always the joker.

Jennifer sat up and shivered. 'What's going on around here?'

I looked about. The lines of Fructa bushes that usually grew beside the lake were gone; torn from the soil by the force of the wave. Beyond the immediate devastation, the trees were listing, their roots exposed as they were wrenched from the ground.

In the sky above the storm still raged. Sheets of water poured down, filling every available indentation in the ground.

I stood up. 'You two need to get on your feet right now and head for home. If this storm is as widespread as I fear, the kids'll be in a real panic.'

'What about you?'

'I'm going to get some answers.'

Without looking back, I ran towards what was left of the forest.

******

The focal stones shone like beacons in the dark; drawing me closer.

I was cold, wet, and exhausted, yet it didn't matter. Anxiety drove me up the steps and into the temple.

I came to a halt and looked around.

Trilly stood motionless on the central platform in some kind of catatonic trance. With hands raised above her head, her face bore a mask of total concentration. Her entire body was encased in a bubble of pulsating psionic energy.

I knew I wouldn't get any answers from her.

At first it looked as though she was pulling energy from the stones. After watching for a few minutes, I realised the opposite was happening. The stones were drawing energy out of her; draining her life force for their own purpose.

She was giving herself to save the planet.

Tentatively, I walked up the last few steps until I stood in front of her on the dais. As I came closer, my body started to tingle, the skin mirroring the patterns of colour that ran through the psionic bubble.

Shielding my eyes from the glare, I stepped into the energy vortex.

******

'What should I do?'

'Open your mind. Feel the mass; it's like a gravity well.'

'I feel it. What now?'

'You are a pattern, Angie. A rhythm. A design. Let the archetype within your soul come to the surface. The stones will do the rest.'

'What have I become?'

'Every Manyarnern is a power source. Except in your case you're more like a power station. Together we fuel the planet. You were warned by the Elders that the population was declining. Today we reached the point of no return. If this were Earth we'd call it a brownout. But in our case we didn't just lose the lights; we lost control of the weather. If we're lucky your help will stabilise the situation.'

The final thread of my life clicked into place. I was a geometric shape with infinite complexity.

Now I understood.

Energy surged out of me with explosive force. I could have sworn the stones leaned closer; like animals eager to drink from the well of life. And like animals they were greedy.

I let go of myself and became the shape I was always meant to be.

At last the stones quenched their thirst.

The storm passed. Clouds dissipated.

As the sky turned back to a gentle lilac I felt the warmth of the sun on my back.

I sighed heavily. 'I'm glad that's over.'

Trilly stepped down from the platform, straightening her plaited hair as she walked. I followed.

'Sorry, Angie, I didn't mean to give you the wrong impression.'

She didn't need to explain. The sadness in her thoughts said it all.

It wasn't over, not for me.

'Do Mother and Father know?'

She nodded. 'They know that you are the most important being born on this world for five thousand years. That you are the Premier, the one who will bring stability back to the planet.

'How do the Lenses know what I am and why I'm here? If this is my specialisation, why was I created? And more importantly, by whom?'

She looked down at her feet. Despite her shield, I could sense the dilemma in her thoughts.

The image of Iain's face flashed across my mind. 'For fuck's sake, Trilly. You just asked me to sacrifice my life to Manyarner. You've got to help me out here. Tell me everything you know.'

******

'The age of conflict doesn't have a very cryptic name. It was a time of great civil unrest. For over three centuries, psionic war raged between the Academic community and the Liberationists.'

She sounded like my old tutor at the Academy, recounting the sacred texts almost verbatim. I wasn't in the mood for a school lesson.

'Yes, I know all this. We learnt the Chronicle of Grimloch in our first year at the Academy.'

'Be quiet, Angie. Do you want me to explain?'

I sighed and motioned for her to continue. It looked like I was going to get a lecture whether I wanted it or not. I felt images forming in my mind as she supplemented her words with telepathic transmissions.

'The age of conflict was a dark chapter in our world's history. Mind was set against mind in the most brutal way possible. Battles raged across the four continents, scorching the ground and stripping the life force from every living thing.'

Dressed in the brown uniform of the Liberationist tracker squad, I smiled to myself as I crept up behind an academic foot soldier. She was young, barely ten years old. Her untrained mind was scanning no more than a few metres in front of her. My face went blank as I moved my psi-awareness through my opponent's neural pathways. The soldier let out a cry of pain, then collapsed onto the ground; her brain reduced to ashes inside her skull. I looked down and laughed. The body of the girl soldier was nothing but a lifeless shell at my feet.

'The two opposing factions believed they had right on their side. The Liberationists fought for freedom of thought. They still wanted to use psionics, but they also wanted to choose their own life path - to select their own specialisation. The Academics, led by the Lenses, wanted to retain the old order of living by the role given you at birth. A way of life perpetuated through our people's religious practices and worth preserving.'

Now I was jostled by an angry mob. A thousand individuals chanted in unison.

'Liberation. Liberation.'

In front of me was a grand administrative building. The elegant stone architecture had rows of high windows between which were a series of statues. The roof was topped with a massive dome, constructed from glass panels held together by fish-like spines of steel.

'What gives them the right to monopolise such wealth when it's our sweat that built it in the first place,' I pathed on the public frequency.

Shouts rang out as the crowd surged forward, their collective minds pushing against the ornate wooden door. With a loud crash the door caved in. I was swept forward on the tide of fury.

Crossing the threshold, I spotted a group of old men running for their lives. *'Get them!'*

To my right the massive door lay on its side, two Elders crushed beneath its weight.

There was mayhem as the mob ran past me into the building, tearing down artwork and burning everything in their path. I felt no remorse, this was war. Satisfied by the outcome of today's rally I marched forward into the building.

The image dissolved away to leave me staring at a featureless desert. At first the landscape appeared empty. As I looked deeper, I noticed remnants of stone columns lying haphazardly amongst the dunes. Here was the grand building from the previous scene, buried beneath the endless sands. I looked down at my body. I was wearing a

213

long gown, my hair tied into a braid that reached almost to the ground. Summoning a familiar meditation, I lifted and flew away.

The vision suddenly stopped, pulling me from my reverie. I opened my eyes, Trilly was staring at me. 'Who won the war?'

'Wha...How should I know?' I paused to think. 'Of course I do know. It was the Academics. We still have Lenses and specialisations today.'

'You're wrong. The Liberationists won. That's why we have Clause Thirty-One of the constitution.'

'Well I'll be damned.'

We walked out through the stones and sat together on the steps of the temple. Now the rain had stopped, the extent of the damage could be seen clearly. Trees lay on their sides all around us, debris piled against them. The forest path was hidden beneath a layer of murky water, fish and other drowned creatures floating indiscriminately on the surface.

My mind filled once again with the image of the dead soldier.

Such a waste, I thought.

Trilly's shield lowered, I felt her sorrow. Dragging our eyes away from the devastation, we took a deep breath and together recited a familiar meditation; focussing ourselves back onto the story.

'You know the official version of history because it's what you were taught at the Academy,' said Trilly. 'What you don't know is that each of the Chronicles' have details that the Lenses never tell the people.'

'So why are you telling me now?'

'You're not just anyone, you're the Premier. I've decided that you deserve to know the truth.'

'Will you get in trouble?'

'The Senior Lens of my temple won't be happy, but I can handle her. After what you just did...' She pointed back towards the centre of the shrine. '...Even she won't deny you the information.'

I smiled and took Trilly's hand, forging a strong link with her mind. *Then this is my first day of school.'*

'The psionic war not only destroyed many lives, but also wrecked the planet's ecosystem,' she began.

Images of rolling hills teeming with life gave way to desolate dust bowls.

'When the fighting was over, a Liberationist soldier from the most feared Tracker Squad seized power of the Ruling Circle.

I stood beside a tall, lean, man. Despite his tattered uniform, the narrow face, arrogant jaw and rigid spine denoted someone formidable. Smoke rose from the smouldering remnants of the tented settlement before us.

I scratched at my unkempt beard. 'What are your orders, Sir?'

'Can you taste it, Worrel?'

'Taste what, Sir?'

'Freedom.' Trynax stepped across a semi-decayed corpse that lay on the path and marched forward.

'Looking about him, Trynax realised that if he was going to restore the planet, he would need to take radical action. He decided to open up the Archive of Knowledge.'

I pushed the vision aside. *'Wait just a minute. Are you telling me the chronicles are historically accurate? I always thought that the Archive of Knowledge was a myth. No one's found solid evidence that it ever existed.'*

'Oh, it existed, but only the Academics knew where it was and how to read it.'

Now I could see a massive stone vault. The walls and ceiling were decorated with colourful pictograms. There was a low rumble like thunder and part of the right hand wall collapsed, revealing a group of people brandishing pickaxes and shovels. Pushing past them, Trynax strode into the room and grinned. He spotted me kneeling on the central dias. Our eyes and minds locked in mortal combat.

'I knew it,' he seethed. 'I knew the academics were keeping secrets from the people.'

'You will never understand,' I said as my life force slipped away.

Trilly continued. *'When he discovered the archive hidden beneath the capitol building of Chenlin Province on*

215

the First Continent, Trynax recognised that he had found something of immense value. Here was technology beyond anything that Manyarner possessed before the war. It had the potential to turn him into a great leader.'

'Or a cold-blooded despot,' I added.

'Trynax had a problem. No one knew how to translate the archive. Then he learned that an old comrade, Grimloch, had been found living amongst the last remaining Academic community. He coerced him, and his sister Fayuun - who had accidentally become his Joining Partner - to help him decipher the texts.'

'Accidentally?'

'That's not relevant right now.' She rushed on with her story. 'Over the next few years, Grimloch and his sister translated knowledge on agriculture, medicine, structural engineering and much more. In addition, they found details of an unlimited power source that although useful, had the potential to destroy the entire planet.'

I sat at a work bench, flicking through a pile of note books crammed full of scribbled glyph sequences. The door opened and I looked up apprehensively.

'Did you hide them?' I said.

Grimloch walked over and sat down beside me. 'For the time being, yes, but I still think we should destroy them.'

'I can't believe you'd even consider it. The archive is the most precious artefact in Manyarnern history.'

'And the most dangerous. You said it yourself, Fay. If Trynax finds out what we know, they'll be no stopping him.'

I closed the book in front of me. 'So we make sure that he never finds out. We've accessed and translated data from eight of the twelve stones. There's enough technology here to keep him busy for years.'

'I certainly hope so. You don't know him like I do. We served together in the combat zone for five years. Under those conditions you really get inside someone's head.'

His comment intrigued me. 'So what's inside Trynax's head?'

'Death, killing and power. It's all he knows. I'm sure he believes all the things he says about rebuilding Manyarner, but he's not doing it for the good of the people. It's all for the good of Trynax. He wants absolute rule and will stop at nothing to ensure he gets it and keeps it.' Grimloch put an arm around my shoulder. 'Once the temples are working again, we'll not only be back in control of the weather, we'll have an unlimited power supply. If he discovers that some of the stones were control circuits that can turn them into a weapon he'll...'

'You worry too much.' I looked deep into his eyes. The inkling of our rapport was still clinging to my psyche. 'They're hidden right?' He nodded. 'So the knowledge of their whereabouts must be hidden too.'

I felt myself enter his mind. Trynax wasn't the only soul scarred by the endless bloodshed of the psionic war. I pushed past Grimloch's sadness and remorse, past the endless images of the thousands he'd killed. Eventually I found the active memory store for the past six hours.

'Once I do this you won't even remember that we discussed it. As far as you'll know there were only ever eight stones.'

'Just get on with it, will you. I've wiped enough minds in my time to know how it works.'

With a deep breath I moved my psi-awareness into the cells of his brain. Scanning the chemical and electrical bonds, I purged the stored data in one quick burst before retreating into the comfort of my own mind.

Grimloch scanned my face. 'Sorry, Fay. I've got a bit of a headache. I think we've stared at these books enough for one day. Would you like to go into the courtyard for a walk?'

I stood and picked up the note books. 'Sure, just give me a minute to put these into the strong box. We don't want the cleaners reading them, do we?'

He smiled and we walked hand in hand from the room.

******

Breaking the link, my head cleared of the visions.

'The power they refer to was in fact the power of the peoples' minds.'

She nodded. 'Yes, indeed. They discovered a way to fuel the planet using Psionic energy.'

'So what made this any more dangerous than what they were already capable of?'

'Imagine a bomb. Even a nuclear bomb used by the Humans has a finite amount of power. They measure it in megatons, I believe. Now imagine a bomb that once it starts to explode goes on exploding indefinitely, drawing on the almost unlimited power of the people.'

'It couldn't go on indefinitely because eventually everyone would be dead.'

She nodded again. 'Very true and that's what they wanted to avoid. They knew Trynax was unstable. He was paranoid that someone in the Circle might depose him.'

'I see... at least I'm beginning to.'

'Unfortunately, Grimloch and Fay were so caught up in their work that they underestimated Trynax's resourcefulness. Neither of them guessed that he'd been studying in secret, gradually learning how to translate the archives for himself. When Trynax learned, not only of the weapons they had denied him, but also of their treachery, he confronted them in the chambers of the Ruling Circle.'

My mind filled with familiar images. I'd experienced the mortal battle waged between Trynax and Grimloch on numerous occasions; as a child, at the Academy and on Captain Fern's ship - the last time I was really close to Andranovich. Even after all these years, the violence with which the two men ripped each other apart appalled me.

'Eventually Grimloch won this epic struggle and took charge of the Circle himself.'

She paused and looked out at the trail of destruction left by the storm. Her thoughts had a ring of sadness to them.

'So what happened next?'

'Patience never was your strong point, Angie.'

'I'm sorry... but can't you be more succinct? None of this explains why I'm the Premier.'

I felt her mind enter mine as the psychic link reasserted itself.

'I'm getting there.... Grimloch didn't approve of what Trynax had done, but having opened up the archives, he could see the advantages of using the stored knowledge. He and Fayuun learned a great deal about, chemistry, physics, biology, and genetics. They knew that it would take decades for the ecosystem to recover naturally, but if they used these new sciences the planet would recover much quicker.'

Now I could see people constructing dwellings to house those displaced by war. Irrigation systems bringing life-giving water back to the barren plains - turning them into lush pasture once more. Finally, I saw medics administering treatment in modern-looking hospitals.

'All this rapid change would need power, so they secretly deployed the ancient way of extracting psionic energy from the people. Between them they rebuilt the planet and in doing so earned the name the 'Architects of modern Manyarner'.'

'If the Archive of Knowledge really existed, where did it come from? And where is it now?'

She dropped the link. My mind felt suddenly empty.

'It was a gift from a race called the Cruxions. They visited Manyarner thousands of years ago, leaving behind knowledge of their technology. At the time, no one knew what to do with it, so it was sealed away for future generations. Over the years, people forgot where the archive was hidden and how to translate it.'

Something prickled at the edge of my psi-awareness. Her words sounded rehearsed. Something was wrong with this story.

'So how come the Academics knew about it?'

'Knowledge is our way of life.'

Her response was frustratingly cryptic. She knew I wanted to know more, but her mind was closed to me. Premier or not, there were still things she wasn't willing to tell me. Never mind, I thought, there was plenty of time for me to coax it out of her.

'Go on with the story,' I urged.

'It soon became apparent that Grimloch and Fayuun were leading Manyarner down a dangerous path. If the population became unhappy, war could flare up again. They weren't the only ones who knew how to use the Cruxion technology. There was now a whole collection of scientists all eager to experiment with the new disciplines. They were worried that someone might see the weapons potential in these new ideas. A way had to be found to prevent that ever happening.

'Fayuun hit upon the idea of introducing a specialised virus into the people. It was designed to genetically map everyone's DNA, at least that's what she told the unsuspecting population. At the same time, this virus re-wrote people's genetic structure fixing them into their specialisations at a biological level. She believed that if people were born knowing exactly how they fitted into the grand order of things they would never become discontent and war, like the one they'd just had, would never occur again.'

'That was very underhanded. Why've the Lenses kept this quiet for so many years?'

Trilly turned to face me. 'Why do you think?'

'Go on, go on.'

'Grimloch and Fay were the last two surviving Academics and technically their side had lost the war. They re-wrote Clause Thirty-One of the constitution; allowing people to disregard their specialisations, even leave the planet, if they so wished. Of course, this was unlikely to ever happen. The population was now pre-programmed into a fixed way of life. Having extracted all that they could, Grimloch destroyed the archive.'

I shifted my weight, allowing irritation to show in my thoughts as well as my body language.

'This is all fascinating, but you still haven't answered my original question. How did I get my specialisation? We've had a Ruling Circle for millennia, why did they think it necessary to have a Premier?'

'By genetically engineering the population, Fayuun had sent Manyarner down an evolutionary dead end. The people would never evolve or adapt in the future. Even though it was unlikely, over time some people might use Clause Thirty-One and that could lead to a drop in the population, or there might be a natural disaster that killed lots of people. If that happened, some of the specialisations might be lost and with them a lot of the planet's power source. So she created the pattern for you and placed it on a sort of delayed timer. Your DNA contains a special pattern for enhanced psionics. That's what makes you such a power house and logically our leader.'

I wasn't so sure about her logic, but she'd explained quite a few things. 'So when the population dropped, I came to the boil.'

She laughed. 'That's one way of putting it.'

'But why wasn't I told about this sooner?'

Trilly looked thoughtful. 'When you take part in a blending ceremony what do you see in your visions?'

'All sorts of things, why?'

'Have you ever seen the future?' I shook my head. 'Ever wondered why?'

There it was again, that feeling that something wasn't quite right. There was no deception in her mind. She really believed what she's telling me.

Trilly smiled warmly. 'It's okay, I didn't really expect an answer. As I've just explained, everyone's life is mapped out at birth, at least to some degree. They know what is expected from them and how they fit into society. So their future is set.

'You're very different. Although you carry the pattern for Premier within you, it's not known when, if at all, your specialisation will be needed. There have been others before you who carried this pattern. Some were told of their potential, others were not. If, during their lifetime, the population remained buoyant enough to sustain the planet, they never came to power. A Premier's future, your future, is not set. Your personal myth is in a state of flux.'

'Flux?' She nodded. 'How do you know all this?'

Trilly lifted her hand towards the nearest column. 'It's written on the stones.'

I sighed. 'Let me get this straight... You're saying that although you know I'm the Premier, you don't know when I'll be needed to fulfil this role?'

'No we didn't. Not until today.'

I stood up and looked around. 'I concede I was definitely needed today. That storm was dreadful. If you can't predict my future then how do you know I'll be needed again? I could sit here for the next fifty years wasting my life away and...'

My mind raced. Could it be that simple?

I'd never seen my future during a blending, but those other visions...

'I know that look, Angie. You can't avoid the inevitable.'

'But it's not inevitable, don't you see? If I was here my energy would just diffuse into the planet and we'd never know. We'll only be sure if I leave and another crisis occurs.'

I bolted down the stairs, heading rapidly towards my family estate.

She stood on the temple steps watching me disappear among the upturned trees; her mind caught between fury and despair.

You can't do this, Angie. Manyarner needs you. The purpose of the Premier has been set ever since Fayuun created the genetic codes. If you leave, the whole planet will be in jeopardy. Do you want our destruction on your conscience?'

******

I ran into the house. The family sat on cushions in the central well of the living space, wrapped in the beach towels we'd brought with us from Earth. They looked up as I entered their faces weary from the day's events.

'Seb, Jen, go pack your things, we're leaving,' I said.

'What?'

Sebastian waved to the others and they fell silent. 'What's going on? We thought you were Premier now. Aren't you staying?'

'It's a long story. I'll have plenty of time to tell you when we're on board ship. If I... we, go quietly it'll cause the least amount of fuss.' I looked at each of them in turn. 'Pack now, please?'

They scattered to do my bidding, leaving Gabkhan and Susie starring at me.

'What about us?' Susie's tears were barely kept in check. 'We're not Joined. You said we can stay, now you tell us we can't... What if we never come back? Dad won't agree to Join us. If we go back to Earth we'll be separated forever.' She sniffed loudly. 'It's not fair.'

I stepped forward to embrace them both. 'No one's future is set in stone.' The irony of the phrase made me smile. 'Right now I need you both with me. No arguing, no delays. Just pack up your things as quickly as possible.' I looked about. 'Where's your brother?'

'Here.' Kohlarn strode into the room, some kind of musical instrument under his arm. 'I take it the holiday's over? I'm not surprised, this place isn't us. It's not our true home.'

I was so proud of him. He'd arrived as a boy and now...

******

Half an hour later, the family met on the lawn at the back of the house; each carrying a small suitcase. We piled these and some other souvenirs on the grass beside us.

I looked around the group. Gabkhan cuddled Susie reassuringly, her eyes red and swollen from crying. Kohlarn carried his new acquisition under his arm. He'd grown up considerably in the past few weeks. Eddie and Charlotte held onto their mother's hands, her proximity holding back their fear. And Seb... his mind was preoccupied with images of the storm. He tried to hide his disquiet by fussing over the luggage.

Jennifer finally put her anxiety into words.

'Are you sure it's safe? What about that star that went nova?'

'That's just an excuse to stop people leaving.'

'You're not going anywhere without an Eilad.'

We swung around to see my parents standing behind us.

'Daughter, you know what you are and why you must remain. Agree to that and we will release your friends and family.'

'Release.' I flew into a rage. *'So it's just as I thought. We're prisoners!'*

'We will do whatever is necessary,' replied Father. *'The future of the planet is at stake. Compared to that, the lives of these humans are insignificant.'*

Gabkhan let go of his sister and lunged forward, Kohlarn grabbing him by the shoulder as he passed. *'What good's that going to do?'*

He stopped, his mind full of regret. *'I just saw red for a moment. I'm fine now.'* He eased backwards into Susie's waiting arms.

'Primitives!'

Pulling myself up straight, I stepped forward. 'Mother, you... If there had been any chance that I might have remained, that last insult just blew it for you.'

She didn't bother to shield. I could feel the full force of her hatred. 'You father's comment still stands. You can't leave without an Eilad.'

An elfin creature stepped out from the undergrowth. He removed his hat with a flourish, bowing low. 'Westler Topynkin at your service, Madame.'

'Who the hell are you?' demanded Father.

Ignoring everyone, Westler walked briskly across the lawn, his antennae twitching as he approached me.

'Right on time. You truly are a man of your word. Where's the ship? We'll need to get underway immediately,' I said.

'I brought it into geosynchronous orbit, using only thrusters, as you suggested. Then teleported down.'

'Good. Let's get going. Eight passengers, one pile of luggage.'

I pulled a teleport control from the pocket of my gown and handed it over for Westler to enter the coordinates. His fingers flashed across the keys.

'How did you manage to hide a huge cargo ship where no one could detect it?'

In reply Westler looked up at the Manyarnern moon, which hung low on the horizon.

'And what did you do up there for the better part of two months?'

'I sat counting the credits in my ever-increasing deposit account.'

I sighed. 'This trip is going to bankrupt me.'

I leant down to press execute on the teleport control. Before I could complete the movement, Mother sprang forward.

'Angie, no!'

I felt her try to wrench the control form Westler's hand with telekinesis.

My anger flared.

I didn't stop to think whether it would hurt her. My mind picked her up, throwing her body high above the trees.

In the next instant we were inside the flight deck of Westler's vessel.

'So where to?' Westler took his place in the pilot's seat, starting the pre-launch sequence.

'Earth.'

******

Walking into the state room, I was jollied by the happy scene. Westler may have been an unscrupulous rogue, but he knew how to live well. The room's opulence wouldn't have been out of place in the halls of O.P.U. Assembly.

Since we'd teleported from the surface, no one had mentioned my attack on Mother. They were all too stunned by recent events to pass comment. It was good having my family around me; all but Iain, whose absence felt like a hole in my heart.

Stop it, you'll see him soon enough, I thought.

Jen, Seb, and the children sat around a huge conference table, laughing and joking while stuffing their faces with some kind of confectionary.

Seb looked up as I entered. 'It's called Kylinkaylinmi... sod it, it's some kind of cake from Westler's home world and it's delicious.'

'Dericious,' repeated Eddie, lime green fondant oozing from the corners of his mouth.

I smiled. 'If it's that good, I'll join you as soon as I get a drink.'

I ran my eyes around the lavish furnishings. Spotting the food dispenser on the far side of the room, I began to skirt around the table, smiling as the children helped themselves to more of the cake.

There was a piercing whine. I stopped walking and shook my head.

'What was that?'

'What?'

I took another few steps and this time the whine was accompanied by intense pain all over my body. I stumbled backwards, steadying myself on the back of the nearest chair. Then it came again, the noise, the pain and this time a discharge of energy that enveloped my body.

Colour drained from the world.

For a fraction of a second, I saw the others rise in open-mouthed disbelief. The alien teleport tore my flesh into a billion, billion pieces and I was gone.

******

Chapter 11

I regained consciousness some time later. Opening my eyes, I looked about the strange room. The unnatural atmosphere, and gentle background rumble, indicated that I was still on a space vessel of some kind.

This isn't Westler's ship, I thought.

Reaching out my psi-awareness, my whole body was struck with pain.

'Ouch.'

Inhaling deeply, I used a Manyarnern meditation to regain some equanimity then forced myself to stand. The room was small, about eight square metres. The grey-green walls and ceiling looked coarse and scaly like the skin of a huge beast.

I wondered whether the alien vessel was grown rather than built. I'd heard of races that used organic processes to fashion their transports.

Apart from the rough surface, three of the walls were devoid of other features. Opposite me, protruding from the fourth wall, was a waist-height table littered with unfamiliar technology. Amongst them was one piece of equipment I did recognise; a psionic inhibitor.

A telepathic cry for help was out of the question.

'A wise decision.'

A green, jelly-like creature rose up from the floor beside the bench, taking on a roughly humanoid form as it oozed towards me.

That's a clever disguise, I thought.

'I am a citizen of the Order of Planetary Unification. You have no right to kidnap me like this.'

'We have every right,' seethed the alien. *'We are the Valcrumny. The O.P.U. disallowed our application for entry. After today, our species will have a sudden reversal in fortune.'*

The latest security bulletin had spoken of this race. The Valcrumny were scavengers who live off neural energy. Presenting a risk to telepathic species, they were banned from access to any O.P.U. world.

'You are quite right. But Earth is not an O.P.U. member. R.A.W. planetary systems and every telepath on them are ripe for the picking.'

Panic overtook me. Once they've had their way with me, they intended to go after Iain and the kids.

I knew I had to find a way out of there.

Sensing my plans for escape, the Valcrumny oozed back into its globular form and started to slide closer. *'There's no escape. Let it be over with and your discomfort will be much less.'*

'NEVER!'

Summoning all my strength, I broke through the intense pain; directing a stream of telekinesis at the creature. It burst as its internal juices boiled.

'Take that.'

I stood in the centre of the room enjoying my moment of victory.

There was a sloshing noise behind me. I swung around. Two more blobs rose up from the floor, two slid down from the wall and one dropped from the ceiling.

'It would be unwise for you to try anything like that again.'

This came from a creature slightly larger than the others. I assumed it was their leader.

'I am Angeriana'asusilicana of Manyarner.'

'We know exactly who you are.'

'What do you want with me?'

The leader slithered forward. I stepped aside as it passed. When it reached the table a sort of bud appeared in its side. I watched as this lengthened until it resembled long, spindly fingers. *'Now that we're sure you're the Premier, we'll have to increase our inhibitor's strength. That containment field was meant to be the strongest setting. We underestimated the psionic energy at your disposal.'*

It passed the glutinous tendrils across the output dial on the front of the inhibitor.

I sank to my knees, the pain was intolerable.

None of this made any sense.

'You're not very bright are you? You hold more psionic energy in one cell of your body than we could find in an entire non-telepathic race. You will sustain our species for many years to come.'

In the last twenty-four hours, I'd drowned, fled my home world, I'd even attacked my mother. I didn't want to play anymore.

'Why don't you get it over with? Come on, kill me and take what you want. I don't care.'

The creature let out a maniacal laugh. *'Kill you? Why would we kill our prize cow? Dead flesh is useless to us. We'll drain you, little by little, and if the O.P.U. wants you back they can bargain for your life. What's left of it.'*

'Manyarner... if I die what will happen to Manyarner?' I mumbled.

'What do you care? We were informed that you were leaving.'

How did it know? The image of Nyaseema's face flashed through his telepathic signal.

'Mother!'

The Valcrumny leader turned towards the inhibitor once more.

'At last she sees it all...'

I gave into pain and despair, fainting onto the cold floor.

******

It was very dark. Where was I?

I tried to open my eyes.

I couldn't feel them. I couldn't feel my body at all.

Never mind, I thought. At least the pain's gone.

How long had I been there? It could've been minutes, hours or even days. There didn't seem to be any way of measuring the passage of time.

I thought through my meeting with the Valcrumny. What did it say?

R.A.W. planetary systems and every telepath on them are ripe for the picking.

229

They had been testing me. They knew I'd fight back if my family were threatened.

Reality hit home.

I was unconscious on the floor of a holding cell in the Valcrumny ship, my physical self at the mercy of the psionic inhibitor. Those slime balls were planning on draining my neural energy; no doubt, very slowly and very painfully.

And who was responsible for all this? Mother.

There was no way the O.P.U. would strike a bargain with these parasites. She must have known that. I suppose this got me out of the way, without killing me herself; leaving room for a more cooperative Premier to be born.

If the planet survived that long.

I was unconscious, but I was still alive. I wondered whether my psi-awareness still worked.

Reaching out I felt absolutely nothing.

I abandoned that idea.

What now? I thought.

What did the Valcrumny leader say?

Why would we kill our prize cow? Dead flesh is useless to us...

The Valcrumny believed that they were in a win-win situation. The inhibitor quashed my brain function, but kept my body alive. They would offer to exchange my freedom for entry to the O.P.U. While they were waiting for a decision they could suck me dry. And if the O.P.U rejected their proposals they would just carry on indefinitely.

Their physiology was designed to live off neural energy. While I was alive, I was still generating neural energy. What if I had none? What would they do then?

What can they do? I speculated, apart from throwing my body in the garbage or ejecting it into space?

So to survive, I had to die.

******

The room spun round as my vision returned.

Sebastian was somewhere close by.

A gentle hand lifted my head, stroking the hair from my face.

'Are you all right?'

My eyes came into focus.

'Not you as well?' I sighed. 'How were you captured? Where're the kids?'

He gave me a very subtle headshake and I fell quiet.

There was a groan from beside me, I turned over to see Jen, her eyes just opening. Like Seb, she wore a tattered space suit, devoid of helmet. Her glasses hung sideways on her face, the lenses broken.

She'd looked better.

Shuffling across the floor, Seb leant over his wife. I watched as he brushed the back of his hand gently over her cheek, then straightened her hair and glasses.

'I'm okay, Seb. Don't fuss.' He helped her to sit up.

Allowing them some privacy, I stretched, stood up and walked away.

I wondered how long I'd been out for.

Looking around, I could see a Valcrumny guard stationed behind us. I'd not noticed before, but a subtle change in the wall's rough surface indicated a doorway. The guard stood beside this; if a living piece of pale-green jelly can stand. Apart from this new information, nothing in the room had changed. Except... lying on the table was a shot gun and a sort of home-made sword.

I glanced back at my friends, raising an enquiring eyebrow.

Seb coughed nervously. 'It's a long story.'

Why had the Valcrumny left weapons in the room where they were holding us prisoner? It doesn't make any sense, I thought. Then again, none of this did.

I walked back until I was standing over Jen and Seb.

'How come I woke up? Did they turn the inhibitor down?'

He nodded, indicating for me to sit on the floor and huddle close.

'Those things,' he pointed across at the guard, 'are

231

deaf and blind. As long as we don't use telepathy they can't hear what we say.'

'Yes, but they know where you are, so they can scan your brain.' I glanced up at the guard. 'Very clever, they're not as stupid as they appear.'

Sebastian scoffed. 'Clever. A slug probably has more intelligence.'

I shot them both a serious look. 'Don't underestimate the Valcrumny. We can't take the chance of giving anything away by even thinking about the things I think you want to tell me.'

They nodded in agreement.

'So what do we do?' asked Jennifer, hugging her knees to her chest. 'Sit here in silence, trying not to think about anything?'

'Yes, that's exactly what we do.'

******

We felt the ship shudder with the force of the explosion. The lights on the inhibitor unit flashed then went out. For the first time in hours my head cleared and I knew what to do.

I jumped to my feet, Seb and Jen following my lead.

Sensing our movement, the guard glided towards us. As it neared Sebastian, he sidestepped and ushered us across the room.

Jennifer got to the shotgun first. She raised it level with the approaching creature.

'Give me that, woman.' Sebastian snatched it from her hands. 'Even if you could see, you don't know how to fire it.' She looked a little hurt by his brusque tone.

Now Seb levelled the shotgun at the approaching guard. 'Don't come any closer.'

Jen sighed. 'They can't hear, remember... *Stop right there or we'll shoot.*'

'*You have nowhere to go. You may injure me with that primitive weapon, but there's many more of my kind just outside the door.*'

Almost on cue, the invisible doorway slid open on our left. Ten more green blobs entered; the leader at the head of their column. We backed away.

'So the O.P.U. has decided to fight for its citizens - a grave mistake on their part - but of no consequence. We will absorb the tremendous energy stored within the Manyarnern Premier and use it against them.'

Sebastian fired the gun.

The pellets tore into the closest guard. It stopped moving.

'Yes.'

His triumph was short lived. We could see the metal pellets lodged inside the creature. As we watched they started to dissolve, digested by the Valcrumny's internal juices. A few moments later, the creature recovered from its wounds moving towards us once again.

Seb fired again. This time it had no effect.

The leader chuckled. *'Pathetic.'*

Dropping the spent shotgun, Sebastian reached for the makeshift sword. He swung it towards the advancing alien. This was much more successful. The blade slashed through the outer membrane, spilling the creature's contents onto the floor. A pungent smell filled the room, the deck fizzing as the corrosive fluids attacked the surface.

Jen stepped backwards away from the caustic liquid. 'Urgh.'

A different alien slid forward to replace the one Seb had just killed.

'Human sentimentality is your weakness. I have ten thousand warriors all willing to sacrifice themselves for this cause,' pathed the leader.

The Valcrumny continued their slow, relentless attack.

Sebastian swung the blade again, another of the creatures fell; then a third and fourth.

He was tiring now; each cut of the blade was a little shorter and more shallow.

'Is this the best the Premier of Manyarner can do? You don't actually believe you can fight your way out of

here with that one weapon?'

Egged on by the leader's taunt, Sebastian raised the sword high, bringing it down with renewed vigour.

'Wanna try me?'

Still they advanced.

We stood with our backs to the table, Seb's determination keeping the aliens at bay.

Despite the carnage, my thoughts were elsewhere.

I'd never received training, but realised I instinctively knew how to summon the light.

Holding my right hand aloft, a flash of psionic lightening ripped into the Valcrumny leader. Its outer membrane dissolved, the fluid interior boiling away in an instant.

I smiled. 'He was getting on my nerves.'

'That was amazing,' shouted Jen.

I lifted my hand again and blasted the next Valcrumny. As I did so, the door opened and ten more of the aliens entered to fill the places of those we'd killed.

'Let's see if they can cope with this.'

I waved my arms together unleashing bolt after bolt of fire towards the aliens.

Their numbers dwindled and the advance slowed.

'Stay back, I don't want to kill any more of you. Why don't you just let us go?'

There was no response. Their momentum quickened again.

'I mean it.'

Sebastian stopped his defences with the sword, which had been blunted by the corrosive fluid from the interior of the aliens he'd killed.

He turned to stare open-mouthed at me, Jen followed suit.

'My god. Look at you, Angie. What's going on?'

I looked down. My entire body was glowing with iridescent light.

With each second that passed, my psi-awareness grew in intensity. I could hear my friends' hearts beating and feel the beads of perspiration on their bodies. I also perceived the gelatinous fluid that made up the

234

Valcrumny. With a little more focus, my mind slipped to the microscopic level. I became aware of the synthetic bone structure and dermoplastic compounds that made up the fabric of the ship itself. And not too far away I could sense the twins.

Rearranging the particles in the atmosphere to form a protective shield, I prepared for my final surprise.

For some unfathomable reason a human nursery rhyme came to mind. Tinker, tailor, soldier, sailor, rich-man, poor-man, beggar-man, thief. I smiled to myself. I had so much potential that I was all of these things and more.

Summoning a huge wave of energy I propelled it outwards destroying everything in the room. Not only did the Valcrumny disintegrate in an instant, the bench and equipment turned to piles of molten metal.

When the energy pulse subsided, I let out a sigh of relief.

It was Jennifer who spoke first. 'I never knew you could do things like that.'

'Neither did I, until I actually did it.' I shrugged. 'Okay, you two, tell me everything.'

'What about them?' Sebastian pointed towards the door. 'You said we mustn't think...'

'It's okay, they're busy appointing a new leader. No one's scanning us at the moment. How did you find me? Where're the kids?'

'We left Susie to look after Charlotte and Eddie back on Westler's ship,' began Jennifer. 'It's hidden in a crater about three kilometres from here. We gave Westler strict instructions to take them home if we didn't return in 12 hours. '

'And where exactly is here?'

'We're currently parked on a moon orbiting what we guess is the Valcrumny home world. When you were teleported away we knew you couldn't have gone far. We scanned for hours and were about to give up when this weird alien race came on board and told us where to find you.'

'How did they know?'

'They said they were chroniclers of Manyarnern history. A race called the Cruxions. They talked a lot about temporal flux and predicting the future. Most of it went over our heads, but the gist of it was that we had a fighting chance of saving you.'

'Now that's very interesting... go on.' I started to pace up and down in front of my friends, assimilating this new knowledge.

Don't get ahead of yourself. Two plus two doesn't necessarily make five, I thought.

Seb took up the story. 'That's not all they told us. They downloaded security files from the O.P.U. data base into Westler's computer. It recommended that if we were going to fight these things, we'd need to use swords rather than blasters. So we made some.' He swung the blunted weapon in his hand. 'Do you like it?'

'Very nice. But where did you get the shot gun?'

'It was a present from my parents...'

Jennifer frowned. 'Which he and Iain have kept hidden in the lodge for the past six years.'

'We agreed that it might come in useful if the locals got too suspicious.' He reached out and pulled her into an embrace. 'You must admit it came in handy.'

'But how did it get here, Seb?'

'I brought it with me in my luggage. It made me feel... safe. Safer than having nothing. It was a big deal for me, Jen and the kids to leave Earth; even if we were only going on holiday to Manyarner. I've never been amongst aliens before, apart from you, that is.'

I nodded and smiled. 'And the boys?'

'When we got on board we split up. Gabkhan had this idea of downloading a virus into the Valcrumny main frame. He thought, if he could simulate an O.P.U. attack, they might give you up.'

I smiled to myself. The scheme sounded awfully like the plot of one of Iain's favourite movies.

'Not a bad idea. Whatever he did was more than a virus, but at least it cut the power to the psionic inhibitor. Do you have a rendezvous organised?' Jen shook her head. 'How did you expect to contact them without using telepathy?'

'It all happened so quickly. We agreed to spend no longer than eight hours looking for you and then, successful or not, we'd head back to the ship.'

'How long do we have left?'

Seb heaved at the thick binding on the sleeve of his space suit. Glancing at his watch, he stiffened. 'That was eleven hours ago. Jen and I ran into a bit of trouble in the Valcrumny hatchery, we're lucky to be alive. We were dragged in here and Jen collapsed. There's not much else to tell. Even if we get out of here, we'll never get back to the ship in time. Westler's not going to hang around. I'm sorry, Angie, instead of rescuing you, we've just made things worse.'

Stopping my frantic pacing, I patted them both on the shoulder. 'Rubbish. You've done great so far. We're together, we're alive and I've found a way to fight them. Let's get out of here.'

Sebastian moved over to the door. It slid open and he looked out into the corridor.

'What can you see?'

'Shit! Hundreds more of the bloody things have massed just outside. D'you think you can deal with them?'

'We won't know until we try, but I'd rather go down fighting.'

******

Emerging into the corridor, the creatures retreated.

'That's better they're scared of us now,' remarked Jen.

Seb pulled her close. 'Let's hope it lasts.'

We edged our way up the corridor with me in the lead; a hand held above my head, primed to blast any Valcrumny stupid enough to approach us. I didn't know where we were going, but at least we were putting distance between us and the holding cell.

Reaching an intersection with two other corridors, I stopped.

'Which way?'

Seb glanced around the bend to the left and then the right. 'I don't know... it all looks the same. I think they brought us in from that direction.' He pointed up the left hand corridor. There should be a lift somewhere down there. When we were caught we were half a dozen floors down.'

Jen glanced behind us. 'Make up your minds, they're gaining on us.'

I turned around to face the Valcrumny now massed behind us in the corridor.

'Get back, or I'll...'

I didn't finish the sentence.

We hadn't noticed the group of aliens clinging to the ceiling above out heads. Without warning, they dropped down on us. Seb stepped backwards, pulling Jen out of the path of the falling Valcrumny. I stepped forward widening the gap between myself and my friends.

Then it hit me. An intense pain swept through my body as a new inhibitor was activated. Clutching my aching head, I sank to my knees. Seb caught Jennifer as she was also overwhelmed by the inhibitor's strength.

I tried to focus, but it was no good.

The creatures closest to me reared up like animals about to pounce upon their prey. I looked up as they attacked; their gelatinous forms engulfing me in an instant. The agony in my head was nothing to what I felt next. The aliens' internal juices started to dissolve the skin off my body. Eyes, hands, mouth, ears the acid penetrated every contour. I couldn't see, I couldn't move. All sensation merged into one silent agonising scream as my flesh was digested.

'Angie no!' Sebastian's anguished cry was the last thing I heard before I died.

******

238

Chapter 12

Dozens of Valcrumny piled on top of one another in a feeding frenzy.

Sebastian stared at the horrific scene. Disbelief stealing his will.

After a few seconds, survival instinct must have kicked back in because he looked around. His face brightened a little when he saw that the aliens were ignoring him and Jennifer. He still held his wife around the waist, her limp form leaning against him for support.

'We must get out of here.'

Dragging her forcibly up the corridor, they retreated from the scene.

A few metres further on they stopped in front of a door. It slid open and Sebastian jumped with surprise. He held his breath waiting for more Valcrumny to emerge.

Nothing happened. The elevator was empty.

Glancing from side to side, he stepped inside heaving Jen in behind him. The doors slid silently closed again.

'What now?'

With a jolt, the transport started to descend through the ship.

When the doors opened again, Sebastian edged towards the opening and peered out into the corridor beyond. It was devoid of alien life forms.

'So far so good. Come on Jen, stay with me.' He shifted her body weight.

'I'm okay, Seb.' She managed to stand unsupported. 'The inhibitor isn't as strong now.'

Together they left the elevator and headed up another empty, featureless corridor.

'Do you have any idea where we're going?' Seb shook his head.

After a few minutes, they neared an intersection with yet another corridor. They paused to listen. There was a rhythmical noise coming from something out of sight. Muscles tensed in preparation for fight or flight.

Gabkhan and Kohlarn sprinted around the bend and ran into them.

'Oh my God.' Seb patted his chest. 'You two nearly gave me a heart attack.'

Gabkhan smiled at them. 'It's good to see you too.' He paused. 'Where's Mum? Did you find her?'

Jennifer nodded. 'Yes, we were thrown into a holding cell together. That's where we just escaped from.'

'So where is she?' demanded Kohlarn.

'We're very sorry, she's...' Jen lifted her broken glasses, wiping a tear from her eye. 'There's nothing we could do. Those things...'

Seb stepped close, placing a reassuring arm around her shoulder. 'Angie would want us to get you two safely out of here, so that's what we're going to do.'

He and Jen started to walk away.

My sons didn't move.

'Dead? She can't be dead. She's the Premier. Fighting them would be as easy as swatting a fly.'

Sebastian swung back around to face the two young men. 'I'm sorry, Gabkhan. There's no easy way of saying this. We saw the aliens smother her.'

'So what? Did you check she was actually dead? Did you feel a pulse? Had she stopped breathing?'

Jen glanced about nervously. 'Boys.' Her sharp tone quelled their argument. 'This is not the time or place for a discussion. We saw Angie fall beneath the aliens. She didn't fight back because of this damned inhibitor. The Valcrumny started to...' she swallowed hard, 'digest her. While they were busy we managed to slip away. You must accept it. Now let's get going.' She beckoned them towards her.

Staring at one another, Gabkhan and Kohlarn remained still.

'So you just left her there, at their mercy. Even if she was dead, you ran away leaving her body?'

The two brothers marched off in the opposite direction.

240

Seb waved after them. 'No, come back. We don't have time for this. Gabkhan, Kohlarn. Don't be so stupid.'

He glanced towards Jennifer. 'What do we do?'

'We go back.'

******

The scene played out in front of me. It was like watching a TV screen. No… more like a 3D movie. It wasn't really in front of me either, more like all around me. One moment, I was viewing it from above as if I was hovering on the ceiling, the next I was inside the wall. And the next I was standing right beside my sons, wanting with all my heart to reach out and comfort their grief.

Non-corporeal existence is the weirdest thing I've ever experienced. It's not something I'd recommend, yet it was necessary.

With ease, my consciousness followed them along the corridor and into the elevator. Once inside, I effortlessly synchronised my mind with the controls.

Making our ascent towards the correct level of the Valcrumny ship, brought us back within range of the psionic inhibitor. This device could no longer affect me, but little by little it jabbed at Gabkhan, Kohlarn and Jennifer's minds.

When I opened the doors on the correct floor, they were barely able to keep themselves upright. Through sheer force of will, they stumbled out behind Sebastian and headed back to the spot where I had succumbed to the Valcrumny horde.

Seb arrived first, coming to an abrupt halt a few metres away.

I was astonished by the sight before me and could tell by his expression that he was too. My body lay almost untouched on the floor; my arms pulled up protectively around my head and my legs bent double beneath me. What's more, there were no Valcrumny in sight.

Kneeling down, he rolled my body onto its back.

I felt strangely detached from the scene. The corpse looked like me, yet it didn't feel like a true representation of my self.

I'd left Manyarner wearing a brightly coloured translucent gown typical of a Lens. It was a gift from Trilly. This was similar to the garment Iain had used to warm me on that bitter cold morning all those years ago. The delicate fabric was now partially dissolved. Beneath what remained, I could clearly see patches of missing skin, most notably across my left cheek, breast and thigh. Beneath these wounds, the muscles and tendons were exposed and, in a few places, the bone below. Matted together with alien slime, hair was stuck unevenly across my neck and back.

Iain loved my hair. And I loved cuddling up to him on cold winter nights while he played with the long, black, tresses.

Memories of Iain suddenly burst upon me. His gentle face smiling down, the feel of his hand in mine as we walked in the garden, his unshaven chin tickling my face when we kissed good morning.

How could I live without him? How could I go on, knowing that I'd never experience these sensations again? This was worse than dying.

Stop it right now, I chastised.

Grief is a selfish indulgence you can't afford to give in to.

You've been selfish all your life, seeking instant gratification for everything, avoiding any situation that brought you despair.

Your sons and your best friends are still in mortal danger. They need your help. Succumbing to this pathetic display of self pity is a waste. It's time for you to grow up and face your responsibilities.

By now, Jen, Gabkhan and Kohlarn had caught up with Sebastian where he leant over my body.

'She's hardly injured at all.' Sebastian wiped slime away from my face, rubbing it absentmindedly onto the leg of his suit. 'Her skin's blistered in places.' Lifting the tattered robe, he peered at the area where I'd lost most tissue and winced. 'Okay, there're a few places with worse injuries, but apart from those, she actually looks quite peaceful.'

He glanced up, noticing for the first time how pale and drawn the others looked.

I noticed it too.

That damned inhibitor, I thought.

I fled the scene, searching, probing, running along power conduits, in and out of ventilation shafts. It was less than a minute and then I was on the bridge. A group of the aliens were huddled around a particular console. They had once again taken on humanoid form and were using tendrils of jelly like fingers to manipulate the ship's flight controls.

There's no way this vessel was built by the Valcrumny. They must've stolen - or been given - it.

This latest revelation was interesting, but far from my main objective. I focussed once again on the task in hand.

Running my mind along the banks of equipment, I found what I was looking for. The power distribution network used photonic injection units and plasma relays to boost the signal. Linking with the device, I opened the injectors to maximum and closed down the relays. I then locked them both in that position.

Easy as falling off a log, I thought. That was one of Iain's favourite's, too.

A light blinked on the control board, slow at first and then with more insistence.

If I could have smiled, at that precise moment I would've been grinning from ear to ear.

With the Hyperlight generators on overload, I left the room and raced back to my friends and family.

Any minute now they were going to need my help.

******

There was a deafening bang and the ship lurched sideways, almost knocking them off their feet. A panel in the ceiling fell down showering the group in sparks. For a

243

few seconds, the lights flickered wildly before plunging them into darkness.

Jen let out a stifled scream.

After a brief pause, the muted emergency systems kicked in and a ribbon of miniature lamps illuminated beneath their feet.

'Thank god for that,' exclaimed Jennifer. 'I was on the verge of passing out. What d'you think happened?'

'Doesn't matter, at least the inhibitor's out of action.' Gabkhan shook himself, a look of determination on his face.

I'd seen that look before.

He bent down beside Sebastian and lifted my body up over his shoulder.

'We're not leaving her behind.'

Awkwardly Gabkhan stood up again, his brother rushing forward to help him adjust the weight of the load. Together they strode back in the direction they'd come.

Sebastian glanced towards Jennifer and shrugged.

They also headed towards the elevator.

******

The group turned a corner, the twins in the lead.
'Dead end.'

Moving into the floor below their feet, I energised the thread of emergency lighting.

'No, there's a door on the right. See?' Jennifer pointed at the doorway set almost seamlessly into the bulkhead.

They approached.

'I wonder how we open...' The whole wall peeled back to reveal a cargo bay.

Shifting my body weight over his other shoulder, Gabkhan led the way inside. The group ran across the large expanse until they were safely hidden between two storage containers on the far side.

'So far so good,' whispered Sebastian. 'At least we don't have any more slime balls to fight off.'

Jennifer gave a deep sigh and sat down on a crate. 'Can we rest here for a while, please?'

'Great idea.' Gabkhan laid my body gently on the floor. 'I'll find a way to hack into their computer and find out what's going on.' He strode off into the distance.

'That should keep him busy,' remarked Jennifer. 'I don't think he's handling things very well.'

'None of us are,' replied Kohlarn, tears running unchecked down his cheeks.

She reached out and beckoned him into her arms, whispering motherly words of comfort until his grief abated.

Thank you.

A few minutes later, Gabkhan looked up at a computer terminal. It was situated at the top of a ladder that led onto an upper gantry. He climbed up, his feet making a loud clanking noise as he stood on reach rung. When he reached the top, he glanced about nervously before moving onto the exposed balcony. The terminal jutted from the wall just ahead of him. As he approached, I switched on the display. His face lit up with the reflected glow.

Gabkhan flexed his fingers and started flicking through the menu. Meanwhile I moved into the terminal and interfaced with the central processor; interpreting the data into English. When the words changed into meaningful patterns, he paused and blinked repeatedly. I could tell that he didn't quite believe what he was seeing.

Come on. Think like your father. Put two and two together.

He shrugged, dismissing what had happened, then started reading the screen.

The fire suppression system was activated in the engineering section. Orders had been issued to the crew to converge in that area of the ship. This accounted for the lack of Valcrumny in the corridors. The ship, having lifted off from the moon just prior to the explosion, was now moving under emergency thrusters towards the planet.

I changed the view, displaying details of the scanners and weapons systems. The Valcrumny had seen through his ruse and purged the false information from their systems. The weapons were now fully charged and on alert in case a real O.P.U. attack occurred.

I moved on through the files until I brought up a cargo manifest. He read the information twice before its significance sunk in.

Running back, he explained what he'd found to the others.

With his brother's help, Kohlarn picked up my body; heaving it onto his shoulder.

'Lead on...'

Together the group made their way into the next compartment.

******

The shuttle was very small, just large enough for them to lay my body on the floor and huddle around the flight controls.

'D'you think you can fly this thing?' asked Sebastian.

Gabkhan sat down in the pilot's seat, running his hands over the instruments.

This confirmed my suspicions. The Valcrumny wouldn't have fitted inside the craft, let alone be able to handle the manual systems.

'Yes, probably.'

Sebastian didn't look too convinced. 'Are you sure? It's very different from the Eilad.'

'Oh, I can fly it easily enough. But that's the least of our problems. How are we supposed to get off the ship?' He pointed towards the enormous cargo bay doors. 'D'you reckon they can be opened manually?'

They fell silent.

I considered my options.

If I headed up to the bridge to interface with the computer main frame, would I be able to get back into the shuttle in time? It was bad enough existing like this when I was close to my family, I didn't think I could stomach being left behind with the Valcrumny.

During our escape, I'd not had time to consider my impossible existence. Was I physically there? Was I

246

energy, spirit, or pure consciousness? How was I managing to interface with the ship's technology?

One day pupils at the Academy were going to spend hours debating this fascinating topic. If any of us survived long enough to tell the tale.

I was drawn from my musing by Kohlarn's sudden movement.

'Wait here.' He opened the shuttle door and climbed out. The others watched him head at speed towards the bay doors.

Patting Jennifer on the shoulder, Seb followed him.

What was he thinking? I also left the shuttle.

A few minutes later, Sebastian caught up with Kohlarn beside a particularly large container. 'What's up?'

Kohlarn didn't even acknowledge his presence, he was too engrossed in studying the information displayed on the side of the crate.

'If I'm not mistaken,' he said at last. 'This is an O.P.U. language. Andranovich taught it to me. I think it says danger from explosion.'

Good boy, I thought. Remind me one day, to tell you how bright you are...

They smiled at each other, then jumped into action, tugging vigorously at the lid until it burst open.

Some minutes later they'd removed three containers of ionised caesium disulphide.

'I wonder what they use it for?'

Kohlarn shrugged. 'Dad would know.' He sighed. 'It hardly matters. Our problem is how to ignite it.'

Jennifer arrived at a run. 'You two were gone so long, we started to worry.' She looked down at the canisters. 'What're you going to do with those?'

Kohlarn chuckled. 'Make one hell of a bang.'

Together they lifted the first of the canisters towards the cargo bay doors.

******

Sometime later they were back in the shuttle

debating their next move. The discussion had gone round in circles for the past half hour and was obviously getting them nowhere.

'I know we've been avoiding telepathy, but why don't we link minds and use pyrokinesis to ignite the liquid?' suggested Kohlarn. 'Once we breach those doors the Valcrumny will know our location. What difference will a few more seconds make?'

The others were surprised by the simplicity of the plan and nodded in agreement before taking up positions behind the pilot's seat.

Gabkhan depressed the ignition button, the thrusters fired and the little ship lifted a few meters into the air.

'Ready?'

Sebastian stood beside Jennifer, watching her face as she joined minds with the others. I couldn't help from this distance so I took a chance and rushed towards the barrels. Feeling the chemical composition of the caesium disulphide, the molecules began to excite. In the split second before the critical point for detonation, I dashed back inside the shuttle.

There was a huge explosion. The shock wave hit the cargo bay doors wrenching them from their mountings, exposing the compartment to space.

Crates and containers of all sizes were pulled into the void, some thumping the hull of the shuttle as they passed.

'Now!' They screamed in unison and Gabkhan threw the lever forward. The craft lurched towards the opening, quickly passing the skin of the secondary hull.

Kohlarn leaned over the pilot's seat. 'Can't we go any faster? They must've realised what's happening by now.'

A flash from the Valcrumny blasters passed close on the port side.

Sebastian strained to look out through the left view port. 'Stay close to the hull and swing round behind them. They can't fire at us if they don't have a suitable angle.'

'They won't risk hitting parts of their own ship,'

added Jennifer.

'Will you shut the hell up and let me concentrate.'

Gabkhan took the small craft towards the rear of the Valcrumny vessel, travelling close to the surface of the ship. Once we were past the scope of the main blasters, which were mostly forward facing, he let out a sigh of relief. 'Let's hope the drive system is still out of action.'

The shuttle moved off into open space.

The progress of the little ship was pitifully slow. While Gabkhan was busy with piloting, the others craned their necks and looked at what was happening behind us. The lumbering Valcrumny ship slowly turned about until the blasters faced us again.

'Shit,' exclaimed Kohlarn. 'Now would be a good time Gab, to find some extra juice in those engines.'

I rushed into the drive unit, infusing the plasma flow with energy.

We gained speed.

It wasn't enough. The next shot caught the shuttle on its side. We spun out of control, rolling and tumbling through space.

Gabkhan fought the controls, eventually bringing stability back to the shuttle.

'One more like that and we're...'

There was a flash from the thrusters then silence. The engines had failed.

Gabkhan flicked switches, pressed buttons and turned dials, but the controls were dead in his hands.

'That's it. We've lost all power. We're sitting ducks.'

No. I won't let it end like this.

Think, Angie, think.

There was something happening... A build up of static...

Around the shuttle, space itself began to shimmer. Something was coming...

An unknown vessel materialised from hyperspace immediately behind us. Half the size of the Valcrumny ship, it was in direct line of fire from their blasters and took the next shot on its flank.

The communications array flashed.

Reaching past an astonished Gabkhan, Sebastian flipped a switch, opening a channel. A large, humanoid, face appeared on the viewer.

'I am Loftori of Paldrin. Myself and my crew have come to repay the debt of life owed to the Manyarnern Premier.'

It was the engineer I'd saved on the Gretin station.

'You better get out of here. The Valcrumny are pretty pissed off with us,' said Seb.

'It is already too late. Our structural integrity has been compromised.' His face displayed no sign of tension as he spoke. 'As I said, we are here to repay our debt and will shield you from their aggressive intentions as long as we can.'

The viewer went blank.

'Whoever they are, they've got impeccable timing,' mumbled Jennifer.

We watched through the window as the blasters ripped into the hull of the Paldrinian ship. Slowly they turned to face the advancing Valcrumny.

'They're going to ram it.' exclaimed Jennifer, burying her face into Sebastian's shoulder.

The battle played out in silence.

It wasn't really a battle. The unarmed Paldrinian ship couldn't have fired on the Valcrumny even if they wanted to. The ship was wrecked, most of the crew were probably dead. They fought back in the only way they could. Slowly they advanced on a collision course.

The Valcrumny fired a volley that tore through the smaller ship. Despite damage to the engines and lower decks, momentum alone drove it on.

They fired again, an almost continuous beam of energy slicing through the hull. Debris flew off in all directions, yet the core of the ship remained intact.

It was right on top of them now. I had no sympathy for my captors, but the Valcrumny's desperation felt almost palpable.

When the impact came, it felt like an anti-climax. Their respective hulls breached at the point of impact, engulfing them both in flames.

The ensuing fireball extinguished quickly in the void of space.

A fraction of a second later we were hit by the shock wave, throwing us into the reach of the Valcrumny home world's gravity field.

******

Chapter 13

'Brace yourself, we're going down,' screamed Gabkhan, punching every button and lever he could in a futile attempt to restart the engines.

Not if I could help it. I rushed into the drive system. The increased plasma flow had fused the manifolds. Nothing was getting through from the fuel cells.

Damn!

Could I bypass the system? Maybe if I used my own power? Dumping it directly into the thrusters. The control circuits would need to be overridden.

I headed into the computer unit.

******

Buffeted by atmospheric turbulence the shuttle tumbled towards the rock-strewn surface of the planet.

Seb fell backwards, pulling Jen down with him. They landed heavily on the floor. Kohlarn lost his footing, and stumbled sideways, knocking his head against one of the instrument panels.

In the pilot's seat, Gabkhan fought frantically with the controls.

If Iain were here, he'd probably jest that this shuttle had the gliding angle of a brick.

For a few seconds I managed to lift the nose of the vessel.

Too late, the ground was upon us.

I'm sorry Iain, I tried.

A huge dust cloud rose into the atmosphere as the shuttle impacted on the ground. Driven forward by its momentum, the ship's outer hull was twisted and mangled on the rough surface. Eventually the friction decreased our speed and we came to a shuddering halt.

******

I felt the ship around me, it was wrecked.

Sebastian was pinned beneath a piece of what was formerly the flight console. A gash in his thigh poured with blood.

I was worried until I saw him open his eyes.

Beside him lay my body. The face turned upwards, eyes wide open. He jumped when he saw it and pulled away.

Then I noticed that he was lying partially on top of Jennifer. She was regaining consciousness too.

He smiled. She wriggled free from beneath him and stood up.

'Are you okay?' he asked.

She nodded. 'Your leg looks bad.'

Bending down, Jen used telekinesis to partially repair the torn flesh. After a few seconds the bleeding subsided. 'That's the best I can do, I'm not Angie.' She heaved herself up again. 'I'll find something to bandage the wound.'

At first she tugged at the material of her space suit, but it was too resilient to tear. She then scanned the broken metal and debris that littered the ground around them. The only material available was the remnants of my gown. Carefully tearing some fabric from what remained of the sleeve, she tied it around his leg.

All the while, Sebastian lay silently watching her, his features grey and drawn. I could only guess at the dismal thoughts that passed through his brain.

'Thanks.'

'Where's Gab?'

I was suddenly aware of Kohlarn sitting behind us propped against what was left of the bulkhead. He rubbed his temple and groaned.

Jen and Seb looked about the wreckage.

'He's not here,' remarked Jennifer, her face showing the strain. 'I'll go outside and look.'

Sebastian pulled himself up. 'I think we should all get out.' He reached towards Jennifer. 'Give me a hand.'

Once outside, they spotted Gabkhan a few meters

away from the wreckage. He was still strapped into the pilot's seat which had been wrenched from its mountings and thrown clear when the craft broke up.

Jennifer ran over. 'He's alive. Still unconscious and with a nasty wound on his forehead, but I don't think it's too serious.' She started to unbuckle the seat belt.

Kohlarn joined her and between them they carried Gabkhan back towards Sebastian.

'Over here.' He pointed at the nearest rock.

Sitting on the ground, Sebastian helped them lower Gabkhan down beside him. He rubbed his leg. 'We need to salvage what we can from the shuttle.'

'No problem.' Kohlarn turned and padded back into the wreckage.

When he returned he was carrying my body over his shoulder. He dropped me onto the ground.

'Whoops, sorry, Mum.'

Jennifer smiled. 'Did you find anything useful?'

Kohlarn shook his head. 'There's no sign of a medi-kit or any emergency rations.' He sighed heavily.

'Never mind. Sit down and rest,' she said.

They sat in silence, a shroud of gloom descending on the scene.

'You do realise that this is the Valcrumny home world?' muttered Sebastian, sometime later. 'As soon as they locate us we're done for.'

Jennifer shot him an angry look. 'Don't be such a defeatist. We managed to walk away from that.' She waved her hand in the direction of the ruined shuttle. 'Those people on that ship. They sacrificed themselves to save us and all you want to do is give up?'

'Let's face it, Jen, there's no way out of here.' He pulled her to him and gently stroked her hair.

'Thirsty.'

The group glanced around at Gabkhan, breathing a collective sigh of relief as he regained consciousness.

'Jen, I'm thirsty d'you have any water?'

'Just lay quiet and I'll see what I can do.'

Kohlarn looked at her, his eyes wide. 'What did you say that for? There's no surface water and even if there was any, I wouldn't recommend drinking it.'

Sebastian stood up awkwardly and limped away. 'It would've been better if we'd all died in the crash.'

'Don't talk like that,' said Jennifer, bursting into tears.

More alert now, Gabkhan pulled himself up onto his elbows. 'I'm sorry, Jen. I really am.'

She sniffed. 'It's not your fault. It was thanks to you the thrusters fired at the last minute levelling our descent.'

'No they didn't. The drive section was completely dead in my hands. All I could do was strap myself in and brace against the impact.'

Sebastian sat down abruptly. 'Yes they did, I distinctly remember the feeling of lift.'

All eyes turned towards Kohlarn.

'Don't look at me. All I remember is the terrible scraping sound as we careered out of control along the ground. How could it've happened if the thrusters were completely fucked?'

The question hung in the air between them.

Come on... come on, think.

'Maybe we used telekinesis?' Kohlarn didn't sound convinced by his own suggestion. 'It could've been an instinctive survival sort of thing. What d'you think Gab?'

'Influencing such a large object is way beyond any of us. Even our combined powers wouldn't be strong enough to make a difference.'

Kohlarn's face lit up. 'I know this sounds crazy, but there is one amongst us who would have enough power.'

Jen was first to her feet. She rushed over to my body and bent down, feeling for a pulse.

'Well?'

She shook her head. 'Definitely dead.'

Slowly Jennifer returned, flopping down on the dusty ground beside Sebastian.

'If I was religious, I guess this would be the time to start praying.'

Seb put an arm around her shoulders. 'I've been doing it all day, sweetheart.'

255

******

Next morning the remains of the shuttle were shaken by a low rumble coming from over the horizon.

I watched as they awoke and jumped up.

In the distance, and approaching rapidly, was a huge tracked vehicle.

Sebastian climbed awkwardly onto a nearby boulder to get a better view. 'That's it, the games finally up. We wouldn't have made it through another day out here anyway.'

Gabkhan glanced around. 'We can hide somewhere?'

'Why bother, we've no food or water.' Seb clambered back down from the rock and rubbed his injured leg. 'Why postpone the inevitable.'

Jen spun around and slapped him in the face. 'For god's sake, Seb, can't you even pretend?' She darted inside the wreckage of the shuttle. 'If I've got to die then I'm taking some of them with me.'

Scanning the floor, she picked up a piece of metal, then ran outside again and began to sharpen the edge on a nearby boulder.

The others sprang into action rushing into what was left of the small craft.

All the while, the rumbling noise grew louder as the craft carrying the aliens came closer.

Sebastian pulled at a large metal plate wedged between the ruptured fuel tanks and a structural beam. As he dragged it clear, a tangle of micro-fibres from the ships computer unit fell onto the floor at his feet.

'Did you see that?'

'See what?' Gabkhan looked across from where he stood sharpening the crude sword in his hand.

'There was a flash of residual energy.'

'Impossible. This ship has no independent power source. It relies on energy converted from the liquid fuel cells.'

Sebastian bent down closer. 'There it was again.' He started to pull at the mangled mass of fibre optics and bioelectric circuitry. 'Perhaps there's enough residual energy to get the communicator working and call for help.'

Jen looked in through the gaping hole in the side of the ship.

'Whatever you're going to do you better make it quick. Here they come.'

Leaving their vehicle, the Valcrumny slithered across the dust bowl towards us.

Sebastian tugged angrily at the fibres and they came away in his hand.

He gasped.

I rushed up his arm; running along the nervous tissue in a flash. As I entered his brain, the situation became crystal clear.

We started to laugh.

'Seb, what the hell's got into you?'

Unable to respond, we pushed Gabkhan out of our path and hobbled from the shuttle.

Once clear of the wreckage, we dashed forward to confront the multitude of advancing green blobs.

Like a swarm of army ants, the Valcrumny raised up their gelatinous form for one combined assault. They oozed across one another as they surged towards us.

We lifted a hand above our head, summoning the light.

The atmosphere around us crackled.

The others looked on, dumbfounded, as a fireball flashed outwards from our fingers to engulf the nearby creatures.

They exploded, filling the canyon with acrid smoke.

But it was not over yet, the fireball did not abate; instead it grew in size until it filled the vista as far as the eye could see.

The noise was deafening. In all directions the air was alive with fire and light.

We could no longer contain the wave front.

With the force of a nuclear explosion it discharged outwards, leaving us safe in the epicentre. Moving rapidly across the planet's surface, the explosion increased in intensity as it progressed. The savagery of the destructive force consumed everything in its path. The rock-strewn landscape dissolved into liquid magma as we watched.

In a matter of seconds the Valcrumny's presence on that inhospitable world was totally obliterated.

******

Eventually we stood alone in the silence. Seb's body depleted, his eyes vacant.

Jennifer ran over. 'What the hell was that?'

Without responding, we walked over to the corpse laying on the ground a few metres away.

Bending down, we touched the forehead.

I inhaled and opened my eyes.

******

I recovered fairly quickly. The others helped by massaging life back into my stiff limbs.

Once I was able to stand, I waved them away.

'Step back.'

Enveloping myself in a cocoon of psionic energy, I regenerated the tissue eaten away by the Valcrumny.

'That's better, I look presentable again,' I said, a few minutes later.

No one spoke. Not even Seb who was gradually coming to terms with the psionic abilities I'd left behind in his mind.

The experiences of the last few days had taught me much about the extensive powers at my command. I'd already accepted my calling as the Manyarnern Premier. I'd taken on board everything Trilly said about my specialisation.

What her explanation didn't prepare me for was the omnipotent nature of my gifts.

Part of me cried out to reject it, yet I enjoyed the sovereignty the power afforded me. Since waking, a particular human saying had been playing around my thoughts. Power tends to corrupt, and absolute power corrupts absolutely.

It both thrilled and terrified me.

I'd used the power to kill them, all of them. I could've, should've, stopped. But I wanted to punish them, every single slimy... I not only killed the aliens who were attacking us, I wiped every snivelling green lump off that stinking planet.

And I enjoyed it.

Eddie had been right. I was evil: a monster capable of genocide. In fact, I'd been a monster all my life. I'd killed or caused the death of so many innocent people. The irony was that I thought I was choosing to disregard the Manyarnern way of life. In reality, the choices I'd made had far worse consequences than if I'd left well alone. I couldn't blame anyone else for the deaths that had followed me. It was time to admit it. Everything had been my fault.

Do I deserve to live amongst normal human beings, I thought.

I looked around at my family, forcing myself to put these issues aside. I needed to concentrate on getting us all back to civilisation.

History would judge me for my crimes.

It took very little effort to call Westler to our position. He hadn't followed Jennifer's instructions to leave after twelve hours.

I think Susie threatening him with a blaster had a lot to do with it.

'How could you leave me alone with them?' He climbed into the pilot's seat. *'Human children are harder to tame than Lafta cats.'*

He looked up, smiling. 'Next stop Earth.'

'No.'

Everyone stared.

'Take me back to Manyarner. There are questions I need answered.'

******

We dropped out of Hyperspace and the shield

259

lifted.

'What's going on?'

Crowding around the view screen, we gawped at the uproar below.

The planet was smothered in swirling cloud cover. Massive hurricanes sped across the continents, accompanied by electrical storms that spat tongues of brightness into the stratosphere.

Westler read out data from the sensory attuner. 'There's seismic activity off the scale down there. I'd guess the continental plates are breaking up.' He looked me in the eye. 'You don't expect to teleport down?'

'Not any more. We'll land the ship.'

Westler went quite pale. 'Look, Lady. When I agreed to this charter the contract said transport to and from the planet. There was no mention of brain-sucking aliens, insane human children or piloting through...' He pointed at the largest hurricane which could be seen sweeping in from the ocean to attack the First Continent. '...that.'

'Hazard pay. What about a nice fat bonus if you get us down in one piece.'

His antennae twitched, a tell tale sign that I had him on the hook, all I had to do was reel him in.

'How big a bonus?'

'I happen to be Premier of one of the richest planets in the O.P.U. and you're about to save that planet from destruction. I suspect they'll be very grateful and very generous.'

'Okay, people, strap yourselves in. This is going to be a bumpy ride.'

******

The ground quaked beneath me. Fissures opened in the top soil, zigzagging their way across my path as I flew towards the temple. The whole world was convulsing in agony as it neared its end. I'm not sure what was more deafening, the howling wind, the rumble of rock scraping rock as the continents shifted or the telepathic scream of despair.

My feet barely touched the steps as I entered the temple.

I came to a sudden halt.

The place was crammed full of people.

In the very centre were two dozen Lenses their arms raised towards the focal stones, faces upturned. Amongst them was Lara, Andranovich's Joining partner.

I scanned the crowd. He wasn't in the temple.

I hoped he was okay.

Surrounding this central group, the Circle of Elders knelt, hands joined, heads bowed, minds uniting with one desire... to live.

Away from the dais others congregated in family groups. Embracing, wailing, holding onto each other, both physically and mentally, because they didn't know what else to do.

There were more citizens here than I'd seen in a lifetime.

Lifting over their heads, I landed on the central platform amongst the Lenses.

They were too preoccupied to notice me.

Following their lead, I looked up and punched the air with my fist.

'Let's hope I'm not too late.'

I felt energy pour out as my consciousness entered the link.

The world turned white, bleached of colour by the burning intensity of the psionic field.

Minutes passed.

A rainbow of colours flashed through the energy beam; first blue, then green, violet and red, dazzling to the eye and the mind.

Finally the planet had drained all it could take. The storm abated and the spasms beneath our feet died away.

Manyarner held its breath.

The Lens closest to me lowered her arms and opened her eyes. Like the others, her mind was dazed, body limp, and shield low. Feeling my presence, the young woman grinned and pulled me into her arms; showering me with kisses. I hugged her back, her joy was infectious.

Gradually a happy murmur spread around the temple, relief uppermost in people's thoughts.

But the interlude of blissful release was short lived. *'What are **you** doing here?'*

I spun around. Mother was marching across the temple toward me.

'You are not welcome, you chose exile.'

'It didn't feel like a choice,' I pathed.

She stopped her approach and I felt her mind withdraw as she strengthened her shield. With ease I cut through the barrier.

'That won't work, not any more. I am what you made me. My mind is stronger now than you can imagine.'

I opened up to those present, allowing them to experience in an instant the tortures of the past day. On the edge of the group consciousness I felt Father's mind, astonished by her actions.

'You thought they would keep me alive indefinitely, bleeding off my power. But I died. That was something you didn't expect.' I waved toward the devastated countryside. *'**You** are responsible for this.'*

Mother sunk to her knees. *'It was for Manyarner... everything was for Manyarner.'*

The Circle stepped away from her, eyes averted.

The mind of a senior Lens rose above the others. *'Thank you, Premier, for returning to us. How can we be of assistance?'*

'I have questions that need answers.'

She nodded. *'Go ahead.'*

'Who are the Cruxions?'

The assembled Lenses gasped, trying to hide behind a combined shield.

'I want the truth.'

'Very well. The Cruxions were a race who visited our planet thousands of years ago...'

'Bullshit! You've lied to the people for too long. Tell me the truth.'

A familiar face peered around the assembled throng, she winked.

262

'Trilly, come forward.' I beckoned her towards me. There was a hint of jealousy in the others' minds.

She glanced at the senior Lens as she passed. Anxiety flashed through her, quickly replaced by a resolve to reveal the truth.

I didn't have time to play verbal games. *'The Cruxions were Manyarnerns, weren't they?'* I asked.

Trilly focussed her gaze toward me. *'At the dawn of time there were two tribes. One lived a mechanised lifestyle using technology to provide for their needs. They were known as the Cruxions. The Manyarnerns lived a spiritual life employing psionics. These tribes inhabited different continents and rarely had contact with one another. One day the Cruxions came forward and suggested that they combine their technology with psionics for the advancement of the whole planet. They were very persuasive and eventually the Manyarnerns agreed to their plan. The outcome was a disaster of global proportions. The fifth continent was blasted from the surface of the world.'*

A collective gasp spread around the temple at the speed of thought.

'Guilt over what they had done drove the Cruxions to destroy the technology, sealing the knowledge away forever in a secret location. But this wasn't good enough. The Manyarnerns demanded retribution. The Cruxions took their own lives in a ritual mass suicide.'

I smirked. *'But they didn't die, did they? They left their bodies and took on a non-corporeal existence.'* She nodded. *'They weren't psionic, but they found a way to live on; guiding the planet through writing on the temple stones, educating the people in the use of psionics and guarding the Archive of Knowledge. The Cruxions are the Lenses... or should I say the Lenses are the Cruxions?'*

She nodded again. *'The Cruxions inhabit the bodies of those identified as Lenses shortly after birth. We don't mind, it's a mutually accepted symbiosis. The Cruxion within each of us doesn't dominate our will, rather they add their immense knowledge to our own as a mentor and guide whenever we need it. All Lenses welcome this* relationship; the whole being greater than the sum of the parts.'

'Am I also a Cruxion?'

She smiled, looking down at her feet. I waited while she gathered her thoughts. Perhaps she's consulting the Cruxion inside her?

'Yes and no.'

'What's that supposed to mean?'

'You have many abilities that the early Cruxions possessed, you can interface with technology, you can leave your body and enter another. Does it feel like there is someone else inside you?'

'No, not really.'

'Then you have your answer.' Trilly paused, playing absent-mindedly with her plaited hair. 'It wasn't the Cruxions who made you Premier. They're as baffled by recent events as you are, but they're also very grateful.'

I sighed noisily. 'One more question. In the years since the Age of Conflict how many people have left the planet?'

She looked puzzled. 'What makes you ask that?'

'Excuse me.' I turned around. Father now stood on the bottom step of the platform. 'May I answer on behalf of the Elders?'

My excitement was rising. I'd always suspected that he knew more.

'Certainly, Father.'

'Over the centuries eight million souls, perhaps ten million, have left the planet. Some became explorers, others joined the O.P.U. The diminishing energy reserves forced us into the hope that you would replace them.'

I waved people away as I walked over to stand beside him. 'Look around, Father. Have you ever seen so many of our people gathered in one place? This planet is big enough to hold billions, yet the population numbers in the millions. Where are the others?'

Trilly's thoughts sang in my mind once again. 'Remember what I told you about Fayuun?' Now I nodded at her words. 'About the virus she administered to lock everyone into their genetic specialisations? Do you think they allowed her to do that willingly?'

'They left didn't they...those who didn't agree with Fayuun's plan left the planet.' I looked at her over my shoulder. 'Where did they go?'

Trilly shrugged.

I gasped and swung around to face Father. 'The O.P.U? You've been manipulating the O.P.U to search for the missing Manyarnerns.'

'And we found them.' Mother's wretched thoughts could barely hide her hatred. 'Half-breeds and mongrels, interbred with races throughout the galaxy and beyond. They are not worthy of being called Manyarnern.'

'Be quiet woman!' barked Father.

She briefly looked into his eyes, then turned and ran from the temple. I watched her leave, but all I felt was the gulf between us. My mind quickly returned to the missing Manyarnerns.

'The genetic tags...' How stupid I'd been. Why hadn't I seen it before?

I leapt down the steps, pushing people out of my way. I could feel the confusion in their minds.

Coming to a halt, on the edge of the stones, I turned around to face Trilly and Father. They stood together on the central steps. I felt their concern at my sudden exit.

'I'll be back. I swear on my life, I'll be back before you know it.'

I flew away from the temple at great speed.

******

Seb, Jen and the kids were just disembarking from the ship when I landed beside them.

'What's going on? Have you sorted everything out?'

I ignored them. 'Westler, I need to borrow your ship.' I flew up the entrance ramp and headed for the flight deck.

He came running after me, panting heavily at the exertion.

'Oh no you don't.' He pulled off his hat and cloak, throwing them to the floor. 'Premier or not, I won't let you take my ship.'

I dropped to the ground and waited for his stumpy legs to catch me up. 'Very well, you can come along. But you're not going to like it.'

******

Chapter 14

'So, where to?'

'Earth.'

'You wish is my command, Premier.' Westler chuckled. 'That bonus better be worth it.'

He trotted over to the console and started the pre-flight checks. I stepped forward, removing his stubby hands from the panel.

'We don't need to use the engines, at least not yet.'

'Huh?' His antennae twitched wildly. 'Now look here...'

I held my right hand out in front of me. A ball of pinkish energy gathered around the finger tips.

I could feel Westler's trepidation. 'What are you going to do with that?'

'You'll see.'

Slowly the energy pocket enlarged until it filled the flight deck from floor to ceiling. The event horizon swirled and pulsed in an ever decreasing spiral until it folded back on itself. The very heart of the vortex was black: Dead space, absolute nothingness.

Disengaging from my hands, the bubble moved out until it dissolved into the fabric of the walls.

We waited for something to happen. The metal bulkhead started to shimmer, becoming translucent as we watched.

Sensing the astonishment in Westler's mind, I chuckled as the walls, floor and ceiling disappeared.

My elfin friend rubbed his eyes and stared at the floor. It looked as if we were standing on empty air. 'Am I seeing thiiinnnggggssssssssssssssssssssss...........'

The cargo ship and everything within it vanished from space time.

******

The ship settled itself down on the edge of the scrubland, the displaced air from the thrusters making the palm trees thrash about violently. Loose branches and other organic debris were thrown high into the air as we descended. Startled wildlife scurried away.

The bulk of the craft wobbled unsteadily for a moment as its six huge support legs sank into the soft black earth. Then all went quiet.

Silently the forward facing cargo doors swung open, the ramp descended and we emerged to survey the surrounding countryside. Westler sniffed the air, intrigued by the sweet scent of exotic flowers that drifted past his sensitive nostrils.

He looked up at me. 'What now?'

'Now we go and look for the source of that lovely smell.'

******

An hour later we emerged from the tree line onto a broad flood plain. Laid out before us were grasslands that stretched to the horizon. The meandering of a wide river, which snaked its way from south to north across the vista, broke this immense carpet of lush green-grey pasture into a patchwork of disjointed fields. As these water-meadows neared the river's banks the grasses gave way to rushes and reeds; their erect fronds fudging the boundary between land and water.

'Quite nice here isn't it.'

Westler gave a snort. 'Sure if you like this sort of thing. Where're we heading?'

I pointed across the river at a low range of hills in the distance. Silhouetted against the dark rock, three pointed structures could just be seen. The smooth white faces contrasted with the black stone beyond. The top of each was capped in gold that glinted in the bright sunshine.

'What're they?'

'Ships.'

'They're not O.P.U. design. Where did they come from?'

'Manyarner.'

Ignoring his puzzled expression, I set off towards the vessels. Westler remained still. *'They're covered in gold, Wes. Wherever you go in the Galaxy, that's a precious metal.'*

I smiled to myself as he ran to catch up.

'Hurry up, then.' He glanced up at the blazing sun 'That's quite some trek ahead of us.'

******

I'm not sure how long it took to cross the river's flood plain, but in the intense heat it felt like an eternity. The humidity climbed as we neared the bank and the ground underfoot became waterlogged. Insects buzzed around us, nibbling at exposed flesh. Westler's jacket and long pantaloons afforded him some protection, however my tattered gown was no barrier to their insistent bites. After a while I gave up swatting them away, instead passing a tiny psionic pulse across the surface of my skin. The static charge deterred any that flew too close.

'It's all right for some,' he commented from beside me, as he flicked a mosquito off his crooked nose.

'I'm sorry, it looks like we arrived during the rainy season.'

'Can't we just fly?' he asked, looking down at his sodden boots. 'It'll be much quicker. We've still got to cross that.'

He pointed at the torrent in front of us. The river was bulging with accumulated flood water collected from across the continent. I looked down at the swirling eddies, the level was rising rapidly. Perhaps he was right. With the water running so fast, swimming across was not an option.

'I know what you're thinking. They're Manyarnern and we can't surprise them. But things aren't that simple. We'll head to the narrowest point, just there before the river meanders in a wide arc and reassess the situation. Until then, would you like me to carry you?'

269

He scoffed. I knew I'd offended his dignity.

We trudged onward.

By the time we neared the appointed section of river, the bank had disappeared beneath the murky water; firmer ground marked only by a strip of rushes that thrust themselves towards the heat of the midday sun. We waded forward, sinking further into the silt with each step.

Stopping, I felt the slimy mud seeping between my toes. There's a time when even I will admit defeat. Grabbing Westler's shoulder I lifted us both up; the thick mud resisting my pull. Eventually we were bobbing about a few metres above the water; brushing the worst of the black earth from our legs and feet.

I looked across at my companion.

'Happier now?'

He wrinkled his nose, running muddy fingers along his antennae. 'Much.'

Our progress was quicker now. We crossed the raging flood heading on a direct course toward the little cluster of Manyarnern ships. Looking down I spotted a lone temporary shelter, standing beside a bend in the river.

Where is everyone? I thought.

The flood was not as pronounced here and we grounded on solid earth.

'Wait here,' I whispered.

The shelter was little more than a tent, woven from thick white fabric stretched over a cross-frame of long poles. It was square in shape with a tall opening on one side covered by a curtain. Around the top ran a band of red and blue embroidery.

A breeze came up from the river making the fabric billow gently, the unexpected sound made me jump. When the wind died away, I became aware of the strong aroma form an incense burner; Lotus flower and Balsamo wood mixed with Kyphi - smells familiar to me since childhood.

My nerve almost faltered as I approached the shelter. I was out of my depth, but knew I had to see this through.

Taking a deep breath, I reached out my psi-awareness and gasped. A solitary female lay on a mattress inside the shelter; she was meditating and had not, as yet, noticed my approach. I scanned her unshielded mind as she performed the ancient ritual.

The scene was perfectly Manyarnern.

With the intense sun at my back, I stepped forward and lifted the curtain.

'Hello Fayuun, I thought I'd find you here.'

Jerking awake, Fayuun lifted up her hands, shielding her eyes from the glare of the sun. I watched as she scanned my silhouette.

'Who are you?' I could sense her disorientation. She thought I was a native.

'I am Angeriana'asusilicana. But please call me Angie.' I turned around and beckoned Westler towards me. *'This is Westler Topynkin my travelling companion.'* He waddled over to stand just inside the opening.

'Angeriana is a Manyarnern name. Everyone's still in slow sleep. How did you get off the ship?'

I took a step closer to her, allowing her eyes to see me properly.

Fayuun's shoulders tensed and heart rate quickened, her confusion giving way to panic. It was like looking in a mirror. She was the exact image of me right down to the freckle on the underside of my chin. In fact, I was an exact copy of her. Why she fashioned me in her own image, didn't matter. We had more important issues to discuss.

'Well I'll be damned,' exclaimed Westler, flopping down on the ground.

'W... what's going on? Who are you people?'

I sat on the mattress beside her and smiled. *'Five thousand years ago you genetically engineered our race. By doing so, you locked the planet onto a path that would lead to its ultimate destruction. Thankfully, you had the forethought to factor in a being who could restore a dying planet to its former glory.'* I turned to face her. *'Perhaps I should introduce myself by my official title. I am the Manyarnern Premier.'*

Fay's face was suddenly very animated. A host of emotions swam across her thoughts as her mind raced through various scenarios. How could I have found them? Perhaps the ships had landed back on Manyarner? Why after five thousand years should I seek her out? Had they really been in flight all that time? The ships chronometer read that their flight took a little over two hundred years. What had gone wrong? Had her home world been destroyed? What of her brother - did he send this woman and her strange companion to look for the settlers?

I held up my hand. *'Wait a minute. You're getting ahead of us. Before you go speculating about what's become of Manyarner let me ask you a few simple questions.'*

Fay relaxed a little. *'Sorry Angie but you're the last person I expected to meet here today.'* She adjusted her sitting position. *'I had myself woken before the others so that I could meditate in peace for a while.'*

'I know... Time is not an issue. Shall we meditate together and discuss things later?'

She shook her head. *'No, we've started now.'*

I smiled. *'Let's begin by you telling me what you planned for the Premier?'*

'I never really planned anything.' She sighed. *'It was my own arrogance that made it necessary. When I infected everyone who stayed behind with the retrovirus I was attempting to lock them into their specialisations. I suddenly realised that this action would bar any future development. Evolution doesn't stop, but I had, in effect, caused it to. If the planet changed - let's say all the environmentalists died in a freak accident - then others should be able to adapt and take their place. I'd prevented this. The only way around the problem, as I saw it, was **not** to infect my brother with the virus.'*

'But how...'

'It wasn't so difficult. Everyone agreed to be genetically screened and it was during those tests that I slipped the virus into their systems. All except my brother, who I treated slightly differently.

She scanned her eyes across my face.

272

'Uncanny... Grimloch wanted to join with me, you know.'

'Wanted to? History records that you were partners.'

'No, it never happened. He joined with my clone... a creature grown to house the soul of the person he truly loved. Their offspring created a bloodline free to mutate and respond to random evolutionary changes.'

I was confused. Years of O.P.U. science had taught me more about genetics than she could know. The Manyarnern trait for black hair and red eye pigment was due to the action of a single gene, but specialisations are a form of polygenic inheritance. Sometimes this effect is continuously additive, but mostly the genetic component accumulates to a threshold level before the trait manifests itself. It would be impossible to develop a virus that could map the billions of potential combinations across a whole species and then fix those sequences in place.

'No, that's not what I did.' She grinned. *'Sorry to read through your shield.'*

'It's okay.'

She looked at me questioningly. *'How are we given our specialisations?'*

'The Lenses read a baby's code and interpret it for the parents.'

'And how do they know?'

I laughed aloud. *'I always suspected... they don't know do they, it's just a guess?'*

Fayuun nodded. *'A good guess based on centuries of experience, but a presumption none-the-less. Everyone has traits that show themselves early on. Some children are slightly more withdrawn, some creative, some physical. Manyarnerns chose to believe what the Lenses tell them and then gear a child's education to enhancing those abilities.'*

Everything I'd challenged in my lifetime now made perfect sense. *'Not everyone complies with the Lenses. That's what caused the war.'*

She grinned at me. *'Oh you're good, very good. I took the idea and ran with it until I'd found a solution to the*

273

planet's problems. My virus made it look like I'd genetically engineered the race, but in reality I infected them with an obedience gene. Something to make them utterly subservient to the will of the Lenses... all except my brother's blood line who have a recessive trait towards individuality.'

An image formed in my mind of my own base pair sequences. Like a 3D computer graphic they twisted and turned to reveal their hidden message. Suddenly everything made perfect sense.

'So the Premier is the person who can stand up to the Lenses and take control in an emergency?'

'Yes. If a natural disaster occurs, the planet needs a leader capable of...' I felt her probing my memory store. '...Thinking outside the box. That's a human phrase from your Joining partner's home world, isn't it?' I nodded.

An image of Iain's face flashed across my thoughts. Joining with him was definitely something different.

'It's strange that you're the first Premier to realise what she is. Others should have popped up before now.'

'They have done, but how can someone who thinks originally live amongst a bunch of sheep, bred to blindly follow the flock? Many of my ancestors - from within the direct family line and beyond - have invoked Clause Thirty-One and either abandoned their specialisations or left the planet. Now the population has fallen to such a low level that there's not enough power to sustain it.'

I sensed a new train of thought forming in her mind, but ignored it. There were more pressing matters to be resolved first.

'I have one more question, Fay. You explained why the Premier has political power. Why do I have so much physical power as well?'

She scratched her head. 'Hmmm... That's the genetic tampering no one knew about. It enhanced the psionic potential in my brother's offspring.'

'You did that alright. You also created a whole prophecy for me to live up to and a religion based around that prophecy.'

'I never meant for any of this to happen. No one was supposed to know about your increased power. Sometimes political power is not enough to rule.'

I sighed heavily. 'When you left, it was just after a devastating war that decimated the population. You then took half of the remaining people with you.'

'Two thirds,' corrected Fay. 'We left in twenty ships each carrying a million souls. They travelled in groups of five on headings that would take them to the four sectors of the galaxy.'

'Okay, you left with twenty million people. On most planets the population rises over time. Thanks to Clause Thirty-One the population has continued to decline. After five thousand years of migration, there isn't enough energy left. Manyarner is dying. At the moment it's my enhanced power that's keeping it going.'

'I'll accept that this may have happened. What I can't understand is why you keep saying five thousand years has passed when we were only in flight for two hundred years.'

'That's right, your flight was relatively short. You've landed on a planet called Earth just a little way across the galaxy from Manyarner. I've travelled here from much further away. I came looking for you across time, as well as space.'

'Amazing. Manyarner has developed the ability to time travel.'

I shook my head. 'No. I have the ability to time travel. It's a by-product of all that enhanced psionics.'

She scrunched up her nose. 'Sorry.'

'Don't be... It brought me here. I never asked to become Premier. I don't want it, but the planet needs me as an energy source. I came here looking for something to get me out of these obligations.'

'So much power and you want to give it up. When I was adviser to the Circle, my brother had more political influence than he knew what to do with. There was so much he could have achieved. It takes more than being democratic to be a good politician. Sometimes you have to be ruthless to achieve your goals. Trynax understood that.'

She sighed heavily. *'My brother was always sharing decisions. He consulted the Elders before he did anything. If I'd been stronger… But it wasn't to be.'*

'Why d'you think I came all this way looking for you? I could have sought out your brother, but it's you I need. You're right, Fay. You are more worthy of the title than me. You developed the skills to change a whole race. You had the ingenuity to lead a band of settlers out across the galaxy in search of a new way of life. I'm not the one who will heal the wounds that afflict our world. Come back with me, bring the people back and then you can put your talents to work restoring the planet. Fay, you should be governing Manyarner not I.'

She jumped up. I could feel the excitement mounting in her mind. Here was the chance she'd craved all her adult life. Dare she seize it?

'It's getting very stuffy in here. Will you walk with me?'

'Sure.' I followed her to the opening and lifted the curtain.

'What about him?' Fay pointed towards Westler who'd sat cross-legged on the ground during our exchange.

He opened his eyes and crawled on all fours across to the mattress. *'I think I'll take a nap. All this talk of genetics is making my brain hurt.'*

Fay's eyes widened. *'The creature is psionic?'*

I nodded and followed her out into the blazing sunshine. *'That's a very long story, best kept for another day.'*

As my eyes adjusted to the increased light a figure came into view.

My heart sank.

'Mother, how the hell did you get here?'

'Hiding myself on that rascal's ship wasn't difficult.'

'But what are you doing here?'

'I knew you would stir up more trouble. The moment you walked back into the temple I could feel it. And I was right. You're giving away the Premiership to her.'

I stepped to the side. *'My apologies, Fay. This is my mother, Nyaseema.'* She nodded curtly. *'She's a little upset by the offer I just made you.'*

'You can't give away what should never have been yours in the first place.' I could feel the contempt in mother's mind. *'The Premiership should have come to me.'*

I couldn't believe it.

'You never asked did you, never asked about my specialisation. You took it for granted that I was an Elder, that I became a member of the O.P.U. Assembly, but you never stopped to ask what I was born to be. The Lenses groomed me for the role; years of my life wasted in meditation. But they kept saying the time wasn't right, the crisis hadn't been reached, that I must wait for my calling. Then you were born and they named you as the one who would heal wounds and bring cohesion... The Premiership was so close. You snatched it away from under me.'

'Why didn't you tell me?' I said, straining to keep my thoughts calm.

'Believe it or not, to spare you. I know what it's like to have all your dreams pulled from under you.'

As she spoke, Mother prowled around us. She looked like a caged animal about to launch an attack on her keeper.

Had she hated me all my life?

Fay stepped between us. *'I'm sorry. All this is my fault. Please calm down, both of you. We are all of the same family. The same blood line. Surely we can find a compromise.'*

'I've had enough of compromises,' spat mother. *'I accepted a long time ago that it was her, not me. I gave Angie everything to help her along the path. What did she do? She threw it back in my face. The Academy wasn't interesting enough for her. She wanted to go off-world. The Species Recognition Programme couldn't hold her attention either.'*

I was dumbfounded. *'It was you who fast tracked Iain through to me that day.'*

'We had to keep you amused, to keep you from wanting to leave the station.'

Still she circled around me. I kept myself facing her by walking slowly in an arc.

Where is all this leading? I thought.

'And then you found rapport with him. The future leader of the most important planet in the galaxy was throwing herself at... a wild animal.'

My anger was rising. *'So why didn't you terminate him? You had enough opportunities.'* I reached into her mind, pushing easily through her shield. *'The explosion on the Gretin Station. With all your scheming and controlling you didn't foresee that he would save me.'*

She laughed acerbically. *'That's the one thing we did see. If you died before the time of crisis Manyarner would be lost. Earth seemed as safe a place as any to confine you while we waited. But typical of you, you got too comfortable. I knew I'd never persuade you to leave. So I had to...'*

The tension between us was unbearable. I sprang forward, pushing Fayuun aside and grabbed Mother by the arm. Shaking her body angrily, I screamed. 'You killed them, you bloody bitch. You murdered Julia and Tony.'

I let go, swung my hand back and slapped her across the face. Her knees crumpled and she fell to the ground at my feet.

'Is physical violence something you learned on Earth?' She sneered up at me. *'You've become as barbaric as the rest of the humans.'*

I was panting heavily, trying to keep my gaze averted while I quelled my fury. Eventually I turned back and looked her in the eye. *'Mother, if you understood the monster you created in me, you'd see that physical violence is nothing compared to what I'm actually capable of. Do you know what I did to the Valcrumny? I killed them. The entire race of slimy green blobs were snuffed out at my will. I melted the surface of their planet with a mere thought. If you'd left me alone, my powers wouldn't have been so...'*

I used telekinesis to pull her onto her feet. She stepped backwards, away from me and towards the river. I followed pleading for her understanding.

Was it too much to ask?

'I never wanted to be Premier, to have this much power. I never asked for it. I can't change my biology, but I can choose to walk away from the trappings of the title.' I started to chuckle. *'All my life, I thought I was rejecting the religion, now I see that I was the only person actually following the doctrine.'*

Mother stepped back again. I could sense that she was scared of me now, but that didn't stop her from digging the knife in further.

'You never followed anything in your life.'

'Fate, Mother. It's all about fate.' I turned towards Fayuun who stood a few metres from us. Her eyes were staring into nothing, her body rigid. *'Fay, what is the meaning of fate?'*

She jerked her head up. *'What? Oh, fate. It means... a future that is predetermined and unalterable; that unfolds by itself and we have no influence over.'*

I swung back around to face Mother. *'See... Unalterable. But you tried to change my life. Every step along the way, you prodded and poked and interfered in my destiny. I may have rejected the religion, but I allowed events to unfold for themselves. It was your meddling that twisted and distorted my personal myth. Well not any more. I have seen a different future for myself and I intend to follow that path where ever it may lead.'* I looked around at Fay once again. *'Do you accept the Premiership of Manyarner? I'm offering it to you freely.'*

'I... ummm...Yes, I accept.'

Letting out a sigh of relief I nodded. *'Thank you.'*

Slowly Mother edged towards the water. *'You're forgetting one thing,'* she said. Her mind was detached, unemotional. *'Andranovich.'*

I marched forwards, stopping beside her on the bank. Below us the swollen river dashed past. *'What about Andranovich? What have you done to him?'*

'He has a myth of his own.'

The ground shuddered. I glanced over my shoulder. The flood waters had undercut the river bank, gouging out the soil that was supporting us. It gave way under our combined weight and we slipped towards the murky torrent.

Dark earth covered my vision, my mouth filled with dirt. Something sharp smacked against the back of my head.

'Ow!'

A few seconds later, my knees found solid ground again. I pushed the accumulated soil off me, spitting and wiping my face.

I could see with my eyes, but not with my mind. The rock had blunted my awareness.

The immediacy of the situation hit me. I looked about.

'Mother?'

My eyes scanned frantically for a sign of her, eventually fixing on a pale figure almost submerged in the water; one hand wrapped around the long stems of some reeds. The fragile roots embedded in the silt below me, was all that prevented her from being washed away.

Her grip was faltering.

I spread out on my mound of earth, reaching into the water as far as I could.

'Fay, help me.'

I felt firm hands take hold of my ankles.

'Take my hand, mother...' I stretched as far as I could toward her. 'You have the same powers as me, you just never used them. Try, now. Pull yourself out of there.'

She looked up with sadness in her eyes. 'Do you think you have a monopoly on fate? I have also seen my future. And this is it.'

Her fingers uncurled and the river swallowed her up.

'MOTHER!'

Freeing myself from Fayuun's grasp, I dived in after her. The force of the water hit me in the chest, spinning me around like a leaf caught on the breeze. Eventually I righted myself and made a futile attempt to swim against the undercurrent. But I wasn't strong enough. An eddy caught me, my head went under, I was heaved sideways away from the bank towards the area where the flow was fastest. When I resurfaced I gasped for breath and looked about. I was moving fast now, tossing and turning at the whim of the flood. Mother could've been right beside me, but I wouldn't have known. My vision was obscured time and time again as the river pulled me down. I fought with all my strength to keep my head above water.

Something wrapped itself around my torso, holding my limbs rigid. I was suddenly yanked from the river by a strong telekinetic force. I strained to look over my shoulder. Fayuun and Westler stood together on the bank, their arms outstretched toward me.

'Keep still, we've got you.'

'No, put me down. I have to find her, to save her.' I tried to wriggle free, but the psionic field held me firm. Slowly I was pulled back over dry land and then lowered down until my feet touched the grass.

I leant forward, hands on knees, panting for breath. 'What did you do that for?'

'You're too valuable,' said Westler, wrinkling his nose. 'I don't want to be stuck five thousand years in the past. How will I collect that hazard pay?'

'He's right. Nyaseema has played her part in this story. Now it is our turn, yours and mine to bring the people back to Manyarner.'

She was right. The empty place in my psi-awareness where mother's consciousness should have been told me all I needed to know. Nyaseema had reached the end of her personal myth, now my own had to play out.

******

Chapter 15

'Let me get this right,' said a bewildered Uri, as he paced up and down the little tent. *'You want us to go back where we just came from? We only just got here. The settlers are still asleep in the ship. What'll they say when they wake up to find themselves back where they started?'*

Fayuun stepped close and took his hand. *'They won't be back where they started because things have changed on Manyarner. It will feel just as new as settling here ever would. From what Angie tells me, the planet has been through some major upheavals, so there are trials ahead every bit as challenging as settling on a new world.'*

I was glad she was the politician not me. I couldn't have stood it if I had to spend a lifetime squabbling with people over minutia. If she could at least bring a few hundred thousand back, that would go a long way towards solving Manyarner's energy problems.

'The settlers expect to awake on a new world, like I did just now. Not to be confronted with this...' Uri looked down at me. *'This turn about. That's what they voted for before we left. What gives us the right to change the agreement?'*

'So we wake them up and ask them what they want to do. Go or stay? I don't think it's our right to make that sort of decision for them. Besides, ours is not the only group. There are two more that landed successfully on other continents.'

'Do you know how long it will take to decant five million souls from slow sleep?' He started pacing again.

I smiled to myself. Watching them argue was rather amusing. Their rapport was obvious, yet they couldn't see it for themselves.

In the six hours since we woke Uri, I'd sat quietly on the mattress beside Westler. He was curled in a ball still asleep, his head in my lap. It felt strangely comforting to gently stroke his antennae. If Seb were here, he'd probably make some innuendo.

The thought caught me by surprise.

I'd been avoiding this. Avoiding anything to do with the family for fear of what she meant. I pushed images of Mother's body - which we'd pulled from the river a few hours earlier - aside. Could I have saved her? Should I have tried harder? What was Father going to say? I felt uneasy. I should be grieving, but I knew the tears would never come. What did she mean, I thought. *Andranovich has a myth of his own.* What did she know that I didn't?

I shook my head. Concentrate on getting everyone back safely. That was my priority right now.

The couple in front of me were still wrangling over what to do.

'Excuse me, but we don't need to wake them up.'

Uri and Fay looked at me, unanswered questions, and more than a little anxiety, building beneath the surface of their minds.

'I can blend with them while they're still asleep,' I added.

'All of them?' asked a disbelieving Uri. *'You're that powerful?'* I nodded. *'Even those thousands of kilometres away?'* I nodded again.

I was sure I could. It was nothing compared with what I'd done already.

'They won't all agree.'

I stared down at Westler, stopping the gentle stroking movement.

'Keep going, I was enjoying that.' He chuckled. *'I always said you'd fetch a good price at market. Ever fancied a job on the pleasure planet?'*

I snatched my hand away and pushed him off me. *'Why won't they all agree?'*

'It seems to me that the clues which led you here were made by yourselves - or by other Manyarnerns. If they hadn't been available you may never have worked it out. If you go straight back, taking all the people and artefacts with you, then they'll be no clues to follow. You'll create your own temporal paradox.' He stood up and

283

shook himself, then sniffed the air. Noticing the plate of food at my feet, he grabbed a handful of spicy cake, stuffing it noisily into his mouth. *'Messy things, paradoxes. Someone must be destined... that's a Manyarnern word isn't it?'* I nodded. *'Someone is destined to remain and create the clues that will lead you here in the future.'*

'Alright,' said Uri. *'Let's assume that some of us agree to go with you. How do you intend to bring us back to Manyarner? This was always designed as a one-way trip. Our ships are completely spent. The engines have powered down, and there's no way to re-ignite them.'*

Westler grabbed more of the cake. *'That's easy. We brought transport with us.'*

******

People came running from the temple as the freighter landed in the grassy clearing. The air displaced as we materialised from the wormhole, whipped at foliage still standing after the earlier storms. When the cargo bay doors opened the Elders walked forward accompanied by the Senior Lens with whom I'd spoken the previous day. Although from their perspective it was probably about five minutes ago.

Walking down the ramp, Mother's body floated before me. When Father saw us he dashed forward, taking her into his arms. Despite the distance in both time and space, he had felt the moment of Mother's death.

I reached out to touch his hand.

'It's all right, she's at peace now.' He slowly walked away.

The senior Lens stepped forward. *'Premier, I sense that you have much to tell us.'*

'No,' I smiled, *'but she has.'* Stepping aside, to reveal Fay, the crowd gasped. *'This is Fayuun, the architect of Manyarner, and now the leader of this world. She has returned with three million souls to rebuild our planet.'*

The Lens bowed to Fayuun. *'Premier, we have much to discuss.'*

Fayuun stepped forward to address the crowd. *'The time for words is passed. Now is the time for toil.'*

She gave me a cheeky grin as she walked down the ramp and into the hearts of the people.

You're welcome, I thought.

Focussing once more, I scanned for a familiar mind.

'Trilly where are you?'

'Here.' She grounded beside me. 'What's wrong?'

'Where is Andranovich?'

I felt her anxiety rise. 'He had no choice. His visions...'

'What visions?'

'Ever since he was young... During the blending, he saw... he knew it was his destiny to kill his father.' Anger flashed across my features. 'Please, Angie, you must understand. He fought it... he stayed away... but he couldn't deny his own destiny.'

I flew into a rage. 'Why didn't you tell me? Did she have anything to do with it?'

'In a manner of speaking, yes. Nyaseema interpreted the vision when he was a boy. He knew there was no alternative way of making you come back. It was his fate to be the one to remove Iain from your consciousness. None of that applies any more. Now you can go to Earth and stop him.'

I shook my head. 'You know I can't do that. Fate, destiny... They're written in the stones. It's already too late.'

******

I stepped from the shadows of the room. Clara sat on the sofa staring dispassionately into the embers of the fire. The carved highland scene on the wall above her looked uncannily real in the half light.

'Hello Clara. Where are they?'

She jumped and turned toward me.

'Angie. Oh my god. You made me start. I thought you were a ghost.' She let out a huge sigh.

I could feel her mind. It was old, older than I'd ever known and fragile. Holding back my impatience, I walked over and sat beside her on the sofa; a burst of pyrokinesis rekindling the warmth of the fire.

'All right, tell me what's happened.'

'I got a call three days ago saying that Iain was in the private hospital on the outskirts of Fort William. He'd collapsed at the office and was in an inexplicable coma. He stayed like that for two days then suddenly woke up. When I eventually spoke with him alone, he said they had surgically removed his transceiver. The doctors thought it was a brain tumour.

'We came back here together to try and contact the O.P.U. using the hyper-whats-it-communicator thing.' She straightened the folds of her pleated skirt. 'Then earlier this evening Andranovich arrived in an Eilad. He said he had important business with his father. They spent hours down in the workshop arguing. They thought I couldn't hear.'

'What were they arguing about?'

She looked up, eyes full of tears. 'You.'

'I know.' I patted her reassuringly on the shoulder. 'It's okay, Clara. Take your time...'

Time was no longer an issue for me.

'Tell me what happened next.'

She sniffed. 'Iain was angry that he'd parked his space ship right outside the house. He shouted about compromise to the family's security. Then he took off.'

'Where?'

'No literally, he ran out of the house and into the thing, Andranovich followed. It took off over the loch.'

Tears started to roll uncontrollably down her face. 'I'm sorry, Angie... All I could do was watch... The ship, it wobbled, spun out of control for a moment. Flames came from underneath. Then it crashed down into the water. I didn't see either of them again.'

I jumped up. 'When was this?'

'About an hour ago.' She looked up, her thoughts full of questions. 'What are you going to do?'

'You may have to catch me as I fall... '

******

I floated just below the ceiling. Water had already filled the small bridge to a level well above the instrument panels. Iain, his head wrapped in a bandage, was treading water beside Andranovich who had a bad cut on his forehead. Dark purple blood trickled from the wound, down his cheek and into the water. They both shivered.

'I'm not going to argue with you. Get out of here now!'

'No, Father, you go. She needs you more than me.'

I felt the turmoil in Andranovich's thoughts. Years of belief told him it was his father's destiny to die here tonight. Mixed up with this were feelings of betrayal and remorse. He loved Iain and had fought all his life to prevent this event from happening.

The reason why he'd stayed away suddenly hit me.

'Rubbish, Manyarner needs both of you,' said Iain.

'I've always believed in fate. Every blending I ever had showed me this moment. That I would be here in the loch when...' Grimacing, Andranovich wiped his forehead. 'Now I realise that it doesn't have to happen that way.'

On cue the ship rolled and a surge of icy water from the breach in the hull rushed into the small space.

The air pocket wouldn't hold out much longer.

'I never thought I'd hear myself say this, but you've been right all along,' began Iain. 'Just because I'm going to die doesn't mean you have to.' Iain patted Andranovich affectionately on the head; the action causing him to slip beneath the water. He bobbed back up again, pushing the hair from his eyes. 'Look, son. If one of us doesn't get into that access tunnel in the next few seconds, the controls will be under water and the hatch won't blow. You're more important than me. Get the fuck out of here, go back to Manyarner and tell her... tell her how much I loved her.'

My heart leapt.

'Tell Gabkhan, Susie and Kohlarn too. Tell them I'm sorry.'

It was unbearable to watch. I felt helpless, but couldn't interfere. Fate had to play out.

287

Faith in Manyarnern ideology finally won Andranovich's internal battle. Reluctantly he swam over to the portal in the far wall. Holding onto the top rung of the ladder, he opened the hatch. Water rushed inside, half filling the small tube beyond. He took a huge breath and with Iain's help, climbed in, feat first.

'I'll tell her, Father. I'll tell them all.'

Between them they forced the hatch closed again.

Iain reached up for the manual controls. He pulled open a small panel and turned the charging handle.

The water rose again, pushing his head closer to the ceiling of the compartment.

When Iain pressed the button explosive bolts blew off the outer door, sucking Andranovich out of the tube. With regret in his mind, he pulled himself around and swam for the surface.

I watched Iain. His face turned upwards, lips pressed against the ceiling. He gasped the last few mouthfuls of air before the compartment was completely filled. When he was totally submerged, he stopped moving, allowing himself to sink down to the bottom. His cheeks and eyes were bulging, his lungs straining; desperate for the breath that would never come.

I waited.

Iain couldn't hold out any longer. His chest heaved as the lungs took in water. His brain sucked the last vestiges of oxygen from the remaining blood supply and then his heart stopped.

I was amazed that the scared young man I had married now faced death with such dignity. He didn't panic, he just closed his eyes and let his life slip away.

******

Stepping into his mind, the spiritual connection felt more real than anything I've ever experienced.

'Hello, Iain.'

'Fucking hell!' Relief flashed through his psyche. 'You're back. You'll never believe what's been going on around here.'

288

'I wanted to help you earlier. I'm sorry but I couldn't.'

I moved closer. Although in this static moment of time between life and death the notion of distance barely applied.

'We need to talk, but before we do I think there are things I should share with you.'

He immediately knew everything that had happened to me in the past few days; and I knew all that had happened to him. The knowledge was painful for both of us.

He was trying to think, trying to make sense of events. 'If this is all true, shouldn't I be dead on the bottom of the loch?'

'I was hoping to spare you this, but your usual stubbornness makes it necessary. You're right, you are dead.'

'Wow...' I gave him a few moments for reality to sink in.

He's taking all this remarkably well.

'How else can I take it?'

'How did you?'

'Joined minds, Angie. They removed my transceiver so I'm not telepathic, but our minds are still in synch. Isn't that what the Joining is all about?'

'That can be easily fixed. I don't know why I didn't think of it before. I can change the neural connections in your brain to make you properly psionic... If you want?'

'If I had a living brain. I'm dead, remember? Is that something else you can fix?'

'Yes, actually I can. Although your body has died, your mind still holds a residual spark of life. I'm holding you here until we sort things out. Since we met I've died three, maybe four times. It's happened so often in the last few days that I've almost lost count.' I laughed at the absurdity of what I was saying. 'It's a consequence of... I guess I'm descended from a Cruxion.'

'If you can bring people back to life, doesn't that make you... God?'

'Yeah, sort of. I'd rather not think about it in those terms. I guess it all depends on what you believe.' I sighed mentally. 'But that's not the point. If I bring you back then it must be what you want.'

He scoffed. 'D'you think I wouldn't want to live? That anyone wouldn't want to live given the choice between that and dying?'

'I didn't really mean that. I know you want to live, but do you want to live with me? After everything that's happened, to us, to our family. After everything I've done?'

'None of that was your fault. Don't they say to err is human, to forgive divine? I can't say I'm happy Nyaseema killed Mum and Dad, but I have to admit it, I'm sorry she's dead. I forgive her, and so should you. There's someone else you need to forgive too.'

I was puzzled.

'Forgive yourself, Angie. Whether our lives are governed by fate or choice doesn't matter. You've done the things that felt right for you at the time, just as I have. We all make mistakes. You've made some pretty big ones. Let's put them behind us and move on.'

In a flash the events of the past twenty years resonated through my psyche. 'I don't know. What's been the point of it all?'

'Hah! You've done so much. You saved Manyarner, you pulled it all together. You worked it all out. You've raised great kids. You've influenced the lives of so many people, but most of all you influenced my life in a way I could never have imagined possible.'

'You make it sound so simple.' My mind turned dark. 'I committed genocide, Iain, and I enjoyed it. It was a monstrous thing to do. Do you want to remain Joined to a person capable of killing with a thought? You've always kept me grounded, kept me sane. Now I've found all this power. I'm not safe to be around.'

'You did what you had to do to survive. I never understood the Manyarnern inclination for sharing yourselves, but I do know this. I've never met anyone who loves as much as you. What you did, you did out of love. Love for Jen, Seb and the kids. You saved their lives too, remember? You're not the monster, the Valcrumny were. They hurt you, and countless innocent people before you. Fuck it, Angie. No one's gonna blame you for wanting revenge. I'd probably have done the same thing. Now you see how easily the power could corrupt you, you'll never give in to it again. Whether you're some kind of deity is irrelevant. Together we'll never let it happen again.'

'You still want to be Joined to me?'

'Of course I do, stupid.'

'Even after all the things mother did? She pushed us together to fulfil her own agenda. She only allowed us to Join to get me away from the station to somewhere safe. She used you like a body guard. Think about it. If we'd met in another time or place would I have been the one you chose?'

He paused and I saw an image of my younger self through his eyes. It was the first time we met as he awoke on the trolley in my lab.

'I'm very flattered, but I was never that beautiful.'

'We fell in love on our own. Regardless of what your mother did. We made it work. You're a challenge Angie, you always have been. Life with you has never been straight forward.' I could feel his contentment and my mood lightened. 'You know what? I've loved every minute of it. It's all I've ever wanted.

'When I was abducted it was bloody scary, but it was also one hell of an adventure. Everyone before me freaked out. You know why I didn't? Because I'd wished for something like that to happen to me for... forever. Yeah, I missed my home, but being there with you on the Gretin station was the biggest thrill. Better than sex; more addictive and compelling than drugs. I don't want to change any of what we have. I get the feeling that you're here in... what? my mind? my soul?... because you think that I'd want something different. No. I want you, Angeriana, and all the trappings that come with you. You're my destiny.'

I couldn't believe it. Even Andranovich, despite his beliefs, had tried to fight his fate. He knew it was Iain's personal myth to die here, yet he argued with his father to the bitter end. Iain, on the other hand, the human who was always so vocal in his denial of Manyarnern philosophy had become the true inheritor of the wisdom of those beliefs.

And me? I'd spent my life trying to reject my specialisation and be different. But being different was my speciality all along. I was and always had been a square peg in a round hole, but until now I'd found it impossible to define myself. I couldn't blame the gene that pushed me towards individuality, even selfishness. It gave me distinctive, yet essential, abilities that I'd used and enjoyed. It also made it impossible for me to settle to anything. I was caught in the ultimate circular argument, I didn't want to be what I was, but being what I was, was the thing that made me dislike it. I had to both accept and reject Manyarnern philosophy in the same thought. These ideas made very uncomfortable bed fellows. Years ago, Iain had described me as unique and told me to accept it and get on with life. He was absolutely right, that was the only thing I could do.

I felt ashamed. He'd accepted my people's way of life much more than I'd accepted it - and much more than I'd accepted a human lifestyle. I wondered whether I'd find anywhere that would ever really feel like home.

'I've never given Earth much of a chance, have I?'

'I won't argue with that. You lived here, but you never really fitted in.'

'So why didn't you make me? I could have adapted more, become more human.'

He laughed. 'You... more human? Pull the other one. There's never been anyone more Manyarnern than you, Angie.'

'Really, you mean that?'

'I fell in love with this beautiful and exotic alien. I brought her to Earth. Did you think I wanted you to suddenly act like a normal woman? That just isn't you. Even all this fuss over Gab and Susie Joining, I knew I'd give in eventually. I never meant it to cause a rift between us.'

'I was so cruel. The things I said.'

'Were the right things. You don't belong here, especially now. You can choose to live anywhere in the galaxy. Maybe I should say **we** can live anywhere.'

'You still want to be with me?'

'Of course I do, the adventure never ends.'

******

...and so we found ourselves standing naked, with the rest of my extended family, in the temple which we'd built on the highland estate, by the shores of Loch Ossian. In early summer, the loch was particularly appealing and I was longing to dive into its depths. To feel the uniquely sensual qualities created by the molecular structure of the water as it flows across the skin.

But I knew there wasn't time for such revelry. The Eilad waited for us to embark.

There were new horizons to explore.

Iain had explained to Sussia'ficalasa and Gabkhan, just a few minutes earlier, how he would scramble their individual brain patterns during the ceremony, and then reformulate them in perfect synchrony. A process that binds the Joining partners together for life.

Obeying his sub-vocal commands they knelt, lowering their heads to receive their father's touch...

Every action ripples along the threads that bind us together, to touch the lives of others in some way...
The Chronicle of Grimloch

Epilogue

Petulia sat enthralled, sharing her mother's consciousness. Her mind a vibrant palette of images.

Obeying his sub-vocal commands they knelt, lowering their heads to receive their father's touch...

The vision faded as the telepathic link was broken.

There was a long pause while Petulia played with her hair. Fayuun could sense the questions bubbling below the surface of her daughter's mind.

'Well?'

'Is it true that the chronicle of Angeriana'asusilicana is the most insightful of all the myths?

'Yes. I believe so.'

'I was told at the Academy that if I study hard, I will come to know its meaning.'

Fayuun smiled down at her daughter. Of the many fables told on their world, this was also her favourite. I wonder how long it will take for you to realise its significance, she thought.